THE MONSTERS WE MADE

THE
MONSTERS
PEYTON JUNE

WE MADE

NORTON YOUNG READERS
An Imprint of W. W. Norton & Company
Independent Publishers Since 1923

For Max, who was there when the monsters felt too real

Printed in the United States of America
First Edition

For information about permission to reproduce selections from this book, write to
Permissions, W. W. Norton & Company, Inc., 500 Fifth Avenue, New York, NY 10110

For information about special discounts for bulk purchases, please contact
W. W. Norton Special Sales at specialsales@wwnorton.com or 800-233-4830

Manufacturing by Lakeside Book Company
Book design by Hana Anouk Nakamura
Production manager: Delaney Adams

Library of Congress Cataloging-in-Publication Data

Names: Peyton June author
Title: The monsters we made / Peyton June.
Description: First edition. | New York, NY : Norton Young Readers, [2026] | Audience: Ages 14 | Audience: Grades 7–9
Identifiers: LCCN 2026009854 | ISBN 9781324083436 cloth | ISBN 9781324083443 ebook
Subjects: CYAC: Extraterrestrial beings | Monsters | Video blogs | Hoaxes | LGBTQ+ people |
LCGFT: Paranormal fiction | Thrillers (Fiction) | Novels
Classification: LCC PZ7.1.P498 Mo 2026
LC record available at https://lccn.loc.gov/2026009854

W. W. Norton & Company, Inc., 500 Fifth Avenue, New York, NY 10110
www.wwnorton.com

W. W. Norton & Company Ltd., 15 Carlisle Street, London W1D 3BS

Authorized EU representative: EAS, Mustamäe tee 50, 10621 Tallinn, Estonia

10 9 8 7 6 5 4 3 2 1

ALSO BY PEYTON JUNE

BAD CREEK

So far, Scarberry, Nebraska, had more cows than people. Lenny stopped counting the cattle after three hundred something.

"Two more minutes," Evan said.

How was civilization two minutes away? Was their Airbnb actually hidden in some underground bunker? The last thirty miles had just been withered cornfields, cows, and her trusty Oldsmobile, the *Silver Bullet*. Lenny couldn't remember the last time they'd passed another car or a man-made structure other than a crumbling barn or lonely silo. The too-blue sky felt dangerous. She could already tell Scarberry would be the scariest stop on their trip, and that abandoned prison in Ohio had given her nightmares for weeks.

After two minutes exactly, Evan directed her to turn left, onto a dirt road. As dust collected on the already-filthy windshield, he closed the passenger window, faking a cough. "Ugh. Car probably looks trashed."

"Isn't that a good thing?" Lenny offered. "Won't that make the establishing shot more *authentic?*"

Evan rolled his eyes.

Authenticity. That was their branding. That was what made *Odd Kids* better than their rivals, *Dark Unknown. Odd Kids* was real. Raw. *Authentic.* Evan had used those words to pitch their summer-long road trip to their parents. He'd said that they had to go alone, the two of them. No parents. No extra crew carrying bulky film equipment. Just Evan and Lenny and the *Silver Bullet* on the open road. If they could survive it, Lenny's parents would let them do YouTube full-time. No more surprise college visits. No more pamphlets shoved under her bedroom door.

Authenticity was also the same word that got sponsors interested. Yes, they hadn't caught Bigfoot on tape yet, but wasn't it fun watching these relatable teenagers fall in love while squatch-hunting?

Authenticity.

Sure.

Evan pointed his camera out of the window. "This is it."

Yeah, Lenny could tell from the massive UFO in the front yard.

The saucer was about the size of the *Silver Bullet.* It sat on a tilt, like it was frozen at the moment it crash-landed. Nothing about it looked authentic; the chipped coppery paint and the NO CLIMBING PLEASE sign didn't exactly give off Real Alien Spacecraft vibes.

Behind it was an unassuming farmhouse and an old-fashioned windmill. The farmhouse was white—well, it looked like it *used* to be white—but was now a dusty beige with a red roof that had seen better days. Lenny had expected it to be larger, or at least have a fresher paint job. Maybe the owners of Reed Ranch kept the place dilapidated as part of their brand? But what if Evan was right? What if Scarberry was just a tourist trap after all?

No. Lenny tried to shed the thought. This was the place. It had to be.

She parked the *Silver Bullet* on the side of the road (that was the one good thing about small rural towns: you could park anywhere for free). When she stepped onto the dead grass, she resisted the urge to cover her nose. The smell of manure was bad enough while on the road, but now it was overwhelming.

"A whole three days of smelling cow shit," Evan said. "Awesome."

"It's not that bad," Lenny lied.

They were an hour early, just enough time to get the opening monologue in. They popped open the trunk, covered in worn-out stickers from small towns with big legends: Loveland, Point Pleasant, Dover. There were cutesy illustrations of skunk apes, lake monsters, wolf-people, goat-people, and a faded I WANT TO BELIEVE on the bumper.

Evan practiced his lines under his breath while Lenny adjusted the tripod and placed duct tape on their mark, right in front of the saucer.

"Tuck your hair back," Evan said, instead of brushing the loose strands behind her ear like he used to. It had been forever since he'd tickled her waist while pinning her mic to her shirt. She'd giggle and slap his hand away. Pretend she didn't enjoy his teasing.

Now they were professionals.

Evan clicked Record before coming to stand next to Lenny. She watched herself in the viewfinder and pushed her bangs into place. She looked so tiny next to Evan. It's not that he was freaky tall; he just had inhumanely perfect posture. Lenny was easily eclipsed by his height, by his self-assuredness, by her own slime-green *Odd Kids* T-shirt.

She was a speck of a girl. Blink and you'd miss her.

She took a deep breath and recited the monologue she'd written in their motel room last night. "Strange lights floating above a barn, cattle mutilation, eerie shrieks at night, and sightings of a pale creature lurking in corn fields. In the summer of 1961, this small town had more than a few strange occurrences . . ."

Evan jumped in, "Though Scarberry, Nebraska, isn't far from Highway 80, you won't find it on a map. With a population of only thirteen hundred, most of its inhabitants are farmers. But one of those residents might also be an extraterrestrial."

He delivered the lines Lenny had written perfectly, but she could practically hear him fighting the urge to roll his eyes on that last word—*extraterrestrial.*

They hadn't done an alien episode in over a year, thanks to Evan. According to analytics, aliens weren't trendy. Their channel got better engagement with cryptids and poltergeists. In fact, the next stop on their road trip was supposed to be Harrows House in Arizona, where, allegedly, a demon with a baby face and hooves had been haunting a family for generations. That was where they had originally planned to be today.

But they had also planned to be together forever.

"For the next seventy-two hours, we'll be staying at Reed Ranch, where it all began. The creature known as Old Lucky hasn't been spotted since that fateful summer, but recently a subscriber sent us proof he's returned." Lenny paused so they could later superimpose the low-res clip on the screen, before asking, "Was this little town the location of an alien invasion sixty-five years ago?"

"Or was it all a hoax?" Evan finished. He looked at her and smiled, his eyes crinkling behind his glasses. "Ready to check it out?"

After she nodded, he gave her a kiss—a tradition from their very first video. But that onscreen kiss had actually meant something. Now documenting their "love" for 400,000 subscribers was just a formality.

Lenny secretly hoped a fan would see through the façade. Someone would zoom in on her lying face and analyze the way his lips barely grazed hers. They'd freeze on a single frame of evidence, just like their show often did when dust on the lens looked *almost* like a ghost.

"Let's run it again," Evan said. On every stop on their trip, they had nailed the monologue on the first take, but he wanted backup footage, "just in case." He had taken more B-roll in the past two weeks than he'd had in the two years they'd been doing *Odd Kids*. Either he was getting more paranoid, or Lenny was just noticing it for the first time. Since when was she determined to see the worst in him?

"You kids with the TV show?" a voice called.

A man with an impressive white handlebar mustache stood next to the saucer, wearing a sweat-soaked gray shirt and blue jeans tucked into his boots. It was eighty-five degrees outside; he had to be boiling. Lenny's bangs were soaked with sweat, and all she had were bicycle shorts, her tie-dye shirt, and sneakers.

"Yeah," Lenny answered. *Odd Kids* wasn't technically a TV show, but it was easier to let old people think that. Explaining YouTube to someone who couldn't work a flip phone would prove exhausting for both parties.

"Any, uh, parents with you?" the man asked.

"We're both legal adults," Evan said. Barely. Evan had turned eighteen in the fall, Lenny the week of graduation. That was a month ago. A diploma, adulthood, and a career handed to her all at once.

The cowboy nodded before spitting black goo into the grass. Tobacco. Evan recoiled, letting out a little scoff. He was terrified of anything getting on his brand-new sneakers. His other pair got ruined at their last stop. It had been a classic possession case, except the victim just happened to be a cat. The owners were a bigger headache than their supposedly cursed pet. No one had bothered to mention they were remodeling their haunted house's attic, and Evan had knocked over a can of fresh paint. At least the paint had been a rusty color, so, in the video, they could pretend they'd discovered a bucket of real human blood.

"I'm Jared, by the way. Ranch hand for Miss Reed. I'm s'posed to take ya to your room."

The way he'd called his employer "Miss" made him sound like a time traveler from the Old West. He matched the defunct atmosphere of the rest of the place too. If it wasn't for the bulky satellite on the house, Lenny could have sworn she had accidentally teleported to a pre-television era. The subscribers were going to eat this up.

"Awesome, thank you!" Lenny said.

Evan scowled. If he had it his way, they would run the monologue again. Or better—they'd be in Arizona, investigating demonic infant cries.

"I'll show ya where to park," said Jared.

After they shoved the equipment back in the trunk and hopped in the *Silver Bullet,* Lenny slowly followed the cowboy down the dirt driveway.

"Now would have been a good time to use the body cam," Evan muttered. The "body cam" was just a GoPro on a harness, but Evan liked saying the name out loud. Lenny had accidentally dropped it over a haunted bridge a few weeks ago, and he hadn't shut up about it. She'd taken the blame for that. And she'd take the blame for Scarberry too. The manure smell. The weird old guy. If this leg of the trip went south, it would be her fault.

It won't, Lenny told herself. *This is where you're meant to be.* She knew it deep in her bones.

She tried to change the subject. "Jared seems nice."

Evan rolled his eyes. "Yeah, if you like serial killers."

"If we get murdered, we'd go *viral,*" Lenny muttered under her breath.

Evan gave her an accusatory look as the cowboy pointed out a patch of dirt, where three cars were parked. Lenny rolled down the window, catching Jared midsentence.

"—and right over here is the parking lot. There's a nice spot under a tree for ya."

"Thank you."

She backed into the spot, praying it wouldn't rain. The fluffy white clouds above them were growing denser, and the *Silver Bullet* didn't do well with mud.

She tried to shake the thought. *It won't rain. It won't rain.* She was only manifesting good things now. Foretelling the worst-case scenario was Evan's job, not hers. She couldn't let herself turn into him. But it was probably too late for that. It'd been *two years.* They were intertwined now.

"I can help with bags," Jared said, sloshing the chew in his mouth. Against Evan's silent protests, Lenny let him take some of their luggage. The three of them carried two roller suitcases each as they followed a dirt path through the yard.

Jared was definitely judging all their bags. He must have thought they were shallow city slickers or something. Some suitcases were for equipment: thermal cameras and REM PODs and EMF readers. The rest were stuffed with T-shirts sent to them by sponsors and fans alike. Lenny wore most of them as pajamas after filming, since she wasn't supposed to repeat outfits for videos.

The smell of manure was even more pungent closer to the source. Beyond a metal fence on their right, black dots marked grazing cows across a field that seemed to go on forever, like an infinity mirror. This place was over a hundred acres. When Lenny had typed that stat into her notes, it had felt like an imaginary number. She hadn't really realized just how much land it actually was.

"Gift shop," Jared said, tilting his head toward a white

one-story shed to their left. A faded mural of a green alien gave them a peace sign as they walked past.

"Are you kidding me?" Evan groaned. He lifted his white sneakers to reveal a glob of manure.

"Watch where yer steppin'," Jared advised, too late. Lenny suppressed a giggle.

Now they were getting closer to a red barn. *The* red barn.

Lenny stopped in her tracks. This was it—this was the spot where the iconic photo from 1961 was taken. She'd had a poster of the Scarberry Lights above her bed since she was in middle school. She knew the slant of the barn roof, the crooked square window, but in person, it was a darker red than the grainy black-and-white poster implied.

This was the place she dreamed of every night.

Her heart was buzzing. The next time lights appeared above the peeling roof, she would see them. And she would record them. Proof at last. Screw Evan for not believing in this place, for not believing in *her*. It would all be worth it soon.

They reached a small line of trees, their first respite from the harsh sun. *Thank God*. She didn't want fans to point out any sweat stains when they eventually posted this week's video.

The trail ended with five train cars, all a different color. Each had one window and one door, a welcome mat, and an unlit string of UFO-shaped lights hanging off the flat roof.

Jared gestured to the blue one at the end. "You're in the caboose."

Of course. It was the smallest one—about the size of an

RV. They'd asked for two beds, but Lenny doubted now there would be enough room.

"Outhouse and showers to the right," Jared added after handing Evan the keys, pointing to a cinder-block building. It looked like the kind of structure you'd find in a park or on a hiking trail.

Evan gripped the keys. Being on a break didn't mean Lenny forgot how to read his mind; she knew what he was thinking: *Outhouse? The hotel I booked in Arizona had an actual bathroom. And a hot tub. Why would Lenny make us change course last-minute for a shittier story with shittier accommodations?*

While Evan unlocked the door, Lenny turned to thank Jared—but he had disappeared already. She made a mental note to catch up with him later for an interview. If anything was going on in this place, a ranch hand would have seen something. And this guy, with his mustache and chew, would be a great character for their show.

Evan tore off his ruined sneakers and left them outside.

The caboose's interior didn't look much different from the cheap motels they were used to: beige walls and white blinds, simple wooden dressers, and a dull carpet. But this one had a table lamp shaped like a boot with spurs, and right above the loveseat there was a painting of a cow being beamed up by a flying saucer.

Evan dug through a suitcase on the floor, grumbling to himself, until he pulled out his inhaler.

"You good?" she asked, watching him breathe in deeply. He touched his chest between swigs of it, like he had to check if his lungs were working.

"Fine," he snapped. This was the first time he'd used it since they hit the road. He claimed to only bring it as a precaution. Just like the first-aid kit, the flares, and six jugs of purified water.

"I'm sure they have a hose or something to clean off your shoes," Lenny offered.

"I don't care about the shoes," Evan muttered. Oh no. He got quiet when angry. Evan had never yelled at her. Yelling didn't get results, and Evan was all about results. If he could give a printout of the stats of their relationship, he would.

Dreading the silence, Lenny unpacked her own clothes for the next three days (with backups in case she fell into a pit of manure or something).

"There's probably a map at the gift shop," she said after a few minutes. Evan loved maps. If Lenny hadn't convinced him to create a YouTube channel about the paranormal, he probably would have made his own about maps.

The attempt wasn't just for him, though. The website had called the place a gift shop *and* museum, and Lenny was curious about the museum part. She figured their host would be there. Typically, owners loved to be the spokesperson of places like this. They invited *Odd Kids* for help with hauntings, yes, but also for *exposure*. But Lenny had yet to speak to the owner of Reed Ranch. The bookings were all handled on the website; she hadn't even known the owner was a "miss" until Jared had said so.

At least *Odd Kids* was supporting a woman-owned business.

"I figured we could get some interviews lined up," Lenny added.

"Don't you have a *key witness?*" Evan sneered.

Ah, yes. The only person Evan resented more than the

host of *Dark Unknown* was the nameless emailer. Subject line: "Reed Ranch. June 3rd." Its contents had made Lenny reroute the road trip and completely ruin Evan's life.

But when *Odd Kids* had released a short teaser of the clip, it had garnered more than enough interest to justify an investigation. The subscribers would be happy that their faves stopped in Scarberry.

Evan was just being a baby because he didn't get his way.

"Still no reply," Lenny admitted. "Don't think they'll want to talk."

"That doesn't seem sketchy to you?"

"Plenty of witnesses choose to stay anonymous."

Some people's jobs were reporting paranormal encounters, some people lost their jobs for talking about them. Even if they didn't find the mysterious emailer, the town had to have other witnesses. There was something off about this place. She'd felt it during the drive, and she felt it even more now. The big, open sky was suffocating. No cameras were rolling, but Lenny was sure she was being watched.

"It's a hoax, Lenora." Evan usually called her by her given name to tease her, but right now he sounded like her grandmother. He didn't even like that word, *hoax*. He preferred kinder descriptions like *unsolved* or *incomplete data*.

Apparently, *hoax* was a weapon reserved for the cases Lenny cared about the most. So she hit him back with something just as sharp: "Or maybe, some people care more about the truth than fame."

Then she grabbed the handheld camera and slammed the door on the way out.

CHAPTER 2

CLAIRE

Claire had worked only one job in her life, but sometimes she felt responsible for everything but the Earth's rotation around the sun. Her gig at the gift shop was a Russian nesting doll, containing infinite occupations within. Plumber when the toilets clogged. Firefighter that time someone's cigarette lit the dry grass ablaze. IT expert when the Wi-Fi crashed. Therapist when lonely tourists wanted to vent.

Today, Claire was an astrophysicist.

"The military already has the technology. They just don't want civilians to know about it," said the skinny white dude sporting a patchy mustache and smudgy tattoos on his forearms. "They want you to think it's a UFO so that China isn't suspicious of our spacecraft."

"Wow, that's crazy," Claire said, deadpan. She'd learned quickly that this was the best response for his type. A rebuttal would just make the mansplaining worse. Agree too enthusiastically, and he'd start flirting, even though he was at least five years older than her and the pride flag on her name tag should have been enough for him to get the hint.

"They're not even called UFOs anymore. They're called UAPs," Mustache Bro said, contradicting himself. "I can show you an article."

Reed Ranch didn't get a lot of skeptics. Locals thought it was tacky to discuss the Beast of Scarberry and with their little tourist trap far from a real city, visitors had to show dedication to make the long drive—dedication that nonbelievers typically didn't possess. Yet, every now and then, people like Mustache Bro managed to show up.

Claire's cousin, Bri, was lucky to be stocking shelves right now. Her wiry arms were full of shiny alien plushies. As always, she was eavesdropping. She gave Claire a knowing look from the other side of the store, one that said, *Do you need rescue?*

They always took turns saving each other. From annoying customers. From school bullies. From watching bad TV shows alone.

The thing was, Claire didn't completely disagree with today's skeptic. Though she knew her hometown had never been visited by a UFO (or UAP, or *whatever*), she couldn't say that while on the clock. Reed Ranch's official position: no one can truly know what happened in 1961. But aliens make for easy logos.

Mustache Bro pulled out his phone and read aloud some article disproving the photo of the Scarberry Lights. The same black-and-white image on his screen hung on the wall behind her, surrounded by a collage of old newspapers with headlines like MYSTERY, CONSPIRACY, UNKNOWN and INVASION, followed by gratuitous exclamation points.

"See how the grain around the light looks different from the rest of it?" Mustache Bro pointed out, shoving the phone in her face. "It's edited. And not even edited well. Pre-Photoshop."

"Wow," she said flatly. "Crazy."

Shifts like this, Claire guessed that if someone took her pulse, they wouldn't find one. Maybe she'd feel more alive if she finally screamed at one of the tourists. Not even words. In her fantasy, she stared directly into the eyes of some poor soul and let out an unholy shriek. It'd go on for hours. It'd blow the flimsy gift shop apart. Take off the last of the farmhouse's shingles. Send the windmill into orbit. Claire would be the worst tornado Scarberry ever saw. She wouldn't stop until the town was leveled.

But she was still holding the scream in. Saving it for when she really needed it.

When a car door slammed outside, Claire glanced out the dusty window. Not a new customer, just Mr. J. Porter for the third time this week, clipboard and sweat-stained button-down and one of his trademark patterned ties. The first horseman of the apocalypse wore pineapple print today. How *quirky*.

Mustache Bro had moved on from the photo of Reed Ranch and onto the "totally fake" first moon landing, but Claire kept her eyes on Mr. Porter as he stepped onto the back porch. She hoped Aunt Maeve wouldn't even open the door. The offer wasn't going to get any better, and the way he'd worded it last week hadn't even sounded like an offer but a threat. Almost everyone on this side of town had sold their property already. Mr. Porter probably thought it was only a matter of time before the Reeds would fold too.

Thankfully Bri hadn't seemed to notice the unwelcome visitor. Aunt Maeve and Claire had agreed not to tell her about the first offer. Or the second. Bri had been through enough the past year; she didn't need to worry about losing the only home she knew on top of everything.

Mr. Porter was still lingering on the porch, rocking back and forth in his loafers with poorly hidden lifts. He knocked, more aggressively this time. But the door didn't open. Either Maeve was holding out or wearing her noise-canceling headphones in the bath again. Eventually Mr. Porter gave up and hopped into his shiny new sedan. Armageddon avoided.

For now.

There was a weak ding as someone new entered the gift shop. The girl was about Claire's age, with dark hair cut into a messy shag. She was short, like five-two at most, wearing a rainbow tie-dyed shirt. *Odd Kid*s was printed in neon green on her chest.

Lenny Gilson.

Shit.

Claire expected the other one to follow behind Lenny. The Boyfriend—Claire didn't remember his name—did most of the talking in the videos yet managed to avoid *saying* anything. For all she cared, he was Mustache Bro in a different font. But Lenny came alone. She browsed the shelves like she was at a real museum. Her ringed fingers touched every magnet, every postcard. She even stopped to read the glass-covered original newspaper article where William H. Lamb broke the story to reporters.

Supposedly, Willy Lamb had been parked in a field with his high school sweetheart when they saw strange lights in the rearview window. That was how all these things started, right? A wholesome heterosexual couple getting it on in the backseat until something spooky happens. They rush toward the lights and what do you know, they're right above the Reeds' barn. And conveniently, Willy's girlfriend happens to be carrying a camera with her in nineteen-fucking-sixty-one. She gets the lights on film but fails to take a picture of the ten-foot-tall, long-necked, red-eyed creature that lunges from behind the barn and attacks Willy. The oh-so-brave and chivalrous Willy breaks free and hops back in the truck, but not before the creature takes a big munch out of his shoulder (no evidence of the wound or hospital record). Bleeding and terrified, Willy tries to start the truck, but no dice. The battery's mysteriously dead. They're trapped with a monster.

But then, in a shocking twist, it . . . disappears. Just like that. Allegedly it killed off half the cows at Reed Ranch, but didn't bother finishing off Willy and his girl. So anticlimactic. The story was already bonkers, Willy Lamb ought to have at least ended it with an alien abduction.

No UFOs were spotted. No aliens were captured. Didn't matter. People came in droves to get a glimpse of the lights themselves. Every cow that died that summer was blamed on the town's new pet monster: Old Lucky.

It was bullshit, of course, but the legend paid the bills. Well—it used to. Claire was working on it.

Lenny took a photo of the newspaper and kept moving. Claire forced herself to look away. She had to follow the plan: *Send the footage. Lay low. Play host if you have to, but nothing more.*

Eventually Lenny caught up to Bri, who was sticking barcodes on the back of novelty license plates.

"Hi," Lenny said.

That was all it took for Bri's ears to turn red. She covered them like she could feel them getting hotter. Ever since she'd lost her hair, her ears were her biggest insecurity. *I look like an elf,* she'd said. Claire suggested she wear a hat, but Bri professed that she wasn't a hat girl. She wasn't a short-hair girl either. Since the chemo, she was a hopeless girl. Without her long locks and sun-kissed complexion, she was basically worthless. It didn't matter how much Claire told her the pixie cut was cool and the perpetual bags under her eyes made her look like a very mysterious vampire and plenty of people were into that.

Bri stared at Lenny, eyes glazed over like the taxidermy in Randy's Diner.

"You work here, right?" Lenny asked her.

"Mm-hm," Bri said. Usually she had more words, but she was absolutely star-struck. Shit. At seventeen, Bri was only a year younger than Claire, but sometimes that one year felt like five.

"Cool. I'm Lenny. I do a show about strange phenomena across the U.S." Her words were overenunciated and extra springy. She probably delivered the exact same pitch to every tourist trap she visited. "I'm staying in one of the train cars out back."

Mustache Bro detached from the counter, muttering about tinfoil hats as he left the shop.

Bri nodded with her mouth hung open. *Stay calm.* Claire wanted to telepathically zap the words into Bri's brain. *Stay on script.* Bri said nothing. Just blinked, still holding the price gun pointed at nothing.

"I was hoping to get some interviews about what's been going on here," Lenny added. "There's been no substantial evidence since the lights of '61. But I heard there was another event a few weeks ago."

Substantial evidence? Who talked like that? Even when the cameras weren't rolling, this girl played the part.

"Uh . . ." Bri looked to Claire. She had forgotten her lines already. Claire had personally booked the room for *Odd Kids,* made the bed, sent Jared to greet them when they rolled in. She had done everything but rehearse with Bri.

"Yeah. Yeah but, Claire saw it too. You should ask her."

Lenny's big eyes flicked to Claire. *Crap.*

Lying wasn't part of the plan. Well—not lying to *anyone's face.* Bri was supposed to be the star actor around here. Claire could handle the story and camera work, but she wasn't about to do any improv. As Lenny made her way toward the counter, possible headlines flew into Claire's brain. FAMED RANCH FALSIFYING ALIEN ENCOUNTERS! DISGRACED FAMILY SELLS RANCH POST YOUTUBE EXPOSÉ!

No. Claire couldn't let that happen. She wouldn't let the rumors win, let those bullies like Mr. Porter with their suits and their business cards convince Aunt Maeve to hand over her family's land.

Claire had a new occupation: Alien Invasion Witness.

Lenny pulled out a little notepad and gel pen from her

crossbody bag, jotted something down, then stared up at Claire with her huge doll eyes, green highlights glittering in the inner corners.

"Hi. I'm Lenny. My boyfriend and I do a show about unexplained phenomena."

"Claire. I think I've seen one of your videos."

Bri put her head down, staring blankly at the price gun.

"Someone sent our team some crazy footage from earlier this summer . . ." Lenny began. "It wasn't really clear, but it looked like something was walking on the barn roof."

"Oh really?" Claire managed. She suddenly felt like the alien. Exposed. Observed. She half expected Lenny to pull out a scalpel and dissect her right there.

"Can I show you?"

Claire nodded. This was a flawed interview tactic. If Claire were *really* a witness, wouldn't showing her a video just make her testimony biased? These YouTube people didn't bother with the scientific method at all. Claire had nothing to worry about; there was no way *Odd Kid*s would find the truth because, honestly, they didn't care to find the truth. They just needed to produce their clickbait so they could peddle merch to ten-year-olds. These vloggers were just as much liars as Claire was. But Claire, at least, had a worthy cause.

Lenny played the video on her phone. For the seven hundredth time, Claire watched a cluster of white pixels scurry along the roof of the red barn. If you squinted, it looked *kinda* like a four-armed alien. The creature then disappeared as a flash of light burst into the black sky.

God, Claire was good. Still no obvious faults. She'd watched enough of those fake ghost shows with Bri to know you just needed one clearish frame, and the rest could be obscured with motion blur. She'd only started fooling around with the pirated editing software a few weeks before, but she figured that if she'd taught herself code when creating Reed Ranch's website, it couldn't be *that* hard. To the average believer, the clip was convincing. Totally worth the hours distorting a free 3-D model, rigging it, animating it, tracking it to the barn roof, and scouring forums to figure out why the goddamn export wasn't working. It was a shame she couldn't claim it as her own. This would have been a great portfolio piece if she ever actually committed to film school.

"Do you think it's Old Lucky?" Lenny asked. She pronounced the name of Scarberry's patron mascot with reverence.

"Must be," Claire said.

"Do you have any idea who could have taken the video? It looks like it was filmed here."

Claire sucked in a huge breath. "We get a lot of tourists."

A double lie. The only person to come into the gift shop today was Mustache Bro.

"Could you check your guest list? See who would have been around at the time?"

Damn, she was persistent.

"Um. Maybe?" Claire said. "I can ask my aunt, but it's probably a privacy thing."

The light dimmed in Lenny's shiny doll eyes for a second, but her big smile didn't faulter. "Of course. And I respect that. Totally. Have *you* had any other strange occurrences while working here?"

Claire relaxed her shoulders. "Weird things happen all the time," she said, returning to the familiar script she used on enthusiastic UFO chasers. It wasn't as if Aunt Maeve had ever trained her on what to say. When Claire was old enough to make change, she was put in front of the register, and from there she figured out how to keep the believers satisfied. The biggest rule: Keep it vague. Let the audience fill in gaps on their own. Never deny, but try not to add any new lore. Remind them the magnets are buy one, get one half-off.

Lenny nodded enthusiastically. She set her notepad on the table. Her handwriting was so messy, it might as well have been in another language. "Would you maybe want to talk about your experiences for a video? I mean, after your shift of course."

This wasn't part of the plan. Once *Odd Kids* made it to the ranch, Claire was to remain invisible. Bri could step in as the believer. Get a few selfies with her heroes. Make sure the influencers left with enough to put in their trashy little videos to summon more UFO chasers.

"I work late tonight," Claire lied.

"Oh. The sign said you close at four."

"I help with the ranch too."

Another lie. She had very little responsibility for the cattle. That was Jared's domain.

"Maybe Bri can show you around," Claire offered.

Bri perked up. "Yeah. Yeah of course. My shift's almost over. I can give you the official tour."

"Cool," Lenny said. "Thank you. That'd be sick."

It felt like a natural end to the conversation. She waited for

Lenny to back away from the register, make plans with Bri. But she locked eyes with Claire again.

"Maybe talk tomorrow then? Before your shift?" Lenny asked with unflinching eye contact. There was something desperate about her. Whether she believed her own bullshit or not, she *cared*. She cared like this was life or death.

"Sure," Claire agreed.

So what if she embarrassed herself on-camera? It wasn't like she had a reputation to protect. And if Lenny didn't get enough witnesses, *Odd Kids* could bother Aunt Maeve. And that would ruin everything.

Aunt Maeve didn't know about Claire's master plan. It was easy getting Bri and Jared on board, but Maeve would've said it was too risky. And she would be wrong. She didn't have the savvy to keep this place running; she was afraid to get her hands dirty.

Claire had been born with her hands dirty.

She had indefinitely postponed film school. She had zero friends left (besides Bri) and nothing but time. She was the only one who could do something.

"I'll give you guys my number," Lenny said. "Just text me when you'll be available. I can come to you if you live close by."

"I live here."

"Oh, awesome. I'll see you soon then."

Guilt crept in, but Claire pushed it down.

Lenny was eating it up. Which meant the rest of her subscribers would. *Odd Kids* would get ad revenue for publishing Claire's work, and a new generation would care about the Scarberry Lights, battling to secure a room at the ranch. Buying up merch. Paying for tours.

Everybody won.

Out of all the jobs Claire had worked, saving her family was the most important. And if that meant convincing this influencer that an alien lived in her backyard, then she would be happy to oblige.

CHAPTER 3

LENNY

"Are you being safe?"

"I'm always safe, Dad."

Lenny had said it during every Wednesday check-in, but her father was eternally anxious. He was convinced that his daughter would get snatched up by a masked boogeyman if she took the scenic route. Or her accommodations would be infested with flesh-eating parasites. Or a rogue flame and an inconveniently placed puddle of gasoline would blow up the *Silver Bullet* with Lenny and Evan inside.

At least that way they'd die viral.

"How's the hotel?" Dad asked.

He meant to say: *Has it burned down yet?*

The lights flickered again. Dammit. Her straightener turned off. She'd plugged it into one of the two outlets in the room. Her hair was drenched in sweat, and the humidity wasn't helping calm the frizz. She had to try to make herself presentable for their Night One Investigation—if they could even do an investigation. As soon as she'd left the gift shop it started pouring and hadn't let up the whole afternoon. She had texted Bri that they'd like to do a tour when the rain stopped. But it looked like that would have to be a tomorrow thing.

"Hotel's great. Just like the pictures," Lenny answered.

"How's Evan?"

Still pouting. "He's editing," Lenny said. "There's a lot of footage to go through." Her parents still didn't know they were on a break. If it wouldn't last, why bother announcing it?

"Well, tell him hello from us!" Mom said.

Evan was hunched over a computer, headphones over his mop of brown hair. He hadn't spoken to Lenny since their fight that afternoon. Or moved, really. Every few minutes his left hand would rise from the keyboard to sip his coffee or push up his glasses. And once an hour, he'd take a hit of his inhaler. Lenny would resist asking if he felt okay. Because she knew he'd lie, and he'd only reply with some pithy remark if she told him that she thought the air felt different here. That the presence of Old Lucky could be aggravating his asthma.

We're like magnets, Evan had said in an early video. Lenny had nodded, bobbing her head like a stupid puppet. She didn't speak much at all in that video because Evan had told her she was talking too fast. It was hard to cut up footage when all her words were overlapping.

They were still magnets, but one of them had flipped poles and now they were repelling each other. As much as Lenny wanted to blame him for changing, she knew it was her own fault. They should've taken a *real* break, so she could sort out these conflicting feelings. See if she could manage to survive without him before pulling the plug for good.

But there was no time for that. They had a schedule to keep. That's showbiz, baby.

The entire caboose rattled as another burst of thunder boomed above them.

"What was that?" Dad asked.

"It's raining. And no, we didn't drive in it."

They were to pull over for bad weather, just to be safe. Lenny's father loved safe; therefore, he loved Evan. Lenny had all the ideas, but Evan had the follow-through. *We don't just fit together romantically, but creatively,* she had said in a livestream once. *We fill in each other's gaps. Evan's like my missing piece.*

The memory made her cringe.

"Well, we know you're really busy," Mom said. "Just wanted to check in. We'll let ya go. Love you!

"Talk next Wednesday," Dad added.

"Love you."

Right after hanging up, her phone chimed with a text alert: *Have you arrived yet? Would love on-the-road pics!*

Maria: their social media assistant and secret third member of *Odd Kids*. They sent her selfies, photos of restaurants they ate at, and fans they met. Maria made the captions. She slapped on the hashtags. She altered Lenny's face with enough filters to make her prettier without being unrecognizable. All of the actual footage was edited by Evan for now, while Lenny did most of the research. She wrote the monologues, finding the *heart* in all the strange little towns they visited. Soon, that would all change. Evan wanted to hire an editor. *Every big channel outsources labor,* he said. *It's not unethical. It's smart.* He'd said the same thing when he'd told her to just use ChatGPT to speed up script-writing. *The algorithm likes consistency. Think of how much faster we can upload new content.*

Lenny wished they weren't on the hunt for UFOs. What she really needed was a time machine, so she could go back to the beginning when she was terrified that the tall kid with glasses didn't like her back. When they were making videos to find proof of something bigger, not selling VPNs and subscription boxes. She missed that sizzle inside of her, when she knew she was barreling toward something more. When she didn't have a woman she'd never met IRL telling her to ditch her platform sneakers because the shippers thought their height difference was adorable and they should lean into that.

Evan started to laugh. It wasn't the laugh he did when something was funny—that was more of a wheeze. This was his cynical cackle. He had closed his laptop and stared at his phone.

"One guess where the *Dark Unknown* crew is right now," he said.

He handed the phone to Lenny. The screen showed an Instagram post from Max Malitz, the host of *Dark Unknown*. He had his thumbs up in front of a pueblo-style house with a wavy roof, all the cacti around it brown and shriveled. Lenny didn't need the location tag to know where this was. She knew that house just as well as her own. She had a map of it in her glovebox.

"Good thing we didn't go to Harrows House, huh," she said, returning the phone to Evan.

"We were going to get there first. We would have been ahead of them."

Oh. So it was a bad thing. Lately, for Evan, everything was a bad thing.

"It shouldn't be about getting ahead," Lenny told him.

Evan hopped off the bed and studied the window. The sky looked like a bruise. The un-mowed grass quivered in the wind.

"Can you get off your moral high horse? We're a business. Okay?" he said.

Lenny laughed. She wished he just screamed it like he wanted to. She was so over that gentle, condescending tone. "That's what we are? A business?"

"I meant the channel. And it was your idea to break up, Lenny. Not mine."

"We're not broken up," she reminded him. "We're on *a break*."

"This isn't a break."

As always, he was reading her mind. But she wasn't going to give him the satisfaction of being right.

"Would it be a break if we were at the Harrows House?" she retorted.

He took a deep breath, likely debating if he would retreat or hit her back with something crueler. He could remind her that *his* business skills allowed her to travel the country, therefore she ought to let him decide where to go. Let him hire writers. Plan more con appearances. They would never have to get a real job because of *his* hard work and well-researched strategy. But a real job didn't sound so bad. Lenny thought of the girl at the counter of the gift shop: curvy with a freckled face, long blond hair with dark roots grown out. She wore cowboy boots and ripped shorts and an unbranded tank top. When Claire clocked out, she didn't have to deal with those customers. They came and went. She wasn't glued to any of them. She wasn't forced to share a bed with her work.

She had freedom.

This fight, like the storm, had been brewing since the drive. They had gone the whole road trip without a real spat; Lenny should have seen it coming. But she stupidly thought they were different. That they could take a break without breaking up. Because maybe they didn't love each other *like that* anymore, but Evan was her home planet. Without him, she was floating in space, untethered.

He could still fill in all those gaps. He had to. He was the only one who knew how.

"You need to make a decision, Lenny. If you don't want to do the show anymore just say it," Evan said.

"I didn't say anything about quitting the show. I just can't be *betrothed* before my brain's finished cooking."

She'd told him that when she had invoked the break. When he'd cried and asked why, oh why would she dump him and she searched her mind for a tangible reason. It was supposed to be a brainstorming session for the road trip. She had just pitched they go to the Winchester Mystery House and Evan had debuted his ten-year plan. *By 2030, we'll probably be married, and have at least 2 million subscribers . . .*

That's when she'd snapped. Kicking him out of her room abruptly and asking for *some time to think*.

"Betrothed?" Evan repeated now. "This isn't one of your Jane Austen novels. My God. I told you a million times I wasn't proposing when I said that, just trying to make sure our goals were compatible. Reasonable people make plans. The real world isn't just impulsively driving to the next shiny thing."

"Scarberry isn't an impulse," she said. "I've always wanted to come here."

"No offense, but have you considered that you don't have prophetic dreams? That you just latched on to this place and assigned it meaning?"

He'd tell their subscribers that their Ouija board accurately predicted the latest celebrity death but refused to believe her recurring nightmare meant anything. Had he ever believed in the places they visited? Had he ever believed in *her*? She couldn't just leave before she knew for sure.

"I never said I know what the dreams meant!" she protested. "Just that it's a gut feeling."

"Your gut feeling is making us miss out on getting actual, usable content."

Lenny rolled her eyes. She'd grown to hate that word. *Content.*

"There it is, again," Evan said. "I can feel your resentment every time we're filming. Is it me? Or is it the channel?"

It's all of it! she wanted to scream. *It's living by a script.*

Before she could answer, the dull ceiling light flickered off, and the AC stopped running. They had officially lost power. This night just had to get worse.

There was a beat of silence, and then a new sound from

outside. It was a one-note howl, long and mournful and so high-pitched it hurt. Then, another one. Another one. Overlapping, tinging, like bells.

They both froze for a moment, looking at each other as if to say, *You hear that too, right?* The wails continued. This was real. This was happening. Finally, this was happening. She was where she was meant to be.

Lenny ran outside, hearing Evan unzipping a camera bag behind her. The UFO lights around the caboose flicked on and off. The window AC started and died again. The rain had let up, but it was still dark, and the humid wind blew her curtain bangs around her eyes. She couldn't see anything, but she could feel it. Something was out there with her.

The failing electricity, the strange sound—this was exactly what was reported in the summer of '61.

Yet Lenny couldn't tell what direction the wails were coming from. She stepped away from the cover of trees, brushed her hair back, and looked up at the sky. No stars. No strange lights.

The shrieks were terrifying, but Lenny felt herself smile. Evan was wrong about this place. She had trusted her gut, and her gut had been right.

"We were about to begin our investigation when we heard a strange noise outside of our room," Evan said from behind her in his narration voice. He always spoke clearer when the camera was rolling. He was a natural, while it had taken some getting used to for Lenny. She had to train herself not to talk so fast. Not to mumble. Evan used to squeeze her hand when she got too excited. Lately, she hardly got excited. But now she felt like she was going to leap out of her skin and into another dimension.

Evan focused the lens right at her. "What do you think it is?" he asked.

Lenny pulled a strand of hair from her mouth. For the first time in a long time, she told the camera the truth: "I think it's Old Lucky."

CHAPTER 4

CLAIRE

You can chill with the lights now, Claire texted Bri. She set her phone down and stared between the rotten boards of the garden shed. It wasn't the coziest home base; her butt had gone numb sitting on an upside-down bucket and she wasn't completely sure if the wasp nest in the corner was vacant or not. But the shed gave her cover from the rain and the perfect view. So far, the plan was working. The lights above the train cars stabilized and the happy couple stared at the sky, pointing a big camera at the rain clouds.

"Wait, did it stop?" said the Boyfriend. He had an *E* name. Eddy? Elton? Didn't matter. He wouldn't be here long. They'd only booked the caboose for three days, and if they tried for longer, Claire would just say it wasn't available.

She turned the volume up on her phone. The earsplitting shriek grew louder. The paranormal investigators frantically turned their heads, trying to find the source of it. It was kind of hilarious.

"Holy shit!" Eddyton squealed.

Lenny jumped up and down. "Do you think it heard us?" God, she had such Pomeranian energy, with her big eyes and shrill voice.

"Yeah. I definitely feel . . . watched," Elsworth agreed.

Lenny looked at the camera. She walked backwards, talking with a cadence somewhere between cheerleader and news anchor: "Witnesses from 1961 said Old Lucky's song was at such a high frequency, dogs were affected. Glass would break. People would get headaches and nosebleeds."

Claire had to stop herself from snorting. *Nosebleeds?* She hadn't heard that one before. It only took her thirty minutes to distort regular cow moos into an alien screech. She spent the morning hiding the Bluetooth speakers within a 50-foot radius around the caboose. One in a tree. One in a tipped-over wheelbarrow. One in the weeds around the crumbling windmill (she really needed to catch up on mowing). It wouldn't take a rocket scientist to find them. But these people weren't looking for speakers.

They were looking for the Beast of Scarberry.

The door to the garden shed creaked open. For a horrifying second, Claire thought she'd been discovered. But it was only Bri standing in the doorway, drenched from the rain.

"What are you doing?" Claire whispered harshly.

"I wanted to help."

"You already did your job. You were supposed to stay by the circuit breaker."

"I can't see anything from there. And it's *freezing* outside."

Bri sat on the bucket next to Claire. She was shaking, totally underdressed for the weather. Claire offered her jacket. When Bri put it on, she was absolutely swimming in it. Bri was small, even more so after the chemo, and Claire had always been one of the biggest girls in her class. She had made it her mission to be radically confident. There were about a million corporations who wanted to make money off women's insecurities, and she refused to give them the satisfaction. Claire didn't think there was anything wrong with her body—it was just that *everyone else did*. Especially in a town like Scarberry, where everyone had an opinion on everyone. She knew that she would be treated as infinitely more worthy if she took up less space.

After a few minutes of watching the YouTubers run around in circles, Claire turned off the "Old Lucky" audio on her phone. Lenny and Elmo stopped under a tree.

Lenny looked at the sky. Her man wiped the raindrops away from the camera's viewfinder.

"Holy shit. Evan got new glasses," Bri whispered.

Evan. That was his name. Boring name for a boring guy.

"They're so cute," Bri gushed. "He's so cute."

"Ask him to next year's prom when you give the tour tomorrow."

"Shut up."

"No seriously. Now's your chance to live your dream."

"Being *a homewrecker* is not part of the dream."

"They're probably not even together," Claire theorized. "It's like *The Bachelor* or some shit. It's about views."

"Sorry, I believe in *love*."

Claire snorted. "I believe in love. Just not aliens."

Bri giggled.

Evan yanked off the corded earbuds and let them rest on his neck.

"You can't hear it," he announced. "You can't hear anything over the wind." He took off his (apparently brand-new) hideous wire-rimmed frames and rubbed them on his shirt. "We can just add it in post."

Lenny glared at him like he'd just admitted to manslaughter. "What? We are *not* doctoring footage."

"Told ya," Bri whispered. Though Bri said she watched the show because *it's fun,* she had professed that *some* of it was real. Just like how she thought *some* of the Old Lucky legend was true.

"It's not lying, Lenny," Evan protested. "It was real. I heard it. But the viewers won't be able to."

"So we should stay out all night until it happens again."

Please God, no. Claire's ass already hurt from sitting on this bucket. She wasn't going to hide in the shed all night.

"And if it doesn't?" Evan countered.

"There's more here. I know it."

Lenny kept walking, but she didn't go back to the caboose, like Claire hoped. She went the wrong direction: right up to the shed.

Bri wasn't exactly a light breather, and now that her idols were heading toward them, she was practically panting. Claire covered Bri's mouth. "Shhhh," she hissed.

Evan sighed, long and dramatic, and followed his girlfriend. Claire wanted to look away. She always felt secondhand embarrassment when couples argued. Clearly, they *were* together. There was nothing fake about this argument.

Yikes.

Odd Kids put out a lot of content. But whenever Bri forced Claire to endure their videos, Lenny and her boyfriend hardly disagreed about anything. Either a few hours in Scarberry had already driven them to a breaking point, or the happy couple was pretending to be happier than they were.

They stopped right under the roof. Evan put his hand on Lenny's shoulders. "Finding Old Lucky isn't going to mean anything if there's no usable investigation footage."

Claire couldn't believe this. These people pretended a knocked-over paint bucket contained human blood for a solid five minutes, and Scarberry wasn't spooky enough for them? This wasn't her only scheme of course—she still had the suit. But that was supposed to be the grand finale.

Lenny stood her ground. "There will be. It's just night one."

Evan fiddled with his glasses again, looking more pompous by the second. "Or," he said, pausing for dramatic effect, "we're just wasting time."

Oh, screw you. Now Claire really wished she was watching them behind the safety of a screen, so she could yell at him herself.

Lenny scoffed. "You mean wasting *money*?"

Bri must have forgotten she wasn't watching a reality show. She gasped. Loudly.

Well, *shit*.

Lenny whipped her head around. "What was that?"

"An alien. *Obviously*," her boyfriend muttered. Lenny glared at him, but he shrugged it off. He slung the camera bag over his shoulder and strutted toward the caboose, disappearing into the black.

Lenny pulled out her phone and started typing, big doll eyes squinting at the screen with a scary intensity. Claire flinched as a Bri gasped and grabbed her phone.

"Oh my God. Oh my God," Bri whispered. "Lenny just texted me. Holy shit. I'm gonna yack. She wants to do the tour tomorrow morning. Can you come with?"

This was supposed to be Bri's department. But what if she cracked under pressure again? Bri had frozen during her brief encounter with Lenny. And that girl was all sunshine and rainbows. Evan was going to be much harder to convince. And Bri had an all-consuming parasocial crush on him.

"Yeah. I'll come," Claire said, despite the sinking feeling in her gut.

* * * * * * * * * * * *

Once Lenny returned to the caboose, Claire and Bri made a run for the house, sprinting as fast as they could, as if Old Lucky were really out there. They creeped into the kitchen, careful not to wake up Aunt Maeve (though the woman slept like a rock). She spent her days so stressed that her entire soul left her body come ten p.m. But they were always careful to shut cabinets and took baby steps up the rickety staircase anyway. Every time they left their bedrooms late at night, they were on a "secret mission" even if it was just gathering snacks. If they were too loud, they'd wake up Maeve and the *Old Gods*.

When they invented the game, Claire hadn't known what the Old Gods were, just that Jared blamed them when it rained too much or too little.

But being quiet didn't matter, because moments after making it inside, there were knocks on the roof. The unmistakable sound of hail.

Bri gave Claire a look as they ascended the staircase. It said, *Again?* As if the weather were something Claire could control. This would be the fourth storm this summer. Each getting more and more brutal. The Reeds couldn't afford a patched roof. But it was the farmers who had the most to lose. Half the crops were already goners. She heard the whispers of worry in the grocery store. If Scarberrians needed a push to sell their land to J. Porter and Associates, this was it.

Claire gathered the notes on her bed and headed to Bri's room: their home base for movie nights and hoax planning.

Bri curled up in the bed, swallowed by a dozen Squishmallows. Half her class gifted her plushies during her first round of chemo and now, four months into remission, they lived on. Claire hated their soulless black eyes—she liked to tell herself her disdain was from the uncanny valley, but it was probably because they were a reminder that no one in her class would have sent *her* gifts if she had been the one who'd gotten sick. Claire sat on top of the comforter and pulled open her master-plan document on her laptop.

"We need to get our story straight for tomorrow," Claire started. "I'm thinking, you tell them the sounds started up again in April. Then they became more frequent during the summer. Okay?"

Bri watched the quarter-sized balls of ice slamming against the window. "Mm-hm."

"When you talk about the encounter, don't mention glowing eyes. I know it's in all the papers, but the suit's eyes don't light up. We want to be consistent with our version of the story, okay? And if they ask about other witnesses, tell them Jared saw something. He's already prepped."

Bri wasn't paying attention. She traced the crack in the window with her pointer finger.

"I don't feel good," she whispered.

"Don't," Claire said. Bri always did this when she got stage fright. Claire had to drag her from the bathroom stall before Bri's freshman musical debut.

"I'm serious," Bri protested weakly. "I might puke."

"You're fine. We just gotta practice, run through possible questions they'll ask."

Bri just shook her head and leaped from the bed. She skittered down the hallway and slammed the bathroom door.

Thunder crackled. White-hot veins of lightning streaked across the window.

Claire nearly jumped when she noticed a figure outside in the middle of the yard. Who the hell would be outside in the middle of a hailstorm? She eased toward the window. Lenny was wearing a neon-green hoodie, hands in the front pocket, as tiny chunks of ice bounced at her feet. She stood alone, staring up to the heavens like she was willing the clouds to part. Praying to neighbors from another galaxy to beam her up.

CHAPTER 5

LENNY

Lenny was starting to understand the NO CLIMBING PLEASE sign. The morning sun baked the metal saucer, burning the edges of her vision and the back of her legs. After twenty minutes sitting on the UFO, she couldn't stand it any longer. She finished the last bite of her granola bar and jumped off. The skin on the back of her thigh looked raw. Great. If the marks didn't fade soon, she would have to change into long pants or risk Evan using the heat rash as part of this episode's plot. He'd act like the wounds were proof of aliens and their radiation powers.

In one video, Evan had pretended his cat scratches were done by invisible forces. According to the ever-expanding *Odd Kids* lore, Lenny's occasional nosebleeds were psychic intuition. If Evan tried to lie to subscribers again, Lenny silently vowed to put her foot down. There were plenty of real mysteries already in Scarberry. She knew it.

She checked the time on her watch—9:22 a.m. They had

agreed to meet at the saucer at nine, and there was still no sign of Bri.

She must have been busy with some kind of farm chore. Lenny didn't mind waiting. Anything to be out of the claustrophobic room with Evan. They didn't talk about the shrieking last night. And Evan hadn't even stopped her when she went outside just as it started hailing. He didn't ask if she was okay. They slept on opposite sides of the bed, and in Lenny's dream Reed Ranch was coated in snow. Lenny was on her hands and knees digging through it. Evan stood next to her, holding a camera. He kept asking "What are you looking for?" and she couldn't answer; even as she tried to speak, nothing came out.

Then Lenny woke up, ripped from her dream before anything could happen. Just like always. Only this time she was on the floor of the caboose. She'd fallen out of bed at some point, as if her unconscious were desperate to be away from Evan.

Not yet.

The show would help her get the proof she needed. Then she'd know all of this wasn't for nothing. But the show wasn't hers anymore. It had mutated into this ugly thing that was slowly sapping the life out of her. She couldn't keep going on like this. But she couldn't just quit, either.

Both options felt like losing.

She thought when she stepped foot on the grounds of this place she'd feel a cosmic disturbance. A shaking in her bones, like the stories said. And now here she was, chafing in her bicycle shorts, dehydrated from the heat and last night's tears, standing right below where the lights occurred over seventy years ago, and mostly she just felt exhausted.

Lenny spotted two brown barrels lined up against the barn and headed toward them. One had to be for garbage, right? She needed to get rid of her granola-bar wrapper, but she didn't want to go all the way back to the train car. She wasn't ready to find out if Evan had woken up. For how type-A he was, he always managed to sleep through alarms.

"And you're sure a coyote didn't do this?" a woman's voice asked from inside the barn.

"No, miss. Coyote would have ate it. Mangled it."

Lenny peeked around the corner, where the barn door was wide open. The concrete floor was covered in hay. A single square window acted as a spotlight, revealing every bit of dust in the air with stark clarity. It smelled overwhelmingly animal, though there was only a single cow inside. She didn't have the best view from here, but it looked like a baby.

Jared the farmhand stood next to it. He was talking to a woman with red hair clipped into a half ponytail. She had on a tank top, exposing freckles on the back of her shoulders.

"See, it's all rotten around it," Jared said, gesturing to the widest part of the calf's stomach. "It happened last night, but the wound's already gone bad."

Lenny couldn't see what Jared was talking about. The calf looked fine from this angle. She squatted closer to the door. Oh. Gross. One of the calf's spots wasn't a spot at all. It was shiny with blood. Lenny unzipped the camera bag. Now she actually wished Evan were here; he was better at operating the equipment. She tried to focus on the cow, but no matter how much she fiddled with the lens, the image wasn't clear. She didn't have the right mic with her either. Most of the dialogue was going to be lost.

The woman gave the calf a gentle stroke on its neck. "Are you sure it happened last night?"

"I always keep an eye on the little ones, miss," said Jared. "Extra care. This one didn't have a mark on her yesterday. She seems fine otherwise. I gave her antibiotics for the infection."

"And the others?"

Others?

"Healing up," Jared said.

"Possibly from the storm."

"Doubt a little hail would make a wound this big, miss."

"You know animals can act all kinds of crazy when anxious. Bad weather can frighten them. They might be doing this to themselves. Nothing to worry about."

"How 'bout I call the chief to help keep watch tonight, see what's goin' after them?"

"No need." She gave a loving pat to his shoulder. "You do enough around here. Go home. Get some sleep."

She had to be the owner, Miss Reed. Is this why she didn't make time to see Lenny and Evan yet? Too busy dealing with cattle mutilation? It was too soon to call it yet. They'd have to weed out all other explanations first, but this looked like textbook bovine excision.

Miss Reed turned away from Jared and the calf. *Shit.*

Lenny ducked behind one of the barrels. She clutched

the camera to her chest and tried not to breathe as Miss Reed strutted toward the farmhouse, somehow looking downright regal as she stepped over the minefield of manure.

Lenny leaned against the eroding paint of the barn, trying to catch her breath. It was a close call. The *Odd Kids* legal team had sent some emails to the ranch before their arrival, asking for permission to record the grounds. All the paperwork was in order, but legality didn't equal morality, and most people didn't appreciate eavesdropping. Especially when that eavesdropping involved cameras.

It felt like a century since the last time she'd had to sneak around for an investigation. *Odd Kids* used to film in abandoned buildings all the time. They didn't wait around for permission. They didn't care about private property, only the Truth. Now they were actual adults who could get in real trouble. If they had a video demonetized, that meant money down the drain. Now they had something to lose.

Lenny jotted down on her notes app: *Miss Reed neglects her cows*. No, that wasn't right. Miss Reed seemed almost annoyed that Jared was showing her this. Because she thought it wasn't a big enough concern, or because she would rather him not look into it? The way she phrased things was off.

Are you sure it wasn't a coyote?

Are you sure it happened last night?

Nothing to worry about.

Lenny hit backspace, replacing the line with *Miss Reed knows something*.

"Oh, there you are."

Claire sat on a muddy four-wheeler, staring down at Lenny

crouched behind a barrel like an idiot. Claire looked just as elegant as Miss Reed, but in a completely different way. She had the soft shape of a woman in an ancient Greek sculpture. Her outfit was careless in a cool way: A T-shirt with the sleeves cut off, muddy black cowboy boots, gray denim shorts cropped just above the knee, covered in patches and colorful stitches and Sharpie words and stars.

Claire cut the engine, and she stepped off effortlessly. She must have ridden this thing hundreds of times—she lived here, after all—but she didn't seem like a girl who should be driving an ATV around a cattle ranch. She seemed like she should be driving something infinitely cooler. A helicopter. A hearse.

"You weren't at the UFO at nine," Lenny said, standing up.

It wasn't meant to sound accusatory, but right as it left her lips, Lenny knew it was the wrong thing to say.

"Where's your boyfriend?" Claire asked.

"He's . . . reviewing footage from last night."

Claire nodded condescendingly. Lenny was a bad liar. Always had been. She was one of those see-through frogs that lived in the Amazon. All her guts displayed for easy viewing.

"Is Bri coming?" Lenny asked.

"She's not feeling well."

"Oh. I'm sorry."

"Probably just a stomach bug."

"Oh. Still. That sucks."

"Yeah. But I'm here now, so . . . let's get this going."

Clearly that meant *Let's get this over with.*

Most interviewees were ecstatic about telling their stories. Lenny couldn't get a read on Claire. Maybe she was just the deadpan type, or maybe she was worried she wouldn't be believed. A lot of their sources had their communities shun them for being crackpots. Requesting their faces to be blurred, their voices altered. But Claire hadn't asked for anonymity.

Unlike the emailer.

If Claire was the one who sent the video, why didn't she just admit it? Why did it have to be a secret? Of course, Lenny wasn't sure who'd sent the video yet. It could have been the other girl in the gift shop, Bri. It could be Jared. It could be one of hundreds of tourists.

Lenny flinched as the farmhouse's back door slammed shut.

"Hello there!" called Miss Reed as she sauntered toward them, carrying two mason jars full of amber liquid. She had a floppy woven hat on now. The brim covered her eyes.

"I don't think we've met," she said, thrusting a glass into Lenny's hand. It smelled earthy. The ice cubes clanked around. Iced tea, maybe?

"I'm Maeve Reed."

"Hi, I'm—"

"Hannah! Yes, I've heard so much about you. I didn't realize you were coming after all. Claire doesn't tell me these things sometimes. She's shy."

"No, Aunt Maeve, this is *Lenny*," Claire explained. "With the *YouTube channel*."

Lenny, with the YouTube channel. That was her official title now. She wanted to profess that she was more than that. But she wasn't more. That was what made it so soul-crushing. Lenny took a sip, just to fill the silence, and tried to stifle her gag reflex. It wasn't iced tea.

"Oh." Miss Reed blinked in confusion. "Lenny . . . Well . . . we're so happy to have you here. If you need anything, I'll be around."

"Yeah I actually wanted to talk to you—"

"I'm terribly busy at the moment. Maybe we can catch up later. I'm sure Claire can answer any questions. Or Jared. You've met Jared?"

"Briefly. But I'd like to talk to him again—"

"Claire, why don't you take our guest out for some breakfast?" Maeve went on. "Show her the best of Scarberry?" Miss Reed gave a strained smile. Hannah. Lenny. Didn't matter who she was. Miss Reed wanted her away from the ranch. This was all wrong. Miss Reed owned a tourist attraction. Shouldn't she be hospitable?

"Uh, yeah," Claire agreed. She glanced at Lenny. "I mean if you want to."

They had the next two days to investigate Scarberry. Lenny didn't need to stay at the ranch the whole time. It might be good to get out. They could do the interview over breakfast. Probably. Some places were weird about filming inside, and Evan would have to manually blur the faces of the other patrons. Good. She kind of liked the idea of making things difficult for him.

And anyway, it made sense from a research perspective. She could get acquainted with the other residents of Scarberry. Get a feel for the town and what they believed. It wasn't just the monsters that interested Lenny, it was the people who lived with them. Who feared them, who hunted them.

Ideally, she'd check in with Evan before leaving. But ideally, Evan wouldn't be pouting in the caboose. He'd already be enthusiastically searching the grounds with her.

"Sure," Lenny agreed.

"Beautiful!" Miss Reed said. She handed Claire a credit card, which she shoved in the back pocket of her shorts. "You'll love Randy's Diner, dear. Good home-cooked food. On me, of course. And go ahead and take the kombucha on the road with you. It's good for your gut. Kids your age don't think about that until it's too late."

"Maybe afterward I can ask you some stuff about the ranch. The history?" Lenny asked.

Miss Reed's mouth twitched. "Maybe. I do have my hands full this afternoon. I'm sure Claire would be just as good a tour guide as I would. But we'll see each other again. You girls have fun."

Miss Reed speed-walked away from them, back inside the red barn. This time, she closed the door.

CHAPTER 6

CLAIRE

"Do you like greasy diner food?" Claire asked. She felt morally obligated to give a warning. Lenny had been everywhere, and she'd been raking in the big influencer bucks. She'd likely eaten at five-star restaurants all over the country. "I don't want to force you. I know I hate when plans change."

They were almost to the truck, parked in the muddy lot. Claire tried to remember the state of the bench seat. If she knew she was driving a stranger today, she would have removed the leftover McDonald's bags and her stash of empty plastic water bottles.

"I'm kinda a go-with-the-flow person," Lenny said. "And Evan tries to support local businesses on road trips."

He tries to support local businesses? What a guy.

Claire never understood Bri's crush on him. He didn't have a presence, not like Lenny did. She was practically radiating energy, like she was trying her hardest not to break into song.

Claire still wasn't sure if the girl was hyped up on too much caffeine, playing a character, or if she was just *like that.*

"Oh shit, did you want to ask Evan to come?" Claire offered.

"No," Lenny said quickly. Then, like that needed an explanation, she started to ramble. "He's really tired from the trip. And last night. We hardly get a full night's sleep on the road and this isn't our first stop, you know? We've been at it for weeks. Not that we're going in a specific order—I mean, we *are*—we're working our way west, but it's not in order of, like, best to worst or anything. Actually, I was more excited to come to Scarberry than anywhere else."

"Really?" That had to be a joke.

"Yeah. It's actually what got me into unexplained phenomena and, like, cryptozoology. I probably wouldn't have started *Odd Kids* if I didn't fixate on this place first. I've had a picture of the Scarberry Lights above my bed since I was in fifth grade."

Claire had seen her share of UFO enthusiasts, but no one was *that* excited to come to Scarberry. It was a consolation prize, since Area 51 was super illegal to visit.

Either there was more to it, or this girl just lived and breathed bullshit.

"Sorry for the mess," Claire said as she manually unlocked the driver's side. The key fob to her old Chevy hadn't worked since she'd bought it last year. She'd never minded till now.

She hopped in and reached over to unlock the passenger door.

Lenny slid into the bench seat. "I've been basically living in my car for the past month. This is nothing."

Lenny picked up a CD from the center console.

"I didn't peg you for an ABBA girl," she said.

"They're okay. I'm not really an anything girl."

"Oh. Well. I love ABBA." Lenny put the CD in the player. "I've seen *Mamma Mia 2*, like, a hundred times, and it always makes me cry."

The band made Claire cry now too. But probably for totally different reasons.

Hannah had gotten her into ABBA. Obviously Claire knew about them before. Everyone knew "Dancing Queen" at least, but Hannah had turned Claire into a fan. It wasn't like what she usually listened to, but the funky disco beats and ethereal voices were calming.

Hannah could talk about music for hours. She knew her stuff too. Somehow, she never ran out of recommendations. Every week, she would send Claire a new playlist, or mailed a CD with stickers on the disc. She was a year older—already in college—and she seemed to have lived a hundred lives in nineteen years. Claire had only lived a fraction of a life.

So of course Hannah got bored of her.

During the twenty-minute drive into town, Lenny kept her eyes out the window, as if miles and miles of endless fields and cows were the most riveting thing she'd ever seen.

"Hey, are the fields supposed to look like that?" Lenny asked as they passed the Nelsons' farm. Or, what *used to be* their farm. The cornstalks were barely knee-high, shriveled and brown prematurely.

"No," Claire said. "It's been a bad season."

It had been a few bad seasons. Farming was always a risk.

You were staking your life on other living organisms you couldn't control. But this year, the Reeds were lucky to be in the beef business.

"That happened in the summer of '61," Lenny said. "All the crops failed after Old Lucky was first spotted."

Claire had to hold her breath to resist saying something sarcastic. This girl was utterly delusional if she thought dead corn was caused by extraterrestrials. And besides, Scarberry's luck had been getting worse and worse every year without any Old Lucky sightings.

They waited an eternity at the only stoplight. Claire always got the red light. It was as if the infrastructure of the place could sense she was queer.

Lenny stuck the little camera out the window, snapping a video of the dozen two-story brick buildings downtown. Scarberry had only the mandatory basics: a post office, a church, a courthouse, a single school for all twelve grades, a library, a fire station and police station, a greasy spoon, and a bar.

"Cute," Lenny said, pointing to the white clapboard church on the corner. "It's like a movie set."

"It's not cute when you have to drive an hour and a half to buy oat milk," Claire said.

"No grocery store?"

"Technically yeah. But there's not many options there."

Scarberry didn't pride itself on options. Scarberry didn't *pride*, period.

Lenny turned to look at her. "Really? No dairy substitutes in Cow Town?"

Claire couldn't help but laugh. "Definitely not." She parked in Randy's gravel lot. It was peak breakfast time. She hoped there wasn't a wait.

Once out of the truck, Lenny slid her tiny handheld camera into her holographic crossbody bag and looked up at the sky, as if aliens were going to make first contact any second and if she looked at her feet just once she would miss it.

When Lenny saw the wood-paneled interior of Randy's Diner, her full lips slid into a smile. Because this place that hadn't evolved since the '70s was so *cute* to her. Everyone wanted to see a time capsule, but no one wanted to live in one. Or, maybe some people did. There was a whole demographic who wouldn't mind existing in a "simpler time." Lenny was traditionally attractive (thin) and lived a respectable lifestyle (straight), but the Scarberrians wouldn't put up with her for long, not with all the talk about aliens and the camera working as an extra limb.

Claire grabbed two menus and secured a booth in the corner, far from the gaze of the sun-bleached deer head. The table was still sticky with the maple syrup from the last unlucky customer. There was a flyer taped to the wall, advertising a town hall meeting tomorrow. Lenny smiled as she read it, like even that was *cute*. Then she brushed lettuce off her menu.

"So, what's good?" she asked.

"Not the eggs benedict. Their hollandaise sauce is impressively bad."

"Noted."

Claire ordered her regular chocolate-chip pancakes and side of tater tots. Lenny told their server "Same," which either meant they had similar tastes or Lenny was devoted to following the rules of the locals. Like that would get her in good graces with Old Lucky.

Claire's phone vibrated in her back pocket and her heart did a little flutter. But it wasn't Hannah deciding to unghost her. Not today. Probably not ever.

It was Bri: *Still on for tonight?*

Claire texted Bri a thumbs-up.

Claire hadn't seen her since last night. This morning, Bri was still in the bathroom. Claire had thought her cousin was taking one of her famous hourlong Epsom salt baths (Maeve believed they sucked out toxins, especially when combined with lemon juice). But Claire had heard Bri sobbing. Claire stayed at the door, trying to console her, until Bri screamed at her to go away. That was when Claire knew Bri's nausea last night wasn't just nerves. She probably had the flu or something, and now she'd have to miss her date with Evan the YouTube heartthrob.

She assumed Aunt Maeve calmed Bri down eventually. That was why Maeve was so determined to remove them from the property. She was defusing the bomb that was her daughter.

"Do you think this place would care if I filmed inside?" Lenny asked.

"It's probably fine."

Lenny's little bag held more than Claire expected. She pulled out a camera, a mic, and a tiny tripod. Before she clicked Record, a shadow blocked the dim light above them.

"Long time no see, Reed."

Pale hands with dirty fingernails gripped the edge of their table. Bryce Stern had aged poorly since graduation in May.

His football T-shirt was somehow sweatier. The words on the front were peeling off. The fresh buzz cut showed off his lumpy head shape. Claire heard he was going into the military. But he was still here, terrorizing the locals.

"Hi," Claire said, her voice low and short. She wanted to say, *Fuck off,* but she didn't want to cause a scene, here in the heart of Scarberry. It would just be more proof she was a man-hating lesbian. If anyone in the restaurant didn't already know, then they would soon.

It was her own fault. She shouldn't have come out so carelessly. But that was when she was sure she was leaving the state. Before Bri got diagnosed. When the idea of being the big fat rainbow thorn in Scarberry's side felt like radical defiance. In reality, Claire had incited a war with no army and no weapons. There were allies, sure. But her family had their own bad reputation, and Jared was always working. Downtown was enemy territory.

Another boy barged in, clasping his meaty hands to Bryce's shoulders. Warren Lamb wore cut-off sleeves, showing off his biceps and severe farmer's tan. He used to be a scrawny kid, until one day he drank Hulk Juice and now his neck was about as thick as his head.

Claire used to play on the rope swing at his house. He used to come over to pet the cows. But friendships before high school didn't mean much. As they drifted apart, he never said anything bad about her. He never said anything nice about her either.

They were cordial, still. They had to be. Warren's mom died toward the end of junior year. Every Scarberrian who'd lost someone was required to perform a hospitality. Drop off casseroles and Hallmark cards with encouraging Bible verses.

And his dad was the chief of police.

The boys slid into the booth, Bryce on Lenny's side, Warren on Claire's. She seriously considered stabbing his toes with the heel of her boot.

"What's your name?" Warren asked Lenny. He stole a tater tot from Claire's plate. As if they were still best bros who did stuff like that.

"Lenny Gilson."

"You in town for the fair?" Bryce asked her.

"What kind of fair?"

Bryce snickered.

"It's just the county fair," Claire explained. "Funnel cakes and tractor pulls and shit. It starts this week."

"She's from outta state," Warren said. "Gotta be."

"I'm from Chicago."

"*Ohhhhh Chicago,*" Bryce cooed. "They all have green fingernails in Chicago?"

"Uh . . ."

Warren interrupted, "What brings you to Scarberry?"

Oh. Here we go . . .

"I travel the country investigating unexplained phenomena for my YouTube channel, *Odd Kids,*" Lenny explained. "I want to find out what happened here in 1961. What's still happening now. If you have any stories, I'd love to have you on the show."

I'd love to have you. Not *we*. Evan's name was mysteriously absent from the pitch.

Interesting.

Warren folded his arms and gave Bryce an amused look. If Claire wasn't already a pariah, her reputation would be finished for bringing Lenny to town.

"Hey," Bryce said, shifting even closer to Lenny. Her head was brushed up against the posting for the town hall meeting. "I saw a meme about how your type's gotta have short nails to do the deed. That's how you can tell."

Lenny's eyebrows flipped up. "Tell what?"

"Maybe Reed should explain."

"*Bryce*," Warren growled.

Yes. Warren. Pretend you're so much better than him.

"What? I'm just saying . . ."

Thunder rolled, far away. "Fuck, dude," Warren said, jumping out of the booth. "Let's go. You've angered the Old Gods."

Bryce peeled away, but before leaving he looked Lenny up and down. His thin mouth stretched into a grin. "Hope we didn't interrupt anything . . ."

"Nice to meet you, Lenny Gilson. I'll check out your channel," Warren said, then dragged Bryce to the other side of the restaurant, where a gaggle of other boys were waiting.

"Who were they?" Lenny asked.

"Warren's the big one. Bryce's the dirty one."

"What's Bryce's deal?"

Claire shouldn't say anything mean out loud. Bryce and co. couldn't hear them, but that didn't make her safe. The old couple in the booth next to her went to church with the Sterns. The owner of this place pampered all the football players. There were ears everywhere.

But it wasn't like Claire's reputation could get any worse.

"Typical Scarberry boy," she said. "He's something they call a fullback. He's going into the army or the navy or something. Then he'll move back here and marry his high school girlfriend and they'll pop out a few kids."

Lenny looked up from the tabletop tripod she was adjusting. "Is there something wrong with that?"

Right. Lenny was famously in a heterosexual relationship. She probably had plans to buy a McMansion and vlog about wedding dresses and baby names. Why the hell did Claire say that? She couldn't get too comfortable. Lenny wasn't her friend; she was part of a greater strategy. If this hoax was going to work, Claire had to keep her eyes on the prize.

"No," Claire said cautiously. "His girlfriend is nice. I actually feel bad for her. Bryce is a total dick. He worked at the ranch for a few weeks and Jared fired him, so now he has it out for me."

He had it out for Claire long before then. But Lenny didn't need to know all the nasty details.

"And the other one. Warren?"

"Just the neighbor boy."

Lenny nodded and leaned over the table suddenly. Claire froze as Lenny pinned a lavalier mic to her shirt and plugged the long cord into her phone. She sat back on her booth, pinned a mic to herself and pressed a button on the camera, its black shiny lens pointed directly at Claire's face.

Go time.

"Claire," Lenny started, "one of the boys mentioned the Old Gods. What are they?"

Really? That was her first question? Claire sighed.

"It's a joke. Mostly," she started, trying to remember the

details that Jared had told her once. Growing up in Scarberry meant hearing the references before the full story. "People get weird religious beliefs during bad times. Start creating all this wild folklore out of nothing, ya know? There was a bad blight on the crops, in eighteen hundred something, so . . . the legend goes, they started sacrificing cattle. The Christian god wasn't answering their prayers, so maybe something else would? And *supposedly* it worked. It worked too well. Because some farmer found gold."

She wasn't sure if she should look at the eye of the camera lens or at Lenny. She chose neither. The clock on the wall became her new best friend.

"So, they started digging mines. I guess they heard about the gold rush in California and were feeling extra confident there'd be more of it. Especially now that they had gods on their side. They did more sacrifices and . . . no gold. Some people said the gods were punishing them for taking the land for granted. Some were converted back to following Jesus and wanted to leave the Old Gods bullshit behind. Everything was so tense. Like, *brink of civil war* tense. But eventually, everyone calmed down and went back to farming. The town shifted away from the mines in, like, the '20s or '30s. There's a bunch of buildings from then that are still up. Old Scarberry's basically a ghost town now. The ranch is right on the border."

"Do people still believe in the Old Gods?"

"Pshh. No. It's this big running joke now. Except for Bryce's mom. She's really messed up. She thinks the ranch makes a mockery of the Old Gods. I heard she's got an altar in her house or something."

Claire didn't know how true the altar part was, but if Bryce could spread rumors about her, she was allowed to return the favor.

Lenny nodded. Of course she was eating this up. Small-town hysteria made good content. Especially if the world hadn't heard it yet. But now they would, straight from Claire's mouth.

She could feel Bryce's gaze burning the back of her head.

It doesn't matter, Claire reminded herself. *They already hate you.*

It was just another reason to leave this place.

Claire would be able to, once she knew Maeve and Bri were okay. Once Mr. J. Porter got the hell off their porch. If the business was thriving, if Bri's blood work stayed normal, then Claire would be good to go. Forever. Just not yet.

"But you don't believe Old Lucky is one of the Old Gods?" Lenny guessed.

Claire flinched as a man sat in the booth behind her. "I don't know what he is."

"So, tell me about June third."

"There was . . . something on the roof," Claire began. "And then a big flash and it was gone."

"You said earlier that weird stuff happens all the time."

Shit.

"Yes . . ." Claire hoped Lenny didn't notice the sweat on her forehead. *Think think think think.* She should have practiced lines with Bri before this.

"There's definitely something here," Claire said. "Just,

usually not as dramatic, you know? It's usually limited to noises and stuff."

"Noises?"

"Mm-hm. Old Lucky's song, I guess. It's like . . ." Claire searched her brain for something from the newspaper articles scattered around the gift shop. She didn't want to add anything new, in case she contradicted herself again. "It's like in between a whine and a whistle."

"Does that happen often?"

"Lately, yeah. I mean, it happened last night."

Lenny nodded, her eyes wild. "I felt it too. There's a presence here. I've been to a lot of haunted places, but nothing as supernaturally charged as Scarberry."

Claire covered her mouth to stifle a laugh and nodded.

"The question is though . . ." Lenny continued. "Why Scarberry? Why Reed Ranch?"

"No one knows."

"But what do *you* think?"

"I guess . . . He came here by accident, and he stayed?"

"Why?"

Claire shrugged. "Maybe he liked it here?"

Maybe Old Lucky's planet was full of cows and homophobes too. He felt right at home.

"But why hasn't he been found?" Lenny prodded. "Small towns are hard to hide in."

Ain't that the truth.

Claire shrugged. "Maybe we're so used to him, we've accepted him as a neighbor?"

Rather an alien than a queer girl.

Bryce and co. cackled in their booth.

"So you don't consider him a threat?" Lenny asked. Her fairylike features hardened into a serious expression.

"No," Claire said. Rumors can kill, but the make-believe alien was harmless. Old Lucky had been nothing but an asset to Reed Ranch. He was what kept them afloat. Real or not, Claire owed him that. She'd make him famous again, and he'd make her money.

Lenny nodded, as if she'd fully expected the answer. "What do you think has been hurting the cattle then?"

"What?"

"I saw a calf in the barn. It had some kind of wound on it. And there are others, apparently. At least, according to Jared and your mom—"

"Maeve isn't my mom. She's my aunt."

"Oh, sorry. I just assumed. But uh . . ."

Lenny lost her composure for half a second. She must have been thinking of all the possible reasons one might not live with their biological parents. But she didn't ask about Claire's tragic backstory.

"What do you think is hurting them?" Lenny asked again instead.

"I don't know. I . . . don't even know what you're talking about."

"You help take care of the animals, but you didn't know something has been hurting them?"

"I don't see each one every day."

"But your aunt hasn't told you about what's happening?"

"Probably not a big deal then."

They hadn't had problems with coyotes in years, but the rare sightings did happen. Lenny nodded, but she clearly wasn't convinced.

Claire kept her eyes on her plate. Clearly, Lenny wasn't satisfied with her answers. She wouldn't accept a mundane explanation, even if it was the most reasonable. She wanted it to be an extraterrestrial who liked sucking cow blood. She wasn't just doing this for the show, Claire decided. It wasn't a character. This was how Lenny *existed*. This was the real her.

Lenny desperately wanted to believe.

Claire just had to make sure she believed the right things.

CHAPTER 7

LENNY

Lenny didn't check her phone until she made it back to Reed Ranch. She had hundreds of social media notifications waiting for her, but zero missed texts. It was past noon—which meant Evan had already woken up, discovered Lenny missing from the caboose, and hadn't bothered to check if she was alive. It wasn't like she had disappeared on purpose; she wasn't *trying* to test him.

But it still stung.

She found him sitting at the picnic table in between the fifth car and the caboose.

"Where were you?" Evan asked without looking up from his laptop. So he *did* wonder where she was. He just wasn't concerned enough to look for her. If he found her body eaten by zombie cows, would he cry, or pull out his camera first?

She sat across from him. Their legs touched for a brief moment. She pulled her knees in.

"Interviewing a girl who lives here," Lenny answered.

"Anything interesting?"

"She saw basically the same thing we did in that video. That night in June seemed to be when things started up again. I think she might have sent us the email. Or she knows who did."

"Huh," he said, uninterested.

"So . . ." Lenny continued. "I saw Miss Reed talking to Jared in the barn. A bunch of the cows have been attacked and Jared wanted to do something about it. Miss Reed, like, gaslighted him. Like it was no big deal."

"Maybe it isn't. I know nothing about cows."

He sipped his coffee. Bringing their own espresso machine for the road trip was the best idea they ever had. They both would have gone insane without it. Well, Lenny was still going just a tiny bit insane.

"Jared was concerned," Lenny explained. "He couldn't think of what animal could have made those marks. And when I asked Claire about it, she seemed shocked."

"There haven't been reports of cattle mutilation here for decades," Evan reminded her. So he *did* read her research notes. They just weren't compelling enough to want to come here.

"Yeah. No mutilation since the summer of '61," Lenny confirmed.

"You think the owner of this place has been covering it up? Why?" He glanced at the UFO-shaped lights hanging from the train car next to them. "They seem pretty open about the whole aliens thing."

"I think it's starting again," Lenny said. "There have been no new sightings because there was nothing to see. Until now."

"So Old Lucky left, and . . . came back?"

"I don't think he ever left. And I think he was here before 1961. This town had weird legends from before then. He could have been dormant, hibernating until he got hungry. Humans like to eat every few hours, but maybe whatever he is doesn't have to feed for a long time?"

"So he comes back every couple decades. Like Pennywise?" Evan asked, a smile spreading on his lips. Now that they had an angle, he was invested. Any tension from last night eroded. Suddenly they were a team again. Not as a couple but coworkers.

Not passionate but *functional.*

* * * * * * * * * * * *

They set up tripods and rehashed their conversation for the cameras as if they were having it for the first time. Evan suggested they lean into the murderous alien clown, which Lenny thought was cheap, but she let it go.

Afterward, they lugged their double tripod setup to the red barn. The door was still closed, now with a rusty metal lock attached.

Maybe it was normal to keep a barn locked. Lenny wasn't going to pretend she knew anything about keeping livestock. The biggest creature in her suburb was her neighbor's Great Dane.

But when they arrived yesterday, it was open. Why the change?

Was the lock to keep out Old Lucky? Or was it to keep out Evan and Lenny?

"We could probably get the drone in through the window up top," Lenny suggested. She knew Evan had been itching to use the new drone. The last one had disappeared somewhere in Lake Erie, thanks to a strong wind and Lenny's less-than-stellar flying skills.

"But if the bites are really bloody, we can't show them without getting demonetized," Evan pointed out.

"Maybe we could put the full footage on the Patreon?"

"We don't want to piss off the owners," Evan said. "If they don't want us in the barn, we can't just sneak in with a camera."

He was right. If the Reeds knew something, betraying their trust wasn't the way to get more intel. They couldn't screw this up.

"There's still plenty of people we can talk to," Lenny assured him. "We could track down Minnie Albert."

There were only two confirmed witnesses from that original encounter: Willy Lamb, who was dead. And his high school sweetheart, Minnie Albert. She had to be in her eighties by now, but there was no obituary for her online. She had to still be alive. She had to.

Suddenly, Lenny's eyes stung. A cloud of dust blew into her face as a car pulled into the driveway. Ignoring the parking lot, it whipped around the back of the house, stopping next to the porch. The vehicle was brown and white and ancient-looking. A police car, like the ones from old movies.

Maybe Miss Reed *did* report the cattle mutilation.

The driver stepped out. He wore a brown uniform. He had a mustache, but a lot thinner than Jared's. Patchy. He went right for the trunk of his car, pulling out a crate of mason jars filled with thick, reddish liquid.

Evan pulled his inhaler from his pocket and gave it a good shake before using it. Then he removed the camera from the tripod and headed straight toward the man. Lenny wanted to scream for him to stop.

Cops always had weird stories. Their witness statements usually made great content. But they needed to be careful. Scarberry was different from all the other investigations. They couldn't just do this on autopilot.

"Hi," Evan said. He had his camera down, for now. "We're from out of town. And we were wondering if you could help us w—"

"Not here on duty," the man said. "Just helping the neighbors."

The screen door opened and Claire emerged. The cop on her doorstep didn't seem to bother her, but she gave Lenny and Evan an uneasy double-take.

"Oh, hey," she said as she picked up a crate.

"We're doing an investigation on the Scarberry Lights of 1961," Evan continued, ignoring Claire. "We would love to hear your thoughts!"

Evan loved having "reliable sources" as their interviewees. Doctors, professors, cops. Anyone they would call a professional. To Lenny, the opinions of some guy who went to a police academy wasn't worth any more than someone with no job at all. But this one might be an exception. She reread the name on the badge a few times, just to be sure her eyes weren't playing tricks on her. L-A-M-B.

"Chief Lamb?" Lenny said. "Any relation to Willy Lamb?"

"He was my father," he said, matter-of-factly. Being a small-town cop probably meant he was used to everyone knowing exactly who he was.

"He's the one that first saw Old Lucky," Lenny said.

"Well . . ." Chief Lamb laughed. "That's the story. You want a statement for your little documentary?"

"Yeah," Evan said.

"What do you want to hear?"

Claire took the crate and let it rest on her hip, looking bored. Surely she had heard all the stories before.

Evan propped up the camera on his shoulder, looking through the viewfinder. "Just your impressions on it," he said. "We've read all the papers, but if you can remember any details of what your dad saw—"

"Well, what you kids have to know . . ." Chief Lamb started. "My father had . . . a problem with the bottle when he was young. Our farm is right next door to the Reeds. The trees outlining the properties weren't as dense then. Now, Mary Ellen Reed used to keep swans. Nasty things. They would wander over to our yard and honk at me. I was terrified of 'em. But think about swans. If you're in an altered state and one is flying at you, they could look much bigger."

"So, you think the thing that chased Willy and Minnie was actually a swan?" Lenny asked.

She'd heard theories that most fantastical creatures were just animals. Mermaids were manatees. Mothman was really a barn owl. She thought all those explanations were oversimplified.

Oversimplified and depressing.

"Fits the description, don't ya think?" Lamb said. "White. Long-necked. Mean as sin. Floatin' up to the sky?"

"Swans don't have red eyes and four arms though," Lenny pointed out. "And what about the whistling?"

Lamb shrugged. "Like I said, my old man was drunk. And anyway, you see it all the time as law enforcement; memories aren't reliable. Unfortunately, the truth is boring."

If they kept this footage in, that'd make a great name for the video. *The Truth Is Boring.*

Claire thanked him for the jam. Evan shook his hand enthusiastically. "Thank you so much. It means a lot."

It didn't mean anything. This guy wasn't an expert. They watched him slide back inside the police car and drive away.

Claire lingered on the porch. She locked eyes with Lenny. Did she believe the swans theory? Something about Claire's eyes said she wasn't sure. She sucked in her lips, looked down at her crate of jam, then she turned to go back inside.

Lenny started after her. "Wait—"

Claire paused.

"We're doing our lockdown investigation after sunset. Do you want to help?" Lenny asked. Evan glanced up from the camera to give her a silent *Are you serious?*

"Lockdown?" Claire asked.

"Yeah, it's usually us staying overnight inside a haunted building, but in this case, we'll be locked *outside*."

They'd had guests for their lockdowns before. Historians. Witnesses. It wasn't unusual. Claire could be a huge help. She could give them permission to get inside the barn. And it would be nice to have a tour guide.

And a buffer between her and her sorta ex-boyfriend.

Claire considered the offer for a beat too long. *She's going to say no.* Lenny couldn't blame her. She was probably busy with work. With chores. Or she had an actual life. She had better things to do than hunt for monsters she hardly believed in.

Unless she sent that video.

Claire said, "Yeah. I can help."

CHAPTER 8

CLAIRE

"Thank you, love!" Aunt Maeve skipped downstairs and plucked the crate out of Claire's arms. She set it on the kitchen counter, which was overflowing with herbal tea and cow-shaped cookie jars.

"No problem," Claire said.

Aunt Maeve had been absent for the last few deliveries. Instead of meeting Chief Lamb by the porch every Thursday for the past month, she had busied herself with other duties. She was cleaning the gutters, arguing with bill collection, talking to her friends in the Natural Medicine Moms Facebook group.

Though the cancer had been inside Bri, it affected Aunt Maeve more. She became scatterbrained and obsessed with homeopathic medicine. Once a month she picked a new miracle plant to grow in her garden, just to let it shrivel and die. Her hair grayed as her daughter's fell out. And she didn't blame her new streaks on aging—it was the toxins, of course.

The older Claire got, the easier it was to notice the seams

on people coming apart. Aunt Maeve had always been bleeding out stuffing, but once her daughter got sick, she was on a hopeless search for the perfect needle to stitch herself back together.

Claire had to postpone college until Bri was better. At least, that was the plan. When the last few checkups were positive, she should have applied to schools. But that felt unforgivably selfish. Both Aunt Maeve and Bri still needed Claire to pick up gooseberry jam from the neighbors and assure them everything would be all right.

"I didn't know Grandma kept swans," Claire said.

She didn't know much about her grandmother at all. But over the years she'd gathered that she was not a pleasant woman. Scarberrians weren't permitted to speak ill of their kin. That was one of the secret commandments of the place: *Thou shalt only talk shit about outsiders.*

"Oh, yeah, she was obsessed with birds," Aunt Maeve said. She inspected each mason jar and stacked them inside the cupboard. "The swans were all gone by the time I was born."

Maeve found today's winner. She grabbed a pink ribbon from the counter and wrapped it around the neck of the jar.

"But the chief remembered them," Claire said. Something wasn't adding up. Lamb and Maeve had graduated together. Just last week, they were reminiscing about their twenty-five-year class reunion. They were close, but Claire hardly knew him. She still called him Chief Lamb, instead of Walter. He was a cop first, not her aunt's friend, not her neighbor, not her former best friend's dad.

Maeve must have zoned out. "Hmm?"

"The chief mentioned swans chasing him off the property," Claire explained. "He said that's what Old Lucky really was. Just a big swan."

"That's a good theory."

Whatever Aunt Maeve truly believed about aliens was private. She was considerably less homophobic than the rest of town, but she was still a Scarberry girl. Commandment number two: *Thou shalt not express an opinion on Old Lucky.* He was both Scarberry's god and their unloved bastard child. Their mascot and the thorn inside their cowboy boots. He was the Thing We Do Not Speak Of.

"But you guys are the same age, right?" Claire asked. "Why would he remember swans if you don't? He said he was afraid of them."

"Sometimes us old people misremember things." Maeve grabbed one of Claire's limp waves, scrunching up her face in disapproval. Claire knew she was covered in dirt. She knew she ought to have worn a ponytail or something when riding the four-wheeler, but she liked feeling the wind in her hair.

Maeve's expression lightened. She patted the kitchen counter. "C'mon. Salon's open." Claire climbed up. It had been ages since Maeve had washed her hair in the kitchen sink. After Bri's chemo, their household tried to avoid the topic of hair.

Claire had offered to shave her head in solidarity, but Maeve vetoed the idea. "I just don't think it'd go over well for you," she had said. "Think of the repercussions." What Aunt Maeve meant to say was *Let's be real, Claire. You can't be gay* and *bald.*

Not in Scarberry. Maeve was a saint for taking in her

niece, but she could only handle so much. Surely, the rumors had been bad when Claire's mom first left Scarberry, only worse when she returned pregnant. And Maeve had endured the brunt of all the passive-aggressive prayer requests when everyone learned of her sister's addiction.

Claire let the warm water wash over her worries as Maeve sang. She was terrible at remembering songs, so she always got stuck repeating the chorus on a loop. She massaged Claire's scalp with lavender shampoo. The same scent from when she was a little kid. In the olden times, when her only duty was existing.

The peace couldn't last.

When Claire closed her eyes, all she could see was swans. She tried to distort their image in her mind, what changes she would have needed to make with her editing software for them to pass as aliens. Enlarge the head, add a red glow to the eyes, sub the wings for two sets of arms. Elongate the legs. It was possible, but a lot of work. How many beers did it take to fuck up your vision that much?

Maeve wrapped her hair in a towel, then handed her the ribboned jar of jam. "Will you take this up to Bri?"

Claire accepted the jam and made her way up the creaky staircase. The towel was wrapped too tight around her temples. There was no way Willy Lamb saw a swan. Aunt Maeve could be right about the chief misremembering. He was always a little too sure of himself, handing out advice like he was so *worldly* when he'd never even left his hometown. There really wasn't much to police in Scarberry anyway. Teenage drinking was fine, as long as it was kept to barns and off the street. And even then, the long, flat straight roads didn't get much traffic. The only time people didn't drive 90 miles an hour was when they were stuck behind a tractor.

But Chief Lamb meant well, even if he was annoying. Ever since Bri was diagnosed, Chief Lamb made it his mission to make sure she was cared for. He brought groceries. He filled the truck with gas and sent Warren to mow the lawn. Which he still did, frequently, even though he and Claire weren't speaking. It made her feel a little guilty sometimes. The chief's wife, Myra Lamb, didn't beat her cancer, but Bri was okay, somehow. Life and death were so unfairly random.

Bri's door was cracked open, an unspoken invitation to enter, if you dared. When Claire walked in, she had to stifle a scream.

A pearly white figure stood in the center of the room. Its flesh was inelegantly lined with bumpy ridges. Four spindly arms protruded from its abdomen. Sharp yellow teeth crowded its round mouth. It noticed Claire right away. When it turned to look at her, its long neck wobbled, like it didn't have a solid spine.

You would think a custom suit that cost four hundred dollars would have better construction.

The red eyes popped out a little too much, and the webbed gloves holding the cellphone gave off more of a swamp-creature vibe than an extraterrestrial one. After the initial shock, it was more pathetic than frightening.

"Oh shit," the creature said. "I was gonna jump out and scare you."

"Take it off."

Bri sighed and zipped off the head. She was covered with sweat. The suit couldn't have been breathable. Claire had to commend Bri for her commitment to the scare. Clearly, she was feeling like herself again.

"Mom said you went to town?" Bri asked.

"Yeah we took a field trip to the diner so I could give a statement about what I *witnessed*. I'm supposed to help them with their video tonight."

"You're a *guest investigator?*" Bri stepped out of the suit, letting it crumple on the floor. She dramatically collapsed on her bed. "I'm so jealous. What are they like?"

"I mean, I haven't interacted with the guy much."

"*Evan*." Bri grabbed her dolphin-shaped plushie and squeezed it against her chest, looking up at the poster-covered ceiling dreamily.

"Yeah. He seems cool, I guess." Well, he seemed like . . . a guy. Not a good or a bad one. Just, *a guy*. A stock character.

"Of course you like Lenny more."

Claire rolled her eyes. "I don't have a crush on every girl that breathes, ya know."

"Oh, chill. I didn't mean it like that. You're just both really *intense*," Bri said. "And don't like authority."

"You don't know someone just because you have a parasocial relationship with them."

Bri couldn't just like something; she had to be consumed by it. She couldn't have just one plushie on her bed but a whole menagerie of them. Her favorite K-pop idol plastered her walls and her phone's wallpaper. Claire always thought Bri's obsessive fandoms were irritating. They showed a lack of individuality, a kind of teenage-girl stereotype she couldn't relate to. But during that horrible month when they weren't sure her treatments were helping, Claire had walked into Bri's bedroom to pick out a plushie to take to the hospital. She'd imagined what would happen to this room if Bri didn't make it. If they finally sold the ranch, Aunt Maeve would have to strip the daisy-patterned sheets, tear down all the posters, throw away the pile of overpriced water bottles. Bri's fanfics would go unfinished. The ranch's new owners would know nothing of her. How loved she was.

"Wow, Claire, you're sooooo edgy," Bri teased. "You must be so enlightened, refusing to like anything."

"I like stuff. Just not exploitative clickbait."

"Everyone knows it's just a show. I don't even follow for the cryptids. That's just added flavor. It's about the *love story*."

Claire scoffed. *Love story. Yeah, right.*

"Don't act like you're better than them," Bri continued. "You're the one trying to fake an alien invasion."

"This is different. It's for—" *A good cause.* But Claire stopped herself before it was too late. Bri didn't know just how bad their financial situation was. Maeve hadn't told her daughter about Mr. J. Porter's offer to buy up their land or how Maeve had considered taking it, even though the price was far too low. *A lot of people will be selling,* Maeve had said. And one by one, they did. Rumors spread fast in Scarberry. *Did you hear who's getting divorced? Who's sick? Who's gay? Who's selling their family's land to a random investor who doesn't even have a website?*

"It's a social experiment," Claire finished. "But if you don't want to help—"

"No! Of course I want to! I just mean the show being fake doesn't stop me—or anyone else from liking it."

But it wasn't fake to Lenny. Her eyes lit up whenever Old Lucky was mentioned. She was genuine. It almost made Claire feel bad about her scheme.

Almost.

"If you really want to help," Claire said, "find me some duct tape."

CHAPTER 9
LENNY

Lenny found the next witness smoking a cigarette by the first train car.

Her purple-and-gray hair was pulled into a thin bun on top of her head. She wore a baggy shirt with painted horses—no, *unicorns*—on it. She had a little dog on a leash. It had an unfortunately small head compared to its body and eyes that faced different directions.

Lenny had been sitting on the picnic table, poring over her notes and avoiding Evan, when the woman sat beside her and asked, "Ever been abducted?"

Lenny looked up from her notes. "Not yet."

"Hmm." The woman breathed in her cigarette, then exhaled, hitting Lenny with a wall of smoke. "You got that look."

"Thanks," Lenny said. Though, she wasn't exactly sure if it was a compliment. "Have *you* been abducted?"

"When I was thirteen. Back in Arkansas," the woman said without hesitation.

Lenny closed the folder. Notes could wait. She stared at the woman. She knew it was rude to gawk, but she couldn't look away. With her dyed hair and faded tattoos on her wrinkly arms, this lady clearly lived life on her own terms. If aliens wanted anyone, they'd want someone like her. Lenny was insanely jealous.

"What brings you to Scarberry?" Lenny asked.

The woman ashed her cigarette. "I gotta see 'em again."

"Of course. You want to prove you're not crazy."

"No, hon. That ship has sailed. Ain't trying to prove nothing. Just wanted to catch up with old friends."

Lenny introduced herself and asked if the woman would want to be on the show. She heartily agreed, but kept insisting that she didn't want to be paid for appearing. "Educating the masses" was enough. Lenny went inside the caboose to grab equipment.

Evan was lying on the bed, texting. He looked up once she started fiddling with the camera bag. She was trying to find the lens that was good for portrait shots, but she couldn't remember which bag it was in.

"What are you doing?" Evan asked.

"Interview."

Evan sat up. "Without me?"

"I didn't think you cared," she admitted.

"Why wouldn't I . . ." He trailed off. Then, softly, "That's the wrong lens."

Lenny offered the camera bag to him.

Maybe he finally regretted his bad attitude. Maybe he finally saw what she saw in this town: that Scarberry wasn't a lost cause. But once he followed her outside and saw the woman and her little dog, he let out a dramatic sigh. He turned on the camera, gave Lenny a glare, and mumbled, "Rolling," before bothering to focus the lens.

"Can you state your name, if you're comfortable," Lenny started.

"Susan Elizabeth Wesley," the woman said, lighting another cigarette. "Born October thirteenth, 1961. It was a Friday. Friday the thirteenth. Means I have sorceress energy."

Evan let out a little laugh. Susan didn't notice. But Lenny did, and the mic would pick it up. Their witness told her whole life story without being prompted.

Susan Elizabeth Wesley didn't remember much from the abduction, but she thought she knew why it happened. They wanted her because she had alien blood. Her father wasn't human, she explained, but her mother would never admit that was the reason he was never around. Susan was on retirement now, after her husband died. She got his pension. Best thing he ever did for her was die. Now she could travel. See the grandkids. See some aliens too, hopefully.

"Have you seen anything in Scarberry yet?" Lenny asked.

"Seen? No," Susan said. "But I feel it. Can't you?"

At the same time Lenny answered "yes," Evan let out a flat "no."

Now it was her turn to glare at him. That was against his character for *Odd Kids*. The Hopeful Skeptic was never supposed to give a hard answer. If they couldn't find definitive evidence, they had to at least leave things open-ended. Evan wouldn't act like this if he was planning on using any of Susan's interview. So why volunteer to help? Just to tease Lenny? Tease this poor woman?

"Since check-in, my joints have been achin'," Susan said. "Toothache I thought was gone is givin' me grief."

"Weird," Lenny said. She glanced at Evan. "Kinda like how you haven't used your inhaler in years and suddenly—"

"This place is dusty as hell, Lenny."

"The body knows," Susan said, undeterred. Lenny loved her for it. "These grounds are angry. It's not supposed to be like this. Can't you feel the . . . *wrongness?*" She squashed her cigarette on the picnic table and called out, "Tilly!"

The dog was now coughing up a dandelion. At some point during her monologue, Susan had said Tilly was part pug, part beagle, though she looked more like something ate a pug and spat it out. Susan took the dog inside, leaving her squashed cigarette still smoking.

"She was a *character*," said Evan. *Character* was code for *weirdo*. Lenny liked the weirdos. They were brave for putting themselves out there.

"I believe her," Lenny said.

"Congrats on the open mind, then. No one else is going to buy it."

CHAPTER 10

CLAIRE

Claire used to put on plays in the barn. Bri would always play the lead. Their favorite production was just called *Princess*. They used the hayloft as a tower, and Grandma's dresses from the attic as gowns. Bri's long, golden locks would be made Rapunzel-worthy by a hair-extension T-shirt chain, which would be woven around a ladder. Bri would sing and brush her wig and call out for a prince to save her, and Warren, valiantly, would burst into the barn atop a hobbyhorse. He'd climb the T-shirt rope ladder, and when he reached the tower and asked for a kiss, Bri would kill him. For the first production, she stabbed him. For the encore she snapped his neck with telekinetic powers. The last time they put on the show, she sucked his blood.

The only audience was Jared, Aunt Maeve, and the cattle. It was enough, back then. Because there was always the unreachable promise of someday. Someday she'd make something for the world to see. Claire just didn't think it'd happen this soon.

Now she watched as Bri crab-walked in the Old Lucky suit, warming up her vocals with earsplitting shrieks. They'd spent the rest of the afternoon reinforcing the floppy neck, but it still drooped too much. Claire couldn't unsee all the seams and zippers. Bri would have to be far enough away that Lenny and Evan wouldn't be able to catch up. She'd duck into the barn, stash the suit in Claire's backpack, cover the evidence with hay and come out the other side. Bri had gotten good at zipping the costume off quickly, but it was one thing to run across a bedroom and another to do it outside, in the dark, with her heroes chasing after her.

If this went south, it'd sabotage the whole production.

"Has there ever been an episode of *Odd Kids* where they didn't find anything?" Claire asked as Bri scuttled across the room.

"They always find something," Bri said, her voice muffled underneath the false plastic teeth of the suit.

* * * * * * * * * * * *

After dress rehearsal, there was only one thing left to take care of before that night's big show: Jared. Technically, his duties ended before dark, but ever since the ranch boys were fired, he stayed later and later, so Maeve made him dinner, and Claire delivered it.

The sun was low in the sky when she found him behind

the barn, hunched beside the mower with all its mechanical guts exposed. Shit. It had been breaking down since spring and Jared had spent countless hours trying to keep it running. Maeve wasn't paying him overtime, and he wouldn't have let her if she tried.

"How's the queen faring?" Claire asked, nodding toward the mower.

"She'll live," Jared answered. He wiped his forehead with a bandana and shoved it into his overalls pocket. "Hand me the Allen wrench."

She dug in the rusty toolbox until she found it and asked, "Are you sticking around for Bri's performance?"

"Performance?"

"The suit came in."

"Oh lord."

"It looks pretty good from far away," Claire said, more for her own peace of mind.

"You think they'd let an old fart like me on their TV show?" Jared asked, smiling up at her.

"Totally. You got that Clint Eastwood look going for ya."

"Ha. He's a fake cowboy, you know. Born rich as shit."

She nodded, as if he weren't the one who'd made her sit through dozens of old westerns as homework last year. She'd diligently watched every recommendation and given her review to him the next day. And he'd gladly listened to her trashing his favorite movies, just like he gladly listened to her rant about the homophobic kids at school, even though he was "straight as an arrow" and offered repeatedly to "teach those boys a lesson." And he would have, if she gave the word. But she never retaliated. It didn't matter in the end—Scarberry decided she was a bitch anyway. There would be no prize for her pulled punches.

"They probably will want to talk to you at some point," Claire added. "For the show."

"I'm ready for my close-up."

"Just tell them all about your BFF."

Jared wheezed a laugh. He didn't believe in God or capitalism or Maeve's homeopathic remedies, but somehow, he believed in Old Lucky. It was probably Jared's only flaw. They'd gone back and forth over it a million times. She'd hit him with cold, hard facts and he'd give a chipped-tooth smile and let her have the last word, but he still was a diehard Old Lucky truther at the end of the day.

Hopefully Jared's testimony could make the Beast of Scarberry look a little more legit. What the chief had said was still gnawing at Claire. He didn't need a good reason for not believing in Old Lucky. Why lie about the swans? Unless Maeve was the one who had the timeline wrong.

"Do you remember Grandma's swans?" she asked.

"Yeah. Mean old bird kept even meaner birds."

That was the best thing about Jared, he didn't sugarcoat. He knew Scarberry's small-town charm was the real hoax—this place would be happy to eat their own if they didn't conform. But not Jared.

"The chief said they were around when he was young, but Maeve said she didn't remember them," Claire explained.

"Maeve's snake oil ain't helping her brain much."

"So she had it wrong?"

"Yeah. When I started here, Maeve and your mom were just toddlers. They'd tease the birds all the time. And I said, 'Be careful. Swans are nasty things,' but they didn't listen until one bit your mom right on the thumb and she wailed and *wailed*."

Is that why Maeve lied? It brought back a memory of her no-good dead sister?

The only photos Claire had seen of her mom were from her high school yearbook. She was fat like Claire. She wore her hair long too, but her highlights were chunky, her eyebrows overplucked, and there was a hardness to her face. Claire always thought her mom looked older than a seventeen-year-old should have looked. Maybe because she was a smoker, and the old school building was full of asbestos, and there was a drought that year, so she had to squint to avoid the dust blowing in from the fields.

Claire's mother was just as abstract as the legends about Old Lucky. The tale of Lauren Reed goes like this: She'd tried to escape Scarberry but ended up pregnant with Claire and in a "dark place." She couldn't take care of her daughter until she "conquered her demons," so she dropped Claire off at Maeve's. She never revealed the identity of Claire's father, just that he was another "lost soul." She died of an overdose before Claire turned four. Scarberrians believed that the city would corrupt and Claire's mother was a God-sent cautionary tale to keep the next crop of kids rooted here, even as J. Porter bought up family farms and the corn got obliterated by months-long droughts and violent hailstorms.

But Jared only told the truth. He said *depressed* instead of *in a dark place*. He said *opioids* instead of *demons*.

"That sandwich for me?" Jared asked.

She tossed him the PB&J and can of Coke. They sat together watching the shadow of the barn get longer. It'd be dusk soon. Almost showtime. The thought made Claire's skin crawl. She'd been dreading "lockdown" all day. If Bri couldn't get the suit off in time—if Claire couldn't keep a straight face—it'd all be over.

"Gotta go," Claire said. "Remember me when you're famous."

She reminded herself to breathe. To unclench her fist and her jaw and relax. The plan would work. It had to.

If Bri could play the monster, Claire could play the monster hunter.

CHAPTER 11

LENNY

The last sliver of sun disappeared behind the red barn. Claire still hadn't shown.

Evan demanded they take turns spraying each other with bug spray, even though Lenny hadn't been bit by a single insect since arriving yesterday.

"Isn't it weird there's no mosquitos here?" she asked as she coated the back of his legs.

"Probably a pesticide thing," he said, and Lenny had no way of knowing if he believed that or he was just determined to disagree with her.

Their hair and clothes now reeked of chemicals, but at least that distracted from the manure. Lenny's nose still hadn't gotten used to it. With the light breeze, it only got worse. Evan was getting worse too. Or maybe Lenny's tolerance was. Maybe she was finally cracking, and Evan didn't have the stamina to fill in her missing pieces anymore. She should have been grateful he'd tried for so long.

Maybe she wouldn't be an asshole if she ended it for good. Maybe he wanted her to and was too cowardly to pull the trigger himself.

Evan paced, studying a map from the gift shop. Wherever they went, he bought a map. He probably liked them because they represented order. Everything was correctly labeled. Borders were marked. If you always had a map, you always knew exactly where you were standing. That was why he hated it when Lenny suggested they go on a break. He would rather an official, clean designation for what they were. Now they were in uncharted waters, and he had nothing to guide him through it.

"Did you know half of Scarberry is a ghost town? Not, like, *ghost* ghosts. I mean, abandoned," he said.

Yes. She knew. Claire mentioned that at breakfast and Lenny had told him all the info she gathered from the interview already.

"This map has a bunch of mines on it," he continued. "All closed a hundred years ago. Guess no one found any gold. Maybe we should check them out."

"Why? There haven't been any Old Lucky sightings on that side of town," Lenny said. "Just at Reed Ranch."

"I'm just saying it'd make good content. People love cave divers and stuff like that. Especially the accidents. We could get headlamps and—"

"Not find anything real, but at least we'd be on trend," Lenny finished.

Evan pushed up his glasses and calmly said, "Your witness isn't coming."

Your witness. Because Scarberry was Lenny's idea, and therefore Lenny's fault. The channel was also Lenny's idea, but obviously that didn't matter.

"She'll be here." Lenny decided Claire was just the kind of person who ran late. Evan's least favorite kind of person. "She probably had work."

Evan rolled his eyes and paced some more.

Lenny figured Claire would ride up on the four-wheeler again, but she snuck up on them. One second, they were alone, listening to the wind blow through the cornfields. And the next, Claire was standing there, wearing the same muddy cowboy boots as this morning. With her soft features and her bleached waves down to her hips, she looked more like a mermaid than a farm girl.

She didn't say hello, just started pulling sandwiches and sodas from her backpack.

Evan gave a polite "Thanks," but didn't take a sandwich. He went right to business. "Let's use the saucer as base."

"Do you need me to help carry anything?" Claire asked.

"It's not that heavy," Evan said, voice flat. He hoisted the equipment bag over his shoulder and started walking.

Lenny had to resist apologizing for Evan's behavior. She had gotten so used to seeing them as a unit. His arm was her arm. His mistakes were her mistakes. The thing is, *she* usually did most of the mistake-making. Usually he had to apologize for her.

You can be too much, sometimes, Evan had told her once after a less-than-successful interview. *You make people nervous.* But maybe that had never been true at all. Susan had liked her enough. Claire seemed like a girl who didn't give out trust easily, and Lenny somehow hadn't scared *her* away yet. So Lenny couldn't ask about the anonymous email. At least, not directly.

They followed the path to the metal UFO. After dark, there was no one milling about. Susan and Tilly hadn't emerged from their train car, and it didn't seem like there were any other guests at Reed Ranch. It would have made sense for Claire to lead the way, but Evan had memorized the map. He took long strides so he could stay two yards ahead of the girls.

Evan stopped and dug a tripod into the ground, like he was sticking his country's flag in the earth, claiming this land as his own. Lenny set up the smaller tripod so the time-lapse camera had a view of the house and the barn behind it. Lenny made sure the lens was in focus and pressed Record. She brushed her bangs out of her face as the wind picked up.

"The barn seems to be a hotbed for activity," Evan began, once they were both in position. "So we'll focus on that for tonight's investigation. We also have our sky cam, capturing any anomalies at 4K . . ."

With Claire there, it was like Lenny was watching herself from outside her body. She saw the filming process for what it was: ritualistic and passionless. Lenny had always noticed the way Evan's voice would change for the camera, but now she worried that hers did too. Or even worse: Lenny had started doing "the voice" one day and never stopped. Her original voice had died a long time ago.

After two more takes for posterity, Lenny pinned a mic to Claire's jacket. The black denim was sprinkled with sewn-on patches. Some with bands Lenny recognized, some with profanity, some with flowers, some with constellations.

"Is that a death's head moth?" Lenny asked, pointing to the purple patch on Claire's shoulder.

Claire looked down at herself, like she couldn't remember what she was wearing. "Yeah."

"Where'd you get it?"

"I made it."

"You *made* that?"

Lenny had never created anything tangible—she was more of an *idea* girl. If it weren't for Evan, she probably wouldn't have started *Odd Kids*. Just watching Evan work with their editing software made her nauseous.

"It's just fabric and embroidery floss," Claire explained. "My aunt would die of shame if I got a tattoo, so every time I want one I just make a new patch."

"That's so cool." Lenny tried not to show how insanely jealous she was. Claire had the time to do things *just for her*. No one expected anything else. Well, her aunt expected her not to get a tattoo. But that seemed like a fair deal.

Evan was still fiddling with the tripod. Of course. He had to double-check all of Lenny's work. Always.

Evan groaned. "We have to roll again."

"I think we got it," Lenny said, for Claire's sake. She was used to redoing the same lines over and over just for Evan's piece of mind. She wasn't going to subject Claire to it.

"You didn't turn the camera on," Evan said.

Lenny could have sworn she pressed Record. The red light had flashed and everything.

"Let me see." Lenny pulled the camera off the tripod and looked at the viewfinder. The screen was totally black. She pressed the On button. Still nothing. "It must've run out of batteries."

"No," Evan said. "That's impossible. It was charging all afternoon," he added.

"Maybe it wasn't," Lenny suggested.

"It was plugged in. It had a full battery before *you* touched it."

Was it at full battery? Lenny wasn't sure. She wasn't sure of anything when the rest of the world seemed to be. It wasn't just Evan. Susan didn't doubt her memory of a UFO abduction. There was intent in every stitch on Claire's jacket.

"So . . . we take a break and charge it for a little bit," Lenny offered.

"Yeah sure, why don't we just waste more time then?"

They'd had technical issues before. Even if this camera was broken, they had a hefty Patreon fund to update their equipment. It was no big deal.

Lenny didn't want to fight in front of Claire. The last thing they needed was a fan telling social media how much *Odd Kids* actually hated each other. If their relationship was a sham, then their whole show was.

"We just have to use the Nikon then," Lenny suggested. They hadn't used the Nikon at all. It was still in the caboose. And with Evan's body cam strapped to his sweatshirt, they had double backup. This wasn't the end of the world.

"The Nikon can't shoot 4K," Evan reminded her.

"Well, unless you have a better idea—"

She stopped when sticky liquid ran down her lips. She

licked them, tasting a nasty cocktail of sweat and blood. Shit. She had already embarrassed herself enough. Now she had a nosebleed.

Evan said something about grabbing tissues and he took off. Claire looked at Lenny like she was waiting for instructions.

"I'm fine," Lenny said.

Thanks to Evan, fans believed Lenny's nose was psychic. It was a warning that something was coming. Whenever she got a nosebleed during a shoot, Evan edited the episode to make it fit that narrative. Once, when they weren't even filming, a random nosebleed came on, and Evan asked her to change her shirt so he could make it look like it happened earlier. He would want to get this one on camera, for sure.

Lenny pinched her nose and looked up at the sky. The stars in Scarberry were ultra-bright. Each constellation was as clearly defined as it was on Evan's map. There was the Big Dipper. The Little Dipper. All the other ones she forgot the names of.

"I thought stars like this only existed in movies," Lenny said.

"You've never seen stars before?" Claire asked.

"I've seen stars. But Chicago has a lot of light pollution. The sky doesn't get black enough. I've been to other places and got a better view. I guess I thought I'd seen the limit, but . . . this is . . . wow."

"It's not worth it," Claire said. "And you're not supposed to tilt your head back."

"This happens all the time." Lenny pinched harder on the bridge of her nose, but the blood kept flowing. She hoped Evan would grab her a new T-shirt. This one was already dotted with red stains.

"The blood will go down your throat if you do that," Claire said.

Claire tried to gently guide her head forward. But Lenny resisted. She had to keep her head up. Had to keep her eyes on the stars, because one of them looked like it was heading toward her.

"I see something," Lenny whispered, mouth feeling thick. Her ears were ringing so loud she wondered if she even got the three words out.

She blinked, and it was still there. A pale white glow, so intense she couldn't see the edges. There were white spots at the edge of her vision. She knew you could screw up your eyes looking at solar eclipses. But this wasn't a solar eclipse. And it wasn't a lunar eclipse either. Just to her left, she could see the sliver of the moon. Was this a comet, then? She was pretty sure comets didn't hover like that.

Just before it reached the barn, the light stopped in midair. Lenny's eyes were watering. Her contacts were blurring up. She squinted, but the thing was so bright, it was hard to tell what it was. Just shapeless and squiggly and white, white, white. It started to fall again, disappearing behind the peeling barn roof.

Lenny ran toward it. A high-pitched, mournful wail rang out from all around her. She had to fight the urge to cover her ears. She had to fight the urge to blink again. Because what if she did and she woke up in bed? If this was a dream, Lenny hoped it would last until she could reach the other side of the barn. Until she could see if her life had a purpose.

CHAPTER 12

CLAIRE

Some asshole with a laser.

A drone.

A conveniently timed plane crash.

Claire could probably think of other explanations for the light, but she didn't have time.

She pulled out her phone. If Bri had actually followed directions, she should be inside the barn by now, waiting for the okay to sprint across the yard. Claire had to warn her. But her phone wouldn't turn on.

Maybe there was some kind of surge that messed with the batteries of electronics.

The shrieking she heard? No explanation for that yet.

Lenny rested her hands on her knees, panting. "Holy shit!" she cried.

Claire shoved her phone into her pocket and braced herself. She peered around the side of the barn and . . . nothing. There wasn't anything there. Not a crashed UFO or Old Lucky and, most important, not Bri. Lenny brushed her hair behind her shoulders. Her bright sweatshirt was stained all over.

"You saw it too, right?" Lenny asked, wiping her face with her sleeve.

She looked pretty badass, covered in blood and unbothered. *No.* Claire tried to disregard the thought. There was nothing *badass* about Lenny. She used her platform to peddle dubiously ethical subscription services. She even dressed like a walking advertisement.

And her boyfriend was a dickhead.

"The light? Yeah," Claire said. There was nothing wrong about admitting she saw the light. Because surely that was explainable. Tomorrow, people would be posting all about the latest once-in-a-lifetime comet. Or aurora borealis. Maybe this was just another new type of weather they'd have to contend with. Droughts and hailstorms weren't enough. Now the sky was falling.

Lenny knelt and touched the dead grass and muttered, "It should have landed here."

Jared rounded the side of the barn. He was holding a rifle. Claire stared incredulously at the gun. She knew Jared had one. Everyone in Scarberry had one. Jared had stories about scaring off coyotes, and they all involved the rifle. But now that she was seeing it, the metal illuminated under the stars, her stomach tightened.

"You girls need to go inside," Jared said, breathless. "It's not safe."

"What do you mean?" Lenny asked. She was still touching the grass, waiting for the ground to tell her its secrets.

"There's something roaming around. I saw it."

Oh. So this was all part of the bit. Still, the gun was extreme. And it was a waste without a working camera.

Claire inched closer to Jared and whispered, "Have you seen Bri?"

"No." He shook his head. "No. No, I saw him. I really saw him. He's back."

Lenny perked up. Her round, owl-like eyes were practically popping out of her skull. "You mean you saw Old Lucky?"

Jared swallowed, gripping his gun to his chest. Sweat shone on his forehead. He was really giving this his all. "Well, it wasn't a coyote."

Evan stumbled toward them, holding a camera in one hand and a roll of toilet paper in the other. He tossed Lenny the toilet paper.

"Did you see the light?" Lenny asked him.

"Light? No. I went back to the caboose and there was this awful ringing . . ."

"We heard it too."

"What the fuck is happening?" Evan looked to Claire for an answer. She shrugged. And he pursed his lips. He looked . . . angry. But that didn't make sense. He came for spooky lights and alien whistles. He should be grateful. Lenny sure seemed grateful. It was Claire's plans that had gone off the rails.

"It didn't sound anything like last night," Evan pointed out. "It was louder this time. I thought my eardrum was busted."

"Maybe it makes different noises for different reasons," Lenny suggested. "Like, cats hiss and they also meow."

"This isn't a cat," Jared said. He looked directly at Claire and added, "I'm serious, kiddo." Not a cat. Not a coyote. Not a comet. Not the northern lights.

Doesn't mean it's Old Lucky. Doesn't mean it's a fucking UFO.

Jared had to be confused. The old man was sleep-deprived, and Claire's plan had him all mixed-up.

"What did it look like?" Lenny probed. She was smiling like a kid on Christmas morning.

"Long neck," Jared explained. "White skin, almost see-through."

"Twelve feet tall? Four arms? Red eyes?"

Jared shook his head. "More like eight feet. And the eyes were blue. Glowing like a flashlight. Regular arms with long claws. Body looked like a person. That's what I thought until I saw the neck." He shivered.

That didn't sound like the suit. But it was close enough. Like how swans can look close enough. Right?

Right?

"You kids need to get inside," he added.

Their phones buzzed to life, vibrating and whistling with missed notifications.

"Extraterrestrials often manipulate technology," Lenny said, her big eyes staring at Claire. "Whatever it was . . . must be gone now."

Evan fiddled with the camera—the Nikon that apparently sucked because *it can't shoot 4K*. God, how could Lenny stand him?

He pointed the lens up at Jared. "Can you repeat what you saw?"

Jared spat chew into the dirt and recounted his tale. "I was checkin' the fence one last time before calling it a night and I heard this awful sound . . ."

Claire stepped away. This was the perfect distraction. She headed toward the house and texted Bri, *Where r u?* There was no response. Shit. Claire thought about calling. She just had to get far enough away from the barn before she could—

Her boot snagged something in the dead grass. What the hell? She lifted her foot off its white face. She noticed the crowded yellow teeth first. Then the tiny nose holes and empty red eyes, clogged with mud.

The Old Lucky suit.

Claire glanced back at the YouTubers, excitedly chatting with Jared. They hadn't noticed the white plastic in the grass. How did the suit get here? Bri was supposed to discard it after she did her part. She wasn't supposed to leave it out in the open for anyone to see. And she definitely wasn't supposed to leave it shredded. The rest of it was a few yards away. The neck was slashed up, the chest ripped open. Claire gathered the biggest pieces and tossed them into the garden. The dead leaves and shrunken flowers would have to act as camouflage for now. She would gather the rest when she knew Lenny and Evan wouldn't notice.

Claire texted Bri again: *What's going on?*

They'd practiced for hours. Bri could get the suit on and off in seconds. Why would she hack it up and dump it? She wouldn't. Plain and simple. She was excited to be part of the plan. She knew how much money Claire had spent on the suit.

"It was on all fours at first," Jared explained to the camera behind her. "Its neck was almost as long as the body. When it was standing, it had to be eight or nine feet tall. White as a ghost . . . It came outta nowhere, ran off towards the road. But I knew it never left town. It'll come back. It'll keep coming back."

Claire looked up at the house. Bri's room had a light on. Good. She didn't need to be outside. She didn't need to be with whatever tore up the suit. *No,* she corrected herself. *With whoever.*

There was a gentle tap on Claire's shoulder. She whirled around, and her hair smacked Lenny in the face. Oops.

But Lenny was the one to apologize. "Sorry! Didn't mean to freak you out."

"I'm not freaked out."

She was searching for rational explanations. The lights? Could be a secret air force base, just like Mustache Bro had said. Jared? He had crappy vision. And he believed in Old Lucky too much. Everyone had their faults, and that was his.

But the suit. Why was the suit destroyed?

"We're going to check out the road," Lenny said. "See where Old Lucky went."

"You go ahead."

Claire had to talk to Bri. She had to get answers. She couldn't survive another second in this uncertainty.

"Oh, okay. Maybe we'll see you tomorrow?" Lenny asked. "In case we find anything else?"

"Yeah. You have my number."

Claire marched toward the house. All the lights were off in the kitchen. Maeve must have gone to bed already. Claire marched up the stairs, resisting the ridiculous urge to go slowly, cautiously. The old wood groaned with each step. But it always did. Wind snuck through the cracks in the windows. If she focused hard on the sound, she could have mistaken it for whispers.

She punched open the door of Bri's room.

Empty. The K-pop boys on the walls silently stared at her.

The ground became swirly as bad thoughts lurched into Claire's head. *Something happened to Bri.* It wasn't fear, it was a fact. Something got her. *Something got her.* She survived the cancer but not this. Whatever *this* was.

And it was all Claire's fault. How would she explain herself to Aunt Maeve? How would she explain herself to Scarberry? She could see the headline: EVIL QUEER GIRL OFFERS UP HER OWN KIN TO A DEMON FROM OUTER SPACE. The YouTubers would film the townspeople driving up to the ranch in pickup trucks, carrying rifles and pitchforks. Aunt Maeve would give Claire a sorrowful look that says, *I'm sorry. You're not worth protecting anymore.* Aunt Maeve would do nothing as the mob descended on the ranch. And Claire wouldn't blame her.

She felt like she was going to throw up. She stumbled toward the bathroom and turned the knob.

Locked. *Locked?* How was it locked? Aunt Maeve didn't use the upstairs bathroom. Only Claire and—

"Just a minute!" Bri called. Claire didn't trust her own ears. How was that Bri's voice, if she was eaten by Old Lucky? The toilet flushed. The sink ran for a few seconds, and the door opened. There was Bri, unharmed, just a little too pale, with bags under her eyes.

"What happened?" Claire asked. "I tried to text you—"

"I didn't feel good. So I went inside."

Claire put a hand to her forehead. Bri was burning. "You have a fever."

"Yeah, I feel like dog shit."

"What did you do with the suit?"

"I left it in the barn. It's in the backpack," Bri explained.

A million what-ifs ran through Claire's brain. A few inconsequential ones like, *What if a feral racoon found it?* But also *What if Evan found it?* He seemed like an uptight guy. He could have snapped when he realized he was being pranked. He could have destroyed the suit in a rage. He seemed so suspicious of the lights. And clearly he hated this place. Did he hate Claire too? Was he going to expose her?

Fuck.

Bri added, "I'm sorry."

This wasn't Bri's fault. She wanted to help. She was innocent. And now Claire's grand scheme was going to make her homeless.

"I'm not mad at you," Claire said. "It's just . . . I'm glad that . . ." *Glad you're not torn to pieces by an alien roaming our backyard. Glad you haven't been abducted.*

God, these influencers were getting to her.

CHAPTER 13

LENNY

Lenny wished she'd packed warmer clothes. She was still in her *Odd Kids* hoodie, now dotted with blood. Her socks were drenched. Snow creeped up her sweatpants. She could have sworn that when she'd gone to sleep, it had been summer.

But the Dream didn't care what season it was. Or where she fell asleep. It was always winter, and it always started at a different place—the local pool, the farmers' market, Evan's grandma's house—but it was essentially the same. This time, she was at her old elementary school's playground. All the other kids were bundled up in snowsuits and big boots. They invited Lenny to join in the snowman-building contest.

"I'm looking for something," she told them, both as her eight-year-old self and her eighteen-year-old self. Dream Lenny was never a set age. Her appearance was constantly shifting, but she was always underdressed for the ever-changing terrain, and she always had the same goal. She climbed over the edge of the fence and kept going until she was in the woods, where no one could possibly see her. The barren Illinois trees turned into a red barn. A giant windmill, missing one of its metal slats, and the vague forms of cows in the distance. The dream always ended at Reed Ranch, with white lights dancing above her head.

She fell to her knees and began to dig into the snow.

But then she was lassoed back to reality. She groaned, staring at the faded stars on the ceiling of the caboose. Waking up after the Dream always felt like a betrayal. The world looked grayer, inconsequential. She wanted to go back and continue her search, but it was pointless. Dream Lenny never found anything and Real Lenny never found out what Dream Lenny was looking for.

They hadn't bothered to close the blinds when they'd gone to bed, so morning light came pouring through in sharp rows. God, it was way too bright.

Wait. It couldn't be morning yet, could it? The cow-shaped alarm clock on the nightstand was off. Fine, she'd check the time on her phone then. She slowly rolled out of bed, careful not to wake Evan. He'd been at the computer when Lenny had dozed off. After hours messing with recovery software, he had only seemed to get more frustrated. There was six minutes of missing footage on the GoPro and time-lapse cam, and nothing could get it back, so he got to work on the footage they did have. It was mostly just Jared explaining his encounter and pointing to the exact spot he'd seen the creature. Then they drove around on the dark country roads, looking for Old Lucky until three in the morning. Unless Evan managed to make their possum sighting way scarier than it was, they had no tangible evidence.

She crawled to the other side of the room to grab her phone from its charger. Dead. Just like it was last night. Just like the cameras.

What if . . . ? Lenny's heart was buzzing. She rose to her feet and peeked out of the blinds. Yes. There it was. Pretty as the poster in her childhood bedroom. The lights were back, shimmering in the night sky above the barn and beaming into the caboose. She glanced back at Evan. Still asleep. He was missing it. Lenny would have too, if it weren't for the Dream waking her up.

That was the point though, right? This wasn't for him. It was for her. She ran outside in nothing but sweatpants and the bloodstained *Odd Kids* hoodie. As she got closer, she heard screams. But not like the ones last night, and not like the ones from the night before. These weren't high-pitched bells. It was a man, hollering.

What the hell? Then the lights were collapsing. *No no no no.* She pushed herself faster, ignoring the cramp in her side. But she slipped in the dewy grass, looking up in horror as the lights faded. There were no more screams, from Old Lucky or anyone else. She waited by the mouth of the barn, staring at the sky. Five minutes passed. Ten. Thirty. An hour. The sun rose, hot and golden and *normal.* She couldn't help but feel like it was mocking her.

* * * * * * * * * * * *

When she finally trudged back to the caboose, Evan was outside on his phone.

"We're only a day's drive away," he said, using his adult professional voice. "Yeah. That shouldn't be a problem." He paced back and forth, talking into his phone branded with the *Odd Kids* logo on the case.

His back was turned. He hadn't noticed her yet. Who the hell was he talking to?

"Okay. Wow," he said. "Yeah. I guess I'll see you then. Okay, bye."

"Who was that?" Lenny asked.

He paused with the phone still on his ear. Guilty. A little kid caught with his hand in the cookie jar.

She used to worry he would cheat on her. That, surely, this relationship was too good to be true. But if that happened now, it wouldn't be so bad. Then, at least, they could really be done and Lenny wouldn't be the villain for ending it.

"Evan. Who was that?" Lenny repeated.

His expression shifted. Just for a second. An involuntary flinch he probably wasn't even aware of.

She'd had him figured out since the first time she invited him to family poker night. He did this thing with his eyebrows whenever he got really good cards. They would go up, and then back down, all serious. Scrunched tight under the rim of his glasses.

He had some good cards today.

Evan took a breath before facing her. "I got a DM this morning," he finally said. His eyes were rimmed with purple. He shouldn't be making business decisions while sleep-deprived. At least he had his coffee in hand. It was in a generic white cup. While Lenny was outside, waiting for the lights to return, he must have gone to a gas station. Hopefully he brought her back something.

"DM from who?" she asked.

"Max Malitz." Usually his lips curled in disgust at the mention of their rival. But Evan was still beaming. "*Dark Unknown* is at Harrows House," he said.

"I know."

He took a sip from his coffee. He seemed antsy. Erratic. Excited, for the first time on this road trip. "They want us to come," he added.

"*What?*"

The bigger channel hadn't acknowledged them before. They'd both started posting around the same time, but *Odd Kids* still hadn't hit 500,000 subscribers while *Dark Unknown* had skyrocketed to 2 million quickly. "They want us to join the investigation," Evan explained. "Tomorrow."

"We can't leave Scarberry yet."

"Lenny. This is a huge opportunity. Since we did that deep dive of desert hauntings last year, we'll be the experts."

"So basically they want to piggyback off our research?"

"Lenny." His voice was serious. At least he didn't call her Lenora. "The collab will be posted on their channel. Their audience will see us. It's the perfect business move. If you can't beat them, join them."

But it's not about winning, she wanted to say for the millionth time. *There's crazy shit happening in this town and you're leaving to pump up our views?*

It wouldn't just be leaving. It would be joining forces with their nemesis. She thought she'd had Evan all figured out. But she'd never believed he was spineless. And yet, the guy standing in front of her was practically an invertebrate.

"Absolutely not," Lenny decided.

"I already said we would."

"Without asking me?"

"Why waste this chance? We should be grateful."

Translation: Lenny was ungrateful.

"We're not getting anything in Scarberry anyway," he added.

"Not getting anything? You saw the lights last night. And guess what? They came back again. I saw them this morning. This place is crawling with activity."

He set his coffee on the picnic table. There wasn't another one for her. Poetic.

"Let's play devil's advocate," he said. "Say there's something supernatural happening." *As if that were still up for debate.* "Looks like it can't be captured by cameras. Maybe there's a magnetic field. Maybe the aliens have tech to mess up ours. Or . . . it's a hoax. Does it even matter? We won't be able to film it."

"It's been captured before. In 1961, and earlier this month—"

"Are we sure about that?"

She paused. "What?"

"The first night here, I found a speaker underneath the wheelbarrow. I didn't think anything of it, but . . . there was another one in the garden. There's probably a bunch hidden around here. We're being pranked, Lenny."

She shook her head. She felt sick. He was wrong. So wrong. "Then what about our phones?" she managed. "Our cameras?

You've kept your inhaler in your pocket since we got here. And when was the last time I got a nosebleed this bad? Or maybe you haven't noticed the freaky lights in the sky?"

Evan sipped his coffee, unbothered. She was the one shrieking and freaking out, screaming about aliens and, as always, Evan was collected.

"Like I said. Electromagnetic fields," he said in his professional voice. "This place could have some kind of energy anomaly. Maybe there really were aliens at some point but . . . not anymore."

"That doesn't explain—"

"There's probably some sort of pollen I'm not used to. Old Lucky isn't responsible for my asthma, Lenny."

"So you don't believe what Jared saw?" She gave up trying not to sound shrill. She was shaking. He was making her feel insane.

Evan sighed. "I think he works for a ranch that makes its money off UFO enthusiasts."

"So that makes him unreliable? *We* make money off UFO enthusiasts."

He paused. She thought he was actually considering her point. But he was just waiting for Susan and Tilly to walk by.

Evan stepped closer. He took hold of Lenny's hand. She couldn't think of the last time he touched her when the cameras weren't rolling. She wanted to scream.

"I know this place means a lot to you," he said. "But you have a habit of assigning meanings to things without reason. You make them symbols. Do you get what I'm saying?"

He was saying she was delusional. That he knew better

than her. He was so sure, all the time. And Lenny had to put every single one of her thoughts on trial. She had to prove to herself over and over again that she had the right to exist. And Evan was just *so sure.*

What gives him the right?

He kept going, holding his fucking coffee cup in his other hand. "Like, that dream you always talk about? With the snow? Lots of people have reoccurring dreams. It's an anxiety thing."

"You're the one that suggested my nosebleeds are a sixth sense," Lenny said. Her voice sounded so weak. She used to be too loud. And he'd tell her to be quiet so she wouldn't blow out the mic. But that wasn't for the show's sake. It was for his.

"And I love that you're passionate," Evan continued gently. "I love that. I love *you.* But this is what's best for the channel."

And Evan knew what was best. Because he was Evan. Steady Evan. Pragmatic Evan. *Sure Evan.*

Lenny's thoughts were wobbly. Unable to stand on their own. But she couldn't go on like this. She had to learn to walk, eventually.

"So, go," she said. "I'm staying here."

Evan sighed like a disappointed teacher. "*Dark Unknown* wants both of us to come."

He could have said, *I want you to come.* But that wouldn't be true, would it?

"I'm not going."

"Lenny?"

"You asked me to make a choice. And . . . I'm done."

"With me, or the channel?"

A little laugh escaped her. "Kind of the same thing."

"It doesn't have to be."

"Yes . . . it does."

He looked like he was about to cry. She wished she could cry, but no tears escaped her. She was too exhausted, too shocked, but she didn't have the right to be surprised. This was always coming. She'd had an open wound for months, and instead of taking out the bullet, she just thought one day she would wake up and be healed. But that wasn't happening. Evan wasn't going to save her. He didn't even notice her bleeding.

"It's over," she decided. "All of it."

CHAPTER 14

CLAIRE

Claire wasn't very good at giving up. She had been congratulated for it as a child. At a parent-teacher conference, Mrs. Sharpe told Aunt Maeve that Claire was "tenacious." It seemed like a good word at the time. But as she got older, *tenacious* became *persistent* became *stubborn* became *difficult*.

Her future therapist could help her unpack all that later. Right now, she had a job to do.

Today's occupation: detective.

She stepped outside. The screen door's high-pitched whine made her jump. It sounded like the thing she'd heard last night. She still didn't have an explanation for that, and it was bugging her. There was something *extra* about the noise. Something she wouldn't be able to re-create with editing software. It went through her ears and into her insides. The invisible sound waves gnawed at her flesh. Even now, just the memory of it made her shudder.

Obviously, it wasn't Old Lucky. But she couldn't get that

sound out of her head, or the look on Lenny's face when she peered up at the sky, covered in blood.

Claire shoved her hands in her pockets as she stepped through the dewy grass. Mornings at the ranch were her favorite thing. It was a fresh start. A rest. She could pretend she was the only girl in the world, and this was her solitary kingdom. There was no drama, no judgment. No Scarberrians lurking around the corner, ready to gossip about her. When her company was just the open sky and slow, lazy movement of the cattle, it was like Claire had no body, no reputation. She could just exist.

This morning, she couldn't go on one of her solo walks. For one: she'd slept in too long, and two: there was a trampled alien suit she needed to find. She had planned to snag it last night, but while waiting for Lenny and Evan to get out of her way, she'd fallen asleep.

She circled the red barn, and . . . nothing. The suit wasn't there. Last night, she had kicked the bigger chunks into Maeve's dying garden. It had been windy, but was it windy enough to blow the pieces of the suit away? The rubbery material was too heavy, but even if it did move from the garden, the nearby trees should have caught it.

She had no luck, not after five minutes of searching through the weeds. Not after twenty. Not after forty-five minutes of combing up and down the ranch on the four-wheeler.

She had to be honest with herself—someone found it. Jared, she hoped. Maybe he patrolled the place and discovered the scraps. That would be the best-case scenario.

If Aunt Maeve found it, she would just get more gray hairs.

A hoax was too risky for her to stomach. One more negative review on Yelp would send her overboard.

And if Lenny and Evan found it . . .

It had to be Jared. That was the only acceptable result. Usually he would be roaming around bright and early. He would be the only other human allowed in Claire's silent morning kingdom. He wasn't here yet. Maybe he was picking up something for Aunt Maeve.

Even if the suit was safely hidden, that was the least of Claire's problems. She needed to know who'd shredded it in the first place. Her only suspect was Lenny's boyfriend. But how could she confirm anything without giving herself away? Was she better off just saying nothing? Lenny wanted to believe there was something paranormal here; maybe Claire only had to keep *her* convinced. Screw her boyfriend.

She went back inside. Aunt Maeve was in the kitchen wearing a fruit-patterned apron and her hair pulled back in a scarf. She looked exhausted as she cut a slice of pie.

She wasn't alone. A teenage boy with dark, curly hair and a severe farmer's tan sat in the least-wobbly dining-room chair—the one reserved for special guests.

Warren Lamb was hardly special.

Scarberry liked to pretend he was. Apparently, throwing a football really far was impressive. So impressive that the girls in her school fawned over him and his uncomfortably thick biceps and his lack of vocabulary.

Claire could already imagine the scene that had played out: the chief's son stopped by for a quick delivery, and Aunt Maeve had to hold him hostage with hospitality. Demanding he sit.

Have a slice. Hoping Claire would find him there, and they would suddenly become besties again.

"Hey," Warren said to Claire. His green eyes pleaded for help. He probably had better things to do with his summer. He only had a few weeks to live out his small-town football fame before he became a nobody at his big state college.

Aunt Maeve slapped a huge slice of pie on the plate in front of Warren and looked at Claire expectantly.

"I just had breakfast," Claire lied. She was starving but wouldn't eat one of Aunt Maeve's gooseberry pies unless she was literally on-the-brink-of-death starving. Whatever asshole first said a woman's place is in the kitchen never saw Maeve Reed coming. She was convinced gooseberries had magical healing properties and demanded Bri eat as many as possible. Claire couldn't stomach them. They tasted like acidic grapes.

"Is Jared around?" Claire asked.

Aunt Maeve blinked, then looked down at her knife and set it in the sink. "No . . ." She wiped her hands on her apron for a little too long. "He took the day off."

"Really? Why?"

"Flu. Must've had the same bug as Bri. It's going around."

Jared had come to work with a fever before. He had even stayed after he cut off the tip of his thumb chopping wood. He wouldn't miss work for anything.

Aunt Maeve turned her back to them. "How's the pie? I can send some home with you!" She rummaged through the Tupperware cupboard.

"Is Jared okay?" Claire asked.

"I'm sure he is. Did you hang the clothes on the line? I can't have the linens catching mold spores sitting all wet like that. I really can't."

"I can hang the clothes. Sorry."

"Your cousin really isn't feeling well today."

Ah. That explained it. Maeve only got that twitch in her eye—that panic in her voice—when her baby girl was threatened. It was like she couldn't accept that Bri truly was better now.

But what about Jared? Aunt Maeve hardly seemed concerned.

Just like she wasn't concerned about the cows.

Claire shooed away that thought. Lenny's theories didn't matter. This was the same girl who tried to summon Bigfoot with a mating call. Even if Lenny really believed in the paranormal—even if it wasn't all for show—that didn't mean any of it was real.

Claire found the basket of damp laundry sitting by the stairs and took it outside. She hoped for the briefest second that the Old Lucky suit was somehow mixed in with the stack of sheets and pillowcases. It would look hilarious, tacked to the clothesline, blowing in the wind.

But Claire couldn't have anything go her way this morning. As she grabbed her first clothespin, the screen door whined open. Warren. He didn't head to his ridiculous lifted truck, like expected. He went right toward Claire. Chores were better than Aunt Maeve's poison pie, he probably figured.

He rested one beefy arm on the clothesline's wooden pole. "I hope Bri's okay."

So that's why he was here. Warren had always had a thing

for Bri. That was probably why he was still nice to Claire. Not real nice but Scarberry nice: a tightlipped smile and prayer request.

"She's fine," Claire said. She pinned a pillowcase to the line. "Aunt Maeve is just dramatic."

He nodded at the ground, but he still didn't leave. "Would you tell me if she wasn't okay?"

"Why don't you ask her yourself?"

Even if Aunt Maeve had barred him from going upstairs, he had Bri's number.

"She won't answer my texts," Warren said.

"Why? What did you do?"

"Nothing! I swear."

She couldn't probe him further because Lenny was marching toward them. She was once again dressed in blindingly bright colors: jean shorts and a traffic-cone-orange cropped tank top. One sock was plain white, and the other was dotted with yellow daisies. Her mood did not match the cheery outfit.

"Good morning," Lenny said with zero perkiness. It was like all the light was sapped out of her.

Oh shit.

She found the suit.

Lenny set her backpack on the grass and knelt to unzip it. She looked right up at Claire as she said, "This yours?"

Claire prepared to be shocked. The best way to lie is to convince yourself first. She almost convinced herself she was straight for her first fifteen years. She could be a believer for a few more days.

But Lenny didn't pull out the mangled suit.

She held a black cylinder in her hands. A speaker. Bri said she'd brought all the speakers inside. She must have forgotten one.

"I found it in a tree behind the caboose," Lenny said. "Evan saw more. But they're all gone now."

Evan. *Awesome.* As if she didn't hate the guy enough already.

Claire tried to push down the guilt, pretend the sweat in her armpits was just from the heat. Lenny was smarter than she gave her credit for.

Think. Think . . .

Bri had a phase where she watched confession tapes. Learned how to spot bad liars. Any detective would be on to Claire by now. She was fiddling with the clothesline too much. The dishrag already had one, two, three . . . seven pins on it. The truth had to be on her face.

Focus. It didn't have to be too late. Maybe Lenny would find out aliens didn't really exist one day, but not today. Claire wouldn't be the one to burst her bubble.

"Huh. That's weird," Claire said. "Must belong to one of the guests? We can put it in the lost and found . . ."

Lenny's eyes narrowed. "Old Lucky's song sounded different on the first night. It wasn't as loud. As . . . piercing. None of our cameras turned off. Our phones didn't either."

"Weird."

"I really need you to be honest with me," Lenny added.

Claire looked away. An obvious sign of a liar. *Get it together. Get it together . . .*

Warren stepped forward. "It's mine. Okay?"

Claire didn't have to pretend to be shocked. "What?"

Warren shrugged. "Sometimes I like to pull pranks on the out-of-towners," he lied.

Where did this knight-in-shining-armor move come from? Did he finally feel bad for not protecting Claire from the torment all of senior year? Or was he trying to win her over so he could get closer to her cousin? He wouldn't call a truce out of the goodness of his heart.

Lenny switched to interrogation mode. "So, two nights ago, *you* made those sounds."

"Yeah," Warren said.

"And last night?"

"Last night?" he looked at Claire, waiting for her call. She shook her head. "Last night . . . I was at a bonfire with some friends."

Was he really? Or did he destroy the suit? Did he get one of his cronies to do it for him? She thought of Bryce's smug grin at the diner. *Oh shit . . .*

"Do you have anyone who can vouch for you?" Lenny snapped.

Warren laughed. "Am I in trouble?"

Warren, what the hell did you do?

Lenny glared up at him unflinchingly. "I'm trying to figure out what's going on here. I'm trying to find the truth."

Warren cleared his throat nervously. "Well. That's the truth," he said. "Take it or leave it."

He mumbled a "See ya" to Claire and took off in his truck. Lenny still had the speaker in her hands. Maybe this got Claire out of trouble with Lenny, but this didn't put Warren in the clear. He was up to something. And since becoming besties with Bryce Stern, he could be capable of anything.

"Sorry for accusing you," Lenny said, once Warren was gone. "I just don't know who to trust right now."

That makes two of us.

"It's okay."

"Last night was different, though. Last night was *real.*" Lenny picked up her backpack and slung it over her shoulder. "We were supposed to leave tomorrow, and I don't know if you already have the room booked up. But I'd like to stay. If possible."

"Uh . . . I can talk to my aunt," Claire said. Another lie. She didn't need to consult with Maeve. Claire had been doing all the bookings for the past two years. It wasn't hard, especially since the ranch hardly ever had more than one guest at a time. "How long do you need the room?" Why was she asking that? Why didn't she just try to get rid of her now, before it all blew up in her face? *Stupid. Stupid . . .*

"Just until Wednesday," Lenny said.

"I'll look into it."

Lenny nodded, then walked away. She made long strides for how short she was. Claire had gotten her wrong. Lenny wasn't a vapid influencer. She wasn't a brand with a face. And she wasn't a clueless believer either. She wouldn't be easily manipulated.

Shit. Claire should have told her no. But if *Odd Kids* left without enough footage, would they even put Scarberry on their show? All of this would be for nothing.

Claire's phone buzzed in her pocket. Her heart still did that little flutter whenever she got an unexpected text, as if Hannah had decided to unghost her a year later. But it still wasn't Hannah. It was Warren. The last message he sent her was from over a year ago. He asked her if she had done their history homework yet. She hadn't responded. Now he sent a warning:

My dad says you should stay inside tonight.

CHAPTER 15

LENNY

Evan was good at planning for the worst-case scenario. He had a binder on his bookshelf labeled "If I Die" with all his medical records and social media passwords. He had made his funeral plans in eighth grade and tried to get Lenny to do the same.

"I'm not dying anytime soon," she had told him.

But Evan was always dying. Every bruise was sign of some sort of deficiency. Every headache was actually a budding brain tumor. He needed to pack five portable chargers in his suitcase. Six bottles of sunscreen. He had to read every review for every hotel they stayed in. He kept a satellite phone on him at all times. Because "that's what responsible people do."

Now Lenny wished she had been as prepared for imminent death. Then she would have brought post-breakup snacks ahead of time.

Evan's departure was a blur. He was almost completely packed by the time she returned to the caboose. He spoke in logistics only: "I'm getting picked up at noon. You can keep the Nikon."

And then she was on top of the cow-print comforter, surrounded by granola bars, while *Pride and Prejudice* (2005) played on her laptop. The blinds were drawn and the lights were off, but the glow-in-the-dark stars on the ceiling wouldn't grant her total darkness.

In the movie, Mr. Darcy told Elizabeth Bennet she had bewitched him, body and soul.

Evan had told Lenny she could keep the Nikon.

She had expected an eloquent breakup speech from him. Perhaps the contingency binder never covered that. Or he forgot how to say words that weren't written by Lenny or their social media manager. It wasn't his job to give the breakup speech though, was it? On the record, it was Lenny who ended it. She broke up with him because he was doing his job too well. That's how he would tell the story. And he would tell it *publicly*.

Odd Kids had never had a scandal. Of course, Evan planned their response in case they ever did something to spark outrage. "We'd have to get on top of it," he had said. "React quickly, before new rumors can spread."

When he announced the split to the world, he likely would use a vague cliché like "We still have so much love and respect for each other. But we agreed, mutually, to go our separate ways . . . blah blah blah."

Lenny realized she was getting angry at a social media post that existed only in her head, so she redirected her attention to Keira Knightley somehow pulling off Regency-style dress.

Then her stomach growled. It was four in the afternoon. The granola bars weren't offering much. She needed actual food. Which meant leaving the safety of her misery cave.

She put on her sunglasses and slipped out. Her eyes were still puffy from crying for hours. Lenny hated crying in public even before the channel got popular. And now? It was a PR risk. She didn't need a video of her wandering a farm in Nebraska, all alone, sobbing with chocolate granola bar smudged on her face.

In five days, it'd be Wednesday again, and her parents would expect a full recap of the last week. They'd want to talk to Evan. She'd have to tell them eventually.

She felt like a dead girl walking as she shuffled toward the parking lot. Somehow her ghostly hands could grip her keys. She was half-convinced she wasn't real. She was just a specter now. Vapor. Which would imply that she couldn't live without this boy. *God, that's pathetic.* It was her fault they were done. How could she feel this broken when she wasn't sure if she ever loved him in the first place?

Mr. Darcy and Elizabeth Bennet were definitely in love. No question about it. Even if they didn't make sense together, their love would do all the work.

Lenny and Evan did make sense together. On paper. If Lenny never loved Evan, maybe she could never love anyone at all. She took a sharp inhale, her throat closing as the tears threatened to return for an encore.

"Are you okay?"

Shit. She'd been spotted.

Claire was parked two cars down. Holding open the door to her beat-up truck.

The sunglasses weren't helping Lenny look incognito. Surely Claire could see the tears falling from her chin. And her nose was running. Not blood this time, at least. Lenny wiped her face with her hoodie sleeve.

"I'm okay," she said. "Just haven't eaten yet."

"Same. I was gonna hit up a drive-thru," said Claire. Then, a pause. "I can . . . give you a ride if you need it."

She considered the offer. Lenny couldn't spend all her time hanging out with Claire. She needed to cast a wider net. Gather more witnesses. There had to be people who saw the phenomena in the '60s who were still alive now. But what was the point? *Odd Kids* was over. Surely Evan would take the subscribers in the "divorce." The fans liked him better.

Lenny stopped herself from spiraling. She didn't need someone to interview. She just needed *someone*. And a sandwich.

"Okay, yeah," Lenny said. For the second time, she hopped into Claire's truck.

* * * * * * * * * * * *

Claire drove them through the one-stoplight town, through more fields of dead corn and cattle ranches, until she pulled onto a freeway, where she drove fifteen miles above the posted speed limit. After the third ABBA song, Claire turned down the radio and said, "Sorry for Warren. He's a dick sometimes."

"Is he your ex or something?"

Claire snorted. "No fucking way."

"Oh, I just assumed—"

"I don't even like guys."

"Lucky. They're the worst."

Claire snorted again. "That doesn't make me lucky. Not in Scarberry."

Oh. Duh. Lenny didn't need to double-check an electoral map to figure out this was a red county. She got enough side-eye from the patrons at the restaurant to know this place wasn't used to strangers. It probably wasn't used to gay people either.

God, she probably sounded so insensitive.

"I'm sorry," Lenny said. "I didn't mean—"

"You're fine." Claire pulled into the drive-thru and changed the subject. "What do you want?"

Lenny whipped out her card before Claire could try to pay. Evan forgot Lenny had possession of the *Odd Kids* credit card, and she wasn't going to remind Evan anytime soon. Food would be a good distraction. Another minute with Claire in this car and Lenny probably would have admitted that she and Evan broke up. That wouldn't have gone well. Claire wouldn't want to hear the privileged straight girl whine about boy drama.

After grabbing the food, Claire sped off again. "Oh yeah," she said, one hand on the wheel, the other holding a sweet tea, "we don't have any reservations after you. You guys are clear to stay."

"Oh. Cool . . ."

Lenny forgot she had made that request. She had still been a full person a few hours ago, hot off the last argument with Evan, barreling toward another one with Claire. But thankfully Claire had proved she wasn't in on it. There was something off about the Warren guy though. And Maeve was sketchy too. Lenny didn't have time to mope over Evan and the stupid show.

Scarberry had secrets, and Lenny still had a chance to uncover them. She could still solve this place.

This is where you're meant to be. That's what the dream was trying to tell her.

"I wanted to talk to Jared again," Lenny said. "See if he's noticed anything else weird. Maybe get a look at the cows."

Claire didn't respond. She just bit her lip as she sped past a tractor.

"What?" Lenny pried.

"It's just . . . Jared didn't show up to work today. He's never done that. My aunt says he's sick, but I don't know."

"Contact with extraterrestrials can result in a litany of side effects," Lenny offered. "Burns, heatstroke, personality changes, amnesia . . ."

Claire gave her a side-eye. "So have you *made contact?*"

"Not yet."

Claire nodded, like that was the exact answer she was expecting. Like she knew from the beginning that Lenny didn't know what she was doing.

"Jared doesn't live far," Claire said. "I kind of want to check up on him on the way back. If that's okay with you."

Lenny nodded. She didn't have any cameras besides the Nikon and her phone. No tripod. No mic. But oh well. She could take notes. Best-case scenario: Evan waited to go public with the breakup. She'd have the next four days before she had to tell her parents and drive back to Chicago to start her new, exciting life as an ex-influencer.

In the meantime, she could solve one last mystery. Her way.

Claire took a sharp turn and another car came toward

them. It was boxy, black, and driving down the center of the road. Claire swerved to avoid it.

Lenny tried to get a look at the driver, but the windows were tinted. "Asshole. Who drives like that?"

"They're not from Scarberry," Claire said. Her voice was flat, as usual, but her words were tinged with worry. "No one here has a car that nice."

She pulled up in front of a double-wide trailer. Claire punched at the stereo dial, shutting off ABBA. "There's not anything else for miles," she said, unbuckling her seat belt. "That car was definitely leaving Jared's."

CHAPTER 16

CLAIRE

The door was cracked open.

People in Scarberry didn't lock their doors. But that didn't mean they left them open. Claire's heart clenched. This was wrong. This was really, really wrong.

There was no truck in the driveway. Where would Jared go? Nowhere, if he was gravely ill. *Burns, heatstroke, personality changes, amnesia.* It was total bullshit, but Lenny's insane theories replayed in Claire's head anyway.

She jumped out of the driver's seat. Maybe she could leave a note or something. Jared never answered his phone.

Lenny followed behind her. She looked vigilant, owl eyes wide. It was like even when she didn't have a man-made lens to do it, she was always snapping pictures, inhaling the world around her with ferocity. She was so fascinated by this place that she hadn't even sent a text to the Boyfriend on the drive over.

"Look," Lenny said, pointing to the edges of the doorframe

where part of the plywood was splintered. More shards of wood peppered the linoleum floor. "It's like someone kicked it."

Claire liked to think she would have noticed that on her own eventually, but in that moment, she was grateful to have Lenny there. The YouTube show was likely super fake, but Lenny was decent at investigating things. Maybe the Boyfriend was good at it too, but Claire didn't care to find out.

She called out Jared's name. Of course there was no response. He wasn't home. He couldn't be. He would never let someone kick in his door and get away with it.

Jared was a private person. Claire knew he didn't have any kids. That he hated billionaires and country music stars who pretended to be rednecks. But she had no idea if he had any friends in Scarberry.

Or if he had any enemies.

She stepped in, feeling Lenny's breath behind her. Claire had expected Jared's trailer to be tidy, like the last time she was here. He hated overconsumption. He believed everyone ought to clean up their own messes. But the place was in shambles. There were a few pictures on the walls: old-looking paintings of cowboys in landscapes much more epic than Scarberry's. Some of them were crooked. One was a spider web of cracked glass. The floor was littered with broken mason jars and papers and books. Couch cushions and pillows were scattered everywhere.

"Yikes," Lenny said.

Claire's stomach churned. The chicken sandwich she'd just eaten was threatening to crawl up her throat. Why didn't she check that black car for a license plate?

Lenny whipped out her phone and clicked the camera app.

"Dude," Claire said. "You can't just record someone else's house."

Lenny looked up, thick eyelashes fluttering in confusion. "But what if we find a clue?"

"A clue?"

"What if he's been abducted?"

Lenny asked it so casually, like *of course* that was something they should be considering.

Claire rolled her eyes and snorted. Then she remembered she was supposed to be playing a believer. She had to keep the act going or Lenny would see through her.

"We have to explore all other explanations first, right?" Claire offered, hoping Lenny hadn't already noticed her mask slipping.

"It's a pretty crazy coincidence," Lenny said. "He saw Old Lucky last night. Then *told us* he saw it, and now, he's disappeared and his house is a mess."

"He hasn't disappeared," Claire said. "It hasn't even been a day."

Lenny gave her a sympathetic smile. "Most abductees are returned in less than a week. I'm sure he'll come back fine. Wherever he is."

Claire didn't believe in UFOs with tractor beams or little green men. Lenny's reassurance didn't do much to quench the fire igniting in her belly. Whatever had happened here looked violent. It was like a tornado had run through this place. The worst Scarberrian-on-Scarberrian violence was withdrawn invitations to Christmas parties, or "this seat's taken" at church potlucks. Gossip was the currency here. No one ransacked each other's homes. No one abducted anybody.

Claire tried not to panic. Maybe Jared had a family emergency and took a flight somewhere far away, and a few of his former farm boys threw a party in his absence. But this hardly looked like a party scene. Could it have been a robbery? Clearly someone was looking for something.

They had to report this.

Lenny started down the hallway. Claire went after her.

She caught up to Lenny in the bedroom, staring at a wall covered in overlapping paper. Crude drawings of monsters and black-and-white photos of circular wounds on the sides of horses, goats and cows. Magazine cutouts. Newspapers.

She knew Jared believed in Old Lucky, but he was always so nonchalant about it. He didn't seem like the kind of guy to have a conspiracy wall in his house, red string and everything.

Lenny grabbed a paper that had fallen on the floor. Claire looked over her shoulder to read it. *Hello Nebraska, 1962* was written on the top corner. The rest looked like it was typed with a typewriter.

"It's a transcript," Lenny said.

Well, part of one. Whoever made this copy was only interested in one exchange:

Burt: So, Willy. It's been a year, and you still haven't found your alien?

Willy: I won't, Burt. No one will.

Burt: Think it went back home? (*Audience laughs*)

Willy: No, Burt. It never existed. I made the whole thing up. (*Audience gasps*)

Burt: Now, why would a good man like yourself do something like that?

Claire didn't know Willy had recanted his story. It didn't exactly line up with what the chief had said. According to him, his dad had made an honest mistake. This transcript made it seem like a full-blown hoax.

It sounded exactly like what Claire was doing.

Was someone screwing with her? Pranking the prankster? Claire could handle that if it meant Jared was all right. She couldn't imagine Warren doing this. Too much commitment. And his dad would kill him for breaking and entering.

But she did know someone who had nothing but audacity, and after getting fired from the ranch, he definitely had beef with Jared.

Bryce Stern.

He already hated Claire, losing his summer job at the ranch could have been his last straw. That would explain why Warren covered for Claire's prank with the speakers. He knew Bryce was up to something worse.

"Okay. Strike the abduction theory," Lenny said. "I don't think anyone was beamed up. It could have been the military. Could have been the Men in Black. Don't know yet." She panned her camera over the wall, hovering in front of a yellowed newspaper clipping with the headline COVERT COVER-UP?

"But clearly," Lenny said, "your friend knew too much."

CHAPTER 17

LENNY

"Should I be more dressed up for this?" Lenny asked, trailing behind Claire. She didn't realize town hall would be held in a church. She had noticed the poster back at the diner, but there was no official venue listed. No dress code either.

"You're fine," Claire said. "I just have to talk to Chief Lamb."

Right as they left the Jared's trailer, Claire had demanded they go to the authorities. She didn't seem to agree with Lenny's theories, which was understandable. Abduction was a lot to take in. Not everyone could be Susan, welcoming it with open arms. Lenny was just grateful Claire was still letting her tag along.

When they stepped inside the clapboard church, Scarberrians turned around to stare. All the men wore flannels and denim. All the old ladies had long dresses or skirts and short permed hair. Lenny felt as if she'd walked into a Norman Rockwell painting. She stuck out with her neon-orange cropped tank top. She hoped no one here recognized her. They were the only teenagers there, so it was unlikely any of these people subscribed to *Odd Kids*, but the fear lingered. Her face was still red and puffy from crying all day. And she wasn't prepared for anyone to ask, *Where's Evan?*

Who cares?

There might have been an actual alien abduction. Her stupid ex shouldn't matter. Still, she was used to Evan guiding her through big crowds. Squeezing her hand when she talked too excitedly, when she missed a social cue. And on the ride home, he'd tell her where she fucked up so she'd never do it again.

Lenny and Claire sat in the back. The wood was cold against her thighs. The woman in the pew ahead of them kept glancing back at Lenny, eyeing her up and down in disgust. There was no way she noticed Lenny's phone, facedown, recording audio. Maybe the woman was mad at her outfit. When Claire had said they had to go the town hall meeting, Lenny had been excited to meet other potential witnesses. But she could feel the tension in the air. She was choking on it. She tried to tell herself the bad vibes weren't her fault but she couldn't be sure without Evan telling her so.

"Good evening," said a muffled voice through speakers. An old man with muttonchops stood behind a podium, speaking too close to the mic. The chief sat in a foldable chair next to him. He leaned back, legs spread.

Muttonchops said, "It's a beautiful day."

"It's a beautiful day," echoed everyone but Lenny and Claire. After repeating her line, the woman in front glared at Lenny again.

"That was creepy," Lenny whispered.

Claire smirked. "Isn't creepy your thing?"

Yes. It was. But she was hoping Claire would at least give her some sort of context.

"Don't want to keep us long," said Muttonchops. "Just have a few announcements then we'll open up to the floor." He shuffled papers on the podium, the mic catching every movement in all its earsplitting glory. "County fair volunteer sheets will be posted outside. Now, as most of us know, Bethany Randall won't be our ticket booth hero this year. We'll all be praying for her recovery, but meanwhile, we'll need an experienced cashier to lend a hand . . ."

"What happened to Bethany Randall?" Lenny whispered.

Claire's voice was flat. "Cancer."

Muttonchops droned on, "And of course no one could replace our longtime auctioneer, Jerry Collins . . ."

"What happened to Jerry Collins?"

"Don't remember. Brain tumor maybe?"

Lenny felt a chill on the back of her neck. "Do a lot of people in Scarberry get cancer?"

"Cancer isn't exclusive to Scarberry."

"Like, how many other people?"

Claire gave a look that said *Are you stupid?* and Lenny wanted to melt into the pew. Was that a bad question to ask? She wanted to be a serious journalist, but Claire was all she had in Scarberry. Lenny needed her if she was ever going to find Old Lucky.

But Claire's expression softened. Her eyes gestured to the wall on their right.

There were little paper cutouts of angels, tacked to the

bulletin board. There had to be at least a hundred of them. *Jerry Collins, 1962–2024* was written on one, name lovingly rendered in cursive. *Rachel Arbor, 1959–1963. Judy Shores, 1971–1984. Emma Shores, 1980–2005. Andrew Siler, 1948–1965 . . .*

How had Claire avoided mentioning this?

Myra Lamb, 1982–2025.

"Lamb?" Lenny asked.

The lady ahead of her turned to glare again.

"Warren's mom," Claire explained. "She died last year."

This was too weird. Lenny was terrible at doing math in her head, but the numbers seemed all wrong. According to the paper angels, dozens of people died of cancer every decade in Scarberry, and many of them were *kids*. This town had fewer than 2,000 people in it. If Evan were here, he'd already know how Scarberry lines up with national statistics. He'd weed out all other explanations. Chemicals in the water supply. Related families. But she didn't have Evan. No, she didn't *need* Evan.

"You don't think it's weird," Lenny started, "that right after Old Lucky popped up, people start getting cancer?"

"They just started the wall around then. Correlation, not causation, ya know?"

"But these dates . . . A lot of them are really young."

Claire bit her lip and stared blankly ahead. "People die every day," she whispered.

Muttonchops finished droning on about the county fair. "I'd like to open the floor to any citizen concerns." Right as he said it, the lady in the pew in front of them shot up. All attention turned to her.

"Here we go . . ." Claire muttered.

"It's been a month," said the woman. Her jaw jutted out when she spoke, each word sounded as coarse as sandpaper. "We lost another twenty acres. Just withered away overnight. What's your plan, Chief?"

Chief Lamb didn't stand from his chair. He stayed slouched confidently with his arms folded. "Gosh, Mary, I don't control the weather."

"Leave the Old Gods to that," a man to their right chimed.

Someone laughed. Muttonchops smiled.

The woman didn't falter. "He wouldn't punish us for no reason. Your leadership is failing us. And He's taken notice."

Lamb's eyes narrowed. But he didn't speak.

"That'll be all, Mrs. Stern," Muttonchops said into the mic. Then people started to leave the chapel, cheerily chatting amongst themselves as if that wasn't the most bizarre meeting ever.

Lenny stopped the recording on her phone. "What the fuck was that?" she whispered to Claire.

Claire shrugged. "I told you. She's delusional. She thinks the Old Gods speak to her through microwaves, *and* her son's a homophobe. Lovely family."

"So, people don't talk about Old Lucky because they think they'll sound like her?"

"Maybe. But honestly? You're gonna have a hard time finding anyone in Scarberry who believes in him."

"Besides you?"

Claire grimaced. "Besides me."

* * * * * * * * * * * *

They caught up to Chief Lamb in the barren parking lot outside, chatting about sports with Muttonchops and another guy, who looked like a shrunken version of Muttonchops.

Claire stepped in between them. "Chief, can I talk to you real quick?" she asked. He nodded at the other men and let Claire lead him away.

"Hello, Lenny," Chief Lamb said, once out of earshot of his buddies. "Catch any swans?"

Obviously it was meant to be playful, but she felt belittled. Evan would have had a professional comeback, but Lenny just clenched her fists and gave a gritted-teeth smile.

"Jared didn't show up for work," Claire explained. "We went to check up on him. The door looked busted-in, and everything was a mess. Broken glass, furniture knocked over. He's missing."

The chief's calm composure faltered. His expression turned serious. "When was this?"

"Just now."

"And the last time you saw him?"

"Last night," Lenny jumped in. "Around one or two?"

"So he's been missing for less than twenty-four hours?"

Oh no. Lenny saw where this was going.

"I can't do anything professionally," Lamb said. "Yet. He's an adult, I can't report him as a missing person so soon. But tell ya what? I'll see if I can track him down. Get some guys to keep an eye on his place, in case anyone comes back. Okay?"

"Okay," Claire agreed. She gave him her phone number in case he had any updates on the case.

Claire gave Lenny an unsure glance. What else were they to do? At least the chief was less dismissive than Miss Reed had been. He'd do *something.* But it didn't feel like enough.

And he'd be looking at all the wrong sources. He'd search the trailer, search the ranch. But no one else in Scarberry would dare to look up.

CHAPTER 18

CLAIRE

It was a long drive home. Lenny didn't spew any theories, probably because she was afraid of being compared to Mrs. Stern now, thanks to Claire being a dick. Claire didn't know how to turn off her cynicism, even when she needed to. God. She almost blew it.

She wished she'd pushed Chief Lamb more, asked him how he planned to look into it. Because if roads led to Bryce Stern, his son's best friend and teammate, would he look the other way?

When they pulled into the ranch, mountainous clouds were forming. There was nothing Claire could do to stop tonight's storm. Nothing she could do to find Jared.

"Let me know if you hear anything," Lenny said before heading back to the caboose.

As Claire lay in her bed, listening to hail hit the roof, she tried to think of plausible explanations for the black car and the trashed house that *didn't* involve alien abduction. But her ideas all went back to the papers scattered on the floor. The artists' depictions of Old Lucky. Lamb's bizarre interview. Why was Jared hoarding all that research?

She dreamed of swans. A big, otherwise-empty room full of them. Claire clumsily tried to grab hold of them, and they didn't try to fly away. They didn't have to. Her hands went right through them, like they were never there to begin with.

* * * * * * * * * * * *

The sun was bright and unforgiving when she woke up. She hoped that all of it had been a bad dream, but when she glanced out the window and scanned the parking lot, there were only four vehicles parked: Her own beat-up truck, Maeve's van, Lenny's little silver sedan, and the Subaru belonging to the woman staying in Car 3. No sign of Jared. He'd never missed a day of work. Now he'd missed two.

She quickly changed and flew downstairs. Maeve had to sense something was wrong by now. Or maybe, miraculously, he wasn't missing. He'd already stopped by that morning and explained his mysterious absence and was now simply running errands. All was well. No conspiracies to see here.

She found Aunt Maeve on the porch, leaning back on her old wicker chair. On hot days like this, when it wasn't any cooler inside, she would live in that chair. She hadn't found the time to sew a new pillow for it this year, so she still had the old one: seashells, though they were a hundred miles from the nearest beach. Aunt Maeve had never seen the ocean.

Claire hadn't either.

It was first on her bucket list. After film school, she was going to buy a van and travel the country. She would drive to the West Coast and swim in the ocean until the salt and the seaweed and the trillions of gallons of shark piss would wash the Scarberry dirt off of her. Then she would be brand-new.

Maeve gave sympathetic nods to the woman standing on the porch: Susan, the loner in Car 3. The one with the dog. There was no dog with her now.

That was the problem.

"She doesn't wander. Ever," cried Susan. "She has separation anxiety."

"Well," Aunt Maeve said, "she can't be far."

"She has a bad hip. Hates walkin'. She wouldn't just take off."

Lenny stood behind the woman protectively. Of course she would have already bonded with Susan. Susan was a textbook UFO chaser. She had told Claire about her childhood abduction during check-in, and when she had bought a Kit-Kat in the gift shop the next morning.

"Aunt Maeve," Claire said, "I need to talk to—"

"I didn't lose her," Susan protested. "She *disappeared* last night. Full-on *vanished*."

"Why don't you girls help look for her?" said Aunt Maeve. "I am terribly busy here, with the bookings and the gardens . . ."

Maeve never did the bookings. And everything in the garden died two hailstorms ago.

"We'd love to help!" Lenny said. She looked at Claire expectantly. She was probably giddy over the word *vanished*. The aliens must have been responsible for the lost dog. No, not aliens. It was the "Men in Black."

Looking for an elderly puggle wasn't how Claire preferred to spend her morning. But if she couldn't find Jared today, she could at least find that stupid dog. Both disappearances would turn out to have a rational explanation. And she had to do something to win Lenny over again. She'd almost ruined everything in the chapel when she forgot to include herself among Scarberry's believers.

"Yeah, of course," Claire agreed.

The screen door clacked shut as Maeve retreated inside. Claire wasn't sure if it was even a good idea to tell her about Jared. If Maeve knew about the state of Jared's trailer, that could send her into a spiral. They didn't know who was responsible yet. But it definitely wasn't Will Smith and Tommy Lee Jones.

Lenny immediately started to interview Susan, holding the mic between them. "When did you last see Tilly?"

"When we went to sleep," Susan said. "She was gone when I woke up. What if it got her? I heard 'em. The other night."

"What did you hear?" Lenny probed.

"The whistle, honey. Old Lucky's song. Woulda been beautiful if it didn't blow out my eardrum. What if it got her?" Susan looked like she was about to start sobbing again.

According to legend, Old Lucky was much more interested in gnawing on cattle than little dogs, but there were a million other things to worry about. Coyotes. Bobcats. The dirt road didn't get much traffic but was still a threat. People drove fast in Scarberry. Was that what had happened to Jared? Did his truck land in a ditch somewhere?

Claire suggested that Susan stay near her train car, in case the dog found her way back. She reluctantly agreed, returning to her post at the picnic table, smoking cigarettes worriedly.

"Have any theories?" Claire asked Lenny once they were alone.

Lenny jotted something down in her little notebook and looked up. "Maybe she got under the fence?" she offered.

There was plenty of room for a little dog to squeeze under. Other farms electrified their fences. The Reeds couldn't afford a guest who didn't follow the guidelines and got hurt. No one paid any attention to the NO CLIMBING sign on the UFO. Some asshole kid would definitely get themselves barbecued on an electric fence.

They started heading toward the pasture. As they passed the caboose, Claire asked, "What's the Boyfriend up to?" She realized she forgot to say his actual name as it slipped out of her mouth.

Lenny didn't seem offended. "Oh, he left. He's . . . working on a different case."

"Puggle abductions aren't interesting enough?"

Lenny snorted. "Apparently not."

Claire wasn't going to pry an explanation from her. She didn't know if the bickering she'd overheard from the couple was normal for them. Even if it was, it didn't seem healthy.

But it wasn't Claire's place to give dating advice. Not when the only girlfriend she'd ever had ghosted her almost a year ago.

Claire climbed over the fence. She debated offering Lenny help, but it turned out she didn't need it. She swiftly climbed up and jumped off, like she had done it a hundred times before.

"Usually when I'm climbing fences, I'm trespassing," Lenny said.

"Really?"

"Why is that hard to believe?"

"No offense, but you give off a student council president vibe."

"That's Evan. Not me."

Oh. So they really were at war. For some reason that made Claire smile.

"Anyway, the most haunted places are off-limits to the public." Lenny stepped carefully as she walked, avoiding the minefield of manure. "You don't find anything if you follow the law all the time."

The cattle gave them confused looks as they went into the pasture. Some stepped back to allow them to move forward. A brown one with irregular white spots on his face followed them on their mission.

"Tilly!" Lenny called. There was a moo in response, but no little bark.

Then Lenny gasped. Her manicured nails grabbed Claire's arm. A cow lay on its side in front of them. Its big brown eyes looked up, pleading for help.

On its stomach was a hole the size of a fist. Just like the photos that were hanging in Jared's trailer.

"It happened again," Lenny said. She leaned toward it. "It looks fresh." Claire willed herself to look closer. She wasn't a huge fan of blood, not on people and especially not on animals. She was the only one in her anatomy class to object to dissecting piglets. Their insides were too close to her own; she didn't need intimate knowledge about what guts look like. Yet she instinctively knew there was something extra wrong about this cow. The blood around the edge of the wound was too dark, its sheen purple in the morning sun.

And it was the worst smell ever.

The ever-present aroma of manure never bothered her. But this wasn't a natural scent. It was chemical, yet sweet. A mix of formaldehyde and old-lady perfume. Not blood. Not flesh.

Not right.

They couldn't leave the calf here to suffer in pain. A few cows stood nearby, urging them to help their fallen brother.

"I need to tell my aunt," Claire said.

"She already knows this is happening," Lenny reminded her.

Aunt Maeve was a farm woman. She could afford to spare only so much empathy for animals bred to be eaten. She didn't love them like pets, but she didn't treat them inhumanely. From a business standpoint, whatever did this would hurt their profit. Maeve couldn't afford that now, more than ever. She would *have* to care.

Claire left Lenny waiting on the porch while she slipped inside the house.

Bri was slouched on the brown leather couch in the living room, watching her current favorite Netflix show.

"Where's Aunt Maeve?" Claire asked.

"She had errands."

Errands. Code for groceries. Bank. Post office. All of her out-of-the-house adult duties were done at once. She would be gone for hours, and she hardly ever brought her phone with her. She was purposefully incompetent with technology. Claire handled the Wi-Fi setup. She kept track of their passwords and logins.

She tried calling Aunt Maeve's cell and, sure enough, she heard the phone ringing in the kitchen.

Claire couldn't tell Bri about Jared. She was too sensitive; it would only cause her to worry. And by the looks of her, she still didn't feel well. She was swaddled in blankets, her new tufts of hair looking like baby bird feathers.

"Season 3 comes out tomorrow," Bri said. She had rewatched this stupid show a good four times. It was an average teen drama, full of thirty-year olds playing high-schoolers and twists that made zero sense. It was awful. It was riveting. It had become a ritual for the both of them.

Claire's phone buzzed in the back pocket of her black jean shorts. *Hannah.* She still hadn't retrained her brain from having that reaction. It would never be Hannah again; she had to get used to the fact.

No, this came from a number she didn't have saved in her phone. It had a Scarberry area code, and Claire remembered she'd given the chief her number for updates on Jared. She opened the message. There was a photo of an unfortunate-looking dog wearing a little sweater. Its glassy, round eyes faced different directions.

This one of yours? the text read. She wanted to correct him. She wasn't responsible for the guests, so the dog wasn't hers, not really. It didn't have to be her problem. But she was hit with a wave of relief. She had a rational explanation for it now. The dog had wandered over to the Lamb property, hypnotized by the chief's frequent summer barbeques.

"Are you going out again tonight?" Bri asked.

Claire's blood ran cold. Did Aunt Maeve tell Bri the same

thing Warren had told Claire yesterday? Forbid her from leaving the house after dark too?

Lenny's words echoed inside her brain: *She already knows.*

"No," Claire said.

"Damn. Was gonna ask you to pick up some Ben and Jerry's."

CHAPTER 19

LENNY

After Tilly the puggle was recovered, Lenny needed a break from the ranch. She figured her next best move was finding other witnesses. Willy Lamb was deceased, so that just left his ex-girlfriend, Minnie Albert. There was no address for her in the bedside table's phone book. So Minnie Albert was either dead or in a nursing home.

She sat sprawled on the bed, looking up the number for the nearest nursing home.

It was eighty miles away. Huh. Scarberry really *was* in the middle of nowhere. She called the number. Anxiety tickled her stomach as she listened to the staticky classical music. Evan was always better at this part. He was good at appointments and schedules and "yes ma'ams." He toed the line between innocent, unthreatening kid and serious researcher. Lenny's nervous desperation shone through every interaction with small-town strangers.

The call was easier than expected. The receptionist didn't have to double check the name.

"Yes, Mrs. Albert is in Room 22."

Her hunch was correct. Minnie Albert was alive. At least something had gone right. Lenny still had no idea if she'd be willing to discuss her encounter from over sixty years ago. But she was running out of witness options.

"Do you have visiting hours?" Lenny asked. "Do I . . . need to schedule an appointment?"

"Kin can visit anytime before six," the receptionist said.

"Awesome." It was just past noon. Plenty of time.

Now she had to tell Claire. Lenny searched her recent calls for Claire's number. She should have probably saved Claire's contact already. But Lenny wouldn't be in Scarberry much longer, so there really wasn't much of a point to add her name in. After Lenny left, she wouldn't see Claire again.

The thought made her stomach drop. Lenny didn't expect it. She had gotten used to losing friends. Evan and the show had always been her top priority. She didn't have room for much else.

She made a new contact on her phone, putting a little alien emoji after the name.

Claire picked up on the first ring. "You've reached the puggle rescue hotline; this is Claire speaking."

"Do you want to come to a nursing home with me?"

"Call me old-fashioned, but why don't you buy me dinner first, and we'll see where it goes?"

"Hey. I bought us KFC yesterday," Lenny reminded her.

"I bought breakfast."

"That was your aunt." Lenny got off the bed and began assessing her pile of laundry. She needed to get out of these clothes. She could still smell that sweet chemical smell from the cow's wound. It had seeped through the fibers of her shirt, but she worried it went even deeper. Was it in her hair? Under her skin?

"Okay, you got me," Claire said. "Do you seriously want to go to a nursing home?"

"Yes. I want to talk to Minnie Albert."

"Who?"

"Exactly. She was with Willy Lamb when he first saw Old Lucky, and no one has talked to her about it. She was only mentioned in, like, one article. I want to hear her take on everything."

She thought, for a horrifying second, that Claire wouldn't want to come along. Lenny knew she'd been asking a lot of her. But Claire said, "Okay. When do you want to go?"

* * * * * * * * * * * *

Driving around the countryside was like driving in the past. There were few clues pointing to what decade they were actually in. Most trucks parked in their driveways were older than Lenny was, the men on their mowers were shirtless, wearing nothing but blue jeans. Clothes hung on wooden clotheslines, and they passed several kids riding horses on the dirt roads. All the other cattle they passed looked unharmed, unaware that only a few farms away, their kind were getting munched on by extraterrestrials.

"Are you sure this lady is gonna want to talk to us?" Claire asked. She switched gears and the truck shivered.

"To be honest? I'm not sure."

After the initial report in 1961, Minnie Albert went the rest of her life avoiding any mention of aliens. The subsequent articles, the fan websites, the subreddits, and that one sketchy documentary from the '90s—they only mentioned Willy Lamb. He got to be the household name, forever in the canon. Minnie was exclusively referred to as "Willy Lamb's girlfriend." Maybe Minnie could help Lenny confirm her hunch: Willy only went back on his testimony not because it had been a hoax but because he was threatened.

Minnie deserved a chance to tell her story. And Lenny needed an opinion from someone other than the Lambs and the Reeds. Claire had been a big help, but her aunt was . . . off. And so were Warren and the chief.

"How do you know it's an alien?" Claire asked as they drove past wilted cornfields. "Not trying to be one of those people, but like . . . how can we be sure that's what Old Lucky is?"

There it was again. Her thinly veiled skepticism showing through. It was probably an asset to the investigation—with Evan out of the picture, Lenny needed someone to keep her grounded. A good investigator couldn't get tunnel vision. She had to want the truth more than she wanted to see Old Lucky.

But after what they'd seen in the sky, after actual cattle mutilation, shouldn't Claire be more receptive?

Especially if she was the one who sent the video.

Lenny was becoming less sure of that now. There was very little she was sure of.

"We know there's something special about the ranch," Lenny said. "I don't think it's a coincidence it's happening again in the same place. And all the dying corn. People getting sick. What if it's all because of Old Lucky?"

Claire sighed. "Yeah. It's just . . . I guess being from here makes it harder to notice when shit's odd."

Claire still didn't sound convinced. At least she didn't put down her ideas like Evan did.

It was probably the culture that stopped her from truly believing. Claire probably endured enough being queer in a place like this, she couldn't afford to be the town's conspiracy theorist.

But she was safe with Lenny. Claire would never be the weird one when it was just the two of them. Lenny just had to keep pushing.

Claire pulled the beat-up truck into the gravel parking lot. They had since crossed into a new town, which was only slightly bigger than Scarberry. They were still in middle-of-nowhere-territory. Lenny stepped out and smoothed her dress. She hadn't packed a lot of "nice" clothes for the road trip, but she'd brought some backups just in case. She knew some elderly people hated ripped jeans and showing a lot of skin, so she wore a babydoll dress and Mary Janes. She even secured her bangs out of her face with flower clips.

Claire, on the other hand, didn't bother to change for the occasion. She was in jean shorts, mud-covered cowboy boots and a T-shirt with the bottom half cut off in a ragged line. The employee at the front desk didn't seem pleased with the outfit, which made Lenny like it better. Instead of trying to always blend in, Claire had doubled down on being herself. Claire was braver than Lenny ever could be.

"We're here to see Minnie Albert," Lenny told the receptionist.

"Any relation?"

"She's my great-aunt." The receptionist did not look convinced. Remembering the lady was pushing ninety by now, Lenny added. "My great-great-aunt."

That seemed to do the trick.

They were directed down a long beige hallway adorned with fake flowers in ceramic vases. When they reached Room 22, the receptionist left, but not without a few backward glances.

"I can wait out here," Claire said. "Unless you need me in more footage."

"She might respond better to someone local," Lenny said.

Claire looked around, clenching and unclenching her fists. "Doubt it. I don't exactly have the best reputation around here."

"I still want your help."

Lenny was used to having a partner. She could do this on her own, but she didn't want to if she didn't have to. Even if Claire was an outsider in her hometown, at least they could be outsiders together.

"Okay," Claire agreed.

Lenny opened the door. The room looked something in between a hospital and hotel room: clean, plush furniture, paintings covering the walls. They seemed to be landscapes. Lenny admired one with an aurora borealis floating above a wheat field.

The white-haired woman almost blended into her beige recliner. She had her hands crossed on her lap like she was waiting for them. Well, maybe she was. Someone could have told her visitors were coming.

"Hello," Lenny said.

"Hello."

There was a ring to the way Minnie said it. Like the word had extra syllables. When the door closed behind them, the woman's wrinkled face was cast in shadow.

"You don't know me. My name is Lenny, and this is Claire."

"Lenny's a boy's name," said Minnie.

It wasn't the first time someone told her that. Her own grandmother preferred her legal name too.

"It's short for Lenora," Lenny explained. Minnie smiled, pleased that she had a proper lady's name after all. Lenny didn't have the time or energy to explain that names didn't have gender. She had to get this woman to like her.

"The youth group came yesterday," Minnie advised.

"I'm not with the youth group. I'm not from around here. I came to Scarberry to find out what happened on July fifth, 1961, and I'd like to hear your side of the story."

Lenny pressed Record on the audio recording app on her phone and presented the first page from her folder to Minnie. The photocopy of the newspaper was one of the forty-seven physical research documents she had for this case. She could have kept her resources digital, but the printouts made it feel tangible. Like real evidence.

Minnie accepted the paper with shaky hands and slowly

brought it up to her face. She reached for the glasses sitting on the table beside her, taking her time to unfold and adjust them on her nose.

Lenny sank into the chair facing Minnie, and Claire leaned against the windowsill, next to a cactus. Minnie stared at the paper for a long time. Maybe she could barely read it, with her aging eyes and the dim room. Maybe she didn't remember. Asking her to recount something that happened over sixty years ago was a stretch. Lenny could hardly remember what she'd had for breakfast yesterday.

Minnie let the paper sit on her lap. "Hmm . . ." she said.

"Would you say that account is accurate?" Lenny asked.

"I suppose." Minnie grabbed her tea from the side table. The cup had pictures of children's faces. Probably her grandkids.

"Did you see Old Lucky after that night? Willy Lamb said he saw it again," Lenny reminded Minnie. She was prepared to show another article, where Willy added details. That was where most of Old Lucky's descriptors came from. Elongated neck. Four arms. Legs bent strangely. Pale skin with a pearly shine to it. Red eyes.

"Well, Willy was a special case," Minnie said. *Special case* clearly wasn't code for something good. "He went lookin' for the thing. I don't know why he did. It hurt him real bad the first time. He thought he was invincible, like most boys did at that age."

"How did it hurt him?" Lenny asked. Willy's injuries had been glossed over in all the sources she could find.

"It clawed at him, bit into his shoulder. Thought he was

a goner. But he healed up fast. I don't remember the thing screaming much. That seems to be what people talk about. I only remember hearing Willy's screams. It happened quickly." She said it all so matter-of-factly, bored almost. Maybe the encounter wasn't extraordinary to her after living with it her whole life.

"And where were you when you first noticed the lights above Reed Ranch? All the articles mention being outside town, on a road people hang out on to . . . be alone. A lover's lane?"

"Can't say Willy was much of lover," Minnie said.

Claire snorted.

Minnie continued: "Yes, we were out mine-side. Near Clawson's."

Lenny turned to Claire. "Do you know where that is?"

Claire nodded. "That's still a hookup spot. Kids with strict parents take their dates there all the time. I mean, that's what I've heard, at least."

"And there were no other witnesses?" Lenny continued, sliding the phone on the table closer to Minnie.

"For a while, it was just Willy out lookin' for it," Minnie said. "I never wanted to see the thing again, but Willy had to be believed. Needed the respect. Soon, others joined the hunt. Mostly out-of-towners. They never found anything."

"Willy went on record saying he made it up," Claire added. Minnie's eyes flicked up. She studied Claire for a moment, and the girl didn't flinch.

"Well, that was his choice," Minnie said, sipping her tea.

"But why would he say that?" Lenny pressed.

Minnie pursed her lips. After a moment, she said, "Last we discussed it, he called the thing a miracle. He was a weird little man."

"Did you paint all these?" Claire probed, trying a different tactic. All the art on the walls shared the same aurora light, but each one was a different color, with different shapes. Puffy clouds in one. Swirls in another. Lights over windmills. Lights over a McDonald's.

Minnie nodded.

"Huh," Claire said. "Looks like the picture from all the newspapers."

"I paint my memories."

"Who took it?"

"Hmm?"

"The photo. You or Willy?"

Minnie hesitated. It must have been a lot, to remember something that long ago. Lenny didn't like how Claire was asking the questions. Like this was an interrogation.

"I did."

"Then you painted on top of it? Sold it to the papers and said it was a UFO?"

Minnie's mouth hung open, then she licked her lips. The tea was shaking in her hands. "No," she finally said. "No, dear. I didn't have my camera with me that night. So I tried to re-create it. To explain. Willy sent it to the press. He's the one who needed to be believed. But I *know*. It's a sacred thing. It's . . . it's personal. But not a lie. Never a lie."

Claire's eyes flicked to Lenny; her expression looked too

close to pity. As if she expected Lenny to crumble at this revelation.

But this changed nothing. Minnie had seen the lights. She had seen Old Lucky attack Willy. Just because the famous photo was an artist's rendition after all didn't mean the legend wasn't true. She'd seen enough to know. She'd felt it. They were getting closer to answers. They had to be.

Lenny cleared her throat. "What do you think Old Lucky was?" she asked Minnie. "In your own words."

Minnie looked at her teacup. Thinking. Claire had her hands on her hips, glaring at Minnie like she'd just confessed to a crime.

"When I was a little girl, my father . . ." Minnie began. "He worked in the mines, like everyone else who didn't have land in that day. It's destructive work. Mean to the land and mean to the men doing those jobs. But they had to dig to make something of themselves. They poked holes. Made the earth bleed. It ruined a lot of good men. They came back wrong, you see. Talking of seeing colors. Hearing messages from gods. They called it mine fever."

"What do you mean, messages from gods?" Lenny probed.

"They thought they were communing with something. My daddy was so sure of it. Came to dinner, talking of 'wonderous things' revealed to him and his crew. No gold. But something better. Then the mines closed. They were unsafe, I guess. Everyone said my daddy was off his rocker. He didn't find anything. Just had the fever, that's all."

"What do you think?"

Minnie took a long breath. "I think there was something down there. Something man wasn't meant to see. That's why they closed the mines. Moved the whole town south."

"So, you don't think Old Lucky was an alien?" Lenny asked.

"Not any more than you and me."

"And you think it came out of the mines?"

"Maybe men like my daddy sealed 'em off. Closed those holes. Now they can't get home. We trapped 'em. For progress."

Huh. It was an interesting theory. One that could explain nearly every cryptid, every paranormal occurrence. Old Lucky was a man-made monster, a physical manifestation of humanity's greed. Proof of what happened when you poke holes in the wrong places.

"Willy wasn't the same, after," Minnie continued. "His body healed up but he was . . . It would be terrible if . . ." She stopped herself, shaking her head.

"If what?"

Then Lenny was hit by a blinding flash-bang. She put her hands in front of her eyes, blinking away the shock. Someone else had entered and clicked on the ceiling light. Two women stood in the doorway. One was wearing scrubs. The other had a severe-looking blazer on, complementing the sharp angles of her face. Her dark hair was smoothed into a tight bun. She would have been beautiful if she wasn't so terrifying.

"Ms. Albert," said the woman in the scrubs. "You have, uh, another visitor."

Minnie pulled down her reading glasses and stared at the woman in the blazer. Clearly she had no idea who she was either.

"Ms. Albert, I'm Agent Brenner." She quickly flashed a badge inside her wallet, then put it back inside her breast pocket before Lenny could get a good look at it. But she was pretty sure it said FBI. Lenny glanced at Claire, still standing by the window. She had her arms tensely crossed, looking at the woman with suspicion.

"I'm here to ask you some questions," said Agent Brenner. She eyed Lenny and Claire. "*After* the room is cleared."

Lenny felt suddenly very protective of Minnie. Lenny had no purpose being there either, but she didn't like the idea of leaving her with Agent Brenner. But she didn't get a choice, did she? This was a federal agent. What were the FBI doing in Scarberry, Nebraska? Could that explain the car leaving Jared's? Was that who messed up his house?

Claire leapt from the windowsill. Lenny rose from her chair. "Thank you for your time," she told Minnie.

They were almost out the door when Minnie spoke again: "You seem like nice girls. If it's back, don't go looking for it."

CHAPTER 20

CLAIRE

Claire knew a grifter when she met one.

She'd always thought the 1961 photo was faked. She never cared how or by whom. Now she knew for sure. Mustache Bro and all his predecessors were right. When you see the iconic photo in high res, the grain did look different on the edges of the light.

Minnie Albert was full of shit. Yet Lenny talked excitedly on the drive home. She was convinced that the FBI woman was proof Scarberry was the next Roswell. She said Minnie's "close encounter" had a "profound effect" on her.

They pulled into the ranch's dusty parking lot.

"So?" Lenny said. "What do you think? Maybe we should check back in with Minnie tomorrow. Ask what the FBI wanted? I didn't get through all my questions either. It's hard to find the data from that long ago, but I was thinking, we should try to find medical records or something. Find out how long people here have been getting sick. Do farmers keep, like, ship logs? Ya know, to record how good their harvest or whatever is? If we can find out when the anomalies started, we could find out when Old Lucky got here."

"Yeah. Maybe," Claire mumbled. She couldn't bear to go back to the nursing home. Her mask was slipping. Hard. If Lenny wasn't on to her, she would be soon. "But let's figure out our next move later. I promised Bri I'd do something with her tonight."

Not a lie exactly. Claire was taking every chance she had to tell the truth. Bri really did want to binge the next season of that stupid show.

Lenny's smile dropped. "Oh. Yeah. For sure."

They both stepped out of the truck.

Before heading for the caboose, Lenny turned. "Hey," she said. "I hope I wasn't being too, like, *intense*. This is a lot. I don't want to overwhelm you."

"You're not. I just . . . made a commitment."

"Right. Right. Of course. I just really appreciate you helping me here. But you don't have to. I know I can be too much sometimes."

Oh God. Now Lenny thought Claire was mad at her. *Fuck. Fuck. Fuck.*

"You're not too much," Claire said. "You're doing your job. And you're good at it. Nobody's even thought about interviewing this lady. You were ahead of the freaking FBI."

She'll be on to you soon too.

Lenny's smile returned. "Okay. Just checkin.' See ya later."

* * * * * * * * * * * *

"She's an idiot," Claire said.

Bri's response was predictable. About as predictable as this episode was so far. "She's in love."

"She shouldn't be. I mean, did she learn anything from Season 2?"

The two of them were in Bri's bed, burrowed under the blankets from their childhood. Claire liked the blanket with the moon on it best. It was scratchy and the moon's face sorta creeped her out, but she was convinced it had been her mom's favorite. She didn't know why she had that idea, but she didn't want it proven wrong. If Claire asked Maeve, she would only get flustered. Maeve's no-good dead sister was just another horrible burden she had to shoulder.

"Jonathon broke her heart," Bri said. She looked like a floating head, her neck peeking out from the blanket. She was surrounded by an army of stuffed animals, some as back support, some strategically placed to prop up milkshakes and bowl of popcorn. The episode ended, and Claire clicked to the next one. It had taken nearly an hour to find a download of the new season. After maxing out credit card number three, Maeve had stopped paying for all their streaming services in March, and Claire got very good at finding free downloads of their favorite shows. Add pirate to her résumé.

The cheesy theme song started up. Claire considered telling Bri about Jared's ruined trailer and the FBI woman, but that would just freak her out. Bri was in a good mood, and for the first time in twenty-four hours she didn't have a fever. Claire could save Minnie's fake-ass painting and ominous warning for another day.

Now the *feds* were involved. Agent Brenner could have been talking to Minnie about tax fraud or something innocuous but still, Claire couldn't think of a rational explanation. And it didn't help that Lenny was totally convinced this was a government coverup. Without the Boyfriend there, suddenly Claire was the unofficial third member of *Odd Kids*.

And the weirdest part? She didn't totally hate it.

Claire couldn't tell Bri about that part either. She'd probably joke about shipping Claire with Lenny. That was Bri's favorite hobby: pairing the hopeless messes on her TV shows together. To Bri, love was best when it was impractical. When it would cause more problems than it would solve. That was when it was *real*.

Bri coughed weakly and sank her decapitated head further into her blanket.

"You can have my milkshake," Bri said. She had hardly touched the popcorn. Maybe she still felt like shit. That would explain Maeve's avoidant behavior. She couldn't handle seeing her little girl in peril, even if it was just the flu. Or was Lenny right about her already knowing about the cattle mutilation?

On the smudged laptop screen, the protagonist walked into a flower shop. Her new man was talking to a woman. His ex.

"Oh shit," Bri said. Shocked, somehow, by the formulaic plot.

"Bryan literally told her it was complicated. She needs to get over this guy," Claire said.

"Just like you got over Hannah," Bri muttered.

"I have. You're the one who keeps bringing her up," Claire

said. She dug for more popcorn in the bowl between them. She found only kernels.

"'Cause you're acting like she was your one shot out of here when you never even met her."

Ouch.

"She's not a catfish. We've done video chats," Claire pointed out. "You've literally talked to her."

Bri paused the video. "I don't mean she isn't real," she said. "Just . . . maybe you're missing a person that only existed in your head. Someone you imagined."

Claire wanted to laugh. That was an absurd accusation. Especially coming from Bri. "You're the one that thinks Jimin is gonna marry you," Claire reminded her.

"I don't actually think that. Obviously. I'll be dead by the time I'm old enough anyway."

"Stop," Claire said. "You're not dying."

"Not living either."

Claire wasn't going to put up with Bri using her illness as a scapegoat this time. She was in remission now. Not a speck of cancer was left in her. She wouldn't die like Warren's mom and the others. She only felt sick today because she had gotten used to being sick. Because Maeve was acting like a regular flu was an omen. Because that was her new normal.

Claire wiggled out of the blankets.

"You *could be* living," she said. "You don't need to rot in this house. You could be going to parties again. Warren practically begged me to get you to talk to him. He's obsessed with you."

She wanted to keep going. She wanted to say, *You would*

rather romanticize all the possibilities than act on any. You would rather criticize me for not putting myself out there.

Claire stopped herself. She didn't come into Bri's room to fight. They had two more episodes to watch. Bri got quiet, staring blankly at the computer screen that was now playing the credits music.

"Yeah, and you said you were leaving Scarberry."

"I'm *not* leaving you."

"I'm going to bed," Bri muttered, shutting the laptop.

Claire picked up both milkshakes and left the room. The hallway was hot without any windows to allow a breeze. This place should have been checked for mold a long time ago. There had to be some hiding in the unfinished basement, or in the old metal heat vents. One of the few pictures she'd seen of her mom was her yearbook photo, and she had too many lines on her face for an eighteen-year-old. She'd smoked; that could have been part of it. Or maybe her mother's face looked so worn because she'd grown up in this goddamn house.

Claire pulled out her phone. No missed messages. She sent Lenny a text without rereading it first: *Are you investigatingg tonight?*

Right as she sent it, she realized her mistake. Oh God. Oh God, *no.* A typo shouldn't have sent her into a panic spiral, but a sense of doom washed over her anyway. Hannah hated spelling and grammar mistakes, and Claire had learned to text like she was writing a college admissions essay. Now her fuckup was illuminated bright blue. The extra *g* mocking her.

She watched three dots appear on the screen. Lenny was typing something. Had she noticed?

Wait. Why the hell did Claire even care?

Lenny didn't need to believe Claire could form coherent texts, she just had to think Claire believed in Old Lucky. Lenny's opinion shouldn't matter. Surely after spending all day with her, Lenny had figured out just how much of a weirdo Claire was.

And the more time Claire spent with Lenny, the more chances Lenny got to discover her lie. Not just a lie, a whole hoax. But nobody else would help find Jared. They needed each other, for better or for worse.

Lenny responded: *Unfortunately Minnie Albert was wrong. I'm not a nice girl.*

Oh thank God. Claire typed her response: *Me neither.*

CHAPTER 21

LENNY

Lenny's heart was beating too fast. It had been hours since she'd left the nursing home. It was past midnight now. Even though there was lightning on the horizon, the ranch was completely quiet. Not even a cricket was chirping. It was the kind of silence she didn't think people were supposed to experience. She felt like she was interrupting something.

She touched the cold metal of the UFO sculpture. Probably a bad idea, with all the lightning, but she needed to do something to ground herself.

Lenny used to be afraid of the dark. That was something she had said on several *Odd Kids* videos. It was part of her persona. She was the Girl Who Used to Be Afraid.

It was a lie.

She was still very much afraid.

She had been to far creepier places. Hotels that had brutal murders. Homes where people claimed spirits pushed them down the stairs and whispered atrocities in their ears.

But never an FBI agent interrupting their investigation. That meant they would have to be careful. It also meant they were onto something big.

She was more scared than ever, yet she felt lighter. There was nothing weighing her down now. Not the body cam or the tripod. Not Evan demanding she say the same thing several times so they could get multiple angles. She just had the Nikon. Maybe it wasn't 4K, but it did well in low light. And it was easy to operate.

It had enough pixels for her.

There was another flash of lightning, miles away. Her subscribers didn't know it, but Lenny had always been afraid of lightning too. Her friends used to tease her, saying her braces would make her more likely to get struck. She knew, logically, that wasn't true, but when her braces were removed, she was relieved. One less thing to worry about.

Despite her phobia, part of her wanted to dance outside during a thunderstorm. It was very rare to be struck by lightning. So if it happened to Lenny, it would mean she was chosen. By whom? By what? She wasn't sure.

Then, after ten minutes of complete silence, something whined in the darkness. Lenny held her breath, scanning the empty ranch for any glowing red eyes, but she only saw a flashlight. The sound had just been Claire closing the screen door. She tiptoed down the porch steps and put a finger to her lips, then silently motioned for Lenny to walk with her toward the barn.

They had agreed over text to focus their investigation on

the cows tonight. Catch Old Lucky while he had his midnight snack. It wasn't late, not by Lenny's standards, but what they were doing felt utterly *scandalous*, like the old days of *Odd Kids*. Actually, it felt better than that.

"Are you gonna get in trouble?" Lenny whispered, once they were safely in the shadow of the barn.

Claire shrugged. "Not really. She's been more paranoid lately, but Aunt Maeve could never commit to a punishment."

The red barn was devoid of any color in the night. Claire's all-black outfit almost blended in. Her dark eyebrows and smudged eyeliner contrasted with her white-blond hair. Once again, she was both part of the landscape and its opposition. She had the coolness of a girl in a postapocalyptic movie who shot zombies in the head without giving a fuck.

After climbing over the fence, Lenny shone her camera's flashlight on the patchy grass in front of her, trying not to startle the cows or whatever might be feeding on them. Claire walked confidently forward, weaving around the dark shapes of the unmoving cattle. Most of the cows were taller than Lenny—walls of a living labyrinth. If Claire weren't guiding her, Lenny would have been lost in the maze of spots forever. Every time she pointed the camera at a cow, its eyes would reflect the light and Lenny had to stifle a scream.

Maybe the swan theory wasn't totally unrealistic. The cows were creepy enough at night. When you were on edge, anything could seem supernatural. This pasture was endless, yet claustrophobic. The big sky of stars didn't offer escape. It seemed to be pressing down on them. Even though it was cooler than the day had been, the air was too thick to breathe. Lenny almost wished she had stolen Evan's inhaler. Her lungs weren't agreeing with Scarberry air.

Lenny had to fill the silence before she shrank into nothing. She was feeling smaller and smaller by the minute. What were they talking about before?

Miss Reed.

"What do you mean paranoid?" Lenny asked, because she couldn't just come out and ask, *Have you noticed your aunt is sketchy as hell?*

"Just her usual shit. If she believes in Old Luckly, he doesn't bother her. She went down this homeopathic deep dive a few years ago. I think she credits Bri's miracle recovery to all the snake-oil shit she was buying, but now it's like *everything* is toxic and she wastes money on pointless supplements. She was fully convinced gooseberries have magical properties. Makes Bri eat at least one jar of jam a week."

"What kind of cancer did Bri have?"

"She had leukemia. I forgot you didn't know. I'm so used to people just knowing all my business before I even tell them."

"That sucks." Lenny meant both leukemia and nosy people. She had zero experience with cancer. Her mom had a suspicious mole removed once, and her dad overpacked sunscreen on vacations because "the sun is not our friend." But that was about it. She *was* used to people knowing more about her than she would prefer. For Lenny, it wasn't her neighbors being nosy, it was strangers. Four hundred thousand of them. And most of what they knew were lies.

It was Lenny's own fault, really. She didn't have anything to complain about.

She hadn't checked her socials all day. What would people comment when they saw Evan hanging with *Dark Unknown* and not Lenny?

Lenora, said a warning voice in her head. Part Dad, part Evan, part her. *This girl is talking about a loved one with cancer and you're worried about YouTube comments?*

"I'm glad she's okay now," Lenny said.

"For a while we weren't sure. I mean, everyone else didn't get better. But Bri did. Aunt Maeve can't just accept that Bri got lucky. She's been in survival mode for so long that she's more erratic. Like, she's feeling all those emotions after the fact. Everyone got so used to the idea of Bri dying, we didn't plan for what to do if she lived."

Lenny only vaguely remembered the other girl in the gift shop. The small one, with the short hair. She was still a stranger. Claire used to be a stranger. That was only a few days ago. Were they turning into . . . friends? Or strictly partners in a platonic, *business* sense. They were like Mulder and Scully, minus the sexual tension.

Except sometimes Claire looked at her a little too long, and Lenny wondered if Claire was checking her out. She didn't feel violated by it. *Honored,* was a better word. And then she felt horrible for assuming that was what the looks meant.

Lenora, be for real. Just because she's gay doesn't mean she has a crush on you.

Lenny should know better. She knew plenty of queer

people. She just had an outsider's understanding of the community. Though, once at a party (back when she had time to go to parties), her friend Addy joked that Lenny ought to be bisexual. "You just have that vibe," Addy had said.

Lenny's response: "It wouldn't matter. I'm with Evan."

Addy had laughed, and suggested Lenny was *Evansexual* and there should be a pride flag for that.

"You're kinda right about Aunt Maeve though," Claire continued. "She's not worried about the cattle. If she was, she would have been telling me all about a *holistic bovine healing salve* she heard about on a Facebook group. She usually worries about everything. It doesn't make sense."

Lenny could relate. She also worried about everything.

They reached the edge of the fence, where bald trees grew in a neat little row. Claire stopped and grabbed Lenny by her sleeve.

That was when she saw it. A portion of the wooden fence was splintered around an unmoving black mass. As they edged closer, Lenny could see the dark shape was a vehicle: a four-wheeler like the one she saw Claire ride.

"Is that yours?" Lenny asked.

Claire nodded. "One of them. We have two. We keep the keys in the house. No one could have stolen it . . . unless Jared was the one who crashed it."

"Do you think he was running from something?" Lenny asked.

What if he'd gone looking for Old Lucky? What if he did exactly what Minnie warned them not to do? Lenny's neck stiffened as a cow mooed mournfully behind her.

Jared was an older man, but he seemed sturdy enough. Farm work was hard work, for sure. But if all the legends were true, then even a tough guy like Jared wouldn't win in a fight against Old Lucky.

Claire called out for Jared, just like they'd called out for the lost dog. She climbed over the fence and Lenny followed, putting the camera in her pocket. She wasn't expecting the fence to be slick. Her hands slipped, but Claire caught her before her head hit the ground.

"You good?" Claire asked.

Lenny wasn't sure. Her hands were burning. Her palms were dark. Dark with blood? Had she managed to get splinters? When Claire shone her flashlight on her hands, the sticky substance didn't shine red but purple-black. The slime was too thick, too transparent, to be blood. Tiny air bubbles rose and popped like it was alive.

"Ew," Claire said. "What the fuck is that?"

At the moment, Lenny didn't particularly care. She just wanted it *off of her*. The burning feeling was only getting worse. "Grab my camera from my pocket," Lenny said. Claire obeyed, swapping her flashlight for the point-and-shoot camera. She pointed it at Lenny's hands for a few seconds.

"That is . . . nasty," Claire said.

Lenny wiped her hands on the grass. If Evan were here, she would have to stand there long enough for the stuff to erode all her flesh down the bone. She could imagine the YouTube thumbnail of her skeletal fingers.

Was this the same too-dark blood she'd seen on the cow? She smelled her hands, fighting the wave of nausea.

It was the same odor: sweet, yet necrotic. A death-scented perfume.

Lenny thought out loud. "I think this is the stuff we saw on the calf."

"Uh. That's not cow blood."

"No, I mean, what if it's from Old Lucky? What if it's like . . . his venom?"

She rubbed the rest of the stuff on her pants. She would burn them afterward. Or maybe sell them at auction after they found the damn thing. No, that was something Evan would do. Lenny would be better. She'd donate them to science.

"Holy shit," Claire whispered. She stepped toward a pile of abandoned farm equipment. "There's more right here."

Lenny inched closer, shoulder touching Claire's. The massive tractor tire was dotted with the purple goo. The grass around it was crispy, more dead than the rest of the ranch. There was nothing in the center of the tire. Was there a hole in the ground? They both leaned in, flashlights shining on the center of the tire.

Lenny couldn't see the bottom of the hole, only a pool of stars.

Rainwater. That would make the most sense. It was just a reflection. But that wouldn't explain how the stars seemed to get closer. They rose up, getting bigger until a white-hot light enveloped the world.

The tire, the dead trees, and every blade of grass lost all definition, consumed under the glow.

Lenny couldn't see her hands in front of her face. She wildly reached out for something to hold on to. Claire's hand gripped hers. At least she wasn't alone in the blinding void.

The ground was snatched from under Lenny.

She was falling.

She was falling.

She was flying.

CHAPTER 22

CLAIRE

Claire had approximately three seconds of clarity before she landed. Lenny's eyes were closed tight. Her hair blew around her face. Her free hand was outstretched, reaching out, and her feet were slowly kicking like she was underwater, trying to rise to the surface. Her other hand held Claire's in a death grip.

It was just the two of them, the black night, and pulsating white stars.

Then she looked down.

If she'd had longer, maybe she would have felt powerful. They were superheroes, floating above the world, observing just how small it was. They were higher than the ranch's tallest trees. Eye-to-eye with the windmill. The cows looked like dots from here. Claire never had a chance to learn if she was afraid of heights. She thought the first time she flew would be in an airplane. Not hovering magically above the ranch, and definitely not holding Lenny Gilson's hand—which, she realized with horror, she didn't totally hate.

The ground was rushing toward them now. Too fast for Claire to brace herself, too fast to warn Lenny. She shut her eyes tight. Her butt slid against something rough, and then she fell again. A smack on her arm. Smack on her leg. She grabbed for safety. Failing and flailing until she stopped.

She opened her eyes. She'd landed in a tree. The branches pulled at her hair, coiled around the buttons on her jacket. Her shoulder was screaming, maybe from the last attempt at grabbing for a branch. At least gravity was a thing again. The tree stayed a tree. Not a black hole disguised as one.

Lenny asked, "Are you okay?"

She was on a branch above Claire, arms hugging the trunk of the dead pine.

"I . . . think so." Actually, Claire was pretty sure her shoulder was dislocated. But she was alive, so that fell into the *okay* category. She eased herself down slowly. She still didn't trust this tree. This branch could turn into a snake at any moment.

Once her feet reached the dirt, she lay on her back. She wanted to be as near to the solid ground as possible. She looked up just in time to see a glowing ball hovering ten or twenty feet above her. Because, sure. Why not?

None of this was real anyway.

Lenny jumped off her branch and knelt down by Claire. She stared up at the swirling mass in the sky. "Holy shit," Lenny gasped. Once it got their attention, the orb collapsed in on itself, fading into wispy clouds and innocently blending in with the night.

That's when Lenny lost it. "Holy shit. Holy shit. Holyshit. Holyshitholyshitholy . . ."

She had a scratch on her chin. Funny. Claire couldn't remember the last time she or any supporting characters were injured in a dream. She also couldn't remember the last time a person she had just met appeared in a dream either. And usually, once she was aware she was sleeping, she would wake up.

Claire put her hand in front of her eyes. Hands look strange in dreams. And counting was supposedly impossible. But she counted all five fingers. Oh no.

She sat up. Her shoulder felt too heavy for its socket. She bit her tongue to avoid crying out.

This wasn't a dream at all. This was real.

"I think . . ." Lenny started. She was pacing. "I think we teleported." She looked at Claire, waiting for her input. As if Claire had any authority to say what the hell had just happened.

"Teleported?" Claire repeated.

"Yes. I'm like ninety-nine percent sure we went into a portal."

"Is that . . . something that happens to you a lot?" Claire managed.

"It's my first time. You?"

She snorted. "Yeah, gotta say I'm a tire-portal virgin."

Why would you say that? She always made crude comments. But now they actually felt dirty.

Lenny looked back at where the orb had been—where *they* had been—only a minute before. "Where are we?" she asked.

There was an abandoned train car not far from their tree. It was covered with sloppy graffiti. "Not far from the ranch," Claire explained. "We're in Old Scarberry. Clawson's Field. Kids have bonfires out here."

There was evidence of the last one. A singed barrel was turned over. There were piles of beer cans and hard lemonade. Claire had been here only once, with Warren. That was before sophomore year, before Claire became the town's outcast.

"Do you think the lights we saw last night . . . do you think they're from a portal?" Lenny asked.

Portal. Dear God. Claire couldn't decide if that sounded crazier than *UFO*. But Lenny had seen the same thing. So either Claire wasn't crazy, or they were both crazy, which sounded much better than being crazy on her own.

"Probably," Claire guessed. "Maybe the lights show up whenever someone goes in."

"Or goes out."

So Minnie was partially right. There weren't just holes in the earth, but holes in the *universe*. Random pockets where the particles glitched. There had to be some scientific explanation. Claire's school didn't exactly have advanced STEM classes, so she had no theories.

She rose to her feet, cradling her elbow to prop up her shoulder. "We should get out of here."

It would be a long walk back to the ranch. She couldn't handle any new discoveries tonight. Or any more time with Lenny. This was all too confusing. She wanted the safety of her bed. Sleep would give her a reset. When she woke up, she would be in the real world again.

"Wait," Lenny said. "I need to find my camera." She kept her head to the ground, searching through the tall grass. Claire knew she should help Lenny look. The sooner she found it, the sooner they could go. She didn't know how long she could last with her shoulder like this. If it still bothered her in the morning, she could make up a story about it and get Maeve to drive her to the doctor. But then Claire's eyes focused on a pop of color by the train car. It was barely visible in the tall weeds.

She froze. She couldn't even alert Lenny. Her throat was clogged and her feet stayed stuck, as if the field had turned to quicksand.

"Oh shit. The screen is busted," Lenny said from behind her. Then, a little quieter: "What is that?"

Claire mustered the strength to move forward. A frayed yellow bandana lay in the grass. This was the hanky that lived in Jared's breast pocket. He used it to wipe sweat off his neck in the summer and blow his nose in the fall, when his allergies were bad. Why was it here?

And why was it covered in blood?

Probably the same reason the suit had been torn to bits.

Old Lucky.

CHAPTER 23

LENNY

This was Lenny's first time calling the police. Technically, it was the chief's personal cellphone number, not the police department. She used Claire's phone to call, while Claire held her shoulder into place, grimacing.

"Where are we again?" Lenny asked her.

"Clawson's Field," Claire said. "He'll know where that is."

Lamb answered on the first ring. "Claire? It's past midnight," he said. "What's going on?"

"Hi, hello, this isn't Claire but we're in Clawson's Field and there's been an accident and Claire might have broken her arm and we found blood and you should get here ASAP please—"

There was a brief pause. "Clawson's?" he asked, his voice even.

"Yes."

"Why are you girls way out there?"

Oh. Right. This was the local lovers' lane.

"We . . ." Lenny looked at Claire. Surely, she didn't expect

Lenny to tell the truth. The chief didn't believe in Old Lucky; he wouldn't believe what happened tonight. "We got lost," she finished.

There was a pause. Fuck. That was a stupid answer. Clearly Claire knew how to get around Scarberry. "Be there in ten," the chief said before hanging up.

"He's on his way," Lenny said, trying to reassure Claire, but she only stared blankly at the dead grass.

"He must have followed it through the portal. Or it chased him," Claire mumbled. "I mean, he saw Old Lucky—or what he thought was Old Lucky. Maybe he stayed up, looking for it." She locked eyes with Lenny. "Did you ever see his truck leave? It's an old white Ford."

"I don't know. I don't think I saw anyone leaving."

At least, not through the parking lot.

"When I saw the lights the second time . . . I heard screaming. But it didn't sound like Old Lucky's song . . . it sounded like man. Do you think that was Jared?"

"Maybe. But if Old Lucky attacked Jared out in the field and he got away, why would he just disappear?"

"Maybe he was scared it'd come back?"

Or Lenny's first instinct had been right. He knew too much. "It could be the FBI lady putting pressure on him," Lenny offered. "He got out before anyone found out what he knew."

Claire shook her head. "He wouldn't just skip town like that. He wouldn't leave me here."

Every theory Lenny conjured was worse and worse. What if the FBI made him disappear? What if Old Lucky swallowed him—bones and all? But she kept her thoughts to herself. Claire looked like she was barely holding it together.

Soon the field was glowing with headlights. Two cars parked ahead. One was a police car, the other was a beat-up SUV. Maeve jumped out of the SUV and ran straight to Claire.

"What happened?" Maeve asked, her thin fingers brushing Claire's hair out of her face.

Claire didn't mention any portals, but explained, in a tiny voice, that she'd found Jared's bandana.

"Oh honey. You're *hurt*," Maeve said, ignoring Claire's words.

"I'm fine. Jared's in danger. We need to find him before *it* does."

"Of course. Of course. Let's get you fixed up. Poor thing."

Claire gave Lenny a pleading look as Maeve dragged her into the SUV.

"C'mon," Chief Lamb said to Lenny. "I'll take ya home."

Shit. Obviously Claire needed to go to the hospital. But Lenny hated the idea of being separated. And the last person she wanted to be alone with was a cop.

Lamb opened the passenger door for her. "Thanks," Lenny said numbly.

She didn't know how to play this. Evan had only been gone for a day, and Lenny found herself in a police car.

She was in the front seat, so she wasn't under arrest at least. Chief Lamb drove fast, even faster than Claire. The headlights didn't do much to illuminate the empty road. There was nothing to see but the endless stretch of blackness ahead.

So far, Maeve Reed was the shadiest person in Scarberry, but Chief Lamb wasn't off the hook. His son, Warren, was weird. And Claire seemed to think his friend Bryce was someone to watch, with his paranoid mom and his beef with the Reeds.

Lenny looked out the window, waiting for her eyes to adjust. She needed to see something to stay grounded. One of those dilapidated farmhouses. A horse. A cow. Anything to prove she was still here on Earth. She had dreamed of discovering magic since she could remember. But not like this. She hated the uncertainty of this informal police custody, and she hated being separated from Claire—the only person who knew she wasn't crazy.

"Are you chilly? I can roll down the window," Chief Lamb said.

"I'm okay."

He was acting like a dad driving home his friend's kid. Clearly he had better things to do, but he wanted to portray some level of politeness. The problem was: he wasn't acting like a *cop*. He didn't ask Lenny what she'd found. Why was she in the field to begin with. She had just called in evidence of a crime, and he didn't seem to care.

"The bandana's right by the train car," Lenny said. "Claire says it's Jared's. That he never goes anywhere without it."

"Don't worry. We'll look into it. I'm a bit more concerned about Claire. I imagine Maeve is worried sick."

"Yeah," Lenny said, brushing dirt off her pants. "Did you know the FBI was in Scarberry?"

"Hmm?"

"We saw a black car leaving Jared's. And then . . . ran into this FBI woman. She said her name was Agent Brenner. Have you seen her?"

He laughed. "Why would the FBI be in Scarberry?"

Lenny almost gave him a look but caught herself and kept staring out the window instead. This place was famous for alien sightings. Why else would they be here? Where there were aliens, there was the government claiming there were no aliens. Either the FBI wasn't working with the local police or the chief was playing dumb.

"Are you going to test the blood, then?" Lenny asked him.

"We'll look into it," he said again. His voice was stern now. He shifted in his seat and let out a big sigh. "I have units watching Jared's property. We're looking for his truck. But I'm going to be honest with you because you seem like a pretty mature kid, okay? The guy was in a heap of trouble in his past. Came to Scarberry to get away from it. Drugs. Gambling. You name it. He's turned his life around, clearly. But a guy like that, if he thought the walls were closing in, if demons from his past found where he was hiding, well, he's just gonna run again. That's how it goes. But like I said, we're keeping an eye out anyway. We protect our own here."

Lenny didn't know Jared beyond a brief conversation about aliens, but Claire trusted him. And Lenny trusted Claire. She had to believe he didn't voluntarily leave Scarberry.

"So, where is home?" Lamb asked, back to chill dad mode.

"Chicago," Lenny answered.

He nodded. "Well, I imagine you'll be heading back."

"Yeah. I guess so." In a couple days, her parents would call. But until then, she wasn't going anywhere.

He slipped into a smile. It wasn't very convincing. He wanted her gone. He wanted her *long* gone. He was already tired of this outsider sniffing around.

Chief Lamb didn't speak again until he pulled up to the ranch.

So, now what? Lenny wondered. Was she free to go? Shouldn't he ask for her to give an official statement? All of this felt too casual.

"Take care," Chief Lamb said.

She nodded and stepped out of the car, closing the door behind her. That's when she saw it: a spot smeared on the passenger's-side door, right under the handle.

It would have seemed like blood if not for the purple sheen. Jam, maybe? This was the car he used to deliver gooseberry jam to the Reeds. But Lenny had to know if it was the same stuff found by the tire.

She swiped her hand over the purple spot and nearly cried out in shock. It burned hotter than the stuff on the fence. She rubbed it on her pants and glanced at her palm. Her skin was already blistering.

The police car disappeared in a cloud of swirling dirt.

Maeve's GPS gleefully announced the route to the hospital would take thirty-two minutes. Thirty-two minutes on the dark, bumpy roads before Claire could get her arm fixed. Before she could look for Jared.

She watched the headlights of the police car get smaller and smaller in the passenger mirror. Maeve kept assuring her they were almost there. Almost there. And Claire thought of what to say. Whether to say anything. But it was hard to form words when every time the car went over a bump, she had to bite her lip to avoid crying out.

While waiting for a doctor to see her, Claire endured the world's most uncomfortable plastic chair and Maeve doting on her, brushing her hair, giving hollow affirmations about how strong she was. Maeve promised in the morning she'd cook Claire a huge breakfast. Everything she could possibly want. She had never been this affectionate. Not to Claire, at least—this sort of softness was exclusively for Bri. It wasn't that Maeve was usually cold to Claire; she was just more direct. Like they were coworkers. This sudden attention didn't feel right.

She was grateful to go into the X-ray room alone. The doctor declared Claire's arm not broken. It was, unfortunately, dislocated, which meant lying on a cold table, where she was held down and had her bones popped back into place. Three hours after entering the hospital, they gave her a sling and sent her on her way.

On the drive back to the ranch, Maeve was all smiles, pointing out the significance of every song that played on the radio—"Remember when you and Bri made up a dance to this Lady Gaga song?" And Claire tried to think of how she'd begin to explain what she and Lenny had discovered. Aunt Maeve would have to listen. Aunt Maeve had always trusted Claire to be reasonable. Grounded.

"It got him," Claire said.

"Hmmm?"

"Old Lucky. That's what got Jared. We were trying to track it . . . We found a four-wheeler crashed at the gate," Claire explained. "And blood. Weird, purple blood like what was on the cows . . ."

"We don't know what happened, hon."

"I touched a tractor tire out back and the next thing I knew I was falling out of the sky." It sounded bonkers when she said it aloud. Shit.

"You mean you fell out of a tree?" Aunt Maeve asked.

"No! I mean, yes, but—"

"I think you may have hit your head."

Claire stared at her in shock. Yes, it sounded absolutely

nuts, but Maeve was open-minded. She believed in the healing power of crystals. Why couldn't she believe Claire? Claire was the one who ran the ranch's website and Facebook page and cleaned up after guests and kept the gift shop open. Had she not proved herself yet?

Maeve bit her lip as she stared forward. Her robe was bunched up by her elbows, and on her forearms were red, angry lines.

"What happened?" Claire asked, reaching out with her good arm to touch her.

Maeve forced the sleeve down, briefly swerving as she took her hands off the wheel.

"The cats. Look at you! You're the one who's hurt!"

There was no way a cat had done that. The latest stray to drift into their barn hadn't been seen in a month.

"I'm sorry, Claire Bear," Maeve said. "I've been expecting too much from you. It's not fair. I know you're legal now, but you're still a kid. You don't need to be responsible for saving everyone. It's not your job to figure this out. Jumping to conclusions . . ."

There she was, playing maternal again. It was a deflection.

"Did Jared ever call in sick?" Claire asked, fighting the bile rising in her throat. "You know he wouldn't just disappear."

"Just let the adults do the worrying. Okay?" Aunt Maeve's voice was stern. She parked the SUV in the dirt lot and hopped out. Claire followed her inside the house. Maeve didn't believe her. Of course she didn't believe her. Claire had thought Lenny was delusional until the truth dislocated her shoulder.

Claire headed straight for the medicine cabinet in the downstairs bathroom. She couldn't find any pain relievers.

Claire swore she'd bought some the last time she'd grabbed groceries.

"Where's the Advil?" she called out.

"You don't need that poison," Maeve said. "We have peppermint oil."

She stepped out of the bathroom to face Maeve.

"But my arm is still hurting," Claire said. "The doctor said to take ibuprofen for the next few days—"

"The doctor is incentivized to keep us sick, dear. Our pain is their gain."

Claire stared dumbly at Maeve. Since when was Advil banned in this house? When did Maeve get this militant about her alternative cures? She hadn't cared about this shit at all until Bri got sick. And Claire always let it slide. It gave her aunt hope. Made her feel in control when her world was falling apart.

"I just think . . ." Maeve continued. "With your genetic history . . ."

"If I take a fucking Advil, I'm gonna end up like my mom?"

Maeve gave a sympathetic look. Yep. That's exactly what she meant.

Claire had dedicated eighteen years to proving she was reliable. Responsible. She'd stayed in Scarberry just to prove she could. And for what?

Maeve still didn't believe Claire about Old Lucky. She still didn't believe Claire could make her own decisions. Fuck this. Fuck *her.*

Claire stomped upstairs. She needed this night over, right now. It was too much. All too much. She couldn't handle any new discoveries. She reached the dark hallway and slammed into a shadow. Someone yelped. Bri. Her curls were moist with sweat. Her blue eyes sunken in.

"Claire! Mom said you went to the hospital?" she whispered.

"Yeah. All good now. Are you . . . okay?"

"What happened?" Bri asked, eyeing the sling.

"Long story. Tell ya in the morning."

"Does it involve *Lenny Gilson?*" Bri teased. She was smiling despite looking like she was minutes from death. She hadn't looked this rough since . . .

"Shut up." Claire pressed the back of her hand to Bri's forehead. "You're burning."

Bri shrugged. "Still not over the flu I guess."

What if it wasn't the flu? If Bri's cancer came back, would Maeve even try to treat her this time? Or would she just feed her gooseberry jam and rare Patagonian roots and throw in some manifestation if things got really rough?

"What if it's more serious than that?" Claire whispered.

Bri backed into her bedroom. "Oh my God Claire. You're seriously worried about me when your arm's in a sling?"

"But—"

"Good night!" Bri called, slamming her bedroom door.

CHAPTER 25

LENNY

The first thing she did when she was out of the chief's informal custody was run her hand under cold water. It looked like a second-degree burn, and it was only getting redder. The second she pulled her hand away, the pain returned with double the severity. She traded the sink for the communal shower behind the caboose. She still had tear-streaked mascara on her cheeks and leaves in her hair and dirt on her skinned knees. The water was so cold she could hardly breathe, but that's exactly what she needed. She watched the rest of the gunk wash down the drain. She was free of it, but she didn't have any evidence. She should have taken a sample of it. But she stupidly forgot. Now if the goo poisoned her bloodstream and killed her, no one would know.

She imagined Evan's next YouTube thumbnail. He'd be fake-crying. The title would be something like *STORY TIME: MY EX WAS FOUND DEAD AT A RANDOM FARM IN NEBRASKA. NOT CLICKBAIT.*

Chill, Lenny told herself. *You're not dying.* No cows were dead. Yet. The goo probably wouldn't kill her. It was the *not knowing* that bothered her. She had to take her mind off it. She had to do something productive.

At two a.m., with her hair still dripping wet, Lenny changed into sweats and a hoodie and took off in the *Silver Bullet.*

She stopped at the first gas station, where she plucked energy drinks and gauze from the nearly-bare shelves. The twentysomething cashier looked even less awake than she felt. Like every Scarberrian, he had a scruffy, weather-worn look to him. He barely paid any attention to Lenny. Just gave a curt hello and her total. He could probably sense that she was an outsider. Did he care?

She felt marked now. Different. The pain in her hand was proof this was actually happening. But it was also proof that the answers might be dangerous. She glanced around the gas station, in case any federal agents happened to be around.

What if Chief Lamb was involved? Lenny had shown too many of her cards. If she called her parents, they would tell her to come home. If she called Evan, he might not even pick up. If he did pick up, he would just say, *I told you so,* and she would say, *You told me there was nothing here, so actually I'm right,* and he would say, *Fine, you're right. How does it feel?* and she would say, *Lonely.*

She hadn't felt the chill of loneliness when she was with Claire. She almost didn't feel those missing pieces when they were sneaking through the pasture. Even when she thought she had wandered into the black hole, she was glad she had been with Claire. Somehow this stranger was more comforting than her boyfriend of two years. What did that mean? Lenny couldn't let her mind wander there. A man was missing and this town's police force might be covering it up.

And she would prove it.

Lenny paid for her items and speed-walked to the *Silver Bullet*.

She texted Claire once she was back in the caboose, ignoring anxious thoughts telling her she was being clingy. Then she grabbed a spare flashlight and the grocery bag with Evan's soiled sneakers and set out for the pasture. She played music from her phone. The last ABBA song she heard in Claire's truck had been in her head all day, so it felt appropriate. The cows were all clustered by the barn now, like they didn't want to be separated. Like they knew what was out there. She almost panicked when she thought she'd gotten lost, but then she saw the crashed four-wheeler. X marks the spot. She climbed over the fence, careful to watch for purple goo this time. The second she landed, the music stopped. Just like she predicted.

At first, the tire looked just as insignificant as it had hours ago. But when she squinted, even from ten feet away, there was a slight shimmer to it. The edges wobbled under the glow of her flashlight, until that too flickered off. Okay. Here went nothing. She chucked the bag of sneakers toward the tire. Her throw was off by a few inches, but it was close enough. Before the bag could land, Lenny's vision went white. She was knocked backward, colliding with the fence.

She whirled around, ignoring the dull ache in her skull. They lasted only a split second, but the Scarberry Lights were unmistakable. White tendrils flashed above the barn.

She was right. The lights showed up whenever something went through a portal. She couldn't wait to tell Claire.

For now, Lenny would tell her journal. Writing things out let her sift through her thoughts. She returned to the caboose and made a timeline of everything she knew and ripped pages out to pin on the bulletin board. She usually wrote neatly for the board segments of their videos. It was more of a visual for the audience than an actual help for the investigation. Now she needed it to feel sane.

Willy Lamb was attacked by Old Lucky, she wrote.

No one believed him. He claimed it was made up.

Swans. Miss Reed. Motive?

Holes in cows.

Holes in the sky.

Cancer.

Nosebleeds. Asthma. Toothaches.

Dead crops.

Purple goo.

Bloody bandana.

Warnings everywhere.

The government is involved.

Hand is starting to itch.

The itch could mean it was healing, or it could be the beginning of an allergic reaction.

She had to stay focused.

What else?

Lenny wrote, *Home???* If it lived here, it had to have a lair. A nest somewhere. Scarberry didn't have many trees or tall buildings. A nine-foot-tall creature would be easy to spot during the daytime, so it had to be nocturnal. Where was it sleeping?

Her writing fugue was interrupted by a heavy knock at the door. She jumped up. The dirty room came into focus, brighter than before. Was it morning yet? She glanced at the UFO-shaped clock. Eight a.m. Yikes.

Lenny rolled out of bed. Her bare feet crunched on a glitter pen. She peeked through the blinds. Claire stood in front of the door. She had her long hair tied into a chaotic bun, with random pieces poking out, framing her face. Her arm was in a bright-blue sling.

Lenny yanked the door open, shielding her eyes from the sun. The heat was already overwhelming. "Hey," she said. "Are you okay?"

"I'm fine." The answer came a little too fast, but Lenny wasn't going to press it. Claire didn't seem like a girl who wanted to look weak. Lenny could relate.

Lenny stepped back so Claire could come in, but she didn't move from the doorway.

Claire glanced behind her, like she feared they were being watched. Then she asked, "Wanna get out of here?"

CHAPTER 26

CLAIRE

Claire would have preferred to drive, but she couldn't with her arm in a sling. She hated feeling helpless. She'd slept fitfully, her room stuffy and her shoulder aching. When she had meandered downstairs, Maeve had already cooked Claire's favorite breakfast: chocolate-chip pancakes. Maeve couldn't make a pie to save her life, but she made pancakes way better than the diner did. She didn't mention their fight from last night. Maybe she truly felt guilty for giving Claire too many responsibilities.

Maybe she felt guilty for something else.

"I tried to tell Aunt Maeve, but she wouldn't listen to me at all," Claire said as she hopped into Lenny's Oldsmobile. The inside smelled too strongly of evergreen. But it was decorated adorably. The seats had lime-green covers; a plastic-sheet ghost hung from the mirror.

"I'm sorry," Lenny said.

"I don't know if she knows something about Jared though. She's probably just as clueless as us. She's in denial."

Maeve had been in denial for a long time, Claire supposed. She wished now that she had intervened before Maeve got this bad. Showed her articles debunking those first magical supplements she'd bought from that Facebook wellness group. Called her out the first time she called vaccines toxic. When she had said Bri's doctors "didn't know a damn thing." But she thought Maeve had earned her frustration. She had needed something to believe in. Now Maeve was in too deep and Claire didn't know how to rescue her from the rabbit hole.

"I didn't tell Lamb about the portal or the goo," Lenny said. "But uh . . . I don't think he's doing anything about Jared. I thought maybe he didn't want some random girl coming to his town and telling him there's monsters that live among us, but . . . more of that purple shit was on his car."

"What?"

"Yep." Lenny showed the palm of her hand, wrapped with gauze. "Couldn't get it off as fast as before. Burned like hell. Do I just keep following this road then?"

"Yep. It'll take ya right into Old Scarberry."

Well, what was left of it. No Trespassing signs were posted on half the abandoned buildings now. Before J. Porter and Associates set their eyes on Reed Ranch, they'd bought up all the useless land here.

"But we have one thing confirmed," Lenny continued. She explained how she threw trash at the tire and, seconds later, the lights appeared above. She thought the screams she had heard the morning of Jared's disappearance had been him, going into the portal.

Claire's phone vibrated in her back pocket. She had two unanswered messages from last night she hadn't looked at. They were both from Warren: *Is Bri okay?* He had sent that one while Claire was getting an X-ray. Why the hell would Warren send that?

Did he know she was sick again? Did *everyone*? Then, just now: *yoooooo*.

She replied with a *why?* Warren had basically ignored Claire for the past two years, now he was texting her nonstop about her cousin. Why was everyone acting so weird?

Warren sent another one, right away: *Are you with her?*

"Everything all right?" Lenny asked. When she asked it, she meant it. It was like Lenny couldn't help but ooze honesty.

Claire felt nauseous.

"It's Warren," Claire admitted. "He's trying to marry my cousin but can't court her without my permission."

Or maybe he knows she's sick again.

"Oh," Lenny said.

"I'm kidding."

"At this point, I'd believe anything you say about this town. This place is insane."

I'd believe anything you say. The words beat against the edges of Claire's brain. She had Lenny fully convinced. She'd gotten what she'd wanted. It didn't feel like a victory, and it didn't feel like a hoax. Not anymore. She had to try to ignore the guilt, just like she'd ignored all her extra heartbeats when Lenny had held her hand.

A new text from Warren popped up: *I was gonna invite her to Bryce's thing but she's not responding.*

Claire typed back, *She has the flu. It's going around.*

She looked up from her phone. "Turn left here. This is it."

Lenny turned onto the narrow dirt road. Rows of corn slapped at the side mirrors.

The observatory (at least, what was left of it) came into view. Dead ivy covered most of its redbrick walls and snaked up the steel frame of the dome. None of the windows had any panes left in them, but there was plenty of broken glass scattered around.

It must have looked like a palace in its heyday. Even in its disturbed, crumbled state, it filled Claire with reverence. This was her holy place.

"Watch your step," Claire warned as Lenny crossed the open doorway. Then cursed herself for saying it. Lenny had been to plenty of abandoned buildings.

"Wow," Lenny said, probably for Claire's sake. Lenny probably didn't even think the old observatory was that impressive. She'd been to castle ruins in Scotland. This was nothing to her. But Claire still wanted to show it off for some reason. And it was the only private spot she could think of.

There were a few instances of graffiti on the inside, the same faded drawings since the first time Claire found it. There were always the same artifacts sitting untouched—a shattered pair of glasses, empty cardboard boxes, dusty scientific books, and unused notepads.

Claire had been on her bike when she found the narrow road into the cornfield. It didn't seem like the local kids had been there, at least not for a long time. No one really went to Old Scarberry except horny teenagers. But they usually just made out in their cars or set off fireworks in the empty fields. They didn't bother the abandoned ruins from a failed gold rush. Soon, the ghosts of Old Scarberry would be bulldozed over, once everyone sold their land. She wasn't sure exactly what J. Porter wanted to do with it. Suburbs? Strip malls?

"An independent lab built this place in the '20s," Claire explained. "Because Scarberry had almost no light pollution. There was a custom telescope right here." She pointed to the middle of the floor, where four steps led to a lower platform. Its tiles were all smashed up, cracked like dirty eggshells. They were white. Marble maybe.

Lenny opened a can of Monster from her backpack. She offered it to Claire. "So what happened?"

"After the mines closed, everyone moved to New Scarberry. Made no sense to live in the middle of nowhere."

"Dude," Lenny said, "*all* of Scarberry is the middle of nowhere."

"Okay. Fair."

"What if . . ." Lenny began. Claire braced herself for a wild theory. "What if the government shut them down because they knew too much? What if the mines closed because they discovered something they shouldn't?"

Claire wanted to roll her eyes. But Lenny had a point. Her aunt was the one who'd told her about the town's history. And she couldn't trust anything Aunt Maeve said. Not anymore.

And the government was definitely interested in Scarberry.

"Maybe," Claire said. Why not? Reality was unraveling.

If Jared could be missing, if Aunt Maeve could lie, then yeah, maybe it was aliens all along. Maybe Scarberry had a portal to the Milky Way.

Claire sat on the steps in the middle of the room and looked up. Most of the panels of the dome were missing, leaving square bits of the blue sky visible.

Lenny looked up too, but she didn't sit. She kept circling. That girl struggled with staying still.

"What did you mean, though, when you said it's not worth it?" Lenny asked.

"What?"

"When I had a nosebleed and you said the stars aren't worth it?"

"Oh, I just meant I'd rather have a starless sky than be in Scarberry."

"'Cause of the lack of oat milk?"

"The lack of everything," Claire said. "I *know* my people are out there. I can't be with them if I'm stuck here."

"Your people as in . . ."

"Queer people. Yes." Lenny didn't get it, of course. She *couldn't* get it. "It's not even about having a girlfriend," Claire added. Even when she'd thought she had Hannah, she was alone. "It's a community. It's not being a fucking outcast. It's not having to ask permission to just exist."

"Why don't you leave?"

"I can't just abandon my family. Someone has to take care of them."

"Why does that have to be you?"

"Because . . . because that's how it is. Not everyone can

just drive around America with their boyfriend and no one to answer to."

Oof. That was too much. This was what happened when Claire opened up. She was a Venus flytrap, ready to bite anyone in her vicinity. Lenny was the only one who actually dared to spend time with her. It didn't make sense to push her away. To blame her for problems she didn't cause and couldn't solve.

Lenny, somehow, wasn't deterred. She sat beside Claire. The little steps weren't very wide, so their knees were touching. Claire put her legs together, but that didn't offer much space for Lenny.

Don't fly too close. I'll swallow you whole.

"I have four hundred thousand people to answer to," Lenny said. "And Evan isn't even my boyfriend."

Claire gave her a look that said, *Elaborate, please.*

"I wanted to do the show. At first. I was the one who was into spooky stuff. It's not even Evan's fault it became what it did. All the ads and the sponsors and analytic data . . . you need it to be successful. And that's what Evan cares about. Having a business. Financial security. But the show stopped feeling real. And then, *we* stopped feeling real. Aaaaaand . . . I broke up with him."

"I knew it was weird he left," Claire thought out loud. *Good riddance.* They didn't seem to get along anyway. The guy seemed rigid. Lenny had a sparkle in her massive eyes—a restless energy to her. One that was too wild for anybody to try to contain. She didn't need someone to keep her in line. She deserved a cheerleader.

"I actually broke up with him weeks ago," Lenny said.

"Well, we called it a break, but it wasn't. Not really. Now it's over for good."

"That's rough," Claire said.

"I mean, I was the one who ended it. Both times. Any day now, he's going to announce it. But I doubt he'll run it by me first. I haven't even had the mental energy to think of my response. Or, like, a *plan*. My parents were only cool with me doing YouTube full-time because they trust Evan. Not me. I don't know what I'm going to do. Or what I even want to do. Eventually, I'll know I made the right choice. But I'm not at that point yet. And I don't know how to get there. I'm in limbo."

Claire nodded. "I guess I'm in limbo too. The thing is, I was gonna leave. I was gonna move to Tennessee with Hannah after graduation. But that fell through when she ghosted me."

"Ouch."

"Yup."

"How long were you guys a thing?"

"Like a year. We never met though. So, it doesn't count. She probably never cared as much as I did. It's pretty pathetic, honestly."

"It's not pathetic. I get what you mean," Lenny said. "About not feeling like you've found your people. I've been to conventions with a hundred fans packed in a room and it just gives me a stomachache. It's like, when I sign my name, it's not actually mine. When you stare at your face on video for so long, it stops being your face . . ." She poked at the dead leaves at her feet with a stick. "People think they know me. But they know a pretend person. And sometimes, *I* even get it confused.

Where my persona ends and I begin. Where the relationship ends and the show begins. And somewhere along the way I've just turned into a hollow nothing."

"I don't think you're hollow."

Lenny was more present than anyone Claire had ever met. Scarberry seemed sullen and gray compared to her. Lenny was all neon pep. Audacity in bike shorts.

Lenny looked up from her leaf pile, making fierce eye contact. Claire's first instinct was to look away, but she wanted to show she was listening.

"Thanks," Lenny said. "I'm sorry your town is shitty to you. But that's just because you're authentically you. You're a *real* person. Anyone who has a problem with that really is just afraid of themselves."

Lenny let the words hang there, eyes still on Claire. The sun was right above the skeletal dome, shining a light on them. Like a classic UFO beam.

It would be a beautiful spot for a first kiss. Right as the thought entered Claire's brain, her face felt hot. She looked down at the energy drink on her lap. There were a million reasons why they couldn't kiss. First of all, Lenny was straight.

And then there was the hoax.

She ought to tell Lenny the truth, especially now that they were baring their souls to each other. Claire owed her honesty. Just . . . not now. Something had happened to Jared. Something was hurting their cattle and making Aunt Maeve behave like a stranger. If Claire admitted to the trick, Lenny might think she was in on the conspiracy. She might not want to help anymore.

She might leave.

Claire's phone buzzed in her pocket. Warren. Again. This time, she was grateful for the interruption. She couldn't handle sitting this close to Lenny for long. Surely Lenny could feel just how sweaty Claire was, and see how the ends of her curls were crunchy from the bad bleach job.

Just tell her to call me, Warren had texted.

Take the hint dude, she wanted to write back. But instead she sent the eye-roll emoji.

"So, what should we do?" Lenny said. "I don't think the chief is going to be much help. He's hoping I leave. He's either embarrassed at the shitty police force, or he's hiding something."

They were back to business. Thank God. Claire couldn't stand this conversation anymore.

"He's hiding something," Claire agreed. The Lambs weren't the only ones who were sketchy. The FBI was here. Maeve wasn't totally innocent. Claire saw that now.

"I think we should talk to Minnie again. And . . . go back to that field," Lenny said.

"Okay," Claire agreed. "Can we *drive* there this time?"

CHAPTER 27

LENNY

The call to the nursing home was quick. Lenny barely got a word in before the receptionist told her, "Ms. Albert is no longer accepting visitors," and hung up. Shit. There goes another lead. Claire was finishing her chores for the day, leaving Lenny to doomscroll on her phone in the caboose.

She had hundreds of unopened messages on Instagram. She used to reply to them, even though Evan had warned her not to. "If you can't respond to every fan, don't respond at all," he'd said. So she had made it her mission to keep up with her inbox, responding to everything except for the creeps and spam bots.

When was the last time she even looked at her message requests? Six months? A year?

She opened the latest one, from XOXOSophieZ: *Hi Lenny. I was going to send this for the fiftieth video but it took a little longer than expected. Hope you like it!* There was an attached image of a colored-pencil drawing of her and Evan.

Lenny knew she should comment something nice, like *Wow, you're so talented. I love it!* but she was trying this new thing where she didn't lie to fans. The artist *was* talented. Lenny had seen the reference photo a billion times, so she knew the likeness was perfect. The colors were vibrant and the details were lovingly rendered. This was the best fan art she'd seen.

But it made her sick to look at.

Ungrateful. She should tattoo it on her forehead.

She checked Evan's account. He hadn't posted the breakup announcement yet. He was probably proofreading it and running it by Maria first. Or, worse, he was making a whole breakup video. It'd probably get better views than the Old Lucky video would have gotten anyway. Ugh.

Someone knocked at the door. Lenny scrambled out of bed and opened it. It was Claire, her knight in shining armor, saving her from another hour of cycling through the same miserable apps.

"Ready?" Claire asked.

"Yep. I can drive us," Lenny offered.

"Alrighty then."

By the time they hopped into the *Silver Bullet,* the sun was sinking behind the corn. Lenny wasn't looking forward to another pitch-black night in Scarberry.

She would have preferred to look for clues in the daytime. That way, they wouldn't have to rely on their flashlights.

And they wouldn't have to worry about Old Lucky.

Lenny didn't blink as she drove on the dark road. She prayed that an animal didn't jump out in front of the *Silver Bullet.* The air was heavy. The sky was starless. Zero light, zero breeze. Zero sound, save for the *Bullet*'s engine, her own heartbeat, and Claire's occasional directions. Finally, Claire said, "This is it." And Lenny gave herself permission to exhale.

They locked the car and moved toward the massive tree they'd landed in last night. Lenny pulled out a flashlight, but she didn't need it.

The other side of the tree was flickering orange.

Clawson's Field was glowing.

"Shit," Claire groaned.

Someone had placed nine tiki torches in a circle around the abandoned train car. Probably the people wearing the hooded black robes.

Lenny dug her feet into the ground. She glanced at Claire, silently asking, *What the hell is this?*

There were five of them, chanting in another language. They danced in the dry grass, arms to the heavens. She couldn't see their faces; they were all shadows.

Lenny grabbed Claire's arm. An instinct, when she was afraid. She always turned into a sloth, grasping on to whatever was closest. A tree. A person. She had been uneasy before, and now she was terrified. She had been expecting aliens, not a *cult*.

The figures stopped chanting. The tallest one broke the circle and started walking toward Lenny and Claire.

Could they make a run for it? The car was parked fifty feet away. Claire didn't seem desperate to escape. She cocked her hip to the side and glared, as if these cloaked strangers weren't a threat to her. They were an annoyance.

The tall one was almost to them now. Lenny couldn't see any features on them. Just that they were broad, and their breath stank of booze and body spray. One hand was in the pockets of their cloak. Reaching for a weapon? Maybe. This place already didn't like outsiders, and Lenny had likely interrupted some important ritual.

The cloaked stranger stopped a few feet away. Claire didn't flinch.

"You've brought us an offering," the figure said. The voice was young, masculine, and slurred. He was clearly addressing Claire. And she seemed to understand what he was talking about. Which could only mean . . .

The offering was Lenny.

Lenny sucked in a big breath. But she didn't let go of Claire. Claire wasn't actually about sacrifice her to some ancient farm cult, right? It was absurd, yet she didn't know what else could be happening.

She had fallen out of the sky. Her hand was still raw from some unidentified goo. Anything could happen.

"Put the hood down, Bryce," Claire snapped. And then—just like that—the robed cult member was actually a boy with a meaty neck and a close-cropped haircut. His paper-thin lips were grinning hard. Lenny recognized him as the guy from the diner, the one who got under Claire's skin. Bryce Stern.

Another kid in a robe caught up to them, his hood already down. This guy was the same physical type as Bryce, but his hair was darker, curlier, and there was a softness to his features. Warren. The chief's son. The epic prankster. What the hell was going on?

"Oh hey," Warren said, eyeing both of them with a furrowed brow. "Did you bring—"

"I told you, Bri's not coming," Claire snapped.

"Oh. That's too bad," said Warren. "Well, we got plenty of stuff here, if you wanted to hang out."

"No entry without an offering!" Bryce hollered. He reeked. Lenny could practically taste the liquor on his lips. Warm and apple-scented.

Claire rolled her eyes. "Don't you have a cousin to kiss, Bryce?"

"She was my second cousin!" Bryce protested. "And I didn't even know, okay?"

Warren gave Bryce a hard pat on the shoulder. "As high priest, I'm letting this one slide."

Warren winked at Lenny like now she was in on the inside joke. But Lenny still didn't get it, and she hated that she didn't get it. This was almost worse than being ritualistically sacrificed.

Bryce returned to the circle, hollering the strange chant, which now sounded like total gibberish. Maybe it had always been gibberish. When Lenny squinted, she could see other faces beyond the circle, people in regular clothes, with red Solo cups in their hands.

"C'mon," Warren said. "We're not so scary." He sauntered toward the tiki torches, checking behind him to see if the girls were following.

"Moonshine," Claire said.

"Huh?"

"You can't get into Clawson's Field parties without bringing any. That's what *offering* means."

"Oh."

"I'm sorry. When Warren said he was going to a party, I should've figured it'd be here."

They stood there, in between the *Silver Bullet* and the edge of the party. Lenny heard the *shhhhh* of a spray-can nozzle, and new fluorescent pink lines appeared on the rusty train car. The chanting had stopped and was replaced by country music.

"So you've been to one of these? This is a *thing* here?" Lenny asked.

Scarberry was officially the strangest place *Odd Kids* had visited.

And Evan was missing it.

"Nah," Claire said. "I'm too scary for them. They're afraid I'll ruin the vibes of their satanic ritual."

"So . . . this is how the country folk party?"

"They do this every summer. They're asking the Old Gods for wishes. Usually to win football games. It's mostly a joke. They're just here to spray-paint their names on the train car and get drunk. They've done this since before my mom was in school. Scarberry tradition."

"Oh." Still strange. But undeniably cool. Lenny's high school was too big to have secret rituals. And by the time she graduated she hardly belonged to those people anymore. She was stretched between Evan and the algorithm, with zero time to make offerings to forgotten deities in the middle of nowhere, unless of course it could be monetized.

"So, what do you want to do?" Claire asked.

"What do *you* want to do?"

"I want to find out what happened to Jared. But I think the scene of the crime has been disturbed now. We can stay or go, it's up to you."

Lenny considered it. She was still mad at Warren for his "prank" with the speakers, and this Bryce guy seemed insufferable. But this could be an opportunity. Every place had its own rules. If she understood these people, she could better understand Old Lucky. And maybe understand Claire.

"Well, I've never had moonshine," Lenny said.

Claire laughed. "I don't recommend it."

It was immediately warmer once they entered the circle of tiki torches. About a dozen pairs of eyes went right toward them. The girls wore little jean shorts and the boys who weren't in black robes were dressed for either war or a rodeo: camouflage and boots and trucker hats. A few were on lawn chairs; the others were clustered around the train car, watching each other spray their names on the door.

"Is your name on there?" Lenny asked.

Claire rolled her eyes. "Jesus Christ, no."

Oh.

What happened to you? Lenny wanted to ask. Claire seemed to hate that Bryce guy, which was fair. But there was no way everyone in this town was an asshole. If Lenny had grown up here, she'd want her name on the train car. There had to be comfort in belonging to the land. It'd be safer than just tethering yourself to a single person or living to appease total strangers.

They passed Bryce on his knees, downing a bottle of

beer. Most of it dripped all over his face. A guy in a black cloak was watching, enthusiastically chanting, "*Chug, chug, chug*." When Bryce was finished, he sat the empty bottle in the center of the circle, right next to a massive white rock. As Lenny moved closer, she saw it wasn't a rock at all. It was a skull, too big to be human. A horse? Maybe cow? Freaky. She appreciated the theatrics.

Warren approached them, with two girls on his heels. He handed Lenny a mason jar of clear liquid. She brought it to her lips but didn't sip it yet. She was surprised how much it didn't smell. Wasn't moonshine supposed to be strong? Or maybe it was severely diluted. Or maybe the moonshine was another joke.

"You're from *Odd Kids*," one of the girls said. She had her hair piled into a bun, and she wore an oversized blue-and-white hoodie with blocky letters warped around a football that read: SCARBERRY LOCOMOTIVES.

"Yeah," Lenny said.

The girls glanced at each other, sharing a secret giggle. "I'm Megan," said the girl in the football hoodie. The one holding a White Claw introduced herself as Mandy.

"You find Old Lucky yet?" asked Mandy.

"No," Lenny said. "Why? Is he here?" She pretended to look around, startled. The girls didn't laugh, but Claire did, at least.

"Where's Evan?" Megan asked.

That question prompted Lenny to seriously consider the drink in her hand. She had been waiting for Evan to be the one to announce the breakup. He would probably prefer that control. Should she let him have it?

Evan would never let her go to a party like this, spooky cult rituals or not. "It could be a bad look," he would say. They couldn't get caught drinking underage. But Evan wasn't here. He couldn't save her, and he couldn't hinder her either. The roof had been ripped from over her head. There was no protection from the elements, but also, there would be nothing stopping her from seeing the stars.

"Evan's gone," Lenny admitted.

She took a long sip of her drink. It tasted chemical, with a subtle earthy flavor. The girls giggled and Warren gave her a nod as Lenny forced herself to swallow.

"How's that taste?" Warren said.

"Warm," she managed.

She imagined the drink searing a hole through her esophagus, bubbling and blistering like it was made of the gooey purple stuff. But she did not suffer any internal burns. Not yet at least. Her hand was still raw. When she had changed the gauze that morning the burn wasn't any worse, but it wasn't any better either. Her days could be numbered. Might as well party in her final hours.

"I'll grab ya some more," Warren said with a wink. He headed toward a plastic table, cluttered with mismatched, unlabeled bottles and two liters of soda.

That was when Lenny noticed Claire had drifted away. She was by herself, far enough from the glow of the tiki torches that she almost blended into the night. She had her head down, searching the grass. Did Claire know these girls? She had to. This was a small town, and she was sort of friends with Warren. He was the leader, clearly. He was the class president, homecoming king, high priest, or whatever Scarberry's measurement for popularity was. Everyone watched him closely like they were waiting for instructions.

The girls forgot their question about Evan and were talking to each other now, mentioning names but not saying anything of note. Jason's new haircut: *It makes him look Amish.* Mary's new man: *I heard he's inheriting a bunch of land from his grandparents.* Which teachers ought to hook up: *Mrs. Andrews is a moron if she doesn't get with Mr. Lasinski. He's husband material.* They talked so easily, a level of familiarity that Lenny didn't have with anyone now that Evan had left.

It made her queasy.

"So, this is where people hang out, right?" Lenny asked them, fighting off the aftertaste of the moonshine. "Have you noticed anything *weird* about this place?"

Mandy glanced at her friend, smiling. "Should I tell her?" she asked with a giggle.

Megan laughed. "I mean, if you want."

Lenny held her breath. Tried to listen closely, but the moonshine was already fogging her thoughts.

"You'll never believe this," said Mandy, "but last summer our cat, Lucy, was outside when a big storm hit. Like, we were in the basement freaking out. Right when it was over we went outside and looked for her but she was just gone. I was so sad."

"She was gonna have a cat funeral," Megan added.

"Seriously! But then, like three weeks later—"

"It was only one week."

"Okay—technically. But it felt like a month basically. I was so messed up over it. But *sometime* later. We were here, doing our yearly offering to the gods and there's Lucy. Just hanging out."

"Literally a miracle," Megan summarized.

Lenny nodded. *Miracle* was a stretch. It sounded like a regular missing-cat story. But what if the cat stumbled upon another portal? Did they all lead to Clawson's Field in Old Scarberry?

"So uh..." Lenny looked around. She felt herself sway. "Why the cow skull?"

"To please the Old Gods, duh," said Mandy.

There it was again. *The Old Gods.* "Who are the Old Gods?"

Mandy found the question absolutely hilarious. "We mere mortals could never know their true names." Once again, an inside joke Lenny didn't get. This whole town was a party she wasn't invited to.

"*Staaaaaahp,*" whined Megan. "They're *false idols.*"

"Chill. It's just a fun story."

"So," Lenny said. "Old Lucky, he's a false idol too?"

"He's a demon, escaped from hell," explained Megan. Was that another inside joke, or was this girl serious? It was hard to tell in this lighting. And with the creeping warmth of the moonshine in her belly.

"Hell, or the mines?" Lenny asked.

"Those have been closed forever," Megan said.

"Mrs. Stern suggested the town is being punished..." Lenny started. Her mouth felt too soft. "Is that why the crops are dying? Why everyone's getting sick?"

"Dude, chill." Mandy giggled. "Not everything's that deep." She whisked Megan away to watch Bryce chug more beer.

Lenny took another sip of moonshine despite it tasting like corn-flavored mouthwash.

She found Claire roaming around the outer perimeter alone. Was she avoiding the party guests, or were they avoiding her? Claire kicked a mason jar in the grass. "Sorry. I'm feeling antisocial."

Lenny nodded, though mostly, she just felt warm. Her insides were burning. But it didn't feel that bad. The party behind them was blurry now, faraway and unimportant.

She had been so jealous when all her old friends spent their weekends at club activities and sporting events and parties. Lenny never had time for these things, even before she switched to online school her senior year. Her life was Evan and the channel. Lenny, Evan, and *Odd Kids*. That was the holy trinity.

He fills in all the missing pieces.

Ugh. She wanted to gag at the memory. She didn't need to be completed—Lenny Gilson was born intact. But like a self-fulfilling prophecy, the sound bite became true eventually. She gave pieces of herself to Evan. Willingly. Some of the parts she gave, he hadn't even asked for. And when he left, he took them all with him.

Now she was really un-whole.

She tried to think about something else. Anything but Evan.

"So are your parents from here?" she asked Claire.

Claire gave a look Lenny couldn't decipher. Was she offended? Maybe it was a rude question to ask. But social rules were getting less and less defined the more she drank.

Lenny was hardly interested in Scarberry right now. She wanted Claire's opinions. Claire's thoughts. She was brimming with questions. No one else in Scarberry would tell her the truth.

"Well, no one would voluntarily move to Scarberry," Claire said. "No one new comes, and no one moves away."

Lenny figured Claire would stop there. Maybe her family was a sore spot. Maybe she only discussed that part of her life with friends. Lenny was temporary. Lenny couldn't be anything to Claire, not with all her pieces missing.

"My mom broke that rule," Claire added. "She moved away. And it didn't go well. She got addicted to a bunch of stuff. She found the wrong guy and got pregnant and didn't know what to do, so she came back home. And after a year dealing with Scarberry again she couldn't take it anymore. She left. Which meant leaving me here with Aunt Maeve. But then she died when I was, like, four. So I never knew her."

"Oh. Thanks for telling me."

Lenny should have said, *That's awful, I'm sorry*. She shouldn't have asked at all. The ground had turned to pudding, and it was hard enough to stay balanced on it. How many sips had she taken?

"Like I said. I'm used to everyone knowing all my business," Claire said. "It's really okay. I don't mind."

Claire kept walking around the back of the train car. Lenny followed, each step feeling like a mathematical equation, but Claire didn't notice her wobbling. Maybe she didn't look as drunk as she felt. She had gone this long playing a role, maybe she was a better actor than she gave herself credit for.

Someone had left a picnic blanket and discarded bottles behind the train car. There was a pack of half-eaten Cool Ranch

Doritos and a lantern too. It was still on. Shouldn't there have been bugs hovering around it? Lenny couldn't remember a time she ever saw a light in the dark that didn't attract moths. Now that she thought about it, she couldn't remember seeing a single bug in Scarberry. She hadn't seen any creature smaller than the livestock. No squirrels in the trees, no dead raccoons on the long stretches of road.

Do you ever see roadkill? Lenny meant to say it aloud. But she wasn't sure if the words ever came out. She hoped they hadn't. The thought was so fleeting, so unimportant, in the grand scheme of things.

They were on the blanket. Both of them. Lenny hardly remembered how they got there. Claire was staring at her. In the light of the lantern, she looked even more like a painting, all soft edges and delicate pink lips and rosy cheeks. She didn't belong in this barren place, hiding in the dark. *She looked like art.* She deserved to be draped in shiny fabrics, in front of a beautiful mountain in Italy. She deserved to be framed in gold, in a museum in France. No, even better, she ought to be someone's muse, inspiring a whole new type of art. Imagining a completely new backdrop worthy of her.

Claire pulled back. They had been sitting so close for a moment. Lenny hadn't realized just how much she was leaning forward. Had she said any of that out loud? Her words and thoughts were all stuck together. She didn't know how to pull them apart.

"You're drunk," Claire said.

"Mmmm . . ." Lenny agreed. Yes. She was drunk. It wasn't a bad feeling, but a dangerous one. She was thinking wild thoughts, and the alcohol almost gave her the bravery to act on them.

"I'll drive us back," Claire said.

"But your arm—"

"It's fine. I just need one hand. At least your piece-of-shit car is automatic."

CHAPTER 28

CLAIRE

Claire couldn't get that line out of her head.

You look like art.

Thank God Lenny had fallen asleep in the car. Claire didn't know what Lenny would blurt out next, and she wasn't ready to find out.

You look like art.

Claire couldn't handle another line like that.

People had a hard time saying nice things to fat girls. Claire already had eighteen years of practice listening to *You have a great personality* and *I bet you give great hugs.*

It was all bullshit. Claire had purposely crafted an unwelcoming demeanor and she had never offered to hug anyone, ever. Yet she didn't fight those comments when they were thrust upon her. She mustered up her fakest smile, uttered a stilted thank-you, and filed the offender in her massive list of Those Who Cannot Be Trusted.

She had yet to encounter someone like Lenny. She didn't know where to file her.

You look like art.

It wasn't backhanded at all. Especially when it was followed by ramblings about silk and golden frames and galaxies. It was sincere. Unguarded. It wasn't a consolation prize.

Claire wished she hadn't heard it.

On the silent drive home, she tried to search her brain for anything Hannah had told her that made her feel the same way. There was nothing she could think of. Their relationship hadn't been built on appearances. It was about *surviving*. It was having someone on the phone while she did homework. It was videogames and promises that were half fantasies. Never *You look like art.*

And never with *that look.*

Claire had thought she noticed it earlier that afternoon in the observatory. Lenny's massive eyes flicked to her lips. There were only a few inches between them, and for some reason Lenny didn't back away. But surely, Claire misread that. Lenny didn't want to kiss her. The Boyfriend was out of the picture, but that didn't mean Lenny was suddenly into Claire. Lenny had plenty of time to mention she was bi or questioning or unlabeled or whatever.

Lenny's mouth hung open as she slept. Each exhale was louder than the last until it turned into a gentle snore. Even in sleep, she couldn't stay quiet. Claire ought to have been annoyed by it, but she wasn't.

She parked at the ranch. For some reason, Claire hoped

to see Jared's truck in the lot. But that was stupid. His truck was still missing, and so was he. Claire shook Lenny awake. "We're home," she said. Though it wasn't really home for either of them.

Lenny lurched, groaning, like the hangover had already begun to set in. She teetered to the side and kept trying to turn around. Claire had to hold on to her arm to keep her on the path. Luckily, Lenny had left the caboose unlocked, so Claire didn't need to dig into her pockets for the keys.

Once inside, Lenny fell onto the bed. Claire removed Lenny's shoes and found a water bottle from the mini-fridge and set it on the nightstand. She should have done more. Lenny could wake up again and barf. She would need someone to hold her hair back, to scrub the floor in case she didn't make it to the toilet. But that didn't have to be Claire's job.

She would have done it gladly, if it weren't for the art comment. If Claire weren't about to explode from the uncertainty. She wasn't ready to go to sleep. After closing the caboose door behind her, she followed her regular morning route, looping around the parking lot and following the edge of the fence. The walk wasn't nearly as calming in the dark. The wind was picking up; her hair whipped around her face, but she didn't do anything to control it. She couldn't see much in the darkness anyway. That was all right. Claire knew every inch of these grounds, even with her eyes closed. Well, she thought she did. The old pile of farm equipment had been hiding a literal portal and she hadn't even known about it. Was it better now that she did?

What if the art comment hadn't been genuine at all? What

if Lenny discovered Claire's lie days ago and, as revenge, she was performing her own hoax? And Claire would deserve it when the Boyfriend jumped out from behind a bush, holding a big camera and saying, "Smile, you're on *Odd Kids* livestream!"

Nah. That wasn't going to happen. Not a chance. Though the pressures of her online persona made her feel like a fraud, Lenny was an *honest* person. Claire wished Lenny would just leave, so she didn't have to admit to the hoax. Lenny could survive without aliens, but Claire couldn't take another heartbreak.

A small part of her held on to another theory. One even more dangerous: What if Lenny *did* have feelings for her? What if it wasn't too good to be true?

The otherwise quiet night was interrupted by a whimper. It sounded just as wounded and scared as Claire felt. At first she thought it was coming from inside of her. She held her breath.

There it was again. Her ears popped. There was pressure mounting in her head. Tears welled up in her eyes. What *the hell* was that?

Again. Louder, closer. This was more of a screech, somewhere between a terrified cat and large predatory bird.

She spun around. The noise seemed to be coming from behind her. She was at the edge of the ranch, where a row of dead pine trees marked the beginning of the Lambs' property. When the noise happened again, she was sure it came from the other side of the trees.

"Hello?" Claire called.

The trees rustled in the wind. Another whimper. This one

had two long syllables, the second was higher-pitched, as if asking a question.

As if saying hello back.

"*CLAIRE!*" Though Aunt Maeve was screaming, it didn't rattle Claire's brain nearly as much as the animalistic *hello* had. She tried to peer across the divide of trees and investigate just what the fuck was going on, but Maeve pulled her away.

There was something wrong about Maeve's face. Her eyes were puffy, her freckled skin was tight and raw-looking. Maeve had been crying. Shit. Aunt Maeve was a worrier, but never a crier. She professed just how upset she was—how stressed she was—but the tears never showed. At least, not in front of anyone.

"Where *have you been?*" Maeve demanded.

"At a party. We just got back," Claire admitted. She felt bad enough for lying to Lenny; she couldn't pile on any more lies now. She had to even out her karma.

Aunt Maeve's expression softened. She looked relieved for a moment, and then she looked over Claire's shoulder, like she was expecting someone else to be listening. Had she heard the whining too?

"You need to come inside," Maeve said. "I'm so sorry, Claire Bear. Something's happened."

"What?"

"I'll make you chocolate-chip pancakes."

Claire didn't want chocolate-chip pancakes, but she let Aunt Maeve lead her inside. She sat at the least wobbly kitchen chair and watched Aunt Maeve mix the batter.

All the kitchen lights were buzzing. The room was too

bright, too cold. Claire had spent the last hour moping, feeling tainted and unlovable and Aunt Maeve's sudden acts of service didn't make her feel better.

She ought to have been tired, but she saw everything in a startling high definition. The gingham window curtains were a more saturated red than ever before. Every crumb on the wood cutting board was crisply defined.

"Bri and I . . . well, we've been a wreck all night," Maeve said.

"What happened?"

Maeve's head hung low, but she didn't look away from the skillet. "Jared. He's passed away, hon."

Claire felt like the air had been yanked out of her lungs. The wrongness was dialed up even more. *No. That can't be true.*

"The chief called us first," Maeve said. "I suppose he doesn't have much family besides us. It's the circle of life. But it's horrible." She flipped the single, giant pancake over. Claire's headache hadn't gone away. It was worse. So much worse. Her ears were ringing. *Jared. Dead.* The words flashed in her brain with neon intensity.

No.

"But . . ." Claire started. "But how—"

"I always knew he'd work himself to death. I always knew that. And I told him. But that didn't stop him. I feel somewhat responsible, you see. Heart attack. They found him in his trailer today."

No. No. That wasn't right. Jared hadn't been home. His truck had been missing. And his place had been ransacked. *No no no no.*

"Who told you this?" Claire managed. "How do you know

it was a heart attack?" She heard Lenny's voice over and over in her head. *Maybe he knew too much.* Did that FBI agent take him out?

Maeve only sniffled and said, "He's gone, love."

Claire shook her head and pushed back the chair. "He wasn't home when we checked on him two days ago. His truck was gone. The place looked torn up."

Aunt Maeve said nothing. She flipped the pancake onto an antique china plate.

"How do we even know he's dead?" Claire continued. "What if he was . . . abducted?"

"Abducted?" Maeve repeated, aghast. "By *whom?*"

"I'm not sure but . . . there's something wrong in Scarberry. You have to know that. It's not normal for this many people to get sick at once. It's not normal for all the crops to fail, for cows to ooze purple slime."

"Jesus, Claire. You sound . . ."

Insane. Like a UFO chaser. Yes. Nothing like practical Claire. Responsible Claire. The girl her aunt could depend on to grab groceries, to hang the clothes on the line, to stay in this place that was suffocating her because *someone* had to keep the business running.

"Did you even *see* the body?" Claire countered.

"The police found him. Like I said."

"And you trust the police?"

Maeve didn't trust authority. She didn't even trust *Advil.* How could she think Big Pharma was out to kill her precious daughter but trust the chief?

"What has gotten into you?" Maeve asked, sounding betrayed.

"I think Chief Lamb got caught up in this. I think someone"—*something*—"is making him cover it up. Maybe it's the government. They have to know the land's gone bad. This place is *killing us*. The cancer. Old Lucky. Everything is connected to these portals."

"I understand you're . . . in shock. I am too. But you can't be talking like this. It won't go over well for you," Maeve said.

There. That proved what Claire had always feared. Aunt Maeve's loyalty was with Scarberry. Not her. Maeve wasn't going to make waves for her. She never had. She hadn't pushed for the school to do anything about Bryce's bullying. She hadn't quashed any nasty rumors his friends spread. She'd only fired him when it made sense for *the budget*.

She'd rather watch the world burn around her than publicly side with Claire.

Maeve set the pancake in front of Claire, along with a fork and knife and maple syrup. Then she set her hand on Claire's shoulder. Maeve's sleeve had moved up to her elbow, revealing more scratches. Some were still bleeding.

"But we'll get through this," Maeve said gently. "We always do."

She kissed Claire's forehead, tightened her robe and went upstairs, leaving Claire alone in the too-bright kitchen.

CHAPTER 29

LENNY

Lenny's fingers were numb. There shouldn't be snow in Arizona, but she shouldn't be in Arizona anyway. She'd told Evan she wasn't going. Yet here she was, on the doorstep of Harrows House. Just like in the pictures, the beige stucco was cracked all the way up to the red roof. The tripod was perched three feet ahead. The blinking red light meant they were rolling. Lenny had a sinking feeling in her chest. Evan's hand in hers didn't offer any warmth.

She backed away, and he gave her a wounded look. "Where are you going?" he snapped. "We have to run the opener again."

No. She couldn't do it. She had other plans. She mumbled, "I'm looking for something," and took off, running through the empty desert suburb until—yes, there it was! There was the metal saucer, the windmill. The red barn, with dancing lights above it. And Claire, waiting for her. It was still summer in Scarberry. Lenny stopped right before she reached the barn. Without snow, where would she dig? She knelt and began to pull at the dirt. Yanking out weeds and rocks and worms. Claire watched her work up a sweat, digging deeper and deeper. Lenny could feel her time running out.

"Help me!" Lenny cried. But Claire didn't move.

* * * * * * * * * * * *

The sound of the phone ringing might as well have been a gunshot.

Lenny jumped from the warm bed, feeling like she'd left a little bit of her soul behind as she ran across the room to find her phone. It had to be under the pile of clothes. Since Evan left, she had let her dirty laundry and food wrappers accumulate on the floor. She would clean it all up once she left Scarberry for good, but she had no idea when that would be, exactly. Probably once she saw Old Lucky with her own eyes. Then she wouldn't have that frustrating dream anymore. She could finally start having a new one.

She found her phone in the back pocket of yesterday's jeans. She couldn't remember shaking them off and chucking them across the room. Or getting back to the caboose last night, either. She had a missed call from Maria, the social media manager, and a text: *Hey girl! Hope the adventure is adventuring. Would love updates!*

So Evan *still* hadn't told her about the breakup. Maria must think she was in Arizona with Evan. This had to be part of his plan. He'd make Lenny be the one to fire their assistant. To announce the bad news to their subscribers. He'd go down in history as the good guy.

Lenny threw her phone onto the pile of dirty laundry and collapsed onto the bed. Light was pouring in through the blinds. What time was it? She hadn't checked. And she just threw the room's only clock out of arm's reach. If she got back up to grab it, it'd just trigger another miserable doomscroll.

How did she get back here last night? She rubbed her face, trying to remember. There was the party. Tiki torches. A pig skull. Black robes. A mason jar with clear liquid. And then she'd found Claire. They'd sat on a blanket, by a mothless lantern. And, *oh shit*. Lenny had said something embarrassing.

Her stomach groaned. She would have to get out of bed and look for food eventually, but she was in no state to drive. What options did she have? She'd run out of granola bars. The gift shop might be open. She could snag a candy bar to hold her over.

Lenny threw on yesterday's pants, a sweatshirt, and sunglasses. She opened the door, braving the harsh sun. She followed the dirt path to the gift shop, hoping Claire wasn't working the register today. Things would be weird between them now, and it was entirely Lenny's fault. What would she have to say for herself? "Sorry, I wasn't trying to flirt with you!"?

That sounded mean.

Mean and untrue.

Lenny didn't know what had gotten into her.

The gift shop was locked. She was partially relieved, but her stomach complained again. She didn't need to figure out what to say to Claire yet, but she did have to figure out what to eat.

A car pulled in. Not cops or federal agents. It was Ms. Reed, with Bri in the passenger seat. Maeve had a big sunhat blocking her face, and Bri was in her pajamas. They hurried inside. The screen door clapped behind them.

When Lenny returned to the caboose, Susan was smoking and eating at the picnic table. Tilly was unleashed, wearing a pink striped onesie. Susan threw food scraps at her.

"Funnel cake," Susan said. Lenny had been staring, accidently begging for a scrap just like the dog. "County fair this week," Susan added. "Do they have those in Illinois?"

Lenny didn't even remember telling Susan where she was from. Evan must have. He always found an excuse to brag about Chicago's history. The World's Fair of 1893 in particular. It was a huge cultural event, influencing the arts and architecture. It also had the first ever Ferris wheel. Evan loved to tell people that, even though he was terrified of heights and would never dare go on one with her. He also left out the part where the mayor was assassinated toward the end of the fair. It was googleable history, easy to fact-check, and yet he couldn't help but to twist the narrative in his favor.

Fuck him.

Claire had said that so easily without knowing him. Lenny had innocently complained about Evan for two seconds, and Claire just knew. She said "fuck him" with ease. She had been right, of course. Somehow everyone on the outside could just tell how incompatible Lenny and Evan were.

Evansexual. Ugh.

Susan rubbed her hands on her long skirt. It was one of those hippie wrap skirts that you could buy at every New Age store. All those places were basically the same. Lenny had been in dozens of them, looking for cheap candles for their videos. Whenever Evan came along, he rolled his eyes at the tarot-card decks and hemp tote bags.

Fuck him.

"Bet they don't have tornados either," Susan said.

"Tornados?"

"Oh, bless your heart. You must have slept through it." Susan tossed another piece of funnel cake at Tilly. "Round midnight, I woke with a start. Hearing this strange whine outside my door. I went outside, thinkin' I'm hearin' an alien, and what do you know, it's a twister."

Lenny would have been at the party around then, and though it was windy, no one had been concerned about the weather getting any worse. Her memory was spotty, thanks to the moonshine. But surely she would have remembered tornado warnings.

"Huh?"

There were no broken tree limbs around them. No flipped tables. The UFO-shaped string lights hadn't even fallen down. How could a tornado hit without her knowing? No. No way.

"Miss Reed caught me outside," Susan explained. "Said I should be okay in the storm basement."

"There's a basement?"

"In the house, hon." She pointed in that direction. Now that Lenny knew what to look for, she noticed the two angled doors on the ground, near the porch. "Me and Tilly stayed there all night. Miss Reed felt so bad, she gave us free passes for the fair. You and that boy should go. Hey, where is he?"

Lenny didn't have the energy to come up with an

explanation for Evan's absence. Claire was exiting the house. Every step was a stomp, as if she were angry at the earth itself. She went right up to Lenny. Was she mad about last night? Was Lenny forgetting some integral part of it? Something too messy and painful for her brain to allow her access?

"Did you hear?" Claire said. She wasn't wearing the sling on her injured arm anymore. Her freckles were obscured by red blotches. Her whole face looked puffy. Had she been crying?

"About the tornado?" Lenny guessed.

"What?"

Lenny turned toward Susan, but she was a few yards ahead now, watching Tilly poop on the dead grass. "Thatta girl!" Susan said.

"Your aunt told Susan a tornado was about to hit," Lenny explained. "She spent the night in the storm basement."

"You and I were out all night," Claire said. "There was no tornado. It was just a little windy."

"I know. So why did Miss Reed say that?"

Claire looked past Lenny, toward the big red barn. "Because she didn't want anyone outside. She made me come in too. But I thought that was just because . . ." Her face scrunched up like she was fighting back tears. "Apparently Jared is dead."

"Really?"

She should have said, *I'm sorry for your loss*. God, she was screwing everything up.

"I believe it," Claire said. "At least, I believe Aunt Maeve believes it. But . . . I don't believe *how* he died. She said he had a heart attack. But that's according to Chief Lamb. He's *up to something*. And Aunt Maeve is too scared to question it, but . . . she must know there's something out there. She might have locked Susan in for her own protection."

Lenny's sweatshirt was too heavy for the heat, yet she was shivering. She never was involved with a case where someone died—well, died while she was there investigating. Almost every location she and Evan visited had a death, but those were from generations ago. They weren't fresh. They were only ghosts.

Right now, this wasn't a history lesson. These were real people's lives. Lenny had been digging so long, she never actually planned to find anything. Was this her fault? The last time Jared had been seen alive, he had been telling the camera about what he saw.

Oh God. Evan had the last known footage of Jared on his computer.

Claire sat on top of the picnic table. Lenny sat beside her, careful to leave plenty of space between them. "I haven't talked to Bri," Claire said. "Aunt Maeve says she's still got the flu and won't let me near her. Maybe she thinks I've figured out something and I'm gonna destroy Bri's innocence. Or maybe she's getting sick again. I don't know. I don't know."

"Your aunt pulled in a few minutes ago. With Bri."

"Fuck. Bri probably didn't even sleep here last night. She could have been at the hospital. But I don't think so. Maeve doesn't trust doctors anymore. God. I don't know what's happening."

Claire ran her fingers through her hair and stared at the dried bird poop on the picnic table. Lenny wanted to give Claire a hug, but didn't know if that would make things more awkward. They would have to talk about last night eventually. But now wasn't the time.

"So you think . . . Bri's cancer's come back?" she asked.

"We all acted like it was a miracle," said Claire. "But maybe it is too good to be true. That's why Maeve doesn't want to listen to me: if the town itself is getting people sick, that means it's not over. And she's totally powerless. She doesn't want to admit it." Claire took a deep breath. "And that's not all. I heard Old Lucky's song last night. I didn't see anything, but it was like it was trying to *talk to me*."

Lenny had missed her chance to see an extraterrestrial. Again. Where had she been this time? Passed-out drunk? *Get it together*, she told herself. She couldn't sink into a puddle of embarrassment. Someone *died*.

"Do you want to get out of here for a while?" Lenny offered. Though the sky was a welcoming blue, the ranch was creeping her out. Every puffy white cloud was like another eye, watching them. "Susan says there's a fair going on right now—"

"God no," Claire said. "Everyone in town will be there . . . wait a sec." She hopped off the picnic table. "All the cops will be at the fair tonight. They never miss the tractor pull. I guarantee Chief Lamb won't be home."

"What are you suggesting?"

"I heard the noise on the other side of the trees. In the Lambs' yard."

"You don't think it was Warren again? Pulling a prank?"

"No," Claire said immediately. "Something's up with the chief. He's wrapped up in this somehow."

"So, what? You want to break into his house?"

Jared's was one thing. They didn't have to bust down a door or break a window. But this was a cop. Lenny wasn't a minor anymore, and if she were caught, the law would see her as an adult.

"They leave their doors unlocked," Claire said. "Everyone here does. We wouldn't be breaking in. It's just snooping."

"What about Warren?"

"He'll be at the fair too. If not. I can lure him away."

Claire waited for Lenny to respond. Like she needed her approval. As if, even after the messiness of last night, they were equal partners in this case.

"You're a good detective," Lenny said.

Claire smirked. "Maybe I'll start a YouTube channel."

CHAPTER 30

CLAIRE

Claire dreamed of the day she'd forget the names of people in her graduating class. There were only forty of them, so everyone knew everyone, regardless of popularity.

None of her classmates would forget Claire's name, but she didn't want to remember theirs. When she was ninety-nine, she would die peacefully in some far-off place. In her final hours, she would gather her great-grandchildren around her deathbed and tell them stories of her adventures. She would remember it all. Crystal-clear. Yet she wouldn't be able to recall the name of her hometown. There was the ranch, of course. She'd never forget this place. Her morning walks greeting the cattle. The quiet summer nights. Doing homework in the hayloft while Jared fixed the ever-failing lawn mower.

Except Jared was dead.

It all came crashing back. Jared's bloody bandana. Bri, sweaty and pale coming out of the bathroom. She'd be next. Her mom and now Jared and then Bri. They'd all be gone.

Claire cleared her throat. She had to stay focused. If she solved this, Bri could get better again. The cattle would get better. The corn would grow and no one would get sick and when all was well Claire could leave without guilt.

That meant getting rid of Warren tonight. He answered the phone on the first ring.

"Hey! What's up?" There was a forced casualness to his voice that made Claire want to gag. As if he hadn't changed this whole time. As if Claire was the asshole who'd ruined their friendship.

"Not much," she said. "Kinda bored. What are you doing tonight?"

"Probably gonna crash at Bryce's."

There he was. Rubbing it in her face. "You guys going to the fair?" Claire asked, trying to cover her disdain.

"I don't have a date."

The fair marked the beginning of the year's social season. It was Scarberry's version of the debutante ball. If you didn't show up with someone, you were a total loser.

Warren refused to be a loser.

They couldn't get rid of him without giving him a girl to have on his arm.

"Have you talked to Ashley?" Claire said into the phone. "What about her?"

"Which one?"

"Ashley Jordan?"

Warren sighed. "Jordy's staying with family in Yellowstone all summer."

Good for Ashley Jordan.

Lenny seemed to think this conversation was wildly interesting. She was bouncing back and forth in the caboose, putting away clothes. She didn't stay productive for long. She kept stopping, listening intently to Warren's responses on the speaker phone.

"What about Ashley Armes?" Claire suggested. It had been three months since graduation, and all their names were fresh on her mind. At least, for this occasion, the info was useful.

"Double A?"

"You're a misogynist." Claire almost hung up the phone. If they publicly made fun of Ashley Armes for her bust size, she couldn't imagine what they called Claire behind her back.

Well, actually, she could.

"Hey, I wasn't the one who started calling her that," Warren said.

"You could be the one who *stops* calling her that."

"Okay. Fair enough. But Do—*Ashley* is going with Stick. See? I call guys by nicknames too."

"Invented gender equality."

"Why is he called Stick?" Lenny whispered.

"Because sophomore year he told girls he would teach them how to drive stick shift, but he actually wanted them to do other activities in his truck," Claire explained.

"So you see my problem?" Warren said. "This summer has been *uneventful*. Guess not for you, though, huh?"

"What are you implying?"

"I mean you had a date last night and I didn't."

Claire wished she could melt into the mattress. She kept her head down, resisting the urge to glance at Lenny.

"It's not like that," she said.

"Oh." Warren paused for way too long. And then, "Does she play for *my* team then? Is she single?"

Lenny leaned into the phone. "Yes, I am."

It was good thinking on Lenny's part. If she went to the fair with Warren, she could make sure he didn't come home early and check in on his dad. But Claire didn't like how enthusiastically she answered. When she said "Yes, I am," did she mean "Yes, I am single" or "Yes, I am straight"? Claire couldn't think of a casual way to ask.

Surely, Lenny wasn't interested in Warren. He was the opposite of Evan. Evan was all wiry with scholarly glasses and straight teeth and a sharp haircut. He had good posture that only came from intentional practice. He shook hands like a salesman.

Warren was beefy and wild and took up more space than he was required to. You could look at him and know he played football, and in case you didn't figure that out on your own he'd inform you that the team almost went to state his junior year.

Warren definitely wasn't Lenny's type.

But Claire wasn't either.

"Does she want to come to the fair with me?" Warren said. Lenny glanced at Claire, with an amused smile. Claire hesitated a beat too long and then said, "I believe she does."

Lenny put her makeup on in the bathroom. She left the door open, so she and Claire could talk.

"Don't move anything," Lenny said, clipping her bangs back

before applying foundation with her fingers. "Just take pictures. Video would be great too. You can use the Nikon . . . What do people wear to these things?"

Claire said, "Anything you want," and Lenny changed her outfit four times, but not in front of Claire. If she had, Claire would have looked away. Lenny emerged from the bathroom, exasperated. "It's too cold for a T-shirt, and my only hoodie that's kinda warm is covered in blood. I assume that wouldn't be appropriate."

"You assume correct."

"Could I borrow something? If that's okay?"

"Uh, yeah."

Lenny was closer to Bri's size, but all of Bri's clothes were in her room. And Claire wasn't supposed to bother her. Because she was "in mourning." As if Claire wasn't too. Claire had texted her last night and twice this morning, but Bri hadn't even read one message.

Because she's sick again.

Claire took off her jacket, ignoring the soreness of her shoulder. She was technically still supposed to wear the sling today, but she could handle a little pain.

"Oh my God," Lenny said. "You're giving me the honor of wearing the patch jacket? I'll try not to bleed on it."

An hour later, Warren was honking in the parking lot and Claire had a fancy camera in her pocket. The fairgrounds were a twenty-minute drive away. It was about six p.m. The sun was starting to hover above the distant trees but wouldn't set for hours. Most rides and food vendors closed around ten. Bryce and his crew would likely stick around, after all the lights had turned off and the old people left, but Chief Lamb would come home right at ten. Anything that happened after close was none of his business. There was no more time for Lenny to teach Claire how to operate the camera or for Lenny to second-guess her outfit.

"Good luck," Lenny said. She gave Claire a hug. It happened so quick, Claire couldn't psychoanalyze it. Lenny hopped into Warren's truck. Claire expected him to take off, but he gave her a glance.

"Hey. I just heard about Jared. That really sucks. I'm sorry."

She gave him a nod, but she really wanted to give him the middle finger. She stepped into the house, and when Warren's truck was gone, she stomped back outside.

Claire found both four-wheelers parked by the red barn. There was a dent on one of them, but it was clear of any purple goo. Someone had wiped away the evidence.

Claire's insides turned to stone again. There had been moments that day when she'd forgotten about Jared. When she hadn't thought about Aunt Maeve's words last night, or the shredded bandana in Clawson's Field. But after Warren's comment, and the banged-up four-wheeler, she couldn't ignore it.

She didn't cry though. There was no time. She had to shift the sadness into anger. Avenging Jared was her job now, not stumbling over her useless feelings.

Claire took the un-damaged four-wheeler and drove it to

narrow hole in the tree line where Reed Ranch converged with the Lambs' property.

Nothing had changed about the big Lamb farmhouse. It had been built around the same time as the ranch, late eighteen hundred something. The Lambs' had fresher paint but was certifiably less homey. The front door was still unlocked.

When had she last come over for supper? Helped Warren with his homework? Sophomore year probably. That was around the time Warren figured out she was gay and, subsequently, figured out everyone else would know eventually. She hadn't come out to him, exactly. He'd just *realized*. It hadn't mattered when he claimed he accepted her. Clearly his teammates didn't. And that was who Warren chose.

The hardwood floor moaned in agony as Claire stepped inside. It was dark. There weren't any windows in the front room. There weren't many windows at all in the Lambs' house at all. She flicked the light switch on the wall. And . . . nothing. The bulb must have blown.

She stepped around piles of dirty clothes on her way to the office. That room was always forbidden, because it was where the guns were kept. Claire and Warren had snuck in several times to borrow scissors from the desk drawer. It held so much mystique back then. She had felt so brave whenever she ventured inside, pretending to be a secret agent.

Now Claire could see the mysterious office for what it was: dull and dusty. No paintings on the wall. Not a houseplant in sight. She clicked the switch for the desk lamp and . . . again, nothing. Maybe the wind last night was stronger than she thought, and the power got knocked out. Usually when that happened, the Reeds would lose power too. Perhaps the Lambs got unlucky this time around.

The wooden desk had a stack of manila folders. She flipped them open, trying to hold back a sneeze, as if a sudden noise would somehow blow her cover. She tried to remind herself that she could make as much noise as she wanted. It wasn't like there was a security system or anything. No one would be home for hours. And besides, Lenny would warn her if anything changed.

None of the folders held anything interesting. It was all old tax stuff. The gun safe was locked. Of course there was nothing to see here. Her next-door neighbor wasn't a *Scooby-Doo* villain waiting to be unmasked. She left the office, closing the door behind her. The kitchen was a wreck. The dirty dishes in the sink smelled like a sewer.

The fridge had a six-pack of beer and thirteen jars of gooseberry jam. There were more jam jars in the freezer. Surrounded by buckets of ice. No way these men were *living* off of jam.

The dining-room table was covered in random junk. Fast-food wrappers. Bottles. It had been tidy the last time Claire had been over, but that was when Mrs. Lamb was still around. Did they really just stop cleaning since then?

There were more papers here. Half-finished police reports about drunk drivers, then one letter with a heading that read: *U.S. Environmental Protection Agency.*

What the hell.

Dear Homeowner,

You or your family may be exposed to an unknown carcinogen.

Until it is identified and eradicated, it is important to cease drinking and bathing with tap water immediately. Minimize time spent outdoors. Do not consume locally sourced produce or meat. If any persons in your household experiences coughing, wheezing, fever, lethargy, migraines, trouble concentrating, or feeling generally unwell, please call the free toll line . . .

She pulled her phone from her back pocket, ready to text Lenny a photo of the letter.

Her phone wouldn't turn on.

There was a tingle at the back of her neck—subtle, but definitely there. Goose bumps rose on her skin. She felt watched. Just like last night.

"Hello?" she called. There wasn't an answer.

Just a scream.

Claire bent over, cupping her hands over her ears. The pitch slid higher and higher, vibrating the air around her, churning her insides. Just when she was sure she couldn't take it any longer, the scream stopped.

What the hell?

It had to be coming from outside.

She put her phone in her pocket and hurried out the front door. The Lambs had a few scattered trees, an old rotten barn, and berry bushes. Otherwise, the land was open. She couldn't see anything out of the ordinary, but she could *feel* it. Her body instinctively knew there was something wrong. Her heart was beating erratically, and every inhale felt too thick, devoid of oxygen. It was here. She knew it was here.

Which meant either Old Lucky could turn invisible.

Or he was in the barn.

The Lambs' barn was unpainted, leaving the wood ragged and exposed. It leaned to one side, like it was frozen mid-collapse. Claire stepped toward it.

The air wasn't any colder, but she was shivering. There was the sound again: Old Lucky's song. It sounded desperate, beckoning her forward.

The barn door had big metal chains around it. And there was a padlock. What person locked their barn but not their house?

Aunt Maeve locked our barn too.

This lock was more symbolic than anything. The wood was so rotten, so fragile, someone could easily punch through it if they really wanted to.

Claire really wanted to.

She used her palm to push hard on one of the boards. It split in half, just like she expected. There was a footlong opening in the wall now. She glanced through it.

Dark eyes stared back at her.

CHAPTER 31

LENNY

The county fair didn't smell much different from the ranch. Except instead of just manure, there was also the scent of popcorn and weed thrown in. Warren paid for both of their tickets at the entrance. He kept glancing at Lenny as he handed over the cash, like he was checking to see if she would thank him for paying.

Claire had been right about the whole town being there. Strollers and balloons and goats on leashes crowded the narrow walkways. There was a Ferris wheel in the distance. The words on the side were all faded, and half the colored bulbs weren't lit. Still, Lenny's heart lurched when she saw it.

"Can we go on the Ferris wheel?" she asked Warren.

"Uh. Yeah. Let's find Bryce and Megan first."

Warren took Lenny though metal buildings with hay covering the dirt floors, and pens of animals lining the walls. A few pens had ribbons tacked above them. Warren watched impatiently as Lenny pet every single sheep.

If Warren considered this a date, he wasn't doing much to woo her. Not that she was wooable. She was here on a mission. Yes, Warren was kind of cute, in a corn-fed, all-American-boy-next-door way. But there was an arrogance about him that the old version of Lenny might have put up with.

New Lenny couldn't stomach it.

They spotted his friends in a building dedicated to poultry. It smelled worse there. And it was noisy with the incessant clucking of chickens. Warren gave Bryce a smack on the shoulder and fist-bumped the other boy. Stick, she assumed. All three wore blue-and-white varsity jackets, with clinking medals and numbered patches. Claire had graduated the same year as Lenny, and the way the boys talked in past tense implied they also had just completed their senior year as well. Were they going to wear their old school merch forever, then?

Quickly the guys moved away from the group, leaving Lenny with the girls. There was Football Hoodie Girl—Megan—and a second girl introduced herself as Ashley Armes.

"So, are you from Stockville or something?" Ashley asked. That was one of the closest nearby towns. Lenny saw a sign for it on one of the food runs with Claire.

"I'm not from here, no," Lenny said.

"So where are you from?"

"I live just outside Chicago. But I was born in Detroit."

"So where are you *from?*"

Truly, Lenny was from both, and neither. She felt indifferent about her first seven years in Detroit and her house in the Chicago suburbs. Those were places she'd lived, not who she was. Her identity was more concerned with a magical future place she hadn't decided on yet. So when *Odd Kids* gave her opportunities to travel, it was like a dream come true.

Now she felt like an alien—homesick for a place she hadn't found yet.

"I swear I've seen you before," said Ashley. Lenny was going to shrug it off. Say it was a coincidence. But then Megan said, "She's a YouTuber."

"Oh my God! That's it!" Ashley said. She looked down at Lenny, grinning.

"She's from *Odd Kids*," Megan added.

Evan used to keep track of all the times they were recognized in public. Even back then, Lenny thought it was a ridiculous metric to keep track of. Unplanned fan interactions always twisted Lenny's stomach in knots. She knew even if she let Evan take the lead, she'd manage to disappoint every stranger who knew her name. And now Evan wasn't here to steer the conversation.

Ashley folded her arms. "I thought that was a dude. The hot guy with the glasses."

"It's two people," Megan explained. "*She's* the other one."

Lenny gritted her teeth. She was the one who came up with the show. She did all the research. But Evan had the business smarts and the dimples and he was good at not talking too fast.

Bryce looked her up and down. Like he was seeing her for the first time. "So you're *famous?*"

Not if you have to ask.

Ashley set her phone on a sticky-looking bench. "Boys!" she shouted at Warren and Stick. "Get over here."

"We were going to play the gun game," Stick moaned.

"We need pics before it gets too dark!"

They fell in line as Ashley started a timer and backed up. Stick grabbed her waist. "Don't you have enough pictures, Ash?"

"C'mon, Stick you can use 'em for your Tinder when she dumps your ass," said Warren.

"She's right," Megan added. "Get them in now before that hairline disappears."

Everyone but Stick laughed and leaned into their assigned positions for the photo.

Lenny felt a weight on her shoulder. An arm, wearing a scratchy blue varsity jacket. Warren. The flash went off. Lenny blinked. As soon as it was over, Warren peeled away from her. Ashley grabbed the phone to review. She smiled at the screen. "Perfect. Go play with your water guns, boys."

Lenny froze. Stunned. She couldn't remember the last time she did a photo with one take. Or the last time she posed for a picture with someone other than Evan. Would Warren with his arm around her read as couple-y?

Shit.

How many followers could this girl possibly have? Lenny wasn't even looking at the camera, and besides, no one would recognize her without Evan. It was fine. Probably.

Warren bought her food. Though they passed plenty of empty benches and picnic tables, the group kept walking as they ate. The girls dipped their fries into their milkshakes and the boys inhaled their corn dogs. They shot water guns at moving targets, until they got bored of that and moved on to throwing rings at fishbowls. They all had comments for nearly everyone they passed. More inside jokes from an inside world Lenny wasn't a part of.

"Courtney's mom looks pregnant," said Megan.

"She's not pregnant," said Bryce. "She just got divorced."

"So?" countered Megan.

Stick jumped in, playfully slamming into Bryce's shoulder.

"Bryce, you do know where babies come from, right?"

The sun began to set, and they still were walking around, talking. It would be easy for them to go on like this forever, sharing milkshakes, making jokes that required seven layers of context. These Scarberry teens *belonged* to this place, and to each other. This is what Lenny had to give up. For the show. For *him*.

They reached the Ferris wheel. Up-close, it wasn't that tall. Barely three stories. Wordlessly, Megan and Bryce jumped in line together. Ashley and Stick followed. Stick slid his hand around Ashley's waist. She smirked and looked around to make sure everyone had noticed.

Lenny and Warren got in line behind the couples, but they didn't touch each other. Lenny secretly wished Warren would try to grab her waist, so she'd have an excuse to kick him in the groin. She still felt the weight of wrongness when he'd touched her shoulder. She knew her resentment was misplaced. Warren hadn't really done anything to her. She should have been mad at Evan. Or really, she should have been mad at herself. Because Evan hadn't stolen anything from her. She'd given it all, willingly.

The bench wobbled as they sat down. Warren grabbed the metal bar and pulled it over their laps. No one checked to see if they were strapped in properly before their carriage started to lift them up, backwards. The medals pinned to Warren's jacket sounded like a jangling dog collar. Their carriage stopped at the very top. Lenny looked down at the tiny people, wondering if she was this high up when she fell from the sky. She shivered.

"Are you afraid of heights?" Warren asked, surprisingly observant.

"No," she said.

"You seem scared."

"I'm not." She folded her arms and sunk into the seat. The metal was cold against her thin jeans. The carriage moved again, slowly floating down to the bottom.

"I was surprised you wanted to come with me," Warren said. "I thought you and Claire were a thing."

Of course he would think that. She went from wearing matching merch with Evan to wearing Claire's jacket.

"No," Lenny said. "I'm not . . ."

Not what, Lenora?

Her mouth went dry. She wished for another sip of a milkshake, but she had tossed the last of it before stepping onto the ride. The carriage kept moving. They were almost to the top again. The sun was gone now. The lights on the Ferris wheel's arms cast a yellow glow over them.

"I'm for the cause or whatever," Warren added. "Equal rights and all that."

"Really?" she asked numbly.

"Of course. Claire thinks this whole town hates her. It's not true. Not everyone is against her. But I get why she's so defensive. Most of Scarberry isn't . . . with the times. I just figured she'd leave right after graduation. Shit, I thought she would drop out. She used to say she was going to customize a van and travel around." He shrugged. "Maybe she's staying to prove to everyone she's tough, or something? I get it, but at the end of the day, you have to live for you, right?"

"Right," Lenny said. They were moving faster now. The bench groaned and squeaked. Warren was a lot smarter than she gave him credit for, but she wished he would shut up. Her stomach needed to chill out. She would feel much better when she was on the ground.

"I guess I'd hoped she found someone at least," Warren continued. "I have to admit, I've seen your show. I know you have a boyfriend, but I figured part of it was fake. For the cameras."

"So that's why you pranked us? To *prove* it's fake?" Lenny said.

"Uh. Yeah. Sorry about that."

She said nothing. It didn't matter now, but she still couldn't forgive him for such an asshole move.

"It's not all fake though, is it?" Warren asked. "Like, the ghost stuff? Like the handprints on your car in that cornfield video?"

"Yes, that was real."

"And now you're investigating Scarberry?"

"Obviously."

Finally they stopped at the bottom. Lenny lifted the safety bar and jumped out.

"Wait!" Warren called, pulling at her sleeve. "Can I show you something?"

CHAPTER 32

CLAIRE

When Claire was eleven, a stray had kittens inside the garden shed. It was early fall, when the days were mild but the nights were biting cold. She had worried the kittens would freeze to death but Aunt Maeve wouldn't let her bring them inside, because Bri was allergic. The kittens' lives weren't worth her daughter's itchy eyes and runny nose. Even back then, Bri was the sick one and Claire was the difficult one.

Claire had gathered every extension cord in the house and turned them into a sixty-foot rope. The megacord ran from the outlet above the kitchen sink all the way to the garden shed and into an electric space heater. Aunt Maeve hadn't known about this plan, of course. She assigned many jobs to Claire, but the most important ones Claire gave herself.

That night, while guarding the kittens in the shed, she'd heard scratching and panting from outside. She'd cracked the door open and a mangy gray coyote stared back at her. She often heard coyotes at night, screaming like little girls. Jared had told her if she ever saw one, she was to yell at it. Make herself big. Claire already felt big, protecting the litter of kittens.

She'd shouted at the coyote, and it had skittered away.

Claire had a feeling that if she yelled at Old Lucky now, it wasn't going anywhere.

For one, it was bound. Layers of chains crisscrossed its torso like a harness. They ended in thick rings, welded into the concrete floor of the barn. Bandages covered the beast's cracked white skin. Its thin, pale body crouched low to the ground, drinking from a water bowl. It didn't seem to care that Claire had stumbled upon its nest.

No, not nest.

Prison.

When it moved, it led with the neck, which was at least a foot and a half long and bent like a snake. She could see every vertebra of its spine—the jagged bones of hips. Its mouth was a gaping circular hole, completely toothless.

So this was Scarberry's Old God. This was what chased Willy Lamb and Minnie Albert. This might have been the last thing Jared saw before he . . .

Died. Jared was dead. Gone. Because of this *thing*.

Brown eyes narrowed at her. Not glowing red like the stories said. And it wasn't nearly as big. Didn't have enough arms. There was no expression on its face, but somehow Claire felt something strange surge through her.

Recognition.

Its empty mouth unhinged as it screamed. Claire resisted the urge to cover her ears. She had to listen, even if it blew out of her eardrums. Because she was pretty sure it was singing for her.

Wait.

It wasn't singing.

It was *crying.*

Had Old Lucky's song always been crying? It sure looked miserable. And so helpless. Maybe Old Lucky hadn't clawed Jared to death. Maybe just the sight of Old Lucky gave Jared a heart attack after all.

The cries faded to whimpers. Then there was a new sound. Tires and a radio, with the bass turned up. Warren. *Shit.* Lenny was supposed to text her when they came back.

Oh right. Claire's phone was dead. She peeked around the side of the barn. Warren's truck with its lifted tires had parked at the edge of the driveway, a good distance from the house—and the barn. Did he know that Old Lucky messed with electronics?

Lenny jumped out of the passenger seat and slammed the door. Weird. Why didn't Warren drop off Lenny at the ranch? There was no way their "date" went well. Lenny would never have been into him and now she was getting over Evan too.

Lenny didn't like anybody. She liked aliens.

And Claire had found her one.

As they approached the house, Warren was doing most of the talking. And Lenny looked anywhere but at him. Mostly, she looked up.

She would be so excited once Claire told her she'd found her precious alien, even though the real thing was pathetic up-close. She might even forgive her for the attempted hoax.

Once they left, Claire would run toward the four-wheeler and head home. It was a miracle that Warren hadn't noticed it yet. The vehicle wasn't exactly hidden, but Warren had his eyes on Lenny, only. *Ugh.* Claire stepped out of the barn, careful not to scrape herself on a jagged wooden beam.

But then Old Lucky let out a long howl. Both Lenny and Warren turned toward the barn.

Shit.

She was spotted.

"Claire," Warren called, marching right up to her. "What are you—"

"How long has that thing been in there?" Claire spat. It sounded accusatory, because it was. He had betrayed her over and over. First he joined forces with homophobic meatheads, then he tried to hook up with her cousin, tried to hook up with her . . . Lenny, *and* was harboring an extraterrestrial in his backyard? She had been right about him.

"What thing?" Lenny asked. Claire stepped aside, revealing the gash in the barn wood. Lenny stepped forward and cautiously peered inside. Her expression melted from confusion to excitement to fear, and to confusion again. She looked at Warren with her face all puckered up.

"Is this another prank?" There was hurt in her voice. And though Warren solemnly shook his head, Claire felt her heart squeeze. Old Lucky was real, but Claire was still a liar. This didn't absolve her of anything.

Warren peeked inside and then immediately stepped back as Old Lucky bellowed again.

Warren covered his ears. "Ow. Fuck."

"Is this what you wanted to show me?" Lenny demanded. "You . . . you kidnapped Old Lucky."

"No. Fuck. I was gonna show you a videogame at Bryce's. I just had to grab the disk from my room. I've never seen this thing before. I swear."

"What did you do to him?" Lenny asked. She stepped toward the barn, and Claire followed her. There was still plenty of distance in case the thing tried to lunge at her. But it didn't look like it could do much damage, toothless and talonless and bleeding.

"*I* didn't do anything," Warren protested. "I swear. I didn't know it was here."

"You didn't know there was an alien in your barn?"

"I've barely been home. Our electricity has been fucked for a while. It's practically uninhabitable here. I'm at Bryce's house on most nights. Ask him, he'll vouch for me."

"How long has your electricity been off?"

"Jesus. Is this an interrogation?"

"Old Lucky messes with electronics," Lenny explained. "He's the reason your electricity is off."

Warren swallowed. "It's been a few months."

"Dude," Claire groaned. "You really expect us to believe you had no idea your dad brought home a new pet?"

"Okay, you want all the juicy details, Claire?" he snapped. "I've barely spoken to my dad for a year. Well, actually, my dad barely speaks to me. Besides telling me when he needs me to deliver jam. Or when the football schedule's released. He hasn't exactly been okay, ever since my mom got sick. He kept ranting about finding a cure for death. That the recipe was here, somewhere. Our ancestors were given it by the *Old Gods*. He's fucking nuts."

"Wait." Lenny glanced at Claire. "What's he talking about?"

"I've never heard that part of the story," Claire admitted.

"It's not part of the story. My dad's just lost his mind. Once, when my mom was in the hospital, I found him wandering around Old Scarberry in a daze, saying he was *gathering ingredients*." He stared at the creature in chains. "Maybe he did find a cure," Warren continued. "Maybe this is it. Or my dad *thinks* it is. I really didn't know. I didn't want to know. And obviously my dad didn't want me to find out. I'm so terribly sorry for trying to act normal. My bad."

It had been about a year since Myra Lamb died. She went out the same way Bri was supposed to. Claire pushed down any sympathy gnawing at her stomach. Warren wasn't her friend. Not anymore. And she wasn't sure if she believed him.

"I'm sorry about your mom," Lenny said. "Really. We're just trying to figure things out. A man might be dead because of this."

"What?"

"Jared. We think Old Lucky attacked him."

"It might be the reason people are getting sick in the first place," Claire added, thinking out loud. Bri had been an acre away from Old Lucky—of course her cancer would return. Old Lucky's presence had been cursing Scarberry for years, and now that it was closer to town, dug up from wherever it had been hiding, whatever cosmic effect he'd had on this place for over sixty years had worsened.

Claire wanted to hit something.

"Claire," Lenny said quietly. "His eyes are brown."

"Yeah."

"Jared said what he saw had blue eyes. Willy Lamb said Old Lucky had red eyes. And four arms."

"People misremember," Claire offered. "Honest mistake."

Aliens were real. The proof was here. Why would Lenny, of all people, get caught up in minor discrepancies? Long neck, white skin. This was it. In the flesh.

Old Lucky curled into a ball and put its head on the hay, looking like the most malformed, horrifying kitten in the universe.

Warren said, "It's dark. My dad'll be home any minute. Lenny, you should post this on your channel."

"You *want* me to post about it?" Lenny asked.

Warren shrugged. "I mean, yeah. If you guys are right, then it's got some anti-electric field around it or something. I can't even get to the end of my driveway without my truck dying. Someone professional should study it or take care of it or send it back to its home planet. My dad has it all wrong. It's not the cure; it's the cancer." His eyes narrowed at the beast, shaking in the corner. "I want it gone."

"What are you going to say to your dad?" Lenny asked Warren.

"Nothing," Claire answered for him. "He's going to say nothing to Chief Lamb. Because then he can keep claiming he doesn't know what his dad's been up to. Just like you didn't know what your BFF put on my locker, right Warren?"

"What?" Lenny asked.

"Junior year, someone graffitied my locker with a lovely little slur and the school didn't do anything, because there wasn't enough proof," Claire explained.

"What?" Warren said. "Who—"

"It was Bryce."

"No." Warren shook his head. "How do you know it was—"

"He had fucking pink spray-paint on his hands. I heard him bragging about it at lunch."

Warren went quiet. He glanced at Old Lucky again. "I didn't know."

"You didn't *want* to know. That's my point. You want plausible deniability."

"You could have told me."

Claire couldn't take this. Warren had abandoned her, just like Hannah, just like her mom. The electromagnetic field or just good old-fashioned rage was making her head pound.

"Just for you to choose your football cult over me anyway?" she said. "Don't pretend you're not complicit. You know how your buddies all feel about gay people even if you didn't see them write it. Don't worry, Warren. I'll do your homework like I always did. I'll tell off Bryce. I'll confront your dad about the fucking monster in your backyard. And you can keep telling yourself you're a good guy."

She stormed off. Lenny let out a little sound of disgust and followed right behind Claire. The farther she got from the barn, the clearer Claire's head felt.

It was all making sense now. Warren knew *something*. He'd only started texting Claire again right around the time *Odd Kids* landed. He wasn't interested in Lenny; he was interested in her audience. Claire only allowed herself to feel the minor relief for a moment. What if Warren wasn't lying? What about everyone else in town who'd died? Did the chief offer his useless "magic" cure to them? Offer a false hope? Is that what Mrs. Stern was talking about at town hall, when she'd ranted about the Old Gods punishing them?

Did she know what Lamb was up to?

They reached the four-wheeler. Lenny stared at the barn like she wanted to take her precious alien legend with her. Then she looked at Claire expectantly.

"Can this thing fit two?" she asked. Claire nodded and hopped on, and Lenny followed, wrapping her arms around her middle. Claire had to remind herself to breathe. Act normal.

Ideally, they would both have helmets on and Claire would give Lenny a whole safety speech and they would go to a beautiful wooded destination, where a picnic with homemade cookies and a bouquet of flowers would be waiting.

Ideally, the Lambs wouldn't be harboring an extraterrestrial, if that was even what Old Lucky was. Ideally, Jared would be alive and Bri wouldn't be sick again and Aunt Maeve would be honest and the crops wouldn't be failing and the water wouldn't be poisoned and Mom would have never left. But there was a small comfort having Lenny there, with her arms around her waist, and her head buried in her back.

CHAPTER 33

LENNY

Claire's long hair flew into Lenny's face as they zoomed around the ranch. Claire smelled like summer rain. She kept asking if she was going too fast, and every time, Lenny said, "Faster." She knew the second they stopped, the night would have to continue. They had to go back to being people, and Lenny wasn't ready for it.

Once they parked in front of the caboose, Lenny couldn't ignore the anxiety bubbling inside her stomach. It was like she had found the dream thing buried in the snow, and it had evaporated in her hands. What was she to do with this discovery if she couldn't have any proof? She had trained herself to have a camera pointed at anything that might be interesting. Evan's policy was always having more footage than you could possibly need, and yet Lenny had missed everything. If what Warren said was true—if this thing really shut down all nearby technology—then this was a hopeless case. Still, there was something nagging in her stomach.

Old Lucky wasn't supposed to have brown eyes.

"What do you want to do?" Claire asked once they were inside.

"I need to work on my board," Lenny answered.

"Your board?"

Lenny grabbed the bulletin board from the corner of the room and spun it around for Claire to see. It had grown rather chaotic. Multicolored string and sticky notes tangled together like a rat king.

"Oh right," Claire said. "Of course."

Lenny needed something to organize her thoughts before she imploded.

Lenny removed her muddy shoes and shed Claire's jacket before she jumped onto the bed.

They had only known each other for a few days, and yet there was no question that Claire would stay by her side. Lenny would have lost her mind if Claire hadn't been there, confirming all of this was real. At least someone believed her.

Claire sat on the bed next to Lenny, watching her hurriedly scratch out notes with a Sharpie. Lenny connected several strings to the Chief Lamb sticky note. But there were still loose ones: She had nothing to connect to cancer. Old Lucky's powers were still mysterious. Jared's death still didn't make sense.

She had some answers, but even more questions.

"You seem . . ." Claire began.

"What? I seem what?"

"Disappointed?"

Lenny rubbed at her eyes. That was something she could do freely now that she didn't have to be camera-ready. Her eyeliner could smear and no one had to know but her. Well, Claire would see the black smudges on her cheeks, but she wouldn't care.

"I told myself I didn't need the show, I just wanted an *experience,* not an audience," Lenny admitted. She wasn't choosing her words that carefully. She could feel a ramble coming on, but couldn't stop it. Didn't want to stop it. She was heading down a dark tunnel, and once she got all the words out, she would be safe in the sun again. "Now I'm worried I won't be able to catch anything on camera. It's stupid. I feel this . . . responsibility. But that's ridiculous, right? I'm a tourist in all this. How am I making it about me?"

She waited for the judgment to seep into Claire's expression. It never came. She actually scooted closer on the bed.

"*Warren* made it about you," Claire said. "He thinks *doing the right thing* counts when someone does the right thing for him. And I made it about you too, I guess."

"It's the other way around. I roped you into my investigation."

"And now I'm not one of those insufferable skeptics. Congrats, you made a new convert."

Lenny laughed weakly. "Welcome to the club."

She wished she could enjoy this moment. Old Lucky wasn't a myth after all. But she wanted to throw up in her mouth whenever she remembered how much he didn't match the drawings she'd studied for years. And she couldn't get the image of the blood-soaked bandana out of her mind.

"What Bryce did was fucked-up," Lenny said.

"It was a while ago."

"Still. You carry that shit with you, right?"

"I guess."

"And I'm sorry about Jared," Lenny added.

Claire shook her head. "I'm not sure it was *that thing* that killed him. But whatever happened to Jared was sketchy."

"What if," Lenny started, "Old Lucky got loose, and the Lambs removed the teeth after they recaught him? What if he was perfectly healthy a few days ago?"

"I wondered that too at first. But I don't know. It's probably been sick as long as Scarberry has. We're all probably radioactive at this point."

They were quiet for a bit. Lenny really should take more notes. Memories weren't reliable. Evan loved reminding her of that scientific fact. The brain had this fickle tendency to rewrite its own data. It was best to record things as soon as possible, while the memories were fresh and untainted.

"So, what do you want to do now?" Claire asked. "That's all I've got. I've done too much thinking today."

"Same. I need to, like, shut my mind off and rewatch *Pride and Prejudice* for the gazillionth time."

Claire shrugged and said, "I'm down."

There were a million things they should have done. Responsible things. But if Lenny even thought about aliens for one more second she was going to crumple under the enormity of it.

So they gathered a nest of provisions. Lenny offered her last can of Monster and Claire stole food from inside the house. They were on opposite sides of the bed, Lenny with her back against the wobbly headboard and Claire on her stomach, head close to the laptop screen. Lenny couldn't see Claire's face from where she was sitting, so the whole time she wondered how Claire felt. Did she think the movie was pretentious and boring like Evan did?

No, it didn't seem like it. Claire had her eyes fixed to the screen, eating Twizzlers. She hardly spoke, besides repeating back some of the lines in astonishment.

"*Most ardently*. Damn."

And then, when it was over, she sat up and said, "That was fun. I just don't like how Keira Knightley talks with her teeth."

"How can you not like *Keira Knightley*?"

"I guess she's a fine actor . . ."

"She's *radiant* in this movie. She was born to play Elizabeth Bennet. And she's basically the only person who can pull off the awkward proportions of Regency-era clothes."

Claire laughed. "Sorry," she said. "I didn't mean to insult your crush."

"She's not my—"

"Oh, *come on*."

"I just think she's—"

"Radiant?"

"I was talking about her *performance*."

Claire gave Lenny a pointed smirk. "Sure."

"If you hate her so much, you would probably like the 1995 version better then."

"I don't hate her nearly as much as you looooooove her."

Lenny couldn't believe that this was happening. She had shown this movie to Evan and her friends (back when she had time for friends). She had always fiercely defended Keira Knightley and no one called her admiration anything other than respect for her craft. Was this just Claire seeing everything through rainbow-colored lenses? Or was Claire the only one brave enough to notice things in Lenny?

Her stomach dropped. She felt like she was still on that Ferris wheel.

"Sorry," Claire said. Serious now. "I was just joking around."

"No," Lenny said. She tried to keep her voice even. "I think . . . maybe Keira Knightley does makes me feel things that might not totally fall under the category of heterosexual. Happy? But it's just this one movie, okay? It's not like I have a poster of her in my bedroom."

There, she'd said it. And the planet hadn't imploded yet. She thought she had crossed some kind of line, like she would be fundamentally changed for putting it in words. Had this been the thing buried deep in the dream snow? Maybe. The difference was, in the dream, she had been digging alone.

Claire nodded in approval. "Right. You have a picture of the Scarberry Lights."

"You remember me telling you that? Oh God, that's embarrassing."

"It's not embarrassing."

"You don't think it's kinda creepy that I've had a picture of your backyard hanging in my room since I was in middle school?"

"You didn't know it was *my* backyard."

"I'm glad it was."

And that's when Lenny started crying. There was nothing pretty about it. She couldn't cry in a cinematic way like Keira Knightley, and she couldn't explain her thoughts as eloquently as a Jane Austen novel. Claire froze for a second. She likely wasn't expecting the tears, and neither was Lenny. But this was a different kind of a cry, not like that hollow shiver in her bones when Evan left. She tried to explain this, through weak gasps.

"It's okay. I'm okay . . . I'm just. . . . relieved? I think," Lenny said.

Claire tentatively put her hand on Lenny's back. "Good. 'Cause you know there's nothing wrong with you, right? Other than your poor taste, but that can be fixed."

Once she calmed down, they put on *Pride and Prejudice* (1995), and Claire fell asleep midway through. Lenny put away the laptop and climbed under the covers. It didn't take long for her to drift off. But she didn't dream. No long-necked aliens or crashed saucers or dusty snow.

She had forgotten what it was like to share a bed with someone. Her body kept waking her up, as if to alert her of an intruder.

No, she tried to tell her brain. *It's just Claire. We're safe with her.* Every time she woke up, she and Claire were closer and closer together, and in her half-awake state, she didn't care. The last time Lenny woke up, she had her arms around Claire's soft waist, and strips of light were pushing through the blinds.

Someone was pounding at the door.

Lenny bolted up. Her sudden movement woke Claire. She opened her eyes but didn't move. "Who's that?" she mumbled.

Lenny squinted through the peephole, half expecting a totally healed Old Lucky, claws rapping against the peeling wood. Instead, Miss Reed was staring right at the glass. She still had that effortlessly cool look to her, but her freckled skin looked thin, colorless. And her eyebrows were pulled together so tight, she had hard wrinkles in between them.

"It's your aunt," Lenny said.

Claire jumped from the bed and slipped on her cowboy boots. "Open it."

Miss Reed gave Claire a double-take, but only addressed Lenny. Her voice was flat and oddly formal, like she was reading from a script.

"I'm sorry for the late notice, but you'll need to leave immediately. We have to fumigate your room. There's an infestation and we need to clear it for the exterminator. I'm very sorry for the inconvenience."

"Wait," Claire said. "What are you talking about?"

"I'm very sorry for the inconvenience," Miss Reed repeated, not looking at her niece, "but my hands are tied. I expect the room to be vacated before noon today."

There were no roaches in Lenny's room. No rodents. No wasp nests. This "exterminator" was a hasty excuse. One Miss Reed didn't even expect her to believe. But it didn't matter if Lenny believed it; she couldn't do anything about it.

Did Warren confess to his dad? He'd sounded remorseful last night, and he had told Lenny how much he respected Claire, how he wanted the best for her. Despite Claire's disdain for him, Lenny's feelings about the guy had changed. He was caught in a bad situation. He was grieving his dead mom. He wouldn't turn on them, would he?

Miss Reed walked away, and Claire leaped after her. Before stepping out the door, Claire told Lenny, "I'm gonna figure out what's happening. You're not going anywhere."

CHAPTER 34

CLAIRE

The ranch that morning hardly looked like the place that raised her. It was too empty. The grass was all dead. Garden decimated. She couldn't hear Jared whistling. There were no cows idling near the edge of the fence—instead they were all clustered farther into the pasture, huddling together for protection. Aunt Maeve trudged ahead and didn't stop when Claire said, "Wait, what the fuck is going on?"

Then Claire rounded the side of the house and saw Chief Lamb's car, parked near the porch. He wasn't carrying any crates of jam. He had a grave expression, one almost as serious as Aunt Maeve's.

Usually, the chief greeted Claire with polite small talk. They had a consistent script they followed. *Good morning,* he would say. Claire would say good morning back and ask him how he was doing and he would either say *Can't complain* or he would report the defeat of his favorite sports team and then ask, *Is your aunt around?*

Today, there were no familiar niceties.

"Claire," he said. Her own name cut her stomach wide open. Though Claire identified as trouble, she had never been *in* trouble. Especially trouble with someone who wore a badge.

Did Warren snitch?

"When did you last speak to your cousin?" he asked.

Huh?

She had texted Bri a dozen times yesterday but didn't receive a response. This had been the longest they hadn't talked since that terrifying month-long stay at the hospital. "It's been a few days," Claire admitted. "She's been sick."

Did Bri do something? She could be impulsive, but hardly *unpredictable*. Anyway, Aunt Maeve said Bri was too grief-stricken to leave her bed.

"And that girl?" the chief continued. "Lenora Gilson?"

Lenora Gilson. Claire had heard her full name in the nursing home, but coming out of the chief's mouth it sounded foreign. It didn't fit her like Lenny did.

"I've been with her for basically the last twenty-four hours."

Well, except for when Lenny went to the fair. *Basically* was doing a lot of heavy lifting, but it wasn't a total lie.

"What's this about?" Claire asked. "I'm not a kid. You can tell me."

Aunt Maeve looked at Chief Lamb. He gave the tiniest nod. Maeve sucked in a big breath and lifted her chin, feigning a confident posture while her eyes looked unfocused and glassy. She was like a marionette doll, unable to stand on her own, grateful to the man who held her strings.

Claire thought about throwing Chief Lamb off his game.

The words were right on her lips: *I know about the thing in your barn.* But then the chief spoke.

"Bri is missing."

"What?"

Claire wished she had never left the warmth of the caboose, Lenny with her arms wrapped around her. She wanted to go back to those few hours when they knew monsters were real but paid them no mind.

Bri is missing.

Chief Lamb said those three words, and Claire's head was ravaged with monsters. The shredded suit. Jared's disappearance. The bloody bandana and his supposedly bloodless death. No. Bri couldn't die too. And how could Old Lucky reach her when it was weak and chained up? When Bri had been holed up in her room? She hadn't gone anywhere near the portal. She should have been safe. She *had* to be safe.

"Pie?" Aunt Maeve squeaked. She didn't sound like herself.

How could she sound like herself if her daughter was missing?

No no no no no. How had Claire gone this long without checking in on Bri? How could she have been out gallivanting with Lenny and ignoring her cousin? Bri depended on her.

Maeve started for the door, and the chief followed close behind her, offering a comforting clasped hand on Maeve's shoulder, and a look to Claire as if to say, *I'm keeping my eye on you.* What the hell was happening?

The chief sat in the non-wobbly chair in the kitchen. He sighed and leaned back. He was acting far too casual. Maeve looked close to tears as she took out ingredients from the fridge.

Apparently *pie* didn't mean she would cut a slice, it meant she would start baking a whole new one, right now.

"Aunt Maeve, please, what's going on?" Claire pleaded.

"I thought we could shake things up. Do a peach this time."

"No, I mean, with Bri? How could she be missing?"

Maeve tossed flour into the big mixing bowl. She missed horrifically. The white powder was everywhere, and Maeve carried on like she hadn't noticed. She cracked an egg on the edge of the bowl, and threw the whole thing in, shell and all. There were more scratches on her hands. Claire didn't believe they were cat scratches.

They couldn't have a real conversation when Maeve's eyes kept twitching to Chief Lamb, begging for his approval for every breath she took.

"Can we talk in private?" Claire asked.

Maeve tensed.

The chief clicked his tongue. "Of course."

He didn't let the door clack behind him like everyone else did. He gently closed it, staring at Claire through the ragged screen. Then he turned and stepped off the porch, taking his time. Claire didn't utter a word until she heard his car pull away.

"Aunt Maeve?" She still had her back turned, aggressively rolling the dough. "Just talk to me. Why would Bri be missing? Why are you trying to kick Lenny out?"

Aunt Maeve whirled around. Her teeth were clenched together, holding back a snarl. "For her *safety*."

Then Maeve collected herself. Softening her grip on the wooden roller in her hand, she said, "I think it's great you've found a girl, Claire. I really do, it's just not a good time. I have so much to do, and I can't have any distractions. What if . . . what if you got out of Scarberry for a while?"

"What?"

"This place is killing you. You've said it yourself." She collected her purse from the counter, transferring the flour from her hand onto the worn brown leather. She pulled out her credit card. "I never gave you your graduation present. You should book a flight. Anywhere. Go crazy. You can bring your girlfriend and—"

"Did you get a letter?" Claire asked. "About the water being unsafe?"

"You deserve some time off, hon. You can't spend your whole life saving us."

"Aunt Maeve—"

"Please go. It's my treat."

"If Bri is *missing*, I want to help look for her."

"The whole town will be looking for her," Maeve snapped. Then, catching herself again, she lovingly rested a floury hand on Claire's cheek. "Oh honey. I'll be okay. I don't need a babysitter. We'll let the police do their jobs."

"We can't trust Chief Lamb. Last night, Lenny and I found something in his barn—"

"Lenny really is a sweet girl."

"Listen! It's Old Lucky. The chief caught it, somehow. It's in his barn and has been for a *long* time. The chief's been messing around with stuff he doesn't understand, trying to find a cure, and it has to do with Old Lucky. I was right. Whatever he's working on is poisoning the whole town."

Maeve smiled dully. "I'm sure the police will find her, same as she was."

Same as she was?

"Is Bri . . ." Claire swallowed. "Is she sick again?"

Maeve flinched. That was her answer. Bri was sick. And she wouldn't make it this time. She'd be like the others. And no one was going to say it out loud. Claire could run the business. Do the chores. But she couldn't know her own cousin—her *best friend*—was dying.

"Fuck this," Claire spat.

She trudged upstairs and went straight to Bri's room. Somehow, Claire had expected her to be swallowed by her big comforter, scrolling on her phone. They'd get in a big fight and then Claire would hold her close and they'd both cry and watch a stupid TV show.

But of course Bri wasn't there. Her phone sat on the bed face-up, glowing with missed calls from Maeve and social media notifications. Apparently, her favorite K-pop idol released a new single. Bri wouldn't go anywhere without her phone. Even if she was grabbing a snack downstairs or running to the bathroom to vomit.

Claire's legs felt wobbly. She had to concentrate to stop them from buckling. She had no idea where Bri was, and Aunt Maeve didn't either. If Bri was missing, why would Aunt Maeve sit back and let the chief handle it? Wouldn't she demand Claire drop everything to search for her precious daughter? This woman used to be a hurricane. And somehow, Chief Lamb had become an even bigger storm, capable of swallowing her up.

Claire didn't plan to run outside, but somehow her body

knew what to do. She stood in the center of the driveway, waiting for a sign to hit her. For Aunt Maeve to run after her and apologize for not ever listening. For Bri to pull in on her bike, or in a car with some new boy she'd fallen horrifically in love with.

A humid gust made the windmill groan and surrounding cornfields shiver. Even the few hundred acres of crops that hadn't completely failed were half as high as they should be this time of the summer. And she hadn't paid it any notice until Lenny pointed it out.

Claire took a deep breath, wiped the tears from her hot cheeks, and stomped toward the caboose.

CHAPTER 35

LENNY

Clawson's Field was already crowded. They all seemed to arrive just as Claire and Lenny did. There was one truck, then two, and suddenly there were thirty trucks, all loaded up with Scarberrians ready to look for the missing girl.

The afternoon sky felt too blue for the occasion. The puffy white clouds were mocking Lenny. They might as well have been cameras. Plenty of *Odd Kids* videos involved missing persons, but those were all cold cases from before Lenny was born. The names of the disappeared and the dead were never in the video titles. The victims weren't nearly as interesting as the monsters that had hurt them. She tried to remember the name of someone, *anyone* hurt by one of the urban legends she'd covered on *Odd Kids*. And when her mind drew a blank, the guilt swarmed in.

This was all her fault. She had dug too hard, too deep. Made too much of a show about it. Lenny came to Scarberry for all the wrong reasons. She had wanted to put this place under her microscope and claim whatever she discovered as her own. Then she had moped about Evan, using Claire as a sounding board for her anxieties. This trip had become Lenny's coming-of-age film. But Bri was a real girl in real trouble.

Claire wasn't angry at Lenny. Yet. For now her rage was directed at Chief Lamb and Maeve and leukemia and "that thing" in his barn. Funny how she wouldn't say Old Lucky's name now. Did she have the same bad feeling Lenny did?

Willy Lamb said Old Lucky had red eyes. Jared said he had blue eyes. The beast she saw had brown eyes and was a dull approximation of the other sightings. Smaller. Only two arms. Something wasn't adding up.

Claire kicked a bottle cap with her boot. Then she sighed and put it in her backpack.

There was a lot of trash leftover from the latest party. Cans, foam cups, vape cartridges. Claire stuffed them in her bag, and when that ran out of room, Lenny helped her stack the rest on the rusted train car. Lenny didn't have to ask why the search and rescue turned into a trash clean-up. Lenny also shared the urge to do something productive in times of crisis.

They were offered sandwiches and bottles of water. Volunteers gave words of encouragement to Claire. "She's a tough girl," one woman with voluminous bangs said. She had brought turkey sandwiches smothered in mayo.

Every time a stranger said something kind, Claire didn't look very convinced, and Lenny didn't know how to help. The situation felt hopeless, and all Lenny could do was be a bystander and help collect garbage.

Bri seemed to be well liked. Why wouldn't she be? She was

the small-town girl who'd survived cancer. The *only one* who'd survived. That was all people seemed to mention. They called her a fighter. One called her a *warrior*. That word seemed far away from the mousy girl Lenny had met in the gift shop.

What would people say about Lenny if she went missing? They'd call her an influencer, for sure. Her name would be next to Evan's in every headline. And Lenny knew she must be more than that, but she had done nothing to prove it. But she could vow to show the world who she really was *after* they found Bri.

There were no signs of her in the field. That was a good thing, probably. Lenny couldn't bear to see Claire's face contort into panic again, in case they found another bloody bandana among the trash. After an hour of nothing, a uniformed officer stood on top of a flatbed truck and began delegating groups to the next station. Another cop stood next to him, but it wasn't Chief Lamb. They hadn't seen him in the search party at all.

"Do you want to go back to the ranch?" Lenny asked Claire.

"I feel like, if it took her, it would have brought her here," Claire said. "But . . . I don't know. What if . . . what if there are other portals?"

It made sense. The tire at the ranch led to the sky above Clawson's Field. There could be more that led elsewhere. They still didn't understand exactly how portals worked. It was possible one could span hundreds of miles, and that Bri could be *anywhere*. But lost was better than dead. They could do something with lost.

"I'm sorry," Lenny said. "I wish I could be more help."

"You're here. You care. That's enough for me."

Lenny grabbed Claire's hand and squeezed it tightly. Claire

locked eyes with her for a moment but then winced and pulled away. Had she done something wrong? What if Claire thought the gesture was totally inappropriate? What if Lenny didn't have good intentions at all and it was just another way she was making all of this about her and her extra-combustible feelings?

Then Lenny saw a boxy white van with painted blood splatters pull up.

"Are you fucking kidding me?" she groaned under her breath.

The crowd converged around the van. Phones popped above heads, trying to snap a pic of the men who jumped out the back door. The first was big, tall, with the baldest head you could imagine. He parted the crowd with one burly hand: Brian, the muscle. Then a scrawny guy, with a beard too big for his face: Chuck, the videographer. He carried a camera with a gimbal that had to cost at least $3,000.

Next came the man himself. The crowd gasped. Ponytail. Bedazzled jeans. Max Malitz: lead investigator, host, face of a dubiously ethical line of energy drinks. He smiled, clasping his hands in gratitude. As if he were a politician at a rally and not an influencer exploiting a search-and-rescue.

Just like you, Lenny.

Evan pushed up his glasses before stepping out of the Bloodmobile. He'd already shed the neon *Odd Kids* merch for a black shirt to match the rest of the crew. There was a bloody logo on his chest, right where humans tended to have hearts.

He looked past the crowd. Right at Lenny, like he was hoping she'd be there. Was he going to wave hello? Was he going to smirk? Flip her off? Nope. He looked away. Was it guilt? Indifference?

"Why is *he* here?" Claire asked. "And what's with the Mystery Machine?"

Lenny inched closer, not taking her gaze away from Evan. She tried to look fierce, though one time, when she'd gotten angry, he'd told her that her nasty look was too adorable to intimidate. That Lenny only looked like "a pissed-off baby deer."

The murmuring Scarberrians quieted as Max started talking to Chuck's massive camera.

"Strange lights floating above a barn, cattle mutilation, eerie shrieks at night, and sightings of a pale creature lurking in cornfields. In the summer of 1961, this small town had more than a few strange occurrences . . ."

It stopped Lenny in her tracks. Those were her words. *Her* words. Years of research were always leading to Scarberry. That opening monologue had poured out of her. It had only taken one draft.

And Evan had given it away to their rival. Just like that.

"Though Scarberry, Nebraska, isn't far from Highway 80, you won't find it on a map. With a population of only thirteen hundred, most of its inhabitants are farmers . . ."

Lenny was done watching from a distance. Evan wasn't going to get away with this. She marched forward, hoping Claire was still behind her to witness it. Lenny wasn't pathetic and heartbroken anymore. She wasn't a tiny girl too small to contain her big feelings. She'd prove it. Right now.

With an audience.

Max finished his take. Adjusted his layers of silver cross necklaces. "Run it again," he directed to Chuck. Evan had his head down, jotting something in a journal. Lenny put her hand over the paper, smudging the red ink.

"What happened to authenticity, Evan?"

He pushed his glasses up. "Nice to see you."

"That was *my* monologue."

"Not like you were going to use it. Thought you were done with the show." So he wasn't denying it. Classy.

"That doesn't mean you can steal my scripts!" Her voice sounded shrill. Not nearly intimidating enough. She was still an angry Bambi.

"Lenny, honestly." Evan closed the notebook. There were white outlines around where *Odd Kids* stickers had been only a few days ago. He'd already ripped them off. "I didn't remember which of us handled that script. When Max asked me to do the writeup, it was so last-minute, I didn't even think twice."

Liar. Liar liar liar. She wrote *all* the scripts. He just made tweaks. He was rewriting history. How often had he done that?

"Why are you even here?" she demanded. "I thought Scarberry was too small-time for you? That aliens weren't *trending?*"

"That's changed. A girl is missing," he said. "I imagine you've heard."

Claire snorted. "As of *this morning.* Not like it's national news already."

There was no way they'd made it here that fast. Evan didn't look at her. He pushed up his glasses again. He was fidgeting a lot. Was he *scared?*

"Your friend Ashley shared a Missing poster on Instagram," Evan explained.

"What?"

He sighed and whipped out his phone. Showing her the profile of AshAsh_1989. She had a Taylor Swift lyric and SHS '26 in her bio. And her two recent pictures: one, a collage of photos of Bri Reed, and the other, a blurry picture of people in front of glowing lights. Lenny had to squint to recognize herself with Warren's beefy arms around her.

So Ashley Armes had tagged her in the photo last night. And Evan had been digitally stalking Lenny this whole time. Cool. *Awesome.*

"Looks like you've made a lot of new friends, Lenny," he added. "I'm so happy for you."

"So that's it? You came back because you're jealous? I don't even *like* that guy."

"*Max* decided to use his resources to help this town. The picture was just a lead."

Odd Kids was over, and he was still using her research to get ahead. Cool.

"You're not here to help," Lenny sneered. "You don't care about these people. This is about your ego."

"Okay, Lenora."

"Behind the tape," commanded Brian. He held a roll of red-splattered caution tape.

Evan gave her a smirk. She knew what he was thinking:

You don't have an ego at all, right, Lenny? This isn't some self-improvement mission for you, is it? Has it worked out? Have you discovered yourself now that I'm not dragging you down?

Claire grabbed Lenny's arm, leading her away. Empty bottles and cans rattled inside her backpack.

"He's an asshole. Don't let him bother you," Claire said.

Max Malitz had moved away from the van, still within bounds of the red tape, talking to two familiar faces. One wrinkled and furry with eyes that refused to face the same direction, and one equally wrinkled, with smudged-green eyeshadow and a cigarette on her lip.

So Evan just didn't steal her script. He tipped off his new show about her witness. The witness Evan didn't believe. He went inside the blood-splattered van, closing the doors. Hiding, like a coward.

"But you didn't vacate Scarberry," Max said to Susan. "Even if it was a risk to your personal safety?"

"I don't believe the fumigation bull," Susan said. "I don't believe the tornados anymore either. *Listen.* I don't think there is a missing girl. I *saw it.* This whole town is a cover-up for a government lab. You think all these people are *farmers?* Not a chance. Their little science experiment got loose last night. And they got everybody tryin' to round the thing back up. If you or me finds it? We'll just get our memory wiped and shipped back to where we came from. Then they'll put it back in their underground lab and run more tests on it."

Max nodded condescendingly. If his mind worked anything like Evan's, he was thinking about future subscribers' reactions, not about the woman in front of him. Or what she'd witnessed.

"Thank you, Susan," Max said. He swiped his hands under his chin, like he was cutting his throat. Chuck pointed the camera down. And just like that, Brian collected the poles holding up the red tape. Susan pulled Tilly away, grumbling.

Lenny and Claire ran up to her.

Susan tapped the end of the cigarette. Red embers glided to the ground.

"Why the long faces, loves?" she asked. "You look like you've seen a ghost. I can't be dead yet, am I?"

"I just heard what you told *Dark Unknown*," Lenny said, breathless. "You *saw* Old Lucky?"

She nodded erratically. "'Bout three a.m., it came creeping out the back door of my room. Its legs were folded like a kangaroo or some shit. It was all white except the hair, and there were little brown curly bits on top."

"What color were the eyes?"

"Blue. Piercing blue. Almost glowing. And it was wearin' *pajamas*. That's how I knew this was no wild thing. It's a *prisoner*. Been staying somewhere. Lab experiment. You get it?"

"What kind of pajamas?" Claire said, her voice thin. Like she was one syllable away from her vocal cords disintegrating.

Susan tilted her head back, as if asking the sky to help her remember. Then, satisfied, she said. "Pink. Pretty sure there were little butterflies on the bottom."

Claire let out a strangled breath. "Bri has PJs like that," she croaked.

"Bri?" Susan asked.

"She's the girl that's missing," Lenny told her.

Susan shook her head. "No girl. An *experiment*." She tossed her cigarette and dragged Tilly away, muttering something about skipping town before they wiped her memories.

Lenny had a million theories she could tack on a bulletin board, but the best one felt too dangerous to say out loud.

"Claire?" Lenny squeezed her hand again. "What are you thinking?"

Claire was frozen, eyes to the trampled grass in front of her. There was another can by her feet. But she didn't pick it up. She put her free hand to her chest like she was checking her own heartbeat.

"I think . . . Old Lucky isn't an alien," Claire whispered.

CHAPTER 36

CLAIRE

"Susan could have been confused," Lenny assured her. She was speeding down the dirt road. Her worried expression didn't match her arm full of colorful wristbands and neon manicure. They would be at the ranch in two minutes and Claire hadn't thought about what she would say to Aunt Maeve.

"So . . . Susan saw a big swan wearing my cousin's clothes?" Claire said, half laughing. Not that it was funny.

"She could have seen Bri and then saw Old Lucky and mixed up the two." Lenny sounded nothing like herself. Yesterday she'd gone on a whole rant about the people who were sure Mothman was really a barn owl.

"I know I seem like I'm totally freaking out," Claire said. "But I would still prefer you to be honest with me."

"I think . . ." Lenny talked slower than normal, like if she didn't say the right words in the right order she'd set off a booby trap. "There's something wrong with your cousin. Maybe she's turned into . . . one of them. Maybe everyone's reports have been so different because there's not just one Old Lucky."

"But why Bri?"

"To test the cancer?"

"So you think it *is* the government."

"Not necessarily. But the FBI is here. We know the chief has custody of one Old Lucky. Anyone could be involved. You're the only one I trust in this town."

Ouch.

Claire's saliva tasted sour. She didn't deserve Lenny's trust. Someday she would confess the truth. But after this was over, once they found Bri. Alive.

Aunt Maeve's strange words from that morning had a new meaning now.

Just as she was.

"Aunt Maeve knows," Claire said. "I thought she was too scared to recognize there was something wrong, but it's the opposite. She's known this whole time."

Lenny pulled into the dirt lot. Susan's vehicle was gone. Obviously. But Maeve's was still there.

Claire jumped out of the car. "I'm going to talk to her." *And make her listen.*

Lenny nodded. "Okay. Do you want backup?"

Claire's insides still burned like acid. Lenny was in this for the long haul. She had ditched the cameras days ago and had stayed a constant support. Claire didn't deserve it.

"Only if you want—

"I do."

So they marched inside together. The house had all the lights on but was too quiet. Claire knew it was empty even before she and Lenny checked all the rooms. The only thing they could hear was the creak of their own footsteps and the *clap-clap-clap* of shutters outside. On really windy days like this there wasn't a single spot in the house where you couldn't hear the shutters throwing a tantrum. Aunt Maeve never got around to fixing them. She was too set on fixing Bri.

"She's gotta be in the barn," Claire said.

They found the barn door cracked. There was no lock anymore. Claire wanted to pretend there was never one to begin with. That Maeve was simply a woman overwhelmed, not someone with anything to hide.

The old wood screeched as Claire yanked the door open.

Maeve had her back turned, facing a calf. She didn't acknowledge them, but the animal looked up at Claire, watching her, as if saying, *Finally, you're here.*

It had a wound on its side. Larger than the one Claire had seen. It was as big as a soccer ball, but Claire didn't get close enough to check for the strange purplish goo over it, because Aunt Maeve had just finished sticking the white gauze over the open flesh.

"Where's Bri?" Claire asked.

Maeve gave the cow a sad pat. There were others in the barn. Ten pairs of sad black eyes stared at them. All of them with bandages on their sides too.

"The chief will find her, hon." Maeve's words hardly sounded like reassurance.

"Is he going to find her alive, or will she have a *heart attack?*"

Claire sneered. Maeve winced. It didn't make Claire feel any better. "Why are you even trusting him?" she added. "'Cause you already knew, right? You knew he's been keeping Old Lucky?"

"This doesn't have to concern you," Maeve said. She faced them now. She looked like she had aged fifty years since that morning. Suddenly her red hair was overtaken by gray, freckles traded for wrinkles. Of course, nothing about her had actually changed. Claire just saw her for what she had been for years: old and tired and helpless.

"That's not fair," Claire said. "You've made me be responsible for everything, and now, all of a sudden, I'm too much of a kid to do anything?"

Maeve sank into a flimsy wooden chair. "I just thought at least one of us should have been spared."

"Spared from *what?*"

"The burden of knowing."

I'm already burdened. Claire had been trapped here, in this place that hated her so much. She had stayed for Maeve and Bri, who were determined to leave her out of the loop.

Maeve sighed and examined the scratches on her arms. She flexed her fingers, like she was testing to see if they were still working. Then she gave an unsure glance at Lenny.

"This can't go on the internet," Maeve said.

"It won't," Lenny promised. Claire wasn't sure if it was a lie or not. She didn't care.

Maeve nodded, tapped her scratched hand on her jeans. She seemed so . . . defeated. It only made Claire feel worse.

"Bri wasn't getting better. You remember how sick the

chemo made her. She was going to end up just like the others if I didn't do something. The chief, he told me he had an old family recipe. He gave it to Myra too late, but it could maybe help Bri. And it did. She was herself again. It was a miracle. That's what the doctors said. You remember that? Right? You *agreed*." She glanced at the dirt floor, and whispered to herself, "A miracle. A real miracle."

"What was the medicine?" Claire asked, voice flat.

"In the jam, hon," Maeve said. "She's had a tablespoon once a day."

"But it's not actually jam, is it?"

"No, honey," Maeve admitted. "It was blood."

Claire was the only one who mopped the kitchen floor. She called the plumber. She ordered novelty key chains. She begged the phone company for a payment extension every month. But she was never allowed to put away the jam. She could collect it from the chief, but it was Maeve who chose what would go in the fridge and what would go up to Bri's room. Maeve was the only one who gave Bri toast. Her PB&Js. Bri never made food for herself. Claire thought it was laziness. Or some mother-daughter bond she didn't understand.

Bri must have not actually known what Maeve was feeding her.

"*Explain,*" Claire sneered.

Maeve took a shaky breath and shifted in her chair. "The chief didn't show me . . . the source, until recently."

The source. Claire's skin prickled.

"Willy Lamb caught it, way back then," Maeve continued. "He kept it hidden. Kept it in the family, using its medicine.

The blood is special. It can heal. Maybe, if it's prepared right, it could mean immortality. He knew if anyone discovered it, game over. So, he kept it safe underground, out in Old Scarberry, and he recanted his story. He only told the chief about it right before he died. And the chief kept it fed and safe but didn't test any of its miracles until—well, until his wife.

"But he'd started Myra's treatment too late. When Bri got diagnosed, he offered to take care of us, but I still stupidly trusted Western medicine. I thought the doctors knew what they were doing." She rolled her eyes. "And then, well, we ran out of options. Lamb gave me the blood . . . But with all the land in Old Scarberry being bought up, the chief had to move the source. And . . . it's turned into a bit of a mess. But I didn't know what it'd do to her, honey. She started to feel weaker, sooner and sooner. She started to require a higher dosage. Then, early this summer, she came downstairs and her skin looked off. Too pale, too . . . stretched. She said her teeth hurt and there were . . ."

She closed her eyes, like remembering was painful. "There were too many of them in her mouth. I thought going cold turkey might help her. Like, flush it out of her system."

All the pieces were being threaded together. Bri's increasing mood swings. The vomiting. Maeve somehow becoming more protective after the cancer was gone.

"But she needed it," Maeve continued. "I could tell she needed it. It was the only thing that could kill the cancer. A few weeks ago, I saw this thing walking around the ranch. Taking a stroll. At first I thought the thing was one of your little pranks . . ."

"By thing," Lenny started, "you mean—"

"I thought it was Old Lucky. Yes. I never believed in it, but I never, *not* believed. I was more open. I guess. After Bri's miracle, anything was possible. But the thing I saw . . . it wasn't Old Lucky. It was her. She didn't seem to know who I was. Just demanded I let her go home. And I said—" Maeve gasped. Tears started flowing. "I said, you *are* home. Let's go inside. She was so *pale*. She practically reflected my flashlight. And her arms were all twisted. I knew it was because of the treatment. But when we stopped it, she would just feel sick again. The chief said he was working on a fix. But she was getting . . . aggressive."

She gave the calf behind her a mournful pat, hesitating to tell the next part.

"Maeve," Claire said, "she *killed* Jared."

"No. She didn't. Just scared him. He had a few scratches, sure, maybe enough for stitches, but he declined my offer to drive him to the hospital. I had to convince him to take the next day off. He was shaken. Obviously, I mean, she chased him all the way to Clawson's."

Not all the way. He'd taken a shortcut. Jared must have known about the portal. He'd known these grounds better than anyone.

"The chief made it in time," Maeve continued. "But Bri kept scratching and biting. We had to give her horse tranquilizers to put her to sleep. When she woke up, she was back to her old self. But Jared. Well. I'm sure it was deeply traumatizing for him, and . . . I guess his heart couldn't take it. The chief went to check up on him the next afternoon. Like I said. It was a heart attack, dear."

"We were *there* the next afternoon," Lenny pointed out. "No one was home."

Maeve sucked in her cheeks. "That's . . . that's all I know about that."

"The chief is lying. How do you know he didn't take Jared out to hide what he's done? How did you let it get this bad?" Claire's mouth was so dry, she expected her lips to crack open and bleed when she said it.

"She would always be fine once she woke up. But today . . . we couldn't find her. I was trying to *save* her," Maeve protested. "I didn't—I *couldn't* know what it was going to do. What it was going to turn her into."

"So what happened to Warren's mom, then?" Lenny asked. Thank God she did. Claire didn't know if she could get another word out without crying or punching Aunt Maeve square in the face. If she made one move, she was going to snap.

"The chief said she rejected it," Maeve explained.

"So, basically he murdered her?" Lenny said.

"Do you know how many patients are killed by chemo? Sometimes the cures hurt more than the disease. Myra didn't take to the blood as well as Bri. It was too late for her. But Bri's always been a fighter."

"Where is she?" Claire demanded, fighting the tears and the urge to claw an eye out. She needed to sit down, but all she could do was stand and shake and look into Aunt Maeve's eyes and try her best to find the woman who raised her. But she was never that woman, was she? Claire had raised herself.

"I don't know," Maeve admitted. "I told you. The chief said the creature tried to escape a few times. It was heading back to where it came from, some kind of hole in the earth. A . . . tear, I think he said. He thought Bri might go there too. It's near the schoolhouse in Old Scarberry, where he used to keep it."

Schoolhouse? Claire had no idea where that was. So many of those decrepit buildings were spaced between miles and miles of fields. She'd never bothered to explore all of Old Scarberry. She hadn't realized just how strange this place was until Lenny opened her eyes. She only saw it as hateful. Dangerous to Claire and Claire alone.

But now it had taken Jared. And Bri.

"Can you take us there?" Claire asked.

"I . . . no," Maeve answered. "I was blindfolded on the drive up. Not sure where it is."

Jesus Christ. Maeve was useless.

"Claire," Lenny said. "Wait a second. Think about it. *Hole in the earth*. Do you think Minnie Albert was right?"

Claire hated admitting the old liar was on to something. But it was right there. Hole in the earth. Old Scarberry.

That fucker had come from the mines.

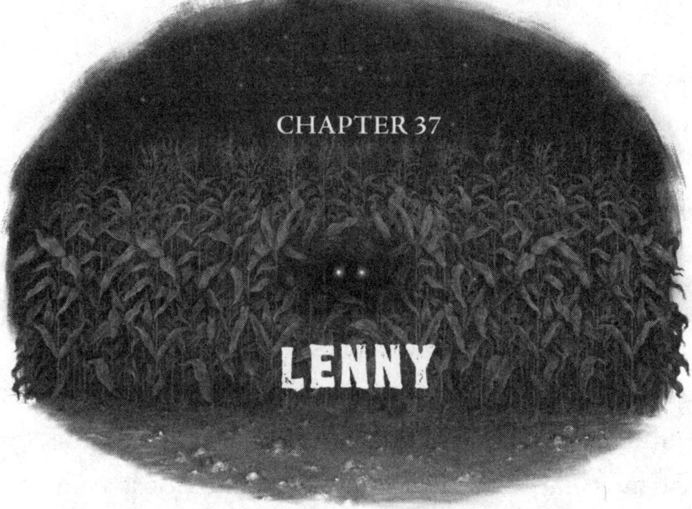

CHAPTER 37

LENNY

Evan would be drooling over all these maps. There were nearly a hundred of them rolled up in the back of the dusty closet. Hand-drawn sketches and official-looking printouts of roads and property lines. Most smelled like an old library. Claire said that was where her aunt had bought them.

If they could find the hole in the earth, they could find Bri. Unfortunately, none of the maps had any portals labeled.

"It's in Old Scarberry somewhere," Claire said. "We just gotta find the map of the closed mines."

Lenny helped Claire sift through them. Their search had made the previously organized gift shop look just as chaotic as Jared's ransacked trailer. Claire had seemed shaken since they'd left the barn, but she clearly didn't want to show it. And Lenny wouldn't be a shoulder to cry on unless asked.

Maeve's words played over and over in her head: *I thought it was one of your little pranks.*

Lenny didn't know what "pranks" was supposed to mean.

Warren was the one who'd set up all those speakers. He was the one pulling practical jokes. Not Claire. Still, Lenny's stomach turned over. She couldn't make this about her messy feelings. There was a missing girl she had to find. They needed to get to her before the FBI. Before *Dark Unknown*. Apparently, the girl was part monster. Which, yes, was a concern. But historically, monsters had always been less dangerous than people.

"I just don't know why Bri would run away," Claire said. She unfurled a map and stared at it for a second. It must have not had anything interesting, because she tossed it aside.

"Old Lucky probably just wants to go home," Lenny offered. "Maybe the blood transferred some kind of instinct to Bri? Or it's like a shared consciousness? It definitely rewrote her DNA."

"Kinda like cancer," Claire muttered. She unfurled a new map. "Found it."

Lenny grabbed UFO-shaped key chains and put them on the corners. The paper was yellowed, and the serif font looked fuzzy. Scarberry looked even flatter in map form. Every road made a nearly perfectly square grid. The red dots marked the locations of mine entrances.

There were seven of them, each corresponding to a range of dates. 1870–1878, 1886–1890, 1890–1901 . . .

Claire pointed to the one farthest from the others. Its last date read 1961.

They followed the GPS coordinates until the road ended and a sparse forest took over. They were miles beyond the abandoned observatory and Clawson's Field. Talk about the middle of nowhere.

"It should be a straight shot if we follow the train tracks," Claire said. "I guess when we find the schoolhouse we'll know we're close." So they continued on foot.

It was unbearably quiet. Even more so when Claire's phone stopped barking directions.

"Phone died," Claire reported.

Lenny checked her pocket. Hers wouldn't turn on either.

They had gone only half a mile when they saw the tape. Actual caution tape that you'd find at a crime scene. *Dark Unknown*'s crew and Evan were posted around the blood-splattered van, but Max wasn't performing another stolen monologue. His body language was all wrong. He was arguing with someone.

"What if we turn the cameras off?" Max was pleading.

"They're not working anyway, boss," Chuck muttered.

"No one is getting beyond this line," replied a female voice. Even and robotic. "For everyone's safety."

Lenny pulled Claire behind a tree to get a better look. The woman wore a sharp blazer, her hair slicked back into a bun. Agent Brenner. Beside her was a guy in a loud tie, holding a clipboard. They were surrounded by a chain-link fence, overgrown with weeds and white, boxy figures holding mechanical devices that looked eerily like EMF readers.

"Are those hazmat suits?" Lenny whispered.

They absolutely had to get through here.

Fast.

"Holy shit," Claire said. "I know that guy. The dude with the clipboard. He's been trying to make Maeve sell our land."

"What?"

"I mean, I hadn't talked to him, but she made it seem like he worked for some private real estate thing. Not the fucking government."

Just then, a shadow blocked their path.

Evan. He'd wandered away from the group as Max was arguing with the FBI agent.

"Out of my way," Lenny snarled.

"You don't want to go in there," Evan said.

He just *had* to beat her to it. He had to win.

"You can't tell me what to do anymore, Evan," she said, pushing past him.

He followed behind, babbling, "Listen. I heard some of them talking. There's crazy nuclear fission stuff going on. Like, unstable neutrons or protons or something. It's not safe."

Lenny stopped behind a gray, leafless oak. The forest was deader and deader, the closer they got to the chain-link fence. For once, Evan wasn't making things up for the show. Scarberry was contaminated, and the government's concern only proved that they were getting closer to the mine that birthed Old Lucky.

"We have to get in there," Lenny told him.

Evan nervously adjusted his glasses. "Look, Max is putting on a big show, but there's no way he's gonna push it. He won't even explore basements because he's allergic to mold. Even those government people are *scared*, Lenny. I guess they've been monitoring this place for a while. You know why half the town is abandoned? Because it was deemed *uninhabitable*. You said it right when we got here. That the air feels different. The second I got out of here, I felt like I could breathe again. I get back, my asthma's worse than ever. You can't get any footage anyway. The van's battery is dead. Our phones shut down. I don't think any of the government people's tech is working right now either. This thing is so unstable they can't even test it."

"We need to get past that tape," Lenny said.

"You can't."

"My cousin's really sick. She might be out here," Claire pleaded.

Evan shook his head. "They won't let you."

"We're not asking permission," Lenny said. "I'm going to do this *my* way. For *once*. It'd be a lot easier if you help distract them."

Evan sighed.

"I told you I had a gut feeling about this place," Lenny said. "Was I wrong?"

Evan sucked in a big breath, closed his eyes and put a palm to his forehead. Then, with a huff, he marched toward his new besties, *Dark Unknown*.

Crap. Was he going to blow their cover? Max went up to him. Lenny couldn't see Evan's lips, but whatever he said seemed to make Max worried. Suddenly, Evan was wobbling, clasping his chest. Max tried to grab his shoulder as he collapsed, body folding hideously into the grass.

Big Brian screamed. Agent Brenner called to her team to assist. It was a brilliant performance from a world-class liar.

This was the window they needed.

"Go," Claire whispered. They ran for it, weaving around the trees, just past the caution tape.

The two of them threw their backpacks over the other side of the fence and crawled up.

The second her feet hit the other side of the grass, the hair on Lenny's arms bristled.

"Do you feel that?" Lenny asked. Claire nodded and they ran until they were breathless. The woods had thinned out, and all the trees were bare, like it was the dead of winter. The grass was brittle. Crunching under every step.

They were getting closer to it. Whatever *it* was. And all of Lenny's anxieties were dialed up to one hundred. Evan's fake fainting spell wouldn't hold them off forever. What if Evan still ratted them out?

What if the portal made her lungs collapse? What if she spontaneously combusted?

What if Maeve hadn't really told them everything?

One of your little pranks . . .

The track started to curve, but Claire said they ought to keep straight. Now they were off the path, but there was plenty of room for them to walk side by side. Lenny's hands were shaking. Claire's didn't seem to be. She marched on, determined.

Lenny stopped and Claire kept ahead. It took a few seconds for her to notice Lenny had fallen behind.

Claire glanced back. "Are you coming?"

"What did your aunt mean, about the pranks?"

Claire's mouth hung slightly open. She tensed up, her grip choking the strap of her backpack. "Um. It's a long story. Maybe after we find Bri . . ."

"Why not now?"

Claire was still five yards away, and she didn't come any closer, like she was afraid Lenny was going to bite her.

"'Cause . . ." Claire looked at her feet. And that cruel voice of reason rose to the surface of Lenny's brain. *If she has nothing to hide, she would have answered right away. If she has nothing to hide, she wouldn't look so scared.*

"I haven't figured out the best way to tell you," Claire said.

"Tell me what?"

Claire took a deep breath. "I sent you that video, okay?"

"I know."

Lenny had first thought it the day she arrived. Though, she didn't know the exact moment it stopped being a theory and became a fact. Claire grimaced. Lenny thought Claire would be relieved now that her secret was revealed. But that wasn't all of it. It couldn't be. Because Claire looked so frightened.

"It was fake," Claire said.

"What?"

The woods were so quiet. She waited for Claire to fill the silence. To say something else that undid those last words. Because . . . no.

That made zero sense.

"I used a 3-D model and motion-tracked it to the barn. I thought if a big YouTube channel posted about the ranch, we'd get more customers," Claire said.

"So, all of this . . ." Lenny started. "Just to promote your family's business?"

Yes. That was her plan all along. And it worked. Because Lenny didn't know the difference between gut feelings and gullibility. She believed every convenient lie she was told. She had believed aliens existed. She had believed Evan knew what was best for her. She had believed she'd be happy once she went viral. She had believed she was straight for eighteen years.

"Not all of it was a lie," Claire said. "Just the video . . . and the speakers you found. That first night, you guys heard edited cow noises. But the rest was all true. I didn't think any of this would end up being real, and I didn't think that I would end up . . . caring about you."

Lenny's guts flipped inside out. Maybe it was because they were closer to the original portal and maybe it was because the Great Big Truth finally smacked her in the face. Evan had exploited their fans' desire to believe and Claire had exploited Lenny's.

Apparently liars were Lenny's type.

"Since I was a little kid," Lenny started, "I've had the same nightmare. I'm trying to find this thing, buried in the snow at Reed Ranch. And I always wake up before I can get to it. I don't know what it is. But I know it'll make me happy when I find it. This morning, I didn't dream at all. I thought it was because I finally beat the riddle. I finally figured out where my happiness was buried. I thought that was *you*."

"I'm sorry," Claire said, voice breaking.

Lenny knew the truth now: there was no one authentic left on Earth.

"Fuck you," Lenny spat.

She took a step back. Then another, then another, until she was certain her knees weren't about to give out. She started to run. Though she didn't remember what direction they came from; she knew she just had to get away, away, away.

Claire called after her, but Lenny was too fast, hopping over fallen logs.

This whole trip replayed in tiny vignettes in her mind. How devastated she was when Evan had left her here. How powerful she'd felt when she thought she didn't need him. The warmth of the lights in the sky, the searing pain in her hands when she'd touched the purple goo. Did it ever mean anything?

What would have happened if she'd gone along to Arizona with Evan in the first place? If she'd called off the break? She'd thought Claire was the special thing buried in the dream snow, when all along she was the ice in the way.

Lenny wiped her nose with her sleeve. It was stained red. Great. Now, she was *bleeding*, too. The universe was laughing at her, making rock bottom extra theatrical. She remembered Claire telling her not to tilt her chin up, so she did it out of spite. And she saw it. There, on the hill, redbrick peeking out from the trees. A building. Clearly abandoned. It looked ready to crumble at any moment. Like the brick was simply giving up. The grass around it was gray.

Was this the spot where Willy Lamb and the chief had held Old Lucky? Lenny stepped closer, careful not to crack a twig under her sneakers. This victory ought to be hers. Not Claire's. Not Evan's. She'd still solve this. She'd rescue the missing girl and expose the cover-up and her name would be on the news and she'd have her own Wikipedia entry and once she earned her dream the nightmares would stop forever.

The door was already wide open. Lenny stepped in. Blood poured from her nose and onto the concrete floor. *Plop. Plop. Plop.* The building reminded her of a one-room schoolhouse. There was a flimsy folding table toward the center and a few cardboard boxes. No sign of Bri—monster or girl. Lenny leaned over a hole in the back corner to find stairs going straight into darkness. She tried her phone's flashlight, but it didn't turn on. Crap. She was looking around, considering her options, when she saw, on the table, a kerosene lantern and matches.

Whoever was here last was used to no electricity.

Lenny lit the lantern and started down the stairs.

CHAPTER 38

CLAIRE

Claire was alone in the woods. She had always felt alone. That bit wasn't new. The sun lazily slid towards the horizon. It'd be dark soon. Her situation was not just pathetic but *dangerous*.

Lenny was alone too. There was a chance she'd made it back to her car without being seen, but Claire hadn't heard the engine start up. There was no sound but her own breathing. There weren't even any birds, any chattering of chipmunks. Animals knew better than to be here.

Ever since they'd crossed the fence, the air had felt electrified. It was as if the molecules around her decided to stop following any rules. Claire couldn't stand it. It made her thoughts feel even more dire. She was falling down a rabbit hole, and she needed someone to come to her aid with a strong rope and a promise that she would be okay.

Claire pulled out her phone. It wouldn't turn on. Shit. She trudged on until she found her way out of the woods. But there was no mine in sight. And it had been closed for over sixty years. How would she even know when she found it?

It could work like the tire portal: you didn't know you were there until you were launched into the sky.

Or *elsewhere*.

There was a truck parked at the edge of the trees with a trailer hooked to the back. It was the kind used to transport cows. She had a feeling there wasn't a cow inside.

Warren was in the driver's seat. He looked shocked to see Claire, but not very concerned. He stepped out, and Claire almost punched him.

"Don't give me that look," Warren said.

"Right. You're just following orders."

"Yes. I am. Yours." Warren sighed and glanced at the trailer woefully. Claire could barely make out its contents through the thin slits in the metal. There was something big and pale inside, and it wasn't moving.

"I'm letting it loose," Warren said. "Even if that means my dad kills me. You're right. This thing doesn't deserve to be stuck here. I'm tired of being . . . comp . . . con . . ."

"Complicit?"

"Yeah."

"Congrats on the character development. Where's my cousin?"

Warren sighed. "I don't know. My dad was looking for her."

"So why are you here?"

"He calls the mines Hallowed Grounds. I thought he was insane, but now it makes sense. Thought I'd send Old Lucky back to another dimension or wherever it came from. I got this far and my truck died."

Yep. They were close. Her phone was still deceased. The buzzing in her ears hadn't let up.

"You might want to back up," Warren said.

Claire stood her ground. Warren opened the trailer. Old Lucky was folded on the hay-littered floor. One brown eyeball stared at them, but the creature didn't get up. Something about it reminded her of a cow. Big enough to kill you if it wanted to. But it didn't want to. Hardly the vicious thing that Willy Lamb described meeting. Maybe Willy was confused. Maybe Minnie misremembered.

"He created another one, you know. Bri's been turning into that thing," Claire said.

Warren glanced at her, mouth open. He had no clue. He really didn't know anything. Chief Lamb had kept everyone in this town as ignorant as possible. "What . . . what do you mean?"

"Jared didn't see old Lucky. He saw *Bri*. Your dad gave her his special cure, and it changed her."

"That's . . . so fucked-up."

Okay, here went nothing. Claire took a deep breath. "Before she passed, did your mom have any . . . side effects?"

Warren glared at her. "What are you asking me? If she grew fangs?"

"I mean . . . kind of?"

Warren scoffed. "She wasn't pleasant, Claire. But it wasn't her fault. The chemo made her awful. I hated being around. The house was fucking freezing, and there was no electricity half the time and she never left the big chair in the living room. She was pissed off and irritable and *wasting away*."

Oh fuck.

Oh fuck.

"She told me she was ready to go," he continued. "That she made peace with it. But my dad wouldn't just let her die. I was relieved when she went to stay at the hospital again. Even though I knew she was going to die. When it finally happened, all I could think was *Thank God*. But that makes me sound like a terrible person."

"You're not a terrible person."

Not any worse than Claire.

"C'mon!" Warren called to the beast in the trailer. He banged on the doors. "Let's go." He pulled something from his pocket. A syringe.

"What's that?"

"Tranquilizer. My dad had a fuck ton stashed in his gun cabinet for when people call in coyote sightings. I probably won't need to use it."

Old Lucky's head poked out of the trailer, followed by its long neck and then its body. As much as "setting it free" felt like the right idea, she had to tell Warren her theory. Even if he still hated her for hating him. Even if it hurt.

"Wait, Warren—"

A scream rang out from behind them.

It sounded like Lenny.

In her future Wikipedia article, there would be a whole section about the fears Lenny had faced: lightning, leafy vegetables, car washes, her own sexuality. This moment, right here, would affirm that she was totally over her fear of the dark.

The lantern wasn't doing much to illuminate the basement stairs. She caught the white streaks of cobwebs, parts of the wall that were crumbling. She should have kept the light down so she could watch her feet. That way she wouldn't have tripped on the last step. She yelped on her way down, landing on her knee. Rough concrete scraped against her unprotected flesh. God, it *hurt*. She resisted the instinct to check for blood. Her shirt was already covered in it. She'd come out of this battered and bruised and triumphant.

Hopefully.

She rose to her feet. Grimacing through the pain.

"Bri?" Lenny called. No answer. She shouldn't have expected one, but it would have been comforting to know she wasn't alone in there. She slowly stepped into the room, knee stinging with each movement. As grateful as she was for the lantern, it didn't let her see much more than five feet in front of her. Her foot brushed up against something soft: a bed. Well, *a mattress,* sitting on the floor. There were moldy-looking pillows. Something shiny.

Chains.

So this was where the Lambs had been hiding Old Lucky. Meaning the portal had to be close. *Bri* had to be close. Besides the chains, this room didn't look much like a prison. It didn't look like a lab either. There was a little shelf, with cups and plates stacked haphazardly. Books. More candles.

Someone had been living here. *Someone,* not *something.*

Maybe a squatter had taken over after Chief Lamb brought Old Lucky home? Lenny shined the light on the walls, illuminating an array of family photos. One with a mom, a dad, and a baby, all of them dressed in white. And a school picture of a little boy, too small to fill out the frame. Then the same boy a little older, proudly holding a fish as his father stood proudly next to him. She'd recognize that mustache anywhere. Chief Lamb. Meaning the little boy was Warren, and that woman was his late wife. Why did Chief Lamb bother to hang these up? He couldn't have possibly spent that much time here.

She ripped a photo from the wall and stuffed it into her pocket. There, evidence. She stepped into another room, pushing open the flimsy wooden door. Lenny nearly jumped out of her skin.

A creature stared up at her. Long neck jutted forward, head

resting on the ground. Four arms were limply hanging from the wall.

Lenny covered her mouth with her hands, stifling a scream.

It wasn't *breathing.* She stepped forward, lanternlight shining on its see-through flesh. Purple veins connected organs that looked like rotten fruit. There were wounds all over its body, shades of yellow and green and black. Its round eyes were open but unseeing.

Old Lucky was dead.

But this was it. This was really it. Twelve feet tall, just like they said. Four arms. Red eyes. Trapped in this basement for God knew how long. How would she explain this to her twelve-year-old self, who'd gazed at the Scarberry Lights above her bed every night?

You get everything you've ever wanted, she'd say to kid Lenny, *and it's awful.*

Her skin prickled. Fresh blood slid to her lips. She knew, even before she heard the creak of the stairs, that she wasn't alone anymore. She turned around and called out, "Hello?" No answer, but she heard another thump on the stairs. Footsteps.

She searched for another exit. The next door led to buckets swarming with flies. Was this supposed to be a bathroom? There were no other doorways. No way out. *Stupid, stupid, stupid.* Why did she come in here alone? They weren't the only ones looking for Bri. The FBI was in Scarberry. Chief Lamb was a wild card at this point. And there was a good chance, if they found Bri, she wouldn't be herself.

Lenny had to take precautions. She searched for a weapon. Nothing but cans of soup and dusty folding chairs. She backed up against the wall, next to the moldy mattress, wishing she could die anywhere but this dark basement.

A form came into focus. It took Lenny a moment to register what she was seeing. Not a monster at all but a girl wearing a butterfly-printed pajama set. Her short curls were drenched. Beads of sweat ran down her forehead.

"Bri?"

She was panting. Eyes wide and terrified. The poor girl looked like she'd been through hell.

"Hey. It's okay. You're all right," Lenny said, trying to console the both of them. She lowered the lantern, gave her lungs permission to work again. "Let's go home, okay?" Bri nodded but still didn't speak.

Lenny led the way upstairs. They'd both feel better once they were out of the dark. Bri followed close behind, but she walked in a stilted way, dragging her feet like her bones were too heavy. Once out of the brick building, Lenny could see just how pale Bri was. Her pajamas were filthy. Had she been hiding in the woods all day?

"Your nose is bleeding," Bri said quietly.

Lenny wiped her face again. "Yeah. It does that . . ."

"When something bad is gonna happen," Bri added.

"That's just for the show," Lenny said. "Evan made it up. He made up a lot of things."

Bri stared at the ground and shook her head.

"Let's go home, okay?" Lenny said again. Honestly, she thought, Bri should go to a hospital. She had deep bruises under her eyes and had apparently spent the last few nights as werelien. But home seemed like a good place to start.

Bri didn't react. She stared past Lenny.

"Let me take you home," Lenny said.

Tears welled up in Bri's eyes. "I can't find it."

Oh. The toxic "medicine" must have made her confused. Lenny's heart broke for her.

Lenny offered her hand. "I'll help you."

"*No!*" Bri jolted back. Folding her arms against her stomach like Lenny had punched her in the gut.

"It's okay. I know you're scared—"

Crack.

Bri's neck sprung back, her head tilted at an impossible angle, so all Lenny could see was the underside of her jaw. Her body stiffened. Her mouth stretched into a scream, but all that came out was a strained gurgle.

"Bri?"

Her two front teeth tumbled into the dead grass. Then went the rest, one by one, making room for new, sharp fangs. Her fingers quivered as they elongated into bony talons. New vertebrae tore through the transparent skin of her spine. She crumpled to the ground.

Run! screamed a voice in Lenny's head.

But she didn't look away as Bri's flesh rippled and bent. Face elongating, eyes shifting apart, neck pulling tighter and tighter. Until, finally, Bri shivered and went limp.

For a split second, Lenny thought the girl wasn't breathing. That she died, just like that. Then Bri sprang to life, snarling.

Oh *shit.*

Lenny backed away. But she tripped on a rock and went down. She'd already messed up her knee, and now her ankle was on fire. She tried to stand, tried to run, but Bri was so close. Lenny knew no matter which direction she went, Bri would catch up.

Bri circled her, slowly. She looked a lot like the thing in the barn, but smaller, even thinner. There were no chains to hold her down. Her partially painted claws were primed to slash. Her eyes were piercing blue—human eyes with human irises and pupils and lashes. Lenny tried to appeal to the part that was human.

"Please, don't! I want to help you!"

Bri bared her overlapping rows of jagged teeth.

So this was how she'd go. Killed by the claws of her own subscriber. Poetic.

Dark liquid spewed out of Bri's Muppety mouth. Lenny rolled out of the way. The grass next to her was a deep purple now, hissing as smoke rose from the goo.

Lenny always sympathized with ghosts. They remained trapped in their worst moments. Unable to move on. She had vowed to never become one. So that meant avoiding an extra-tragic demise or leaving the mortal plane with unfinished business. She couldn't die now. She couldn't haunt Scarberry, Nebraska, forever.

She screamed again. Evan had advised her not to scream when the cameras were rolling. It always blew out the mic, and it wasn't part of her persona. Lenny was supposed to be the Girl Who Used to Be Afraid.

But now she screamed her head off, hoping the whole world heard her.

CHAPTER 40

CLAIRE

Another scream. Claire felt it rattle inside her chest cavity.

Lenny. It was definitely her.

The beast in the trailer leaped out and marched toward the trees. But Claire's only thought was: *Lenny*.

Lenny, Lenny, Lenny.

She'd already broken Lenny's trust. She wasn't going to let anything else happen to her.

Claire sprinted toward the sound, not bothering to look back.

Another scream, fit for a horror movie. *No no no no no*. She pushed her legs to their limits. Her lungs begged for a break. But she didn't stop until she reached a clearing. Lenny was on the ground, grimacing as she tried to scoot backward. A creature stood over her. It wore pajamas and had patches of three-inch-long curls.

Bri.

Well—almost.

Those were her eyes, but they were in the wrong spot. Her nose had recessed to slits in the middle of her face, her mouth was as wide as her head, dripping dark drool onto the butterfly pajama set she'd gotten for Christmas. She was zeroed in on Lenny, tilting her two-foot-long neck. There was a horrifying cracking sound, as if every movement broke her bones.

Someone grabbed Claire's elbow, yanking her back. She whirled around, prepping to pull a punch. But it was just Warren, out of breath, and holding one of those cartoonishly large syringes. He handed it to Claire and then pulled out another one. "You distract her," he whispered, "I'll try to catch her from behind." Then, before she could respond, he backed out of the clearing.

Claire cautiously inched toward Bri. If Bri went after her, oh well. She'd make up for her lies to Lenny. And she'd find a way to save her family.

"Hey!" Claire called. No response. She looked around for something to throw, hoping for a rock maybe. Nope, nothing to see here. She yanked off a cowboy boot and tossed it. Though she didn't make contact with Bri, she did get her attention.

Bri's head twisted all the way around like an owl's, but with a hideous cracking noise. Claire wanted to gag. But she couldn't. Not yet. Lenny was still dangerously close. She had to save them both somehow.

Claire had many jobs in her eighteen years.

Today, she would be a distraction.

Warren was only inches behind Bri now, brandishing the syringe. Claire held hers behind her back. She was shaking so hard her teeth were chattering.

Claire started to whistle, doing her best impression of Old Lucky. Imitation was supposed to be the highest form of flattery, but Bri didn't look very flattered at all. She growled and let out an ear-shattering screech. At least now Bri had forgotten about Lenny.

Bri wobbled toward Claire. It was like her joints weren't quite secure. Her body wasn't pleased to be pulled in all these new directions.

Lenny stood up. She wiped blood from her mouth but otherwise looked unharmed. She stared at Claire, not with contempt but fear. Claire mouthed, *Run,* but Lenny didn't move.

As Bri got closer, Claire could hear her strained breath. She was wheezing, just like that dark week in the hospital when her cold turned into pneumonia and all her doctors recommended they prepare for the worst.

There was another pop, and a crack, and Bri's huge mouth opened into a perfect circle, those many rows of teeth rotating around, faster and faster, like an electric toothbrush. Warren wasn't going to get there in time. Claire had to do it herself.

With one swift move, she stabbed the syringe into Bri's abdomen. She shrieked in agony. The teeth halted, and she went down, neck first.

Claire caught her, guiding her convulsing body onto the grass. *Please, please, please be okay,* she silently begged.

Bri's eyes closed. Her twisted spine shuddered, vertebrae shifting under her pajamas. Her neck shortened inch by inch. Claire could hear the horrific squelch of Bri's organs rearranging. She grabbed Bri's hand, shrinking smaller by the second. Then, after a minute of agony, Bri looked mostly like Bri again. She still didn't open her eyes, but her breathing had slowed, like she was asleep.

Warren knelt beside Claire, mouth agape.

"I swear, I had no idea . . ." he muttered.

"It's okay," Claire said. "It's not your fault."

If Warren hadn't been here, this would have gone differently. If she didn't have that syringe, maybe her cousin would've taken a chunk out of her. Maybe Bri would have gone for the kill.

Claire looked up at Lenny, who was eyeing a crop of dead trees to her right, hands on her hips. "You all right?"

Lenny nodded. Though her knee and her face were covered in dried blood.

"What about the other one?"

"I let it loose," Warren said. "It'll find its way home."

"And the one before that?"

"Huh?"

Lenny nodded toward the crumbled brick building behind her. "I found a dead one in the basement," she said. "Your dad's experiments must have killed the original Old Lucky your grandpa found."

She pulled a slip of paper from her pocket and handed it to Warren.

He glanced at it for a split second and looked up at Lenny, mouth agape. "Where'd you get this?" Claire got a quick glance at it before Warren shoved it into his pocket. It looked like a family photo. She recognized kindergarten-age Warren, with his missing front teeth.

"It was in the basement," Lenny explained. "It's like a bunker.

There's old food and a shit bucket, chains by a mattress. Looks like there was a prisoner in there."

Lenny's eyes flicked to Claire. Was she thinking the same thing? Maybe. Either way, Claire felt like she owed it to Warren. Even if the idea sounded unhinged to say out loud. The truth had to be worth it.

"Warren," Claire said, trying to keep her voice even. "You said your dad tried to save your mom with his cure, but what if she didn't die in the hospital? What if he took her out here instead, but he got nervous when more land got bought up in Old Scarberry?"

"Then he brought her to live in your barn," Lenny finished. "So she'd be close by."

"You think that thing is my mom?" Warren laughed disbelievingly.

"She could have been trapped in the creature's form after taking the blood for too long."

"There was a funeral," Warren said. "No. No way."

"Did she have brown eyes?" Lenny asked.

Warren blinked at her, then gasped like he had been underwater. "This is so fucked. I let it out of the trailer. I didn't even think . . . oh my God. My dad wouldn't let me see her in the hospital. How could he let this happen?"

"Letting go is hard," Lenny said. "Some people will do anything to avoid moving on."

Warren made a strangled choking sound. "What the fuck," he whispered.

"C'mon," Claire said, putting her arm around him. "Maybe she hasn't found the portal yet."

* * * * * * * * * * * *

They carried Bri to Warren's truck, locking her in the trailer, just in case. Maybe if she never drank any more of the blood, she could stay herself. Even if that meant the cancer came back in full force.

Warren pointed them in the direction he had watched "Old Lucky" run off to. Lenny limped ahead. Since when was she limping? Shit. Claire ran up to her.

"Are you okay?"

"Yeah. I just rolled my ankle," Lenny muttered.

"Guys," Warren said. He stepped towards the dead trees. Right as Claire looked in that direction, her eyes started to burn. She saw a white neck twist to look at them. But there was something more too: the air was wavy. Shimmering. This was it: the tear in the earth. The portal. The source.

"Wait!" Warren called, and ran up to the pale beast. Claire couldn't hear what Warren said to his mom, but she saw whatever was left of Mrs. Lamb gently hold his cheek with a talonless claw. Their foreheads touched for a moment, and then, they broke apart. Mrs. Lamb headed past rotted trees and Claire and Lenny followed.

Here, the forest was gray as ash. Beyond the dead leaves and skeletal bushes lay a hole in the ground, about half the diameter of her house. Whatever Scarberrians did to close the mine didn't work for long. The air shimmered above it like the road on a hot day. Claire could feel the hair stand up on her neck. Lenny held her nose, checking for more blood.

A pale beast, which was once a woman, wandered toward

the open wound on the ground, letting out little whimpers and bopping up and down. So this was home—or, at least, the passage to home.

The three of them stood, squinting at the light. Claire rested her hand on Warren's shoulder.

The beast stepped over the edge and the old mine burst to life. It was as if every molecule reflected upon itself. A million little rainbows hovered in the air, sharp and dazzling. So bright, Claire knew she ought to have averted her eyes, but she didn't dare look away. She knew she would never see anything like this again. The beast floated above it, pearly skin shimmering with colors Claire had never seen before.

And then she was floating too. Her feet lifted above the ground, and her jacket, her hair, started to reach towards the mine. She'd let go of Warren. Without a tether, she was being sucked into it. Before she could panic, Lenny found her hand. She had the other one gripped to a tree.

The light collapsed.

The portal was gone, and so was its intended traveler.

Gravity turned back on as if nothing had happened. Claire's feet hit solid ground. Her ears popped, and the heaviness in her chest eroded. She sucked in a big breath. And another. It tasted like heaven. She knew the air in Scarberry had been less than ideal, but she thought that was because of dusty crops and old buildings. Now, though, it was *pure*. Was this what she had been missing her whole life?

"I'm. I . . . I need a second," Warren said. "I'll meet you guys at the truck."

"Okay," Claire agreed. He took off.

Her heart broke for Warren. Claire couldn't believe what they had witnessed. And she certainly couldn't believe that Lenny was still holding her hand. It was bony, and her little metal rings were digging into Claire's skin, but she didn't want to let go.

"I'm sorry for lying," Claire said. "I want to say that's not like me, but it's what I did. It was wrong to bring you here. You're allowed to be mad. Just please don't sue us."

Lenny cracked a smile. "I don't regret coming."

There were footsteps behind them. Warren had come back, Claire figured. She turned to face him.

The chief stood ten feet away, holding a gun pointed right at them.

This was how things ended for girls who pretended they were invincible.

Lenny should have seen it coming. She'd thrown away her safety net when she'd stopped following the script others had written for her. But she'd rather go out like this: authentically.

The chief's eyes were bulging. He looked like a man possessed, and Lenny wished that was the case. It would be a lot cooler to be murdered by a ghost.

"You don't need to do this," Claire told the chief. She stepped back, one, two, three steps, taking Lenny with her. They were still holding hands, and Lenny didn't want to ever let go. She was afraid that if she did, Claire would float up to the stratosphere, never to be seen again.

"Put the gun down. Please." Somehow Claire's voice sounded even. She was brave. She'd had a lifetime of practicing her bravery, and Lenny had only been trying it out for a few days.

Chief Lamb's lip quivered into something resembling a

smile, but he didn't say anything. He wasn't really planning on killing them, or he would have by now. Or delivered a villain monologue at least. But he didn't say a word. The clearing was quiet, aside from the incessant buzzing of Lenny's phone in her pocket. Of course it was back on; when the portal closed, the air had stopped feeling strange. Her nose stopped bleeding.

At least she could check out her notifications before she got murdered.

The chief was breathing violently, his thick chest moving up and down too quickly. He seemed unsure, but the inhuman rage in his eyes didn't make Lenny feel safe. He was waiting on one of them to make the next move. What did he expect them to do? What *should* they do? Plead for mercy? Try to escape? Would he be able to hit them if they ran?

Claire still had the syringe in her hand. She held it behind her back. Was she planning on using it? There couldn't be much tranquilizer left after stabbing Bri with it.

"You'll just go to prison," Claire said, taking another step forward. She let go of Lenny's hand. Her negotiation skills were amazing, but every step Claire took made Lenny want to scream.

Claire had saved her. From the attack, and from herself. And now she was staring down the barrel of a gun. Lenny had to do something. She couldn't just freeze up. She couldn't let their fate be determined by this *asshole*.

"Think about it," Claire continued. "You'll leave your son without anybody."

Could Warren hear them from the truck? Lenny thought

about screaming for help, but her vocal cords weren't cooperating.

"Because of *you*," the chief spat. "You killed his mother."

"Respectfully? Your wife was already long gone. There wasn't any part of her left anymore."

He shook the gun manically. "No. No! I gave her immortality! You've destroyed something you don't understand."

"So now you're gonna kill us? Think about it. Scarberry talks," Claire reminded him. "Everyone is going to find out."

Lamb narrowed his gaze. There was a click as he turned off the safety. "No, they won't."

"People will be looking for us. They'll notice," Lenny said, finding her voice.

Lenny's phone chirped with a text message. That was the notification she had set for Maria. There was another one, from her mom. A buzz for Instagram. All her family and followers and friends, all blurring together. Asking, begging for an update. Everyone wanted to know what was going on with Lenora Gilson. And if she was killed right here, they would never know who she really was.

That's when she got an idea.

"Maeve knows the truth," Claire said.

Good. *Keep him talking.* Lenny needed just a few more seconds.

"Doesn't matter," the chief said. "They'll always believe me. You know, I wouldn't even need to pull the trigger myself? I have this whole town on my side. You, *you* wouldn't make a difference." His eyes flicked to Lenny. "But this one is a liability."

That was when Warren peeked out from the trees. He stopped short when he saw the gun.

"Dad, what the hell?" he gasped.

"Get out of here," the chief growled.

Okay. This could work. With Warren here, they had better odds.

"No," Warren said in a small voice. "Are you crazy? Put the gun down. You're not . . . you're not a murderer."

"*They're* the murderers!" the chief shouted.

"What are you even talking about?" Warren shouted back at him. "Mom was already gone! She told us she wanted to die and you didn't let her!"

"She didn't believe there was a way. I didn't lose hope. This was for all for you, Warren. To have your mother back. I did what I had to do to protect us. That old man was going to hunt down your mother. Sometimes you have to get your hands dirty."

It took a second for his words to click in Lenny's brain, but Claire caught on immediately.

"I fucking knew it," Claire sneered. "You killed Jared."

Chief Lamb gritted his teeth. He wasn't planning on anyone putting it together. He kept the gun steady.

"He was already suspicious," Claire said. "Then he saw Bri that night and you went to his house to make sure he wouldn't talk."

"Life is messy, kids. Especially when you stick your noses in other folks' business."

"But you keeping Old Lucky is what got your wife sick in the first place!" Claire shouted. "If you and your fucking dad weren't so greedy, this town wouldn't be killing us."

"Dad?" Warren asked, horrified. "Is that true?"

With Lamb's focus shifted to his son, Lenny made her move. She pulled her phone from her pocket and for the first time that day, she went on social media. She went right to the livestream button and framed the chief in the center of the shot. His face was in profile, but there was still the gun, pointed at the lens.

Loyal *Odd Kids* followers joined the stream immediately, flooding the chat with comments and hearts. First it was a few hundred. Half a second later, a few thousand. They probably expected on-the-road updates. Lenny and Evan playing relationship games and casually ranking their favorite ghost stories. Nope, they were getting a Real Live Attempted Murder. The sponsors were going to hate it.

Warren stomped toward his dad. "Is she right? Is that the reason why everything's gone to shit?"

"No. No," the chief said. "I was going to save them all. I just needed more time . . ."

"You should have quit after what happened to Mom. Why didn't you just quit?"

"I . . . can't," the chief said.

Chief Lamb's gaze went back to Lenny and Claire. He raised an eyebrow when he noticed Lenny's phone.

"Smile!" Lenny said. "You're on camera!"

Lamb rolled his eyes. "Please. I'll bury that phone with your bodies."

"That's not going to do much good when six thousand people have already seen it."

"Dad!" Warren said, inching closer to Chief Lamb. He was an arm's length away now. "Just drop it. Okay? It's over."

"You're full of shit," Lamb said, uneasily.

"It's nine thousand now. Ten thousand. Eleven . . ." Lenny turned the phone around and gave a peace sign to the camera. She switched it back to Lamb just in time to catch his jaw go slack. His eyes flicked back and forth between them all.

Then he ran.

He wasn't watching where he was going until it was too late. When the portal folded in on itself, it had left a massive crater. Instead of floating up into a prism of light, Chief Lamb went straight down, screeching the whole way. There was a thud as his body landed.

Warren screamed. Claire covered her mouth and looked at Lenny with disbelief.

Lenny limped toward the mine. Each step was agony. She leaned over the edge, pointing her phone toward the bottom. In the shadows, it was hard to see much, but there was a tiny shimmer of a badge down there. It was moving. The chief groaned. He tried—and failed—to rise to his feet. Lenny let the camera linger on the hole in the earth for a second, but after a few moments, when it was clear the chief wasn't going to say "You meddling kids" or anything, she ended the stream.

Warren ran over and looked into the hole. "I'm sorry," he choked. Lenny wasn't sure if that was for them or his dad. But then he looked at Claire, and added. "I didn't know. I didn't think he would ever—"

Claire stopped him. "It's all right."

"Do you guys want to take Bri home? I'll stay here and"—he laughed weakly—"call the cops, I guess?"

CHAPTER 42

CLAIRE

Bri was still asleep in the horse trailer. Her skin was see-through, but her neck was almost normal, and her limbs were all facing the right way. Her mouth was small again, with pink, *human* lips.

They carried her out of the woods, going around the train tracks to avoid the FBI's quarantine zone. Lenny held onto her torso, and Claire took her legs. Bri weighed nothing at first, but as her bones shifted under her pajamas she got heavier. Finally, they reached the car, sweaty and exhausted.

After buckling the still-sleeping Bri into the backseat, Lenny started the *Silver Bullet*. "Where are we going?" Lenny asked. "Back to the ranch?"

"Yeah, unless you have any better ideas," Claire said.

Lenny pulled forward, following the dirt road that ran along the train tracks. The trees gave way to the weathered brick of Old Scarberry. Claire rolled down the window. She couldn't get enough of the fresh air. Her phone vibrated with a text alert. She ignored it.

"So," Claire began. "How are you feeling?"

"Well, I'm alive," Lenny said.

"Wow. Same. What a coincidence. I am too."

There was a beat of silence. Claire bounced her leg in the passenger seat.

"Thanks for saving me," Lenny added.

"What are you talking about? You saved us both with your influencer powers."

Lenny laughed. "Please don't call me an influencer."

"What do I call you then? Are we . . ." Claire searched for the words. "Are we still friends? I would get it, if you hate my guts—"

Lenny cut her off. "I don't hate your guts. If you hadn't sent that video . . . I wouldn't have come to Scarberry. I wouldn't have broken up with Evan. I wouldn't have quit the channel. I wouldn't know that aliens—or *whatever*—existed. And I wouldn't have met you. I think I just need some time to recover from the whiplash of all this."

"That's fair."

More than fair. Claire would do everything she could to prove she deserved Lenny's forgiveness.

A shadow shifted behind her. She caught a reflection in her rearview mirror. It was Bri, sitting upright and rubbing her eyes. Her skin was waxy, and little bruises dotted her collarbones and forearms.

"Bri?" Claire started.

Lenny slammed on the brakes.

Claire unbuckled and turned around. "Hey? How are you feeling?"

"I'm starving," Bri whined.

Hopefully not starving for human flesh.

"Do you remember what happened?" Claire asked.

Bri stared at her knees. "Parts of it," she whispered. Then she glanced up at Lenny.

Lenny got the memo. She put the car in park and said, "I'll give you guys a sec," and stepped out.

Bri tried to brush at the dirt from her pajama pants. She wouldn't look at Claire. And Claire tried not to stare. Twenty seconds passed. Thirty. A minute. Claire knew she ought to break the silence, but had no clue where to begin.

"I'm sorry I ripped your suit," Bri finally said. "I couldn't breathe in it. I felt like I was gonna explode, but my hands couldn't find the zipper. One second it was on and then it broke open and then I was in a field and . . . I think I did something bad. Whenever I leave the house, I do something bad. Sometimes I can't remember. I do, for a bit, but it fades. Like, I'm still not sure if I actually ate cow guts or if that was a dream."

So that explains the cattle mutilation.

"It's not your fault," Claire said. She hated to think Bri felt guilty. She was the only innocent Reed left. "Your mom's been feeding you poison."

"I know. Well, I figured it out. And I think she knows I did, but none of us told each other."

"That's . . . so not right."

"She just wants me to live. Everyone's ruining their lives to save mine."

"Nuh-uh."

"Yes. My mom won't sell the ranch because she thinks it'd wreck me. You wouldn't leave Scarberry 'cause of me. You could have gone away. Gone to Hannah."

"That was my choice. I don't blame you for it. Maeve should have given you a choice too."

"Yeah . . ." Bri muttered, picking at more dirt on her pants. "I'm done taking that stuff. Even if it means I die. I'd rather die as me."

"Any plans for if you don't die?"

"Don't know. Probably join a cult or something."

Claire glanced out the window. Lenny was pacing, staring at her phone.

"It's not too late, Bri," she said. "For either of us."

Bri said, "I know."

Claire's phone rang.

"It's Warren," she said. "I have to take this."

"Oh my God." Bri curled into herself, cupping her hands over her ears. "Please tell me he didn't see me like that. Ugh. This is so embarrassing."

Claire answered the call.

"The fucking FBI is here," Warren started, breathless.

"Figured," Claire said.

"Is Bri awake yet?"

"Yes."

"Is she—"

She glanced back. Bri was picking crud out of her nails. "She's fine. I think as long as she doesn't take any more *medicine* she'll be okay."

Or at least, she wouldn't turn into an Old Lucky clone again. But her cancer could come back. And the chemo could fail again. There were so many unknowns.

"They're calling the fire department to try to get a ladder to get my dad out. He's not happy."

Yeah. I wouldn't be happy to go to prison either. "Do you . . . want to stay at my house?" Claire asked.

"If you'll have me. Thanks. Hey Claire, I didn't get a chance to say earlier, but . . . I didn't know about Bryce. I had no idea that happened. I didn't even see anything on your locker."

"I scratched it out," she admitted.

"If you would have told me, I would have kicked his ass. I would have told the coach. I would have told his fucking army recruiter. You have to believe that."

"I do."

She believed in aliens now; she might as well try to believe in humanity.

The *Silver Bullet* quivered and the open window was flooded with dust. Bri coughed. The beige cloud dissipated, revealing a blood-splattered van.

CHAPTER 43

LENNY

Evan stepped out of the Bloodmobile.

Lenny tried to maintain a power stance as she wiped the dust from her eyes. She had dried blood smeared on her face. Her clothes were filthy. Her bangs had to look wild. And Evan was pristine in his black *Dark Unknown* shirt.

"So," Lenny started. "We go viral?"

He smiled incredulously. "Oh. Definitely."

She laughed. And so did he. And for a second it was as if they didn't despise each other.

"How'd Max Malitz take it?"

"He wants to stick around. He, uh, asked me to ask you to be in *Dark Unknown*'s video. They're thinking of releasing all Scarberry footage as a documentary. Film festivals. The whole thing."

"I'll pass."

He smiled. "Figured."

"So. You're sticking with Max?"

"Feels wrong to keep using *Odd Kids*. It was yours. Without you, it's dead."

Damn right.

"So, no official announcement?" Lenny teased. "No thumbnail with a tombstone that says 'Here Lies Our YouTube Baby'?"

"I'm so sick of making thumbnails. *Dark Unknown* has an editing team to take care of that."

"Are you happier with Max's team?" she asked before she could second-guess it. She didn't realize until just then that she didn't want him miserable. And she didn't want to be miserable either.

"I think so. Are you happy with Claire?"

"Yes."

He nodded, adjusted his glasses. "I guess this is it then."

"I'm sure we'll still haunt each other through our computer screens," Lenny offered. It was hard to avoid Max Malitz's comfortably chiseled grin whenever she browsed YouTube. The only way to avoid her past would mean going completely off the grid. But that felt like hiding. She was so done with hiding.

Evan gave her a weak smile and headed toward the Bloodmobile. Before getting in he turned. "So, was Old Lucky buried in the dream snow, then?"

"No. I think it was just me."

She returned to her own car. It smelled like Scarberry. Or maybe that was her own scent now. She collapsed into the driver's seat.

"They're leaving?" Claire asked.

"Yep."

"And you? Are you leaving?"

She paused. Once Evan had ditched the ranch, Lenny hadn't let herself imagine what would come after she solved this place. But the moment had arrived. She'd found what she'd come for. Twelve-year-old Lenny would be proud.

Soon, the rest of the world would see the video. Lenny would have to explain it to everyone. The authorities. Her parents. Her followers. As always, not everyone would believe the parts about aliens. And some would question why she let her camera linger on Claire for too long. *Who was that girl?* they would say. They would poke and pry and theorize about the beautiful freckled stranger, not knowing that Lenny was just as much of a stranger. Maybe one day, Lenny would reveal more of herself or maybe she'd keep it private. She didn't know which was the braver option. But she would figure it out. There had to be a happy medium between famous and chained up inside a barn. It wasn't like her only options in life were Spectacle or Hermit.

"I need a break," Lenny admitted.

"Right," Claire glanced at Bri in the backseat, her head slumped against the window. "I think we all need a break."

"But I'll come back," she promised. "And to answer your question from before: I wouldn't say we're *friends*."

Claire looked at her hands in her lap, dejected.

"I *mean* . . ." Lenny continued. "I just don't know if that's the word for us."

Claire raised an eyebrow. "What's a better word, then?"

"Girlfriends?"

The two simple syllables made Lenny's cheeks feel warm. But it also felt right.

She drove the *Silver Bullet* down the uneven dirt road. Toward her future, more uncertain than ever.

EPILOGUE
CLAIRE

For the first time, Claire found herself jobless. Well, that wasn't entirely true. She had developed a consistent roster of clients for video editing. Money was coming in, but she felt lazy now that she wasn't in charge of managing the family business.

It had been over five months since the Reed Ranch incident, and even in the brutal Nebraska winter, there were dozens of tourists crowding the place. The rainbow scarf Bri had knitted her for Christmas covered Claire's ears and mouth. It had a few wonky loops, and midway through knitting Bri had run out of red and had to switch to burnt orange. But Claire adored the scarf anyway. It protected her from the tourists and their incessant questions. The sun had just risen over the barn, and already they were wandering the snowy grounds with their cameras out, taking selfies by the saucer and fiddling with novelty EMF readers. There were six more train cars added in the fall, but it still wasn't enough to accommodate the new arrivals. It would get even crazier when nearly every streaming service released a documentary.

Here was the story they'd probably tell.

Scarberry, Nebraska, had an anomaly under the earth. The miners called it many things. A portal. A god. Even after the mines were closed, the holes they had dug festered. The whole town went bad. Crops failed. People got sick. There were nasty chemicals in the soil. Cancer-causing pesticides or nuclear waste. The government didn't have an answer and were dragging their feet about finding a solution. Instead of inciting panic by calling for a townwide evacuation, instead of admitting citizens had been poisoned for nearly seventy years, they discreetly offered to buy up residents' land, without giving the real reason. They sent notices to the homes closest to the mine side of town, telling them not to be alarmed, but also not to drink the water or eat local eggs or go outside for extended periods.

News of the cover-up wouldn't have left the county if it wasn't for *Odd Kids'* last video depicting a deranged policeman with a gun, screaming about aliens and cures that no one had found proof of.

Or, the other theory said . . .

Something had escaped way back when those first mines were dug. Old Lucky didn't come from underground; it came from another dimension. Willy Lamb trapped it and kept it hidden. Then he passed it on to his son.

But then *Odd Kids* shared a seven-second clip that was emailed anonymously to them. This brought the FBI back to Scarberry, Nebraska, to do more tests. They came to find their long-lost monster before those meddling kids could.

Agent Brenner did an interview on Scarberry, denouncing literally every conspiracy brewing online. Even the ones that were almost accurate. She released photos of Claire and Lenny at the nursing home. And at Reed Ranch, calling them UFO chasers. But internal documents revealed the bureau had known about unsafe "anomalies" in the soil for years. Alien or otherwise, people were getting fired. Government reps went on TV apologizing for the slow justice. But it only made the public more pissed off. There were countless little towns like Scarberry with contaminated water, with dying crops and dying people. Where the residents made up wild tales to cope.

Some of those tales were true.

Allegedly the danger in Scarberry was gone. A false alarm, they said. All tests were normal. No one else was getting sick. Nothing to report after the day Chief Lamb fell into a hole.

Claire had declined to comment on any of the documentaries. Lenny was in talks with lawyers. She didn't want her image used—her research used—without her say. And she had her own podcast to promote now. She wasn't going to make content for someone else.

In a few weeks, Claire would start film school in sunny California. A well-written letter and her new-and-improved portfolio allowed her to keep her scholarship while deferring to the spring semester. The ranch's rooms for rent had an extensive waitlist. Claire didn't know the exact numbers. That wasn't her responsibility anymore. Aunt Maeve said she deserved to "be a teenager" until school started.

She was doing everything she could to earn Lenny's forgiveness. It'd take a long time. At least now there was Advil in the medicine cabinet and other bored employees manning the gift shop, warning tourists to avoid the manure and giving nighttime paranormal tours ($40 per person, not included in the room package). Most of the new fans of the ranch were young, around Claire's age. Every few days, one of them would recognize her from Lenny's video. They would look at her as if starstruck, and then ask, "Is it all true?" and Claire would say, "All of it." And then: "Key chains are buy one, get one half-off."

She would spend the day catching Warren up on horrible reality TV while Bri worked on another knitting project. Or she'd spend it with Lenny, talking for hours and watching movies on video chat. After Lenny went back to Chicago, they were a thousand miles apart, but unlike with Hannah, Lenny never felt that far away. Because Lenny hadn't disappeared yet. Just like film school, Lenny wasn't a promise for "someday." She was coming back. In a few months, in a few weeks. Tomorrow. Today.

Lenny was coming today.

The tourists were going to flip once their messiah returned.

Lenny's voice was in Claire's ear, discussing extraterrestrial transplants with a woman who had the ultimate chain-smoker's voice. Susan was an obvious choice for a podcast guest, though half of what she said was absolutely bonkers. But the project wasn't about proof. Lenny had said it best on the first episode:

"It's not about the aliens or the ghosts or the bigfoots. It's about the people who believe in them."

Lenny didn't have a co-host telling her what to do. She could focus on whatever she wanted. Evan was a special guest on Episode 3. Now that they weren't at each other's throats anymore, the awkward tension between her and Evan had disappeared. But Evan's voice became grating after hours of hearing it. It was the only time Claire second-guessed doing sound design for Lenny's podcast. Otherwise, it was a well-paying gig, something on her résumé, and she never loved Lenny more than when she was going on and on about something that fascinated her.

The podcast wasn't raking in the big bucks like the YouTube channel had, but Lenny was fine with that. "It's just a fun project, not my whole life," Lenny had said.

Claire passed the dense line of trees where a tire used to be. That portal had closed up at the same time the main one did. Whatever was in Scarberry was gone, and probably wasn't coming back. Lamb wasn't the chief of police anymore. It's hard to be chief when you've got an attempted murder on film. Jared's autopsy was extra damning. He did have a heart attack, but it was caused by horse tranquilizer, the same stuff the chief had stacked in his gun cabinet. His prints were found in Jared's ruined trailer. He would be in prison for a long, long time.

And though the country was torn about the existence of Old Lucky, everyone agreed that Chief Lamb was the worst.

"And what happens," Lenny's chirpy voice asked in Claire's ear buds, "if you never find the truth?" Susan took a second to respond, probably taking a drag of the cigarette. Claire had chosen to keep the pause in. It added suspense.

"I know my truth, dearie," Susan said. "Fuck 'em if they don't believe me."

The theme music swelled, and the audio ended. Claire pulled her ear buds out. Ep_4_Iswearitsthelastversion-deaRGOD_7.mp3 was ready to send off. The wood didn't creak under her shoe as she stepped onto the porch. Everything was fixed up, compliant with fire codes and everything. Maeve wouldn't be bankrupt while Claire was away. And Bri was back in school. Her hair covered her ears. For now. But there was a chance she'd need another round of chemo. Maeve made sure she didn't miss a single appointment, even when it brought disappointing news. She wasn't out of the woods yet. Apparently her doctors were "hopeful," and for the first time, Bri seemed to be too. She didn't talk about dying anymore, but instead anxiously was anticipating a promposal from Warren before he went back to college for the spring semester. Claire had consulted him on it, though she had refused to make the sign for him. "We're friends again, but that doesn't mean I'll go back to doing your homework for you," she had told him. But she had let him borrow her glitter markers.

Claire flinched as a horn honked behind her. A gleaming SUV had pulled up by the porch. It was all black. At first, she thought it was the feds, until a familiar face jumped out of the backseat and bounced up to her. Lenny had debuted the Haircut a few weeks ago, via selfies. Her waves barely reached her chin now; chaotic layers all flared out. She looked like a mischievous fairy from old legends. But the nose ring was new.

"You pierced your nose?"

Lenny fiddled with the ring. "My grandmother said I look like a cow," she said.

"Well, you're in the right place then."

"Is it horrendous?"

"I love it. Very you."

Lenny dropped her bags and squeezed Claire tight. It was like all those waiting months disappeared. Suddenly it was still summer. It had always been summer and it always would be. Lenny, like the Beast of Scarberry, wasn't a false memory. She was here, tangible, touchable.

A man and a woman stepped out of the SUV. Lenny's parents. They were both short and bouncy like her. They hugged Claire as if they had missed her too, though their only interactions had been polite hellos on video chats. They would follow behind them all the way to L.A., because they wanted to meet Claire, and the last time their daughter went on a road trip, she was attacked by a monster and had a gun waved in her face, so they weren't taking any chances. Lenny wasn't moving to California with Claire—not yet, anyways. She would stay with her parents in Illinois, but eventually, she and Claire would live in the same city. Someday.

Aunt Maeve invited them inside, and everyone sat around the new kitchen table with non-wobbly chairs, rehashing plans and exchanging numbers.

Maeve turned up the dramatics. She cupped Claire's face and said her goodbyes as if they were permanent, and Claire assured her, "I'm going to college, not outer space."

Bri tried to make Claire promise to take photos of her current favorite reality-TV boyfriend's house. "Why don't we go together, when you visit?" Claire suggested. And Bri was satisfied with that.

After the goodbyes, Claire sat in the passenger seat of her truck, and Lenny sat at the wheel. She had been practicing driving manual, so they could take turns driving.

"Wait, shit," Claire said. "I need to send you the audio for Episode 4."

"Don't worry about it. I'll post it tomorrow. I don't really care about a consistent upload schedule."

Claire pretended to gasp. "What would the subscribers think?"

Lenny brushed a curl out of Claire's face and leaned in for a kiss. Claire had been waiting months for this kiss. Months imagining how Lenny's lips would feel pressed up against hers. Part of her had been afraid she would totally mess up. She studied all the kisses on Bri's dumb reality shows so she would know what to do. Tilt her chin exactly 60 degrees. Don't forget to breathe. But all that studying wasn't necessary. Kissing Lenny was effortless. They somehow knew exactly how the other would react to every touch. Like every moment of their lives had led up to this one. They were doing what they were made to do.

Claire didn't want it to end, but eventually, they pulled away from each other, and Lenny gave her another kiss on the cheek.

"Ready?" Lenny asked.

Claire hesitated.

She told herself that when she moved away, she wouldn't look back, but she glanced in the passenger mirror. At Bri. At Warren. At the crumbling red barn and broken windmill and endless sky.

She had always planned to leave Scarberry.

But she hadn't planned to take it with her.

Of course she'd have to visit. Because long country roads

were good for the soul. Because her lungs would need their refill of Scarberry dirt. Because this place made her. And it was not too far gone to be saved.

"Ready," Claire said.

Lenny started the truck and backed out of the snowy driveway.

They would have two weeks on their road trip. On the road, neither girl would be out of place. They would be aliens, together.

ACKNOWLEDGMENTS

Mamma Mia. Here we go again.

Thank you to my agent, Miriam Cortinovis, for enthusiastically championing this story since I pitched "*X-Files* but they're teenage girls and Mulder has a YouTube channel." Thank you to my editor, Kristin Allard, for adopting another monster of mine, and always knowing when to add more blood and guts. Thank you to the team at Norton Young Readers, especially Hana Anouk Nakamura, Rebecca Munro, Delaney Adams, Naomi Duttweiler, Simon Boughton, and Jill Owens Leigh. Thank you to Colin Verdi for another killer cover illustration.

Thank you to my early readers: Jace, fellow doll collector and vampire expert, whom I can always count on to read at lightspeed. To Margot, the Midwest's most iconic drag clown, for the best memes an author could ask for. Thank you to Max "Crazy Effed Up" Nalow and his behemoth of a brain for spackling every plot hole so easily. Thanks to Jimmie and Tiana for long-distance story times when I need a distraction from the Horrors.

Thank you to the adults in my teenage life, who were much more competent than the ones in this book: my art teachers, Mrs. Hefflinger and Mrs. Westhoven, and my guidance counselor, Mrs. Ahleman. Thank you to my mom, Sara June, for letting me stay home from school to watch Syfy's *Face Off* and *Little House on the Prairie.* I think I had a fever dream that combined them and it turned into this book.

Thank you to my brother, Wyatt Lemon James, for his good taste in scary movies. My sister Liv, who is still traumatized by my film recommendations. She wanted my next book to be a cowboy romance, and this is as close as it's gonna get.

To my grandparents, aunts, uncles, cousins, and future in-laws for harassing every person they know with news of my books and making sure I'm aware it's a Very Big Deal that I'm a real-life writer.

To Austin, aka Vampire Boyfriend, who didn't hesitate to say, "Of course the gay cryptid book will get published" and always made sure my M&M's were cold during *Ghost Adventures* marathons.

And to our drooly cat, Azura. The best gray lump in the PNW. She is mostly useless, but her love is pure.

To my Besties. Roomies. Brooks, who went on my first road trip with me. Madelyn, who took my author headshots and was nearly sacrificed in the lake for book one's photos. I owe you a million Red Bull sodas. To my debut group, and my agent siblings, for quelling my 2 a.m. anxieties.

Thank you to the teachers, librarians, and booksellers for promoting curiosity and literacy. Y'all saved my life. Thank you to queer artists and activists. Especially the angry ones.

This is for the small-town kids who left to survive.

And the ones who stayed to make things better.